Prompted by a cryptic message, five polcs secretly leave Teloria to embark on a journey to discover many truths. It is dangerous, in this time of war, and soon our five heroes find themselves travelling to farther lands than they had anticipated, where they discover their Stardust Destinies.

Also by Celinka Serre

Stardust Destinies Short Stories
(found at www.medium.com/stardust-destinies)

Various Fiction Short Stories
(found at www.medium.com/@BinkyInkWriting)

Stardust Destinies

I

Variate Facing

by

Celinka Serre

First Edition Edited by
Marg Gilks,

Second Edition Edits by

Celinka Serre and Cleo Miele

Cover Art by Sophie Brunet

Binky Ink
The literary arm of Binky Productions

www.binkyproductions.com/stardustdestinies

Published by Binky Ink
First Edition Edited by Marg Gilks
Second Edition Edits by Celinka Serre and Cleo Miele
Cover Art by Sophie Brunet

ISBN: 978-0-9919965-2-0

Dedicated to
Milu and Seb

ACKNOWLEDGEMENTS

This book has seen a lot of changes before publication was possible. The journey of these five main characters began when I was only 19. Ideas were fresh, but like our Telorian friends, the journey of writing would soon take me to more places, allowing the story to ripen.

On this journey, there are many people who helped and contributed to making this publication possible.

The first person I'd like to acknowledge is my teacher and mentor from CEGEP, Gary Plaxton at Dawson College, who has sadly since passed away. He read passages of this book, saw a scene become a video in class, and encouraged me to keep writing and to one day publish. Gary was my mentor for several years after I graduated and many of his teachings have inspired me and motivated me throughout the years.

I also need to thank my mother, who was one of my very first test readers. She is the person who has seen me working on this project the most and who has always pushed me when I needed a nudge to pursue this dream and to never give up.

My husband is another person who has seen me work on this, and then talk and talk and talk about it. Simply having someone with whom to bounce ideas around for my publication plans was a great help and motivation when I encountered any challenges along the way.

Next up, when I began searching for an editor, I knew I wanted someone who would provide insight and guide me as I began my publication journey. Marg Gilks ticked all the boxes and we clicked right away. As my editor, she was able to enhance the story in the way that it needed, and at the same time, preserve its authenticity in the way that I needed.

Someone else who is a part of the team is my cover artist. I've known Sophie Brunet since I was very young, both our mothers being long-time friends. I remember speaking to her about doing my cover art way before I had completed writing the story itself. I've always admired her style of painting and knew that together we would be able to shape the book with creative imagery in a way that would reflect the symbols found within its pages.

Last but not least, I must thank all those who helped with promoting this book, friends and family alike, and everyone who has become a devoted reader over the course of this publication process. Our journey has only begun, and the future of our shared experience is written in the stars and prophecised by the dragons themselves.

TABLE OF CONTENTS

Preface

Welcome to the Great Ocean Valley, where magic reigns and the dragons rule the prophecies. I invite you to take a look at *The Stardust Destinies Appendices* that accompany this book to familiarise yourself with this new realm, for the world of Stardust Destinies functions quite differently from many others. You will find them as a free download at:

http://www.binkyproductions.com/stardustdestinies.

In Appendix 1, *Telorian History*, you will learn how the polcs of Teloria exist, and how they measure time and age.

In Appendix 2, *Kaulchèc History*, you will discover how magic came to be in the lands of the Great Ocean Valley.

Appendix 3, *The Magic of Dûnelor*, explores the history of an enchanted people and forebodes some of the events from recent history.

In Appendix 4, *Counting Time*, the seasons and how Telorians keep track of time are explained.

Appendix 5, *Polken Talk*, is a brief summary of speech and spells.

You will also find more complete maps of the Great Ocean Valley and its main kingdoms.

However, it is in Appendix 6, *A Dark Force Growing*, where you will learn about all the evil that has befallen Teloria and its people, and discover the dark lord behind all the attacks – learn about his magic, where he comes from, and what his dark sinister motives might be. The power he wields is unique in Kaulchèc History. Be advised that, although you may look upon these historical texts and study the lore of this world, you should never look into the eyes of the great evil that is Mirauk, for his curse is greater than any magic that has yet been prophesied by any living being, save the dragons.

TIMELINE OF KAULCHÈC HISTORY

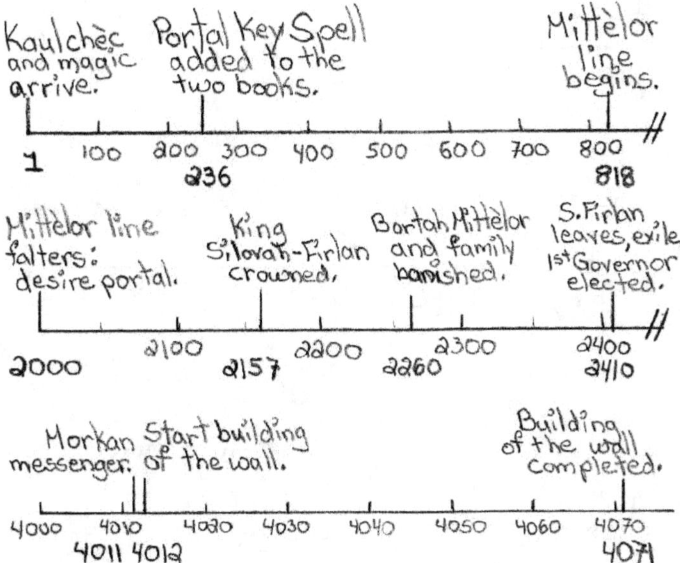

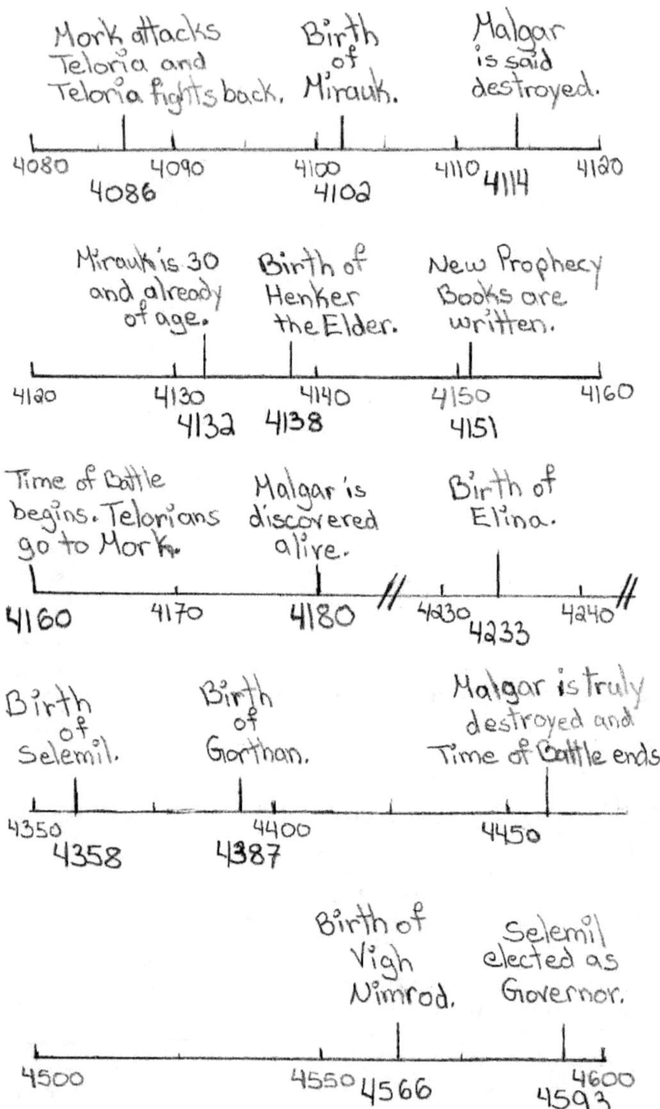
Mork attacks Teloria and Teloria fights back.
Birth of Mirauk.
Malgar is said destroyed.
4080
4086
4090
4100
4102
4110
4114
4120
Mirauk is 30 and already of age.
Birth of Henker the Elder.
New Prophecy Books are written.
4120
4130
4132
4138
4140
4150
4151
4160
Time of Battle begins. Telorians go to Mork.
Malgar is discovered alive.
Birth of Elina.
4160
4170
4180
4230
4233
4240
Birth of Selemil.
Birth of Gorthan.
Malgar is truly destroyed and Time of Battle ends.
4350
4358
4400
4387
4450
Birth of Vigh Nimrod.
Selemil elected as Governor.
4500
4550
4566
4593
4600

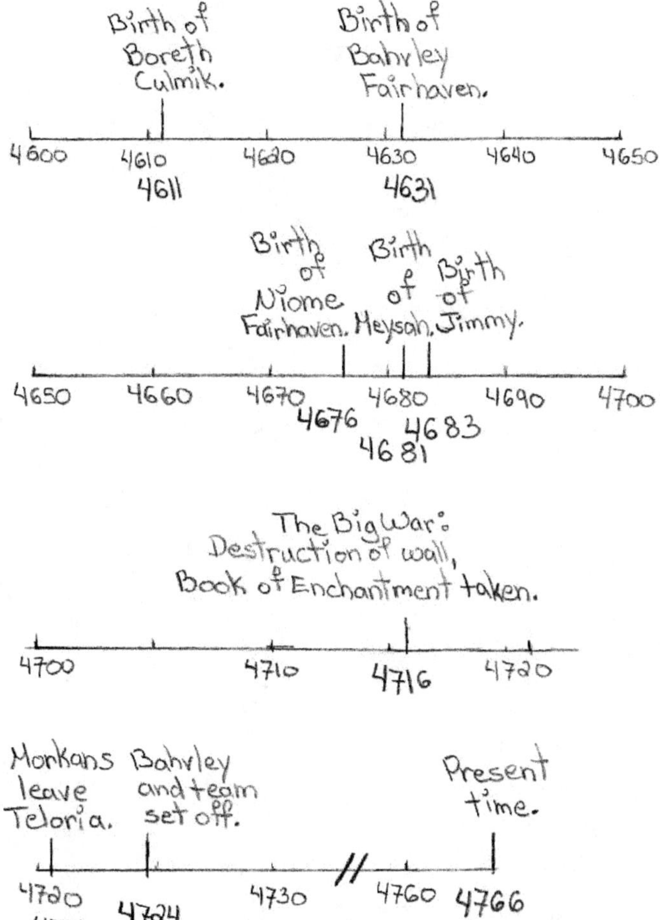
Birth of
Boreth
Culmik.
Birth of
Bahrley
Fairhaven.
4600
4610
4620
4630
4640
4650
4611
4631
Birth of
Niome
Fairhaven.
Birth of
Heysah.
Birth of
Jimmy.
4650
4660
4670
4680
4690
4700
4676
4681
4683
The Big War:
Destruction of wall,
Book of Enchantment taken.
4700
4710
4716
4720
Monkans leave Teloria.
Bahrley and team set off.
Present time.
4720
4724
4730
4760
4766
4721

'Our dear friend, the Great Wizardess Elina, has fallen ill again,' said Gorthan, Chief Swordmaster of all Masters and Knights. 'I fear she may not survive the relapse this time.'

He and the two other polcs present in the small briefing room of the Governor's Hall, once the Royal Halls of Teloria City, had important matters to discuss, especially now that magic was in motion again.

'It has been nearly fifty years since her return from Mork,' said Selemil the Governor. 'She has managed to quell the symptoms before.'

'We do not know the intensity of Mirauk's curse,' argued Gorthan. 'It is her magic that has sustained her for so long. Sometimes I wonder if there is other magic at work.' He shook his head. 'Regardless, we knew that this day would come, when she would no longer be able to fight the illness that Mirauk cursed her with when he looked into her eyes.'

Henker the Elder sat pensive, rubbing his cheek. He stopped. 'If these are the last of Elina's days,' he said, 'then all our hope must lie in Niome, her pupil.'

'Niome is too young still,' argued Selemil.

'She is not much younger than Elina was when she became the best Wizardess of Teloria, even if it did take more time for her to become the Great Wizardess, officially and by title,' said Henker. 'All of Elina's knowledge, all of her teachings – it all rests with Niome.'

'There are other, more qualified wizards in Teloria,' said Selemil. He leaned forward and tapped the table with a forefinger to punctuate his next words. 'We cannot expect a young girl to know how to save our kingdom.'

'Not so much a "girl" as a "woman",' Henker corrected him. 'The polc has come of age.'

'Not much younger than . . .' Gorthan trailed off. He looked at the other two. 'When Elina and the Team of Twelve left for Mork to take back the *Book of Enchantment,* many of them were not much older than Niome is today.'

'And did they return?' demanded Selemil. 'Even the army that left with them never returned.' He closed his eyes and shook his head. 'Whether from spies, messengers, or rumour, there has been no word from Mork. If any from that team still live, they have surely been lost to the darkness of Morok. That mission cost us a slew of talented knights, and our Great Wizardess's health. She is the only one who returned – empty-handed.'

Henker sighed. 'May I remind you that Elina has taught Niome how to guard the *Complement Book*? Should the Morkans come for it, she is prepared and knows what to do.'

'The Morkans better not come before the repairs on the wall around Teloria proper are complete. The Big War caused such damage and loss.' He turned to Gorthan. 'Any word from the guards on the wall?'

'The area at Telor is nearly finished,' said Gorthan. 'The tower at Lani has been reconstructed after long delay. That entire side has been completely rebuilt and is stronger than the rest of the wall. The only area with a few remaining breaches that have yet to be patched is in the south.'

'Has it truly taken us fifty years to rebuild the entire wall around our kingdom?'

'Recovering from the Big War took us fifty years,' said Henker. 'I have never seen such devastation before – the destruction, the famine that followed, the grievous hardship; all that came after. We tended the people, lifted their sorrow. We gave them hope, back then.' His gaze grew distant. 'We must give them hope once more. Teloria is no longer vulnerable. Anyone who was imprisoned in Morkan encampments has been rescued. Yet the people of our kingdom still grieve; they remember, they know, they fear. They fear the army that left fifty years ago has all but perished and they have begun to come to terms with it, but without hope, they will fear that Teloria will fall to Mirauk and his reign of terror over all the lands.'

Henker looked at Gorthan and Selemil. 'The Morkans have left us alone for all these years, but everyone in this kingdom knows as well as I do, they are planning something, perhaps something even bigger than the last time – and they fear.'

'I have no doubt that Mirauk is planning another coup,' said Gorthan, 'and I have trained my knights and masters accordingly. But what is he planning? That is cause for much speculation and much of the fear, as well.'

Henker leaned forward, placing his elbows on his knees. 'With Elina ill again, no one knows what the future holds, not even our best prophets. Not even me. But if we can bestow hope again, then Teloria can win.'

'I hope you're not suggesting we go after the *Book of Enchantment* and send more Telorians to Mork,' said Selemil.

Henker shook his head. 'Despite everything that has happened to Teloria, despite everything that was lost, and everything that is yet to come, there is one who holds that hope.'

'Niome,' said Gorthan. 'She is determined to save us all from evil, even if she has to do it alone. Her valour is admirable, but it is unnerving.'

'Perhaps, but she is young, powerful in magic, optimistic, and determined. She can convey those attributes to the rest of the people,' said Henker. 'Let us give hope to the people of Teloria. Let's let Niome share her strengths.'

'She holds much responsibility,' began Selemil, 'but she is not alone.' He nodded. 'We remain here and wait for Mork to attack. We are strongest here. And we let Niome inspire with her knowledge and magic, and together, we can devise the best plan, should Mirauk attack us again. I've been working on a magical shelter I believe could help us. I think what our people need is purpose.'

'With Niome's aid,' said Gorthan, 'I'm sure we can achieve what has seemed impossible for years.'

'Are we all in agreement, then?' asked Selemil.

Gorthan and Henker confirmed.

The old polc gripped his cane and stood. 'Let us go speak with Elina. If her final days approach, then we will need all the insight she can give us.'

The other two stood. These were grave times; they had been for generations. But magic was in motion, and things were about to change, for ill or for the better. Best they ensure it was for the better.

Niome Fairhaven was a young polc of ninety with beautiful long, dark hair that glistened in the light, and bright eyes of golden green. She most often wore a purple dress that her sorcery teacher Elina, the Great Wizardess of Teloria, had made her. She felt very close to her master, and now that Elina was ill again, Niome felt compelled to wear the dress, almost as though it would keep Elina on their earth longer.

As Niome looked through the ancient scrolls that she was studying, her father, Ceymi, bustled into the room. When Niome looked up and met his dark eyes, she saw the sadness upon his face.

'Niome,' he cried, shaking his head, 'it's Elina! She's . . . her illness, it's worse than ever.'

Worry fell upon Niome's heart, for she had been Elina's apprentice for over thirty years. Dropping the scroll she'd been reading, she brushed past her father and ran to Elina's house.

Everyone, it seemed, was gathering at Elina's door; Niome saw Gorthan the Chief, Henker the Elder, and Selemil the Governor among the villagers; even the tall Telorian who was her and her brother's sword-master was there. *They all know Elina is dying,* Niome thought. *No!* Niome could not conceive that notion yet – the death of her master, the person she trusted most and who trusted her most, the person who was the most versed in magic in Teloria.

Niome entered the house and closed the door quietly behind her, then walked into Elina's bedroom and stopped beside the bed with her head bowed low, trying to remember the few healing spells that existed.

'Niome,' Elina whispered with difficulty, 'you must protect the *Complement Book*. Do not let it get into Mirauk's hands. Teloria's destiny lies with you now.' Niome nodded. 'No spell can heal the curse that has been set upon me. Mirauk's evil was too strong for me alone to destroy.'

'I will find the *Book of Enchantment*,' Niome replied.

Elina smiled and whispered strange words in her last breath: '*Soû lagar andë roc, hëaûbo rede lari verei!*' And then she was gone.

In tearful sorrow, Niome bowed her head even lower, and repeated the words in her head several times to remember them. Whatever Elina said was important and had great significance, Niome knew that much from experience. Then she blew out the candle that sat on the night table. She knew what she had to do to bring hope back to Teloria, but first she had to go out there and announce the bad news to everyone.

No doubt there would be a meeting with the council, and a great gathering to figure out what to do, now that the wisest and most powerful of them had passed away. Everyone proficient in magic was asked to be present at the meeting, but Niome decided that she would be absent. She couldn't stand those types of gatherings. She wanted to be alone and do research of her own, especially now that she had a phrase to decode; that would help a lot more.

Niome left the bedroom and crossed to the door, where she paused with her hand on the latch. Drawing a deep breath, she swung the door open and walked over the threshold and outside.

A spiritual ceremony in Elina's honour marked the day when everything changed forever. It was the eighty-fourth day of the year, at the very end of Winter. The Telorians grieved for a full week before the council meeting took place.

They gathered in the Governor's Hall, a great, dimly lit room large enough to hold all Telorians, young and old alike. Gorthan the Chief, the Swordmaster of all Masters, chaired the meeting, which was attended by Telorians from all of the surrounding villages, even those from the far south and wizards from the far corners, for this concerned the entire kingdom.

Gorthan stood before the people, with Henker the Elder seated on one side and Selemil the Governor on the other. The great hall was filled with chatter that echoed the people's fear, but when Gorthan stepped forward onto a little platform, everyone grew quiet, their impatience and agony hanging heavy in the silence that invaded the room.

Gorthan finally spoke in a deep, loud voice. 'Polcs of Teloria,' he said, 'this has been a mournful time for us all, but we must not lose hope. I know that the warriors have been gone far too long for us to expect their return, but nothing tells us they are dead. Although Mirauk himself announced that he killed them, I am hopeful in my heart that some of those brave polcs yet live. They are powerful and skilled, and whatever dangers they face will allow them to thrive if they survive.' Gorthan paused, wishing he could believe his own words.

'If that is so, why haven't they returned?' shouted one of the younger Telorians, standing next to another young polc.

'Because they are warriors,' replied Henker the Elder. 'They are explorers bound to find peace.'

The boy gave the other a discouraged look.

'There is always determination and curiosity,' Henker finished.

'But what more could they be curious about?' yelled the boy.

'The land, other cultures, making allies. These knights know what they are doing,' said Henker.

'I know that!' the lad retorted. It was the same story that Henker told again and again. 'But what makes you so sure they are still alive?'

'Six hundred and twenty-eight years will get you far in knowledge and wisdom, young polc,' Henker replied.

The adolescent boy stayed silent for a moment, then said, 'Hey, I do know a thing or two about the dangers of travelling. I also know a thing or two about magic. I mean, I *am* a Fairhaven, after all!'

'Meysah,' said Selemil, 'everyone knows you are the son of Ceymi and Latua.'

'And Niome's brother.'

Some of the other adolescents cast annoyed looks at Meysah for his boastfulness, but the young polc next to him only smiled in sympathy.

Selemil continued. 'But you still have much to learn concerning—'

'My brother was the Second Captain!' interrupted Meysah. 'I think I'm entitled to my questions.'

'Indeed,' said Henker, 'indeed, and it is understandable, but you see . . .' He paused as the three leaders scanned the room for Niome to no avail.

Gorthan continued for Henker. 'All is not lost,' he said. 'Perhaps Elina left us, but her spells did not go with her. Niome Fairhaven was her apprentice and knows much. In time, she will become a Great Wizardess herself, so worry not for the future of Teloria – it lies in capable hands: Niome, for great magic, and Selemil, our wonderful governor, who has kept us away from harm for so long.'

Selemil rose. 'That is correct,' he agreed. 'And I have been preparing a secret hideout for us, if ever we are in great danger. So do not fear, my friends. We are safe from the people of Mork, as long as we stick together and help each other.'

The words gave the Telorians a little more hope. Their discord turned into loud rejoicing.

Selemil smiled and stepped forward. 'Telorians, your attention once more!' Their voices died down and they focused on the tall polc's long face. 'This won't be easy and it requires everybody's cooperation. We need each and every one of you to train as a fighter. Most of you have swords or a weapon of some sort; it'll do. We must band together and forge as many weapons as we can, but most importantly, we must rebuild the last section of our barrier, the wall around our kingdom, where I intend to put more watchers than before. Those who can see far into the distance will sound the alarm when they spy the enemy. *That* is when we will hide and wait for the perfect moment to ambush them.'

'How will they not find us?' asked an elder.

'With the little magic that I know, I will prevent them.' Selemil raised his hand, palm towards the floor, and jerked it. A hole opened up and a great light surrounded it. With his other hand, he pulled a crystal orb from his satchel and held it up. 'With this crystal, I can see what goes on in Teloria. And behold, the passageway to the magical hideout. An ancient spell from our ancestors is to thank for this.'

Everyone looked on in awe until, in a flash, it all disappeared.

'We must work in haste. Whoever wishes to assist me today, you may, but I only require your help two days from now.' Selemil glanced at Gorthan and stepped back.

Gorthan dismissed the people. A few hung back to help Selemil organise the remaining repair plans for the wall; the others returned home.

Though baby-faced Meysah was younger than his sister by five polken years, he considered himself to be much more rational than her.

After the meeting, he rushed home, only to discover Niome wasn't there, so he went to the Magic Lab. She hadn't been at the meeting and it was crucial not to miss one, especially in this case, especially because she had been the Great Wizardess's apprentice. It was almost a disgrace! He needed to find out why she'd been absent.

He found her sitting at the desk, looking through one of the books from a pile beside her. Meysah rushed over and grabbed the book from her hands. 'What are you doing here?' he demanded.

'What does it look like?' retorted Niome.

'Perhaps you forgot something?' suggested Meysah. 'Someplace you had to be?'

'I deliberately missed the meeting. I have no time to spend on anything but this,' she said, reaching for the book.

He held it out of her reach. 'Anything but what?' Meysah asked suspiciously, yet his interest in Niome's work grew as she explained.

'When Elina died, she whispered these words to me: "*Soû lagar andë roc, hëaûbo rede lari verei!*" Niome stood and walked towards Meysah.

'What, is that a spell?' asked Meysah, reaching to open the *Complement Book*, which had been left on the desk.

Niome grabbed it and put it in her cloak pocket, where the small book fit very well. 'That's what I thought at first, but then I discovered that the words were in the ancient tongue of the Kaulchèc people. How did I know?' Niome began to pace as she spoke. 'I looked through the language books and history books because I thought it was an ancient version of our tongue, but it's not at all ours. In fact, I read that thousands of years ago, the people who marked their place here among the Telorians, the Kaulchèc, knew great magic, which of course is why we know it here today. The *Book of Enchantment* was a gift from them, before they left.'

'I know my history, Niome,' Meysah reminded her, crossing his arms and giving his sister a lopsided smile.

'Then you know that they used our tongue to create new magic.' Niome picked up a large book. Not to be outdone, Meysah picked up another. 'It says in this book that our spells, our customs, came from an alliance between our ancestors and the

Kaulchèc. So I looked in the *Book of Ancient Tongues* and started decoding.'

Meysah looked at the cover of the book he held; it was the *Book of Ancient Tongues*, an old book with a dusty brown cover embossed with golden scripts. He handed it back to Niome almost reverently, as though it was too ancient and invaluable for him to hold. Right away she opened it, sat back down, and silently continued her decoding. Meysah waited until she finished and leaned back. He looked at her with anticipation. Niome put down her quill, still staring at her page.

'Well . . . ?' he coaxed. 'What does it mean?'

'"*Under the Great Rock, by the river*",' she replied. Ignoring Meysah's puzzled expression, she continued to think aloud. 'The Ortim River has one distinct rock. It's huge, for one thing, and stands out because of the greyish-pink streaks in its centre. I think there might be something hidden there.'

Meysah caught his sister's drift. 'But the Ortim River is more than a week's travel to the north, and then we have to find the rock,' he objected. 'In this time of approaching peril, Gorthan and Selemil will never let you leave, let alone Mom and Dad.' He again crossed his arms at the mention of their parents.

'I'm still going. No one will stop me.'

'What about—'

'I'm going!' Niome glared at him, her mind set.

'Then let me go with you.'

Niome reached for her sword which leaned against a pile of books on the floor and slipped it into the sheath at her belt. Looking her brother in the eyes, she shook her head. This mission was hers, and although she wouldn't mind the company, worrying about his safety would only be a distraction to her at the moment when she needed to focus the most.

They heard the outer door open. Meysah turned around and Niome rushed behind the desk and stuck her head into a random book just before Gorthan entered.

Gorthan stalked over to the desk and slickly lifted the book out of Niome's hands. 'Why were you not there, Niome?' he asked in a stern voice as he set the book down. 'I am disappointed. Selemil was planning on letting you speak.' He waited.

'I apologise, but I needed to figure something out before it was too late,' she answered after a long pause. 'Look!' Niome showed Gorthan the notes she had taken. He studied them carefully. 'I believe whatever lurks there can help us,' she added.

'Well, perhaps once the repairs are complete we can take a look, but right now, no explorer can leave,' said Gorthan.

'That's okay, I'll go alone.' Niome started packing her bag.

'No,' Gorthan said firmly. 'There could be spies out there.'

'Then send someone to accompany me.'

'We need all our best polcs.' He turned to look at Meysah. 'Even our apprentice-knights. I mean, it's over seven days of travel to the Ortim River.'

'Not if I don't stop for the night,' Niome was quick to answer, her words overlapping the end of Gorthan's sentence. Even if he was the Chief, she knew that she needed no one's permission to leave. She only wanted the support of a trusted friend and teacher, out of courtesy.

'And then you'll have to find the Great Rock, then return to Teloria without running into trouble,' continued Gorthan. 'If all goes well and you find allies and explore the region, you could be away for several weeks, at least.' He shook his head. 'No, I won't permit it. It's too dangerous.'

'I can do this! I know how to take care of myself!' Niome exclaimed.

'Can you defeat an army of Morkans if you're on your own? You don't know what they're capable of. You were not on the front lines as *I* was during the Big War.'

'I won't meet any Morkans,' Niome insisted. 'I'll avoid them! I don't understand why I have to stay here. I can't do Teloria any good if I don't know what I should know. Elina told me that for a purpose! Why can't I—'

'I don't want what happened to Bahvley to happen to you!' shouted Gorthan.

Gorthan was right. Even if Niome was correct about the importance of Elina's words, Gorthan knew the dangers better than she could imagine at this time in her life. With danger approaching Teloria, there was no way of knowing what was out there or how soon it was going to come. Even if Niome had other authorities' consent, and even though she need not tell anyone her intentions, if Gorthan said no, it was no.

'You're young, Niome,' Gorthan said in a gentler voice. 'Even with what you know, you're incapable of defending yourself against an army of fully trained warriors – most of us are, alone. Besides,' he added with a sympathetic smile, 'I need you at my side. You're the one who knows the most magic.' He laid Niome's notes on the desk.

Niome remained quiet. She lifted her notes and sat down with a sigh. Gorthan stood silent a while, then glanced at Meysah, who had a sad look on his face at the mention of Bahvley's name. With a last glance back at Niome, Gorthan walked out. Casting a sympathetic smile at Niome, Meysah followed Gorthan out, leaving his sister to her thoughts.

Meysah woke at daybreak to find a note on the bed beside his pillow. He sat up and opened it. It was from Niome. All it said was: *Cover up for me; I'll see you sometime. –Niome.* Letting the note drop, Meysah leapt from his bed and ran to his sister's room. Flinging the door open, he scanned the interior. Though it looked intact, he recognised the absence of what she valued most. *She's gone.* He ran out to the stable and ran along the aisle, looking into the stalls. One of the horses was missing – her favourite mare.

He let out a long sigh. 'She can't survive on her own. I have to help her – somehow.'

Running back into the house, Meysah quickly gathered what he thought he'd need. Then he rushed up the street to Vigh Nimrod's house and hammered on the door until his master opened it.

The lean, rugged polc was one of those who had stood outside Elina's door the day she had died. Vigh was a tall polc, taller than the average Telorian and darker skinned, too, with a medium-taupe tone though he was not of Dûnelorian descent. He often wondered if his lineage dated back to a time before Telorians had lost contact with the fabled Kaltelians.

His pale eyes regarded Meysah and his handsome features creased with concern. 'Meysah! What brings you here so early in the day?'

'Master Vigh, I have a dilemma,' declared Meysah.

'Well, come in.' Vigh held the door open, then followed Meysah into the living room, where warm light from a lone lantern gleamed on the swords and weapons adorning the walls. Vigh barely had time to sit down before Meysah started blurting out words that didn't make sense, so fast was he talking.

'Niome wanted to go to the Great Rock but it was too far – she decoded words, so she had to go – because of the war. Selemil wouldn't have let her and Gorthan refused. We have to help her – she left me a note. It's dangerous out there—'

'Slow down!' Vigh insisted, brows furrowed with concern.

Meysah stopped. He was breathing heavily, out of breath.

Vigh smiled. 'Calm down. Start over – and please, speak clearly so I can understand.'

'When Elina died,' Meysah began, a little too slowly now, 'she spoke some ancient words to Niome, and Niome decoded them. That's why she wasn't at the meeting.'

Vigh nodded and ran his hand through his dark hair, waiting for more.

'They said to go to the Great Rock – the words, that is.' Meysah drew a big breath. 'Gorthan didn't want her to go,' he continued, picking up the pace, 'because it's too far and too dangerous and Selemil would never allow it. But Niome insisted, because she believes whatever's there can help us. She was refused permission to go, but this morning I found a note on my bed and one of the horses is gone. She's gone and she could be in danger and we have to help her to find out what's there!'

Meysah stopped and plopped down on the soft couch, his eyes on Vigh.

'Well,' Vigh said calmly, 'it looks like we have no other choice but to go and find her.'

Meysah nodded vigorously, but added, panic straining his voice, 'What else do you *think* we should do? This is why I came to see you.'

'Calm down. We'll gather a team,' said Vigh.

'But no big team. Not anyone who will bring her home without letting her see what's at the rock,' Meysah said. 'I know this is important to her and to Teloria – and to Elina, if she said it.'

'You believe there's something there also, don't you?'

'Yes.' Meysah nodded vigorously again.

'What will Selemil say?' asked Vigh after a pause.

'We won't tell him. We'll just go. Otherwise, we won't be allowed to go, and it's important that we do,' Meysah blurted.

Vigh looked at him sternly, leaning his chin on his fist. 'Okay,' he said at last. He rose and walked into the next room.

A few moments later, he came back out, now dressed in heavy garments for warmth. He swung a cloak onto his shoulders and pulled the hood up over his head. Then he walked to the wall and lifted down the biggest of the swords and attached its scabbard to his belt. Next came a knife, which he slipped into his boot. He looked at Meysah. 'Come,' he said. 'We shall see who is willing to come with us.' Meysah gladly followed Vigh.

As they passed a red-roofed house, Meysah halted, remembering who had stood next to him at the meeting.

'What is it?' asked Vigh.

'If we want a good team,' Meysah began, 'we have to get Jimmy to come with us. This is his house. I'll go in and wake him. He won't mind being woken this early; the sun is almost completely up.'

Meysah ran up the steps and entered his friend's house without knocking, as he often did. He ran to his best friend's room and jumped onto the bed, bouncing Jimmy awake. 'Wake up, Jimmesh! We have to hurry,' he shouted.

Jimmy reluctantly opened his eyes. 'What is wrong with you?' he grumbled. 'You're yelling loud enough to wake the town. You're lucky my parents are probably out in the garden.' He sat up and rubbed the sleep from his eyes. 'What is it?' he mumbled.

'Niome's gone!' said Meysah.

Jimmy's eyebrows shot up. 'Why? Where?'

'To the Great Rock to find out its secret,' replied Meysah. 'But she went against orders, so she's alone and we have to go after her and help her.'

Jimmy brightened. 'Are you saying we're going on a special journey? You mean, to save us from the enemy?' Meysah nodded. 'Well, why didn't you say so in the first place?' Jimmy flung the covers back and rose. 'I love adventure!' He walked to the window, saying, 'What's the weather like today?'

'Cold,' Meysah said almost apologetically.

'But it's Spring!' exclaimed Jimmy, sounding outraged.

'The weather is as unpredictable as the enemy. *And* Niome. Besides, it's only the first few days of Spring. Hurry, get your things; Master Vigh is waiting outside.'

'To go where?' asked Jimmy.

'I don't know, somewhere to find people who wish to join us.'

'Who wouldn't want to go on such an adventure! It sure is better than staying here and waiting to be attacked.'

'Exactly what I was thinking.'

Jimmy quickly dressed and the boys ran out the door and down the steps.

Jimmy's mother met them at the bottom. 'Where are you two off to so early?' she asked.

'Oh, hi, Missus Hochka,' said Meysah. 'We have an assignment to work on together.'

'All right, then. Just be sure to be back for supper, Jimmesh,' she said.

'Okay. I'll see you later.'

The boys joined Vigh, who was standing on the road, gazing northward. He looked at them but said nothing, he merely led the way down the muddy, snow-scattered road.

They encountered Lóim Weedler, who was Jimmy's age, two years younger than Meysah. He had been at the meeting too, but mostly to mock. He was a boaster who liked to remind others about things they could not have. Not that he had them either, but he pretended to be the best and the luckiest. He had always mocked Jimmy and Meysah growing up, especially Meysah.

'Hullo, lads,' he said. 'Why are you in such a hurry?'

'No reason,' Jimmy said warily. 'We're just off with Master Vigh on a patrol.'

'Says the polc with no master. Well,' Lóim condescended, focusing on Jimmy, 'I am going to train to defend the kingdom, and,' he looked at Meysah, 'I bet I could slay a dozen Morkans at once.'

'Really!' replied Meysah, nonplussed. 'I don't think so.'

'Well, I could slay more than you ever will,' Lóim sneered.

'I think *I* could slay a dozen,' stated Vigh, 'and if you don't watch your tongue, Mister Weedler, I could slay you too! Or at least cut out that boastful tongue of yours.'

Lóim shut up and left, his nose in the air.

A short time later, Vigh stopped at a little hut. 'Wait here,' he said, and went around to the back of the hut.

After a while he came back and signalled for them to follow him to a small door in the back of the hut, so small they had to bend down to enter. There was only one room, warmed by a fireplace before which sat a rocking chair. A table occupied one end of the room. Stairs descended along the far wall, and the young polcs followed Vigh down them.

At the bottom was a large kitchen and a bedroom area and another nook that seemed to be a storeroom for weapons. A short, lean, dark-eyed polc with blond hair, much younger than Vigh but far older than Meysah and Jimmy, waited there. He was leaning against a wall, smoking a pipe, but when they entered he pushed away from the wall and approached the boys.

'I am told you will need my help,' he said.

'This is my dearest of friends,' said Vigh, 'Boreth Culmik.'

'Hullo,' said Jimmy.

'I believe we have met before,' said Boreth, 'though just in passing, and a good while back.'

'Boreth has just come back from Telor,' Vigh told them.

Boreth nodded and shifted the pipe in his mouth. 'I've been there for a long while now, to help train more knights. It feels good to be back home.' He looked at Vigh. 'Funny how we change in so little time!' Then he looked at Meysah, and stared at him for a long time. 'Yes, I can see the resemblance – it runs in the family, eh? Adventure! Seems like yesterday.' His smile faded.

'What does?' asked Meysah.

Boreth smiled again. 'Bahvley, your elder brother, saved my life. I don't know if Vigh has ever told you the story, but I was being held captive at a Morkan camp, and Mirauk's best captain would've slain me himself, had your brother not come with reinforcements. My team, my captain and I came home to help save Teloria.

'This room you see here' – Boreth waved his hand – 'did not serve me as a hiding place during the Big War, but it saved several others, for which I am glad. I believe your sister hid here with a friend of your brother's.'

He smiled in sympathy. 'Bahvley helped many during his trip to Mork. I am gravely sorry for your loss, Meysah. I wish I had known him better.'

'Did you see him slain?' asked Meysah.

'No,' said Boreth. 'He went to Mork and the camp where I was held was too far from Mork to receive any news. Perhaps he was captured; best to hope that. I know you heard from Elina herself that she was told he was dead, but it doesn't necessarily mean he was.' Boreth frowned. 'But then again, if they say that Mirauk killed him himself ... Well, Elina told you the story, no need to rehash it.' Boreth paused. 'I owe him a great debt, and since I cannot save his life, I will save others in Teloria by assisting you.'

Meysah looked cheerfully at Vigh, who was smiling.

'We need no great army if we are to be undetected, as Vigh mentioned before,' continued Boreth, 'but we do need equipment.'

'We have to go see Gorthan,' said Vigh. 'He will be able to provide us with the necessary equipment.'

'What will Selemil say about all this?' asked Jimmy.

'We will first see Henker and Gorthan,' replied Vigh. 'They will advise us well. Gorthan knows that if Niome's gone, he can't do any more about it than to let us go after her. As for Selemil, he may have final say, but nothing can prevent us from going now. Selemil is a polc of tact but knows little of magic on the deeper levels, not like Henker or Niome understand it.' Vigh and Boreth shared a knowing look.

'I sense this may be a case where magic could be our only reliable source,' Vigh went on. 'Selemil knows that the wizards can overrule the governor's choice in certain circumstances. That's how it was in the times of kings and queens. Selemil is playing it safe, but Mork will attack again and Mirauk will use all his best fighters, those strong in magic. We will have to rely on magic.'

Vigh's gaze met Meysah's. 'We must follow our instincts now. I know in my heart that this is the right thing to do and you are our guide, Meysah. Lead us to Niome. She will tell us what we must do.'

They all looked at each other. Boreth put his pipe down on the table and started up the stairs. The others followed.

They walked for a quarter of the day to reach the large house Henker shared with his cousin Gorthan, on the other side of Teloria City. When they arrived, Henker was sitting on the front steps, holding his staff, as if he'd been expecting them. As they approached, he stood and led them inside.

'I have prepared lunch for you,' he announced. 'I knew you would be hungry when you'd get here.'

'But how did you know we were coming?' asked Jimmy.

'I know more than destiny itself,' Henker replied. He led them to the dining room table, where a meal waited. They all sat down and began to eat.

'Gorthan will be arriving soon,' said Henker.

'Henker,' began Meysah, 'I hope you don't think this crazy of me, but I believe that going out of

Teloria is a good thing. Selemil thought it absurd; that's why I mention it.'

'Oh, I understand perfectly,' said Henker. 'It runs in the family, I see, and I am happy it does. This is progress, I know it, and I know why you must go. You are meant to go, all of you. It has been foreseen.'

'Will we succeed?' asked Jimmy.

'That is for you to discover, for whatever I know now of the future may be changed by those involved.' Jimmy cocked his brow and slowly nodded his understanding.

'We'll have to word it carefully when speaking to Selemil,' said Boreth. 'He may get defensive about our safety.'

'Let me talk to Selemil,' said Henker. 'I told him I would have good news for Teloria that would seem like bad news to his ears. And he knows that when I do tell him, he must trust my judgement.'

'Thank you,' said Meysah.

'Hopefully,' said Jimmy, 'we won't run into too much trouble.'

'Oh?' chuckled Henker. 'You may. There is no such thing as "*not too much trouble*". But promise me this: when you come upon a grey house in the middle of a field, you will knock on the door.'

'What's in the grey house?' asked Vigh. Henker did not answer.

'I never heard of a grey house alone in the middle of a field before,' said Boreth.

'It's there,' Henker assured them. 'And you must knock on the door.'

'We will,' said Meysah.

They heard the front door open and close – Gorthan was home. He walked slowly into the dining room and looked at the guests, then at Henker with tired eyes. He let his sack drop to the floor.

'I didn't realise we were having guests,' he told Henker, then he turned his attention to the other four sitting at the table. 'You'll have to excuse my weariness – I was up all night. Remaining construction on the wall has begun and progresses rapidly; Selemil fears an attack soon.' He sighed. 'He's been fearing an attack for the past fifty years.'

'Have a seat,' said Henker. 'We need to ask you something.'

'Oh?' said Gorthan, sitting down.

'Actually,' added Vigh, 'we need weapons.'

'You see,' began Meysah, 'my sister left for the Great Rock, and I know she went against orders, but there's something there that can help us and we need to go help her – Elina told her about it. Besides, the Wizardess of Teloria can defy certain rules, even the Governor's, if she knows it to be good, and with Elina being dead, that leaves Niome as the Wizardess of Teloria.' Meysah wheezed to a finish, and Vigh gestured for him to breathe. Meysah drew in a huge breath. 'We thought, since you're the master swordfighter and a mentor to us all, you could lend us a few weapons . . . if you please.' Meysah stopped and smiled a desperately hopeful smile.

There was a long pause.

'Well,' Gorthan said at last, 'as Chief of Teloria, I forgive Niome and give you the permission to go. I can't blame *any* of you for wanting to go out there and do something. It sure is better than waiting around here. To be honest, I suspected she might go. That is why I insisted so much that she stay. Now that she has gone, it proves to me the importance of her cause. And now that she's out there, she needs all the help she can possibly get, as well as protection; it won't be long before Mirauk discovers she is in possession of the *Complement Book*. But I am not the ruler of Teloria and I'm wondering how to bring this up with Selemil.'

'I will tell him, cousin,' said Henker. 'He will come to see me sometime today.'

'Normally I'd be upset,' admitted Gorthan, 'but deep inside, I was hoping someone would be brave enough to step up and go out and do this rash thing. *I* can't because I have too many responsibilities here; otherwise I would have gone a long time ago, using all the skill in weaponry and magic I know. I don't want to waste time waiting for Teloria's doom, and who better to plunge into this affair than you. When are you planning on leaving?'

'As soon as possible,' replied Vigh.

'Niome was gone when I woke up,' said Meysah. 'She must've left last night or very early this morning.'

'Then we shall leave tomorrow, at the break of dawn,' said Boreth.

'Eat up,' Gorthan bid them. 'I will equip you after the meal.'

After lunch, Gorthan led them to his private chamber. He took out a box and set it on the bed. Then he laid a few garments beside it. 'I have been saving these for those brave enough to venture off,' he said. 'You have shown less fear than most, despite the dangers that await you.' He picked up the warm travel garments and gave them to Meysah and Jimmy. Then he opened the box. In it were sacks of herbs. 'These herbs will help you along your way. They will wake you, heal you, and invigorate you when most needed. They are magical. Take a sack each.'

When each had selected a sack, Gorthan set the box aside and gave Jimmy a sword and a knife. He gave only a knife to Meysah, who had a sword already. Then he looked at Vigh. 'This is all I offer. The rest you have, except this.' He took a smooth stone from his pocket and gave it to Vigh. It fit exactly in the palm of Vigh's hand, and gleamed ruby-gold. 'Keep this with you, close to your heart; it will bring good fortune.'

'Very well,' said Vigh, hefting the stone, which was surprisingly light. 'We thank you greatly.'

They started towards the chamber's door, but then Gorthan halted. 'One more thing,' he said. 'Prepare yourselves! Rest now. Clear your thoughts of anger and vengeance because if your minds are set on negative emotions, Mirauk will detect you and find you with the power of his mind. Do not dwell on him. Concentrate only on the *Book of Enchantment*.'

They all nodded.

Gorthan looked at them and smiled. 'This is good. May the stars shine upon you and protect you all.'

They saluted Gorthan and exited the house.

On their way home they met Selemil, who was walking swiftly towards Henker and Gorthan's house. 'Hello, Meysah,' he said. 'Hello, Vigh; Boreth; Jimmesh.' He frowned as if wondering why the four were together. 'Have you seen Niome?'

'Not yet,' was all Meysah said, but it was the truth.

'Well, perhaps Henker knows where she is. I've been looking for her all morning and I'm getting quite annoyed.' Meysah looked to the ground. 'Oh well,' continued Selemil, 'I will see you later!' He continued walking up the road.

Meysah and his three companions returned to their homes. He was packed for their trip and ready to go by sunset, and slept in his clothes.

Meysah woke early the next morning, so early it was still dark out, but he was anxious to leave and find his sister. He was dismayed when he found his father already up, and waiting for him. *He must have noticed the preparations,* Meysah thought, and wondered how to break the news to his father.

Before Meysah could formulate his announcement, Ceymi smiled and said, 'I've set your things by the door.'

Puzzled, Meysah asked, 'You're not upset?'

'Why would I be?' He held up the note Niome had left, which Meysah had let drop to the floor. Ceymi's smile never faltered. 'You have found the strength to pursue what I was always too frightened to do myself. I knew your time would come. Just promise me you'll be careful and if possible, to return. Don't let Bahvley's fate become your or Niome's fate. Return home after you have found what you are looking for.'

'I promise.'

They embraced, then Meysah gathered up his things.

'Good luck,' Ceymi said, and smiled again. Meysah returned the smile, then stepped out the door.

Jimmy was trotting up the road already. He met up with Meysah and the two best friends continued together to Teloria's main gate to meet Vigh and Boreth.

The officer of the guards on duty there looked at them. 'Henker has informed us of the importance of your departure. You sure are brave. Good luck out there. The Mighty Spirit alone knows what awaits you.'

'Thank you,' said Vigh.

Arrangements had been made to have their horses waiting for them, and Meysah found his Greyer there, eating some hay. Jimmy was given a horse, since he had none at home. Vigh and Boreth had their own there as well. They mounted up and urged their horses towards the gate where Henker was waiting for them. They thanked him again, and he simply smiled and nodded.

Outside the gate, they urged their horses into a gallop, and left Teloria City behind them.

Chapter Two:
The Passing Through Mistoff

After an early start, the four riders moved swiftly, following the main path up along the Stream of Fluidity. Clouds hid the sun, and a mist descended to drape itself around the four travellers. There was still no sign of Niome.

The path they followed intersected with another, and they reined their horses to a stop. 'Well, which way do we go?' asked Jimmy.

'Niome could have gone either way,' said Vigh, 'but which is the safest?'

'This path here leads into the forest,' said Boreth, pointing to the right. 'That explains the mist – that forest is Mistoff.'

'Is it true it's the most enchanted place around?' asked Jimmy.

'The most enchanted it is,' Boreth confirmed.

'It was inhabited by the Kaulchèc, long ago, during their stay in our valley,' explained Vigh. 'At least, that is how history tells it. They created the spells for the *Book of Enchantment* in those woods. I've never ventured into Mistoff, but I hear it is guarded by the ancient Pleessies.'

'Uh, Master Vigh,' said Meysah, trying to remember, 'what are Pleessies?'

'Ah, they are creatures of the night. I cannot describe them to you, for I've never seen or met one, but I have learnt of them.'

'So have we,' said Jimmy, 'but apparently Meysah was dreaming in class, perhaps of the pretty Ihal.'

'No!' replied Meysah, scowling. 'I forgot, that's all.'

The others laughed.

'They are active at night, protecting their realm,' continued Vigh. 'They have strong magical powers. What they use them for, I do not know, but I have my suspicions that the Portal at Darakön was once protected by them. Whether my theory is correct or not, with Mirauk trying to get a hold of the Portal Key Spell, it makes him their number-one enemy, and that makes them our potential allies. Whether they are truly friendly or not, they will appreciate anyone who will try to stop Mirauk and his followers. So I say, let us take the path into Mistoff on the chance that I am right.'

'That sounds like an excellent idea, Master Vigh,' said Jimmy.

'One concern,' began Boreth. 'What if Niome went the other way?'

'We can't split up, Boreth, if that's what you're thinking. We'll have to risk going the wrong way.'

Those in the company shared uncertain glances. Boreth knew his partner well, but he was right – they could not divide their number.

Meysah urged his horse into a slow trot. 'I'm going to Mistoff. Anyone who wishes to join me, let's go,' he called over his shoulder.

'I'm always by your side, my friend,' assured Jimmy, catching up to Meysah. 'It's a promise that I make: to always stick by you, because I know you'd do the same for me, and I don't intend to break it, ever.'

Vigh kneed his horse forward, and a moment later, so did Boreth, muttering, 'I guess I have no choice. I will ignore my fears.'

Vigh took the lead and set a rapid pace, despite the bumpy road. However, the closer to Mistoff they got, the rockier and more potholed the road became, and they had to slow down. By sundown they still hadn't reached the wood, but the horses were tired and refused to go farther.

'We have to stop for the night,' said Boreth. 'There's no point in continuing like this.'

'Agreed,' said Vigh, rubbing stiff limbs as they all dismounted. 'We will start early tomorrow.'

The company set up camp. Vigh ambled into the forest to hunt, while Jimmy and Meysah tended the horses. Boreth gathered firewood and started a small fire, and by the time he was done, Vigh had returned with a rabbit and some edible roots. After a meal of rabbit stew, the group tucked themselves into their bedrolls and within moments, Boreth and Vigh were asleep. Jimmy and Meysah, however, shifted restlessly in their blankets.

'Meysah,' whispered Jimmy, 'I can't get my eyes shut.'

'You're not alone,' answered Meysah. 'I keep worrying about Niome; she's got the *Complement Book*. If we fail to find and help her, I can't imagine how angry Selemil will be – let alone the world, when it's under Mirauk's evil reign.'

'Yah. I have to admit, I'm beginning to get scared as well, considering I'm not supposed to be out here.'

'None of us are, Jimmy. We could be jeopardising Teloria – or saving it.'

Jimmy rolled over and sat up to face Meysah. 'But you're a good fighter. I don't know if I'll be able to fight the enemy if ever we encounter them.'

'Nor do I. Just thinking about it makes me quake.'

'But you've got proper training, Meysah. I know I've received training too, but Selemil doesn't believe I can be a good knight, that's why I still don't have a master of my own. Lóim Weedler loves that. And the farther away from home we get, the more I begin to believe it myself.'

'What about your dream of becoming Master Swordfighter?' Meysah reminded him.

Jimmy sighed. 'I know. I love adventure.'

'There you go, Jimmy. You're just slow at integrating all the new techniques. I think being out here will help you grow as a knight.'

'I'm sure it will. I'm just getting jitters, so I worry about anything. Soon I'll turn into you, nauseous about my fears.'

'Hey Jimmy, you're out here now, and I believe your initial impulse to come was the right one to follow. Everything happens for a reason. We will save Teloria and you'll become a hero and a master swordfighter, and then Selemil won't be able to be as strict with you or me as he is right now. He speaks through fear too; that's why he wants the best to be even better. You'll see, he'll recognise your talent,' Meysah stated with confidence.

'I suppose you're right. He's not here now, so I should probably focus on getting a wink of sleep.'

Jimmy lay back down and rolled over onto his side and shut his eyes. Meysah did the same.

The next morning's journey began even earlier than the previous day's. Jimmy dozed on his horse from time to time, letting his head drop forward. They reached the edge of the wood before midday, and stopped to eat before entering Mistoff.

They progressed slowly and carefully, despite the path they followed, for the woods were enveloped in a fog so thick it swallowed the ground and underbrush – they could barely see the way ahead. It was dim under the trees, and the air was humid, so humid that they had to take off their overcoats. The fog muffled every sound, but they could hear little rustles, as if from scurrying feet, and now and then, squeaks.

'Could those be the Pleessies?' inquired Jimmy.

'I believe so,' replied Vigh. 'I suspect we have disturbed them. They don't normally move about during the day, unless troubled – that is, if the myths are correct.'

'Let us keep going, then,' said Boreth. 'If they wish for us to leave, we will show them we are here in peace and will depart as soon as we can.'

They kept going, moving slowly but steadily in a single line following Vigh's horse. Not having to worry about guiding his own mount, Meysah looked around as they rode. He did a double take when he thought he saw something moving in the leaves.

As Meysah was squinting in that direction, Jimmy halted. 'What's that sound?' he asked warily.

'It sounds like the rapids,' Boreth suggested. He looked at Vigh. 'Can we hear the Twisted Rapids from here? They would have to be quite loud for the wind to carry their sound all the way here.'

'No,' breathed Jimmy. 'It sounds more like . . . hooves.'

The company stopped all movement and listened. Indeed, there were hoofbeats approaching, and quite rapidly.

A dark figure emerged from the fog.

'That can't be Niome's horse,' quavered Meysah.

'To the trees!' cried Vigh. 'Conceal yourselves. Dismount so you're not visible above the fog.'

The group jumped off their horses and pulled them into the trees. Once concealed, they turned to watch the path. They couldn't see the stranger, but they could hear the hoofbeats loud and clear. The sound halted.

'We are almost there, Kuffle,' said a voice.

'All right, then why did you stop to tell me?' said another voice.

'Because I don't like to speak while I'm riding,' the first voice answered. 'Kuffle, once we get there, we must not let anyone out of the kingdom. They can hide in there as long as they want and we are not to enter, for Mirauk's orders are to guard the intersection at the main path. If anyone gets out, we capture them and bring them to Mork, especially if they know certain people, or certain things. Don't get carried away like you usually do! Mirauk wants them unspoiled.' He inhaled loudly. 'Except for the one I'm to deal with.' He chuckled sinisterly.

'Understood.'

The hoofbeats started again. The company waited until no sound was heard but the scurrying Pleessies. Then they slowly got back on the path.

'Guarding the intersection?' said Jimmy. 'Capturing those who wander away? It sure is a good thing we left when we did.'

'Good thing *Niome* left when she did,' corrected Vigh.

'This is the point of no return,' Meysah said solemnly. 'We can't ever go back now.'

'It's clear to me that Mirauk realises the *Complement Book* will leave Teloria, making it harder for him to get hold of it. He will soon be aware that it's not there,' said Vigh. 'We'd better hurry to find Niome, wherever she may be. I was thinking perhaps we could pursue Mirauk's riders and stop them, but by doing so we will only be exposing ourselves. Does everyone agree with me? Meysah, what do you think? I know that—' Vigh looked around. Meysah was not there. 'Meysah?' he said. 'Meysah!'

'Meysah!' shouted Jimmy, looking around.

'He must have been taken, with no chance to shout for help,' concluded Boreth, his eyebrows drawn down in dread.

'Let's look around,' said Vigh.

'Greyer's here,' said Jimmy of Meysah's horse.

But they saw no sign of Meysah.

Jimmy took a deep breath and opened his mouth to yell, but Boreth put a hand over his mouth. 'Not too loud,' Boreth warned.

Jimmy nodded and continued to look around. He was backing away from a tangle of undergrowth when he stumbled, tumbling backwards with a yelp. He disappeared in the dense white fog.

'Jimmy!' cried Boreth, reaching down towards him, but his fingers closed on air. He straightened and whirled towards Vigh. 'They've disappeared into the fog! What are we to do?'

'There's nothing we can do,' answered Vigh. He gestured at the fog that concealed the Pleessies, whose squeaking had grown agitated. 'I think they took Meysah and Jimmy. We must leave, before they take us too. Let's keep going until we reach the edge of the forest. Then the Pleessies will see that we are not hostile, and perhaps they will return our companions to us.'

Boreth reluctantly nodded. The horses had grown nervous, so they continued on foot, leading the four animals. Boreth kept on glancing back, but Vigh looked ahead, observing everything they passed along the way. The day darkened, making it tougher to follow the path.

'Halt!' a voice croaked.

Vigh and Boreth stopped and looked down at a very short and squat creature dressed in green and grey. It glared at them. 'Who might ye be?' it rasped.

'We are travellers,' said Vigh. 'We come in peace.'

'I know ye comes in peace. Otherwise I wouldn't be speakin' to ye. I mean for ye to identify yerselves. Yer names.'

Boreth looked at Vigh and lifted an eyebrow as if wondering if they should trust this Pleessy. Boreth had become suspicious of everything, after he'd been captured and spent time in the Morkan camps.

'My name is Vigh Nimrod,' Vigh told the creature.

'And I'm Boreth Culmik.'

'Then ye are the friends of the boyses. Come with me. Follow up this way and quicken up.'

The Pleessy led them deep into the woods; his eyes seemed to glow in the dark. Boreth tried to steady the horses, but he himself was quite agitated.

The Pleessy stopped at a large tree and lifted up two of its roots, revealing a doorway that spilled light out into the fog. The creature nodded at the horses and swept one arm towards the entrance. 'Bring them in.' The Telorians slowly pushed the horses in and followed carefully, almost hesitantly. When they had passed, the doorway closed up behind them. The Pleessy indicated a stable for the horses not far from the entrance, and the two Telorians left them there.

More roots within the space beneath the tree slowly curled and lifted, forming a stairway. The squeaks of many Pleessies came from somewhere at the bottom of that staircase. Vigh and Boreth followed the Pleessy down.

They entered a garish hall in various shades of green and blue, offset by yellow and red. It was frightfully colourful, a complete contrast to the fog-shrouded exterior. Vigh squinted, looking around the hall at the many Pleessies gathered there. They all spoke in raspy, squeaky voices and wore the same grey hat and grey and green garments as Vigh and Boreth's guide, whose glowing eyes dimmed until they looked as normal as a polc's.

The creature led them across the hall and up a corridor to a room where Meysah and Jimmy sat on a colourful plush rug with a Pleessy clad in resplendent garments, with cut gems for buttons. Unlike the others, it wore no grey hat. It had no crown, but it sat with such dignity, they could not mistake his rank.

The Pleessy rose. 'Greetings,' he said. 'I am Woob, King of my people. This is my servant, Mibb.' He indicated their guide. 'I hear ye are friendly travellers. Sit. Weez will talk.'

Vigh and Boreth sat down next to their companions and the king sat back down. Mibb joined them on the rug.

'Yer young friends tell me ye are looking for another,' began the king.

'Yes,' said Vigh. 'A young girl. Her name is Niome.'

'Yes, the boyses here's sister,' said King Woob, waving his hand towards Meysah.

'Has she passed this way?' asked Boreth.

'I have not seen her,' replied the king. 'Maybe others have. Times are hard.' King Woob gave the Telorians a knowing look.

'My people, weez are magical,' the king continued. 'Weez been here a long time. Weez call ourselves *Piflacatta*, which means "powerful wizards of the misty woods." Pleessies is the name a great Telorian knight gave us long ago. Easier to remember, I suppose.'

'They are quite familiar with the Telorians,' Meysah added of the Pleessies, pointing a thumb in King Woob's direction.

'Yes, weez are. Weez have not been in contact with one of yer people for a long time, but weez always remember a language once weez have learnt it and weez are always ready to help.

'Lately, weez lost our power and cannot protect our forest like weez used to. That is why weez cannot block the paths. There used to be a shield around the area. Weez have been cursed by an evil polc and wicked polcs have been passing through.'

'Yes,' said Vigh. 'We heard them go by. They want to stop any Telorian who tries to go out for help. It appears Mirauk has cursed your forest to tamper with your shield. It is regretful that he has caused so much harm. But now it gets even worse, with the trap they are planning for Teloria.'

'Ye are wise to have decided not to follow. Weez heard them talk of blockading the way and ye shouldn't risk it. Ye should find yer friend and ye should find allies. Weez can help, but weez do not leave our forest. Weez are working on creating enough magic for a new shield, same as ye people are building a new wall.'

'Yes,' said Boreth, 'that's right. And if you can stop any riders of Mirauk's who go by, it would help a great deal, even if it only slows them before they decide to go around the forest. We need to prevent them from spying on the kingdom any way we can.'

'*Karamab,* weez call them: "riders of the evil land." And ye must go before more come,' said the king.

'Then we thank you for your brief hospitality and your advice,' said Vigh. 'We must travel through the night and hopefully we will find Niome soon.'

'I have nothing more to offer,' admitted King Woob, 'but the guarantee that if weez see yer friend, weez'll help. Oh, and this.' He held up a small cube of dim light. 'This'll help ye see through and into the fog, as if it weren't there.'

'This is interesting,' observed Meysah, taking the cube. 'Why don't any of your people use it?'

'Weez need the light in here to feed our eyes, then weez can see well outside. Only that. Weez made these a long time ago for allies.'

'Thank you,' said Meysah, and the others echoed his words.

Mibb led them to their horses, then brought them outside and to the path. 'The others shall be informed of yer presence,' he said. 'They will guide ye as ye need it.'

Vigh nodded, and the little creature scuttered away, disappearing into the fog. They heard the scurrying of the night crawlers as the forest quieted around them. Vigh held up the light-cube and a beam of light shone from it. Then the light dimmed and it seemed to the travellers that the fog had completely cleared away. They could see far into the distance, more clearly than they normally would. When they looked around, they could see that the fog was everywhere, yet the road seemed clear of it.

The horses had calmed by now, so they mounted up. Vigh took the lead, since he was holding up the light. Jimmy and Meysah rode side by side behind Vigh, and Boreth brought up the rear, glancing back from time to time. They were able to set a good pace.

Then Vigh stopped abruptly, and the others practically bumped into him. They followed Vigh's gaze to see many more riders in the distance . . . coming their way.

'Not again,' groaned Jimmy.

At that moment, a Pleessy came out from the trees and said, 'There's no time to run far. Up this tree ye go. I, Munn, shall take yer horses to a safe place, not far from here.'

The four Telorians dismounted and ran to the tree. Vigh interlaced his hands and boosted the others up, then jumped up, grabbing the lowest branch, and pulled himself up. They quickly climbed up the tree. Below them, the Pleessy waved his hand about and the horses followed him calmly, as if summoned. They disappeared into the fog and underbrush.

Vigh quenched the light-cube. Meysah looked down, but saw nothing.

Jimmy was so nervous he started slipping sideways, then watched wide-eyed as his knife slipped from his belt and fell. His heart pounded in his chest. *What if a rider saw it fall, or sees it on the forest floor?*

An army rode past below them. As shadowy riders went by, one clear voice rose above the rumble of many hooves striking the ground. 'Hurry up! Captain Kàtchah is waiting for us. Hurry – to the intersection!'

When they were sure the army had passed, the Telorians jumped down. Jimmy picked up his knife. 'Captain Kàtchah,' he pondered. 'So one's Kuffle and the other who gave the orders was the captain.'

'Yes, and I know that name well,' Boreth said grimly. 'This Morkan is some sort of wizard too. He has a reputation: he will be somewhere only if he will succeed in achieving his goal. I know. I met him while in captivity, though he was not Captain then. This polc is dangerous.'

'Shouldn't we go do something, then?' insisted Meysah.

'Like what?' demanded Boreth. 'I know you want to warn Selemil of this, but if we go back now, we will be captured. Remember what King Woob told us.'

'Boreth is right,' said Vigh. 'The army has passed. It is safer to continue northwards.'

'All right,' conceded Meysah. 'But I wonder, why would they wait to capture the kingdom?'

'Their first priority is to stop all travellers – that, we know,' said Vigh. 'Their numbers are not great enough to take on Teloria alone. They will guard the roads and wait for more soldiers, or orders from Mirauk.'

'Then let us hope the reinforcements don't come while we're in the fields,' said Boreth.

'Is it safe to continue now?' Meysah asked in a meek voice.

'Yes,' said a Pleessy voice, and they turned to see Munn standing with his arm outstretched, pointing at the travellers. 'Here yer horses are. Come back all safe.'

'Where did you take them?' asked Jimmy.

'Down to the curvy tree out yonder,' replied the Pleessy. 'There is a tree hut there. Weez built it ourselves specially for horses.'

'That was very kind of you, to help us in this way,' said Boreth.

'Well, ye are kind too. King Woob had taken ye as friends and chose to find out who ye were in a safe manner for us. Weez cannot do the same with Morkans – too dangerous. But all is well-deserved for ye; it is an honour to meet ye, faithful Telorians. Allies once are allies always, and long ago ye gave weez Pleessies a place to dwell safely; weez owe it to ye to return the favour.' Munn drew himself up. 'Weez live for many ages and remember everything.' The Pleessy smiled warmly. 'Now, ye travellers should not waste time – go now.' He saluted them, then ran off into the darkness of the trees.

The Telorians set off, again with Vigh in the lead and Boreth in the rear, moving slowly and warily, alert for more trouble. Jimmy and Meysah rode in the middle, dozing in their saddles.

Meysah slowly became aware of soft singing and blinked, looking around, thinking he'd dreamt it. But no, Vigh was singing – more chanting, really – an old song Meysah had never heard before.

It was rare to hear someone singing in Teloria lately, for everyone was far too busy working and worrying about Mirauk. Even Elina's funeral had prompted no song, so scared were the Telorians that Mirauk would hear them mourning and exploit that for his own triumph. Meysah and Jimmy, for their part, hadn't sung since their youth. But now, for the first time in many years, Vigh broke the silence in a pleasant singing voice, the kind you want to listen to all the time even if it sings a troubled song, as Vigh's was.

We hear of travellers long ago,
Who slew great beasts and won some gold.
We hear how they overcame all their foes,
Bringing hope and peace, and how they were bold.

But when they die, what happens next?
New fears come home and perils stay,
New heroes come along and there's no time to rest,
For fight they must, risk their lives if they may.

And what about me, when do I go,
And prove myself to everyone?
I will dare to defeat and overcome fear and foe,
I will be as great as the greatest, when I am done.

Now that the shadows are clearly seen,
And the enemy strives to kill,
I shake and shiver – what does all this mean?
I hide away. I cannot find my will.

I fear what is to come,
And question my bravery;
Help I need from some,
To gather up my bravery.

Here Boreth joined in, his voice slightly higher,
and the two voices harmonised sweetly.

So on I ride now with my mates,
Along the path to the unknown future.
We all are scared about our fates,
But fight we will until all is secure.

There the song ended and the older polcs rode on
in silence. The two young polcs looked at each other

and smiled in sympathy but said nothing. So beautiful had been the song, it seemed to resonate in the stillness of the trees. The boys had no desire to break it.

They came at last to the edge of the wood. The sun had risen, sending the Pleessies into their burrows to rest the day away. The polcs rode from the mist into the warmth of the day, which immediately perked them up. Jimmy and Meysah did not mention the song, though Vigh still hummed a bit, for they knew Vigh and Boreth had lived through great hardship and woe during the Big War.

They had ridden only a short distance from Mistoff, the forest still visible, when Vigh scanned the area to make sure there were no riders from Mork in sight, then called a stop so they could eat a light breakfast.

Jimmy looked up at the bright blue sky, his blond hair bright in the morning light. He was only two years younger than Meysah, but in that moment he was as a child, fresh-faced and glowing with happiness. There was a maturity in his adolescent eyes, though.

'Now this is what a real Spring day is supposed to be like,' he declared. 'Warm, sunny, and energising!'

'The days are getting longer,' said Boreth, 'which gives us an advantage if the enemy likes to ride at night.'

'How would we know if they like to ride at night?' asked Meysah.

'If we don't see any during the day!' Jimmy exclaimed with a laugh.

'You shouldn't tease!' said Meysah with a broad smile on his face.

'You're right, Jimmy,' said Vigh. 'So far we've only seen them at night. It's possible they think they've remained unseen, but we will take advantage of that and ride farther by day. They believe they have taken the lead in this race, but we will prove that untrue.'

'I hope they maintain that belief,' said Jimmy. 'Then they won't expect us to win.'

'And we will ambush them,' declared Meysah, getting caught up in the daydream, 'and vanquish them.'

'Yes, I hope so as well,' Vigh said solemnly.

They finished up their breakfast and got ready to depart again. Before leaving, Meysah looked back towards Mistoff. 'Those were friendly people. When they snatched me to learn who I was, and were unsure if I was friend or foe, they were scared. But even then, they were polite and kind.'

'Yes,' said Boreth. 'They are what the stories say of them.'

'It seems funny to say,' began Vigh, 'but I will miss them. We seemed less alone among them. Now we are only four and we'll have to manage on our own.'

'For now,' said Boreth. 'Later we may meet others who will help us.'

'Let us hope so,' replied Vigh, taking out the stone that Gorthan gave him and smiling at it before slipping it back into his breast pocket.

They regarded the wood a while longer, and Meysah expressed a silent goodbye to their new friends. Then they mounted up and trotted away, heading north.

CHAPTER THREE:
The Red Tracks

The day seemed to pass slowly with few landmarks to break up the wide open space the four Telorians rode through. The road ran straight into the distance but they enjoyed the view. The grass was turning from yellow to green, and the sun was melting the last of the snow that clung to the hollows and shaded areas in these northern climes. They passed a carpet of peach-coloured flowers that turned into a thin layer of white snow as they approached the Twisted Rapids.

They dismounted to tend their horses and refill their flasks with fresh cold water.

'Smell the air,' said Jimmy, closing his eyes and taking a deep breath. He stood with his face tipped up to the sun, arms open as if embracing the freshness of the day. 'This trip is better than I thought!'

'Stand like that too long and you'll get a sunburn,' Meysah teased, nudging Jimmy's arm.

A shadow passed over them, and they all looked up. Meysah's jaw dropped in shock. A dragon crossed the sky, wings flapping languorously. It shrieked hoarsely but did not seem to heed them.

'The dragons are already awake,' mused Boreth. 'They can sense what's to come.'

'It's a good thing it didn't see us,' said Meysah.

'Oh, it did,' said Vigh, eyes following the dragon. 'But it won't bother us unless we disturb it first. That's how dragons are. Yet this one seemed . . . I don't know, almost as though it was checking up on us.' He gave his head a quick shake. 'Maybe it's just me. With all these strange things going on . . .'

'Well, at least we'll never have to fight one because we'll never bother them,' stated Jimmy. 'We have no cause to, luckily.'

'I'm afraid that's not so,' said Boreth.

Jimmy gaped at him. 'How come?'

'The Portal lies in their caverns, in case you've forgotten,' answered Boreth. 'In Darakön.'

Jimmy deflated. 'Oh.'

They watched the flying dragon, now just a distant speck in the sky. Then there came another speck, on the ground this time: a rider.

'Is that Niome?' asked Jimmy.

'No,' said Meysah. 'I'd recognise her horse.'

The rider turned towards them as they got closer. Now they saw details they hadn't seen from afar. The rider was clad in full body armour, with a helmet hiding his face.

He halted, keeping over a dozen yards between them, then turned away.

'We've been spotted,' gasped Meysah.

'Shall we go after him?' asked Jimmy, preparing to mount his horse.

'No,' Boreth snapped authoritatively. 'It might only lead us into a trap. It's not hard to be seen in an open prairie such as this. If there is an army, we will see them and take cover.'

The boys remained silent. They mounted their horses and rode onwards.

They continued steadily for quite some time. The faces of the older polcs were peaceful, their thoughts elsewhere. Meysah's thoughts, however, were troubled. He couldn't stop worrying about the doom brought upon them since Elina's death: Niome's 'escape', the riders of Mork, the dragon, the armoured rider – and where was Niome? *What next?* he thought.

Although it hadn't been that long since they had left Teloria, Meysah felt homesick. He had never been away from home before, or away from anyone close to him. He'd never had any worries, other than learning his skills properly. He wasn't used to this sort of life, not like Vigh and Boreth were, but he wasn't one to complain.

It hadn't been that bad so far, he told himself; not compared to what Vigh and Boreth had lived through. *But it will only get worse.* That was too much to bear. Not to mention they'd been gone three whole days and still hadn't found Niome. The last time a member of his family left, he never returned.

Unless Niome had taken another route, they should have reached her by now. Even if she had gone a different way, they would have met up by now. *And she would be guiding the way.*

Meysah's worries overwhelmed him as discouragement filled his mind. A tear trickled down his cheek, and he sniffed. *Please,* he pleaded to the Mighty Spirit, *don't let Niome suffer the same fate that came upon Bahvley.*

Suddenly Jimmy halted. He was staring at the ground. Boreth pulled up his horse beside him. 'Look,' said Jimmy, 'tracks!'

Boreth carefully studied the ground. 'They could be Niome's.'

'Then what are we waiting for!' Meysah urged. 'Let's follow them.'

But night was falling. 'We'll have to wait till morning,' said Vigh. 'It's getting dark. But we shouldn't stay here. We should find shelter or cover within some trees.'

Boreth looked around. 'Over there.' He pointed at a copse of low trees in the near distance. 'We'll take refuge there.'

They guided their horses into the copse and made camp for the night.

When morning came, they returned to the trail and began following the tracks.

'Boreth, does the pattern of steps seem odd to you?' voiced Vigh as he slowed his horse.

'Ay,' replied Boreth. He halted his horse and the others followed suit. 'I observe but one set of footprints – no horse's hoofprints – and the right foot takes a bigger step than the left.'

Boreth dismounted his horse and bent down to take a closer look.

There was a slight deviating twist off the left heel, and the prints of the boot on the right foot pressed more lightly. Only someone with a limp would make such tracks, and Boreth knew what that meant. If these were Niome's tracks, then she had lost her horse and was injured. Boreth shared this observation with the others, and they followed the tracks more attentively.

After a while, the tracks left the road and cut across the field towards the rapids. It was harder to spot the signs on the grass, but Boreth was an expert tracker. He dismounted his horse once more and made sure they were following the right pair of boots.

When they reached the Twisted Rapids, they found no one there. The tracks continued along the bank, visible in the sand. The Telorians walked beside them for some time. Then they all halted.

'What happened?' Meysah asked, confused. 'The tracks, are they—'

'I'm hallucinating,' Jimmy muttered, rubbing his eyes.

'It must be the way the sun is reflecting on the sand,' Vigh surmised. 'It is causing an optical illusion, am I correct, Boreth?'

Some of the tracks had turned red. Not completely red, just a spot on the right side of the right foot.

Boreth bent down once more, touching and smelling what he hoped was just damp sand. He shook his head. 'There is no question, it's blood,' he said slowly.

They all exchanged troubled looks.

Meysah's face paled. 'Are you sure?'

Boreth made a show of examining the trace again, though he was certain. Still, he didn't want to alarm Meysah. 'Let's see, well . . .' He sighed. 'Whoever it's from, I'm afraid it's blood.'

Meysah whimpered. The thought that his sister was severely hurt invaded his mind, and he wondered if she was still alive. *She must be losing blood rapidly,* he thought. He didn't want to find her dead, not until she was older than Henker himself.

Has Mirauk discovered who protects the Complement Book? *Has he captured Niome? Tried to kill her?* These thoughts whirled through Meysah's mind, as fear gripped his heart.

Feeling suddenly weak, he fell to his knees beside the tracks, staring at them as though his sister lay dead before him. *Please let her be all right,* he begged the Mighty Spirit. 'Stars! I've already lost my brother,' whispered Meysah, 'I can't lose my sister, too.'

The tracks blurred as his eyes filled with tears. He sobbed silently for a little while, then wiped his tears on his sleeve.

His best friend helped him up and consoled him with a hug and a smile compassionate enough to make even a Morkan sympathise.

Meysah took a deep breath. 'We're going to find Niome,' he said, determined. 'Or we'll find the bastard who did this.'

They continued on foot, leading their horses behind Boreth as he followed the tracks.

Then Meysah remembered, 'The herbs! We can give her some herbs!'

'The herbs will heal her soul and body, that's true,' said Vigh. 'But even if we found Niome now, as much as these herbs regenerate and disinfect, they cannot stop a bleeding wound.'

'I don't want her to bleed to death,' Meysah murmured to himself. He tried to convince himself that his sister was clever enough to take care of herself and that, hopefully soon, there wouldn't be a residue of blood on the tracks. What offered him the slightest bit of hope was that the blood on the tracks was fresh. Whoever had left them had passed this way only a short time before. They would catch up to that polc eventually.

Boreth suddenly stopped and looked up, his eyes wide with terror.

'What is it?' asked Jimmy. 'Did you find something?'

'Unfortunately, yes,' replied Boreth. He picked up a shiny knife that was stained with blood. He wiped the knife clean and handed it to Meysah. 'Is this Niome's knife?' he asked.

Meysah didn't recognise it. He took it from Boreth and put it in his boot. Then, compelled to find his sister as urgently as possible, he broke into a run, pelting along the track, eyes intent on the landscape ahead.

'Wait, Meysah!' cried Jimmy, running after him. He caught up with Meysah and grabbed his arm, swinging him around to face him. 'It's okay. Niome will be all right. We'll get to her soon.'

The other two came jogging up, pulling the horses behind them. Vigh, Boreth, and Jimmy exchanged worried looks.

'We need to be patient,' Vigh said gently. 'Even if Niome is hurt, we will be able to save her. It's not too late. If she can travel with a bleeding leg, then it's not too late.'

And with that Meysah mounted Greyer and shouted, 'Yah! Find her, Greyer! Go.'

Greyer's mane streamed back in the wind as he led them all onward.

They went only a short distance before Boreth called for a halt. He'd noticed that the tracks had turned back towards the field – their owner had pushed through the grasses and left a telltale trail.

As they turned and slowly followed it, a hollow cold sensation settled in the pit of Meysah's stomach. He had never imagined how frightened he might be once he'd embarked on this journey. This was more than just a search, he realised. Things were becoming complicated.

His stomach hurt. Was he hungry? He brought his hand to his abdomen and rubbed it. His teeth began to chatter. The more he thought of Niome and the tracks, the more his teeth chattered.

'Are you cold?' inquired Jimmy.

'No, my stomach hurts,' replied Meysah. 'It's another one of my weird stomach aches.'

'Nothing weird there,' said Jimmy, 'you've always got those.'

'Are you frightened?' asked Boreth, dropping back until his horse was even with Meysah's.

'I'm dead scared stiff and scareder, even,' admitted Meysah, 'more than I've ever been before.'

'I know it's difficult to ignore it,' said Vigh, also dropping back, 'but you must clear your mind of all this. I know there's not much you can imagine in this state, but you must not let yourself despair.' He rode up close to Meysah and put his hand on his shoulder. 'Take a deep breath and have some water. It'll help.'

'What about the herbs?' suggested Meysah.

'Save them. We will need them at more critical moments.'

Meysah nodded and closed his eyes, taking a deep breath. He drank only one sip of water.

When they stopped to eat a short while later, Meysah, having lost his appetite, only took a few bites. He tried to remember a spell he had learnt long ago – *the* Spell to Heal a Bad Tummy Ache, he had called it. Only bits and pieces of it came to him and not in the right order, so he figured he'd have to rely on mind over matter to help ease his stomach.

The ache started to wear off as they rode on, and the colour returned to Meysah's cheeks, but the ache came back as a piercing, pinching pain when they lost sight of the tracks. The tracks had lost their red tinge, which Boreth deduced meant that the boot had been put back on – a good sign, Meysah hoped – but it made it harder to see any prints in the grass.

'What do you mean, you don't see any more tracks?' cried Meysah when Boreth stopped, looked around, and made the announcement.

Boreth lifted his hands in a shrug. 'They stop. But wait. Let me observe the area and figure this out.' He proceeded to dismount and walk around for a while, eyes scanning the ground. Then he looked up at the sky, where low grey clouds were gathering. 'Rain is coming,' he said.

'Does that have anything to do with the tracks?' asked Meysah.

'Partially,' answered Boreth, crouching over a patch of grass.

'Well then, hurry up and tell us,' cried Meysah in desperation.

'Meysah!' Jimmy snapped in warning, astonished by his friend's tone. 'Let him do his thing!'

Boreth straightened and faced the others. 'There's only one logical explanation for the disappearance of the tracks.' He motioned towards the ground. 'There was snow here before when the polc, hopefully Niome, walked this way. Now it has melted. We have to use our senses and judgement to figure out which way she went. Rain clouds are coming, which explains the warmer air and moist earth. Night is falling, too; I reckon she must have gone looking for shelter. The tracks here are fresh, so wherever she is, she's close. I'm assuming she went down that way to that wooded area.'

The team looked up ahead and saw several willow trees huddled together, creating a shelter, their branches drooping into the water.

'Let's go,' said Meysah.

They slowed their horses as they got nearer; Meysah stopped to listen but heard nothing. The sky was darkening and pink and yellow streaks in the clouds told them the sun was setting. Meysah dismounted Greyer and started walking.

Vigh reached down and clutched his arm. 'Quietly. It may not be Niome after all.'

Meysah nodded, pulled his hood up over his head, and signalled that the others should stay back. He walked into the enclosure created by the willow branches.

There was no one there. He looked around. *Maybe she heard us and hid,* he thought. *Perhaps she was afraid we were those riders.*

A snap behind him made Meysah turn, but still, no one was there. He narrowed his eyes, wondering if the sound had come from above. He clutched the hilt of the sword at his waist, ready to draw it if necessary, and looked up.

Someone pounced on him from above, knocking him flat on his stomach. The polc hunched over him, a knee on either side of him, and, pulling his head back by the hair, placed a knife at his neck.

Then, his attacker quickly flipped him onto his back and, upon seeing his face, retreated.

Meysah rose shakily, belatedly drawing his sword. When he looked up, he saw a fragile, frightened polc standing before him. 'Niome!' he cried. He let his sword drop and ran to take her into his arms.

'I'm so glad to find you here,' she breathed.

'You, find?' Meysah smiled. '*We've* found *you*, at last.'

The others came running up. Meysah sheathed his sword and Niome put away her knife.

'I've been injured,' Niome said, showing them her right ankle, wrapped in bloody bandages.

'How did this happen?' asked Vigh.

'Riders – from Mork.'

'Yes, we've encountered them also,' said Jimmy.

'There was a whole band of them,' explained Niome. 'I got as far away as possible, as fast as I could, but one of them pursued me.' She paused and sat down, leaning against the trunk of a tree. 'I managed to injure his horse, but he tripped up mine and I fell off. It galloped away. I was all alone, facing this enemy, and I was scared and regretted that I'd left without anyone else.' She started weeping.

'It's okay, Niome,' Meysah soothed.

'The rider attacked me,' continued Niome. 'He stabbed me in the ankle. I fell down and struggled to get it out – the knife. I ran a bit and let the knife drop. I looked back to see if he had followed, but surprisingly, he was busy watching a dragon fly by. Then he ran back to rejoin his team.'

'The dragon,' said Jimmy. 'We saw it too.'

'It saved my life, in a way,' said Niome. 'Had it not passed overhead . . .' She stopped again and began gulping air, trying not to cry.

Meysah held her in his arms as Boreth unwrapped the bandage. Pressing on the gash, he looked at it carefully. 'It's not deep. When you were stabbed, the knife cut you diagonally.' Boreth took the pouch of herbs out of his pocket and sprinkled a bit of the mixture on the wound.

'I already put herbs on it; I brought some from home,' said Niome. 'It doesn't hurt anymore, but it won't stop bleeding.'

'I'll put a new bandage on it,' said Boreth. 'Sometimes wounds bleed a long time before healing for good.'

Vigh furrowed his brows in deep thought. 'Niome,' he began, 'the rider, did he leave on his horse?'

'Yes. I hadn't injured it enough to cripple it. Why?'

'Well, I think the rider might have seen us earlier – yesterday,' said Vigh. 'And that was shortly after the dragon flew by. We must be careful.'

'See, Niome?' Meysah said, smiling. 'We were right behind you the entire time.'

A light rain began to fall. 'We should make camp,' said Boreth. 'We need our rest. Tomorrow you will ride with me, Niome, for my horse is strong enough to bear the weight of two without losing speed. If we're to get to that rock, we should do it fast.'

Niome was happy they were going to help her with her mission, but she gave no reply; she merely smiled.

The older polcs set up the tent while the boys prepared a cold meal and cared for the horses. When everyone had eaten, Vigh said, 'Niome, you and your brother and Jimmy can take the tent. Boreth and I will keep watch.'

As the three younger polcs crawled into the tent and settled down for the night, the older two sat down under the meagre shelter of the willow tree's branches. 'I shall take first watch,' said Vigh. 'I'm not tired.'

'All right,' replied Boreth, 'but as soon as you want to switch, wake me.'

Vigh nodded and leaned back against the tree trunk. Boreth lay down between the tent and the tree and dozed off to sleep.

After some time, Boreth woke, troubled. 'Vigh,' he whispered. His friend turned to look at him as Boreth sat up. 'Was I dreaming or did I hear loud thumping?'

'You were dreaming. You're concerned about something?'

'Yes. I can't stop wondering about that rider we saw. What if he was the one who attacked Niome? He's seen us and will have reported us by now. It is too dangerous to stay out here much longer.'

'It's even more dangerous to go back,' said Vigh. 'We may as well go and confront Mirauk himself.'

'I'm frightened that's what we're in for,' admitted Boreth.

'The rain has stopped,' said Vigh, and yawned. 'I need my rest now.'

Boreth nodded and dropped the subject. He rose and stretched, as Vigh lay down in his place.

Morning dawned too cloudy to see the sun. Vigh had to shake the tent to wake the young Telorians. Jimmy and Meysah started to prepare breakfast as Vigh folded up the small tent and Boreth went to tend the horses.

Since no one would let Niome do anything, she went to the edge of the water and sat down. She unravelled her bandage and rinsed away the dried blood. The wound had stopped bleeding, but she washed it all the same and put the bandage back on to keep it clean.

Boreth sat down beside her. 'I'm afraid I didn't say a proper hello. It is easy to forget manners in such times.'

'That's all right,' said Niome. 'I heard you were in Telor. I see you're back now, obviously.' She chuckled self-consciously. 'How did that go?'

'Quite well. Um, it took us a while to find you, you know. Pardon my asking, but which way did you go? Which road did you take?'

'Up around Mistoff. That's where I first saw the band of Morkan riders. They entered the wood from that side, so I avoided it.'

'We saw them also,' said Boreth. 'Almost face to face, in fact. It was when we were in the forest.' Niome looked at him in puzzlement. 'They didn't see us because of the fog. We heard them coming and we hid. The creatures who dwell there, the Pleessies, helped us pass by the riders undetected, but now I fear the Morkans know we're out here.'

'Oh, they know,' Niome confirmed. 'Mirauk knows; I can almost feel it in my bones. And it's not just because one rider saw you that these Morkans know. I've seen two small armies so far, and soldiers in the second one saw me. They all ignored me except for the one who thought he could get rid of me.' She waved her hand towards her ankle. 'No doubt he's reported it to his superior by now.' She frowned. 'I wonder why he was so afraid of the dragon.'

'The Portal lies in their mountains,' began Boreth. 'The dragons hibernate during the Winter and early Spring. If one is out now, then soon they will all awake and fly about. It'll be a good time for Mirauk to enter, when few dragons guard their lair. The Morkan you saw was not *afraid* of the dragon but *excited* by the fact that it's awake.' He paused. 'Is the *Complement Book* safe?'

'Yes, not to worry, I've got it right here.' Niome took it out of her pouch and looked at it for a moment, then put it back and returned to bandaging her ankle. 'Do you think the riders of Mork are planning to attack Teloria?' she asked as she wrung the water from the bandage and wrapped it around her leg.

'Not yet,' replied Boreth. 'From what we overheard, they plan on staying at the intersection to stop those leaving Teloria until they get further orders. Most probably to prevent what we've already set out to do.'

'Niome!' Meysah called out to her, walking towards them. 'Breakfast is served.'

Boreth rose and walked back to the campsite. Meysah helped Niome up.

'I'm not very hungry,' she admitted.

'Neither am I,' replied Meysah. He noticed her pensive expression. 'What is it?'

'Something strange happened to me. When one of the riders looked at me, I sensed evil so strong, it started to choke me. I could hardly breathe, Meysah. My heart was pounding and I thought I was going to die. I don't know how to explain it.' She lifted her hands in frustration. 'I can't explain.'

'It's your magic. You can sense things others can't,' said Meysah.

'Yes, well, I'm not sure what it was; it's only happened once so far. Don't tell anyone yet.'

'Okay.'

They returned together to the campsite and their breakfast.

The sky was covered in grey clouds and continued to darken until the party rode in a gloomy landscape. A cold wind blew, making them draw their coats tighter around themselves and turn their collars up. Eventually fat snowflakes began to fall.

'What's this?' sighed Jimmy.

'It's called *snow*,' said Meysah, as though he were talking to a toddler. 'Can you say "*snow*"?'

Jimmy gave him a withering look. 'I know it's snow. I thought it was Spring. Well, I guess it's the last snowfall before the sun stays out for good.'

'Hopefully by tomorrow, it'll be warm again, Jimmy,' said Vigh.

The travellers paused to bundle up before riding as fast as they could, Vigh and Jimmy in front. Niome rode with Boreth. For two whole days they rode in this way, not even stopping to sleep, only to eat. On the third day, they stopped and rested awhile. The snow had stopped falling but the skies were still grey. They huddled together beside the fire Vigh built and got what sleep they could.

After a short time, Niome woke up with a start. She jumped up and looked around.

'What is it?' asked Jimmy.

'I think someone's coming,' she answered.

They all stood up and looked in the direction Niome was staring. They saw nothing. Then Niome started hyperventilating, pressing her hand against her chest, feeling a sharp, piercing pain in her heart.

'Niome!' cried Meysah. The others gathered around.

'It's the pounding,' she gasped. 'Someone evil approaches.'

Then they all heard it: the sound of hooves. Before the Telorians could break into action, a small band of Morkan riders, maybe ten of them, appeared. They were closing in on them very fast.

'Over there, those are the ones,' a voice called out. 'Attack! Attack! I'm sure Captain Kàtchah won't mind a short delay for this. Attack!'

'Run!' cried Vigh.

They darted to their horses and mounted, then kicked them into a gallop.

'Who's Captain Kàtchah?' Niome asked Boreth.

'The captain of the armies at the intersection,' he answered. 'A very dangerous polc.'

They rode as fast as they could, but the dark horses were faster than theirs were, after being pushed for three days. The enemy riders were gaining.

'Are you ready to fight?' Meysah shouted to Jimmy.

'I may not know much, but I'm prepared for anything. You?' Jimmy yelled back.

Meysah couldn't hide the dread he felt. 'Why must I be so scared?' he moaned, but before anyone could answer, the first of the riders swung his sword at him and he ducked, nearly falling off Greyer. Drawing his sword, Meysah parried the Morkan's next slash, then slipped under the other's guard and stabbed his sword into the rider's stomach. The polc fell off his horse. Meysah sighed in relief, though it was short-lived – now the riders were upon them.

Niome's heart pounded as she saw the tall Morkan approaching her through the fighting riders.

Boreth blocked a side attack, but slipped off his horse. 'Stay on the horse,' Boreth shouted to Niome. He ran forward and swooped in to drive his sword into the belly of the Morkan's horse. He scrambled out of the way as the horse fell and the rider jumped clear. The polc squared up before Boreth, his sword at the ready.

Jimmy was having trouble manoeuvring his horse, so he jumped to the ground and let it go free. Three riders charged towards him. As the first reached him, he swung his sword with all his might and opened a gash across the horse's chest. As the horse went down, he stabbed the rider as he fell.

The other two riders dashed towards him, and one of the riders jumped on him. Jimmy shoved him off him and slashed his arm; the rider stumbled away. The third rider leapt at Jimmy and pinned him to the ground. As he raised his sword high, Vigh came galloping up and swung his sword across the rider's back. The polc fell dead on top of Jimmy, who pushed him off and rolled free. Vigh turned his horse and charged back into the fight.

Meysah found himself fighting two Morkans at once, one on horseback, the other on foot. They were trying to unhorse Meysah. 'Kick 'em, Greyer! Kick them!' he shouted.

Greyer neighed loudly and reared, his front hooves pawing at the air before he came down on the unhorsed Morkan, knocking the polc to the ground. Meysah dodged around the Morkan on horseback and rode to Jimmy's aid. He succeeded in killing the rider attacking Jimmy, but the momentum sent him tumbling off Greyer and rolling on the ground.

Niome saw all of this, all while defending herself. Boreth was still engaged in the sword fight with the tall Morkan and it didn't look like he was faring too well.

Niome backed the horse away and, her voice reverberating, shouted:

'Poû viro depaë, ar ivë! Poû viro deli muerë, briyë!'

Suddenly, all the riders stopped and looked at her, their eyes wide. The Telorians gaped at Niome, and Jimmy dropped his sword. Around Niome shone a faint glow. The Morkans who were still alive drew up their horses.

In Niome's eyes, pureness raged.

The tall rider who fought Boreth hurried to his horse and mounted, but he did not seem amazed by this mystical sight. 'Come,' he instructed his small company. 'Such magic is not for us to fight.'

The riders wheeled their horses and galloped away.

When they were out of sight, the light that shone around Niome faded and she fell off her horse, into Boreth's arms.

'I've never used up so much energy before,' she said, panting. Boreth set her back on her feet and she held onto her horse's stirrup for support.

'I've never fought this well before,' admitted Jimmy, walking over. 'I guess we're all discovering certain . . . powers, if you can call it that.'

'Are you okay?' Meysah asked Niome, looking concerned.

'Yes, quite all right. I'm just low in energy. I had to try out my magic powers to save us from the riders.'

'You did the right thing,' Vigh said gently. 'But don't overuse it if you're not yet ready. The smaller spells will do for now.'

'You think the rider we saw the other day brought this band of riders?' asked Jimmy.

'Either that, or we were seen during the night,' said Vigh. 'I heard them talk of Kàtchah and they will no doubt join him. They may be gathering and waiting, but they will no doubt send a messenger to Mork to report us to Mirauk. Whatever the scenario, our presence has been exposed.'

'Is there not a spell to delay this doom?' asked Meysah.

'I'm afraid not,' replied Niome.

'We should go,' said Boreth, sheathing his sword.

Jimmy picked up his sword and returned it to its scabbard.

Meysah looked around. 'Greyer's gone!'

'So is my horse,' said Jimmy. 'As are the horses of the Morkans we dispatched.'

'Do you know a spell to summon them?' Meysah implored, turning to Niome.

'There is a rhyme to bring precious things lost back to you. This might not bring your horse back, Jimmy, but it may return Greyer to us. Meysah, you are the only one of us who has your own horse, and if he is as dear to you as your life, he will come prancing back.' Meysah smiled widely, hearing this. 'But if he is dead,' she went on, 'it will not bring him back to life.'

Meysah bowed his head, then looked at Niome. 'Let's try it, then. It's worth a try.'

Niome paused to recall the exact words, then pronounced in a clear voice:

> *Ojeb calt sherës, per cynië sherës,*
> *Amalini fid elaës kimers onet sherës,*
> *Rë vûnië amië!*
> *Kwah kilerens oiyt,*
> *Danas moni kûrvuë tes sherës,*
> *Alaros rë vûnië estoy eferiës.*

Meysah looked around in anticipation, but no horse came. They waited a few moments more, but there was no sign of Greyer.

'I'm sorry,' Niome said softly. 'I might have got a few words wrong. Without the *Book of Enchantment*, it's difficult to make sure that a spell is correct.'

'It's all right,' Meysah sighed, feeling dismayed. He loved his horse, he had to trust that Greyer was alive and would find him again . . . someday. Meysah walked towards Jimmy.

'We'll make do with what we have,' said Vigh. 'We can double up, though it will slow us down, as it will put more strain on the horses.'

'Greyer would have been strong enough to carry two,' Meysah murmured sadly.

Niome was mounting Boreth's horse when they all heard a loud neigh. From the horizon Greyer came galloping towards them.

'You did it, Niome!' rejoiced Meysah. 'You brought him back!'

Greyer stopped beside Meysah. The young polc checked him over. 'He's all right.' He looked at Jimmy. 'Shall we ride together?'

'Indeed we shall,' answered Jimmy. Meysah swung into the saddle, then gave Jimmy a hand up to sit behind him.

'Well, it looks like this isn't so dreadful after all,' said Boreth with a grin. 'The Ortim River isn't that far now. We should reach it within a couple of days.'

Chapter Four:
The Old Grey House

*D*espite how near they were now to the Ortim River, the road was beginning to seem long, longer than it should be. Vigh dismissed the younger polcs' complaints with the assertion that it was the extended, tedious time they'd spent in the saddle that was long, and not the road itself.

The morning of the second day since their encounter with the Morkan army was sunny, and the snow that had fallen in the previous days glittered in the sunshine, though it had started to melt and become sticky. As they were relaxing for a few moments after eating breakfast, Jimmy made a snowball and threw it at Meysah.

'Shall we have a snowball fight?' he asked when he had Meysah's attention. He scooped up more snow and formed it into another ball.

Meysah ducked the cold missile and hid behind Greyer. 'I'm sorry, Jimmy, but after that last sword fight, I don't want any fight at all.'

'That's okay, but you have to look on the bright side,' said Jimmy. 'I admit I'm feeling a little childish, but it's sunny and we're safe now, and I have the feeling we will be safe until we get to the Great Rock, at least.'

Meysah joined his friend and together they made a snow sword.

Niome's wound was practically healed by now and she could walk normally again. She joined her brother and their friend and they sat in the snow like little children discovering a new aspect of nature. Vigh smiled at their happiness.

'We only need to figure out how to heal faster,' said Niome. Vigh nodded to himself.

Boreth came up to Vigh and pointed at a spot in the distance.

'Again?' Vigh growled, as the rider observed them from afar. 'When will we ever shake them?' The three younger polcs looked up. 'Is that the rider who attacked you, Niome?'

She squinted, shielding her eyes from the sun with her hand. 'It doesn't look like him.'

'It does look like the one we saw the other day,' voiced Jimmy.

They all watched the distant rider. He did not move but merely remained perched atop his horse, helmeted head turned in their direction.

'Let's get him once and for all,' growled Boreth.

'What if he leads us into a trap?' cried Meysah.

'Then we'll fight them all,' answered Boreth. 'I won't have that spy following us to our destination.'

They mounted their horses and started riding towards the distant rider, who turned and rode quickly away, glancing back at them from time to time. It seemed as if he were making sure they were following.

'Hey!' Vigh shouted. 'Rider! What do you want from us?' He got no answer. The rider kept on galloping. And then he vanished.

'Where did he go?' asked Niome as they all stopped their horses.

Meysah looked around. 'Look!' he said, pointing at a weathered grey stone house with smoke curling from its chimney.

'The grey house Henker spoke of,' deduced Boreth. 'Yes. I'd almost forgotten about it.'

'We should knock on the door,' said Vigh.

'Is it safe?' asked Niome.

'We'll find out,' replied Vigh. 'But it should be.' He dismounted his horse and walked to the door and knocked. A few moments later an old polc dressed in Telorian garments answered the door.

He studied the travellers for a quick moment. 'Ah, come in before you are seen, my fellow Telorians! You have travelled many days, but not in vain.' He turned in the doorway and said to someone inside, 'Clahria, bring their horses to the stable, would you?'

Out came a beautiful polc whose golden hair cascaded down to her waist. Meysah and Jimmy gaped. Clahria approached Greyer and looked up at the two young polcs.

Meysah could not explain what he felt, but it made his heart flutter. 'Oh,' he said, suddenly realising that she was waiting for them. He nudged Jimmy, who slid off Greyer. Then he dismounted, landing on his feet in front of Clahria. 'Um, this is my dear Greyer. Do take good care of him, sweet lady.' She gave him a beautiful smile and grasped the horse's bridle.

Boreth stared at the old polc. 'What stable? There is none.'

The old Telorian pointed to a spot behind them. 'Yes, it's right there.' And suddenly, as if in a dream, there appeared a stable only a few steps from where Boreth stood. The young woman led Greyer and the two other horses towards it.

'Welcome to my home,' the old polc said as the travellers entered the house.

'How come the stable just appeared?' asked Boreth, scowling in confusion.

'Magic,' the polc replied simply. 'My house and stable are invisible at all times. Only friends in need see it. Since I don't know you, I assume a friend sent you?'

'Well, Henker the Elder told us we'd come upon an old grey house,' said Vigh.

The old polc lifted bushy white eyebrows. 'Is he still around? We're competing, you know. I'll be six hundred next season.'

'Ah,' said Vigh. 'But who are you?'

'Why, I'm Drúgan. I live here with my two grandchildren, who took it upon themselves to help me help others. I'm surprised you haven't heard of me – I'm in the old songs, you know. There's even a song about my daughter and her husband, who have their own invisible house.'

'Well,' began Vigh, 'I'm afraid we haven't sung the songs in a long time.'

'I understand,' said Drúgan. 'Let me have the honour.' He cleared his throat and began to sing with gusto.

Up in the north near the Ortim River,
Lives old Drúgan in that land;
And when you go up thither,
No doubt he will give you a hand.

There with him lives Tlúnëe,
The bravest of the warriors,
With his green eyes like the sea
And his silk hat with the feathers.

There also lives young Clahria,
With her long golden hair,
Who, like her mother Maria,
Practices magic in a secret lair.

All three are great, wise sorcerers.
Their house, you will not spot it,
Unless running away from terrors;
The Ghost Rider will bring you to it.

One moment there, one moment gone,
The Old Grey House has smoke puffing out.
What a place to land on,
For the enemy won't find it, even if they search about.

Drúgan shall give you deep information,
He will explain all that is misunderstood.
Help you, he will, with no complication,
As any good old friend would.

Drúgan completed the song and smiled.

'We sure have a lot of questions,' admitted Vigh.

At that moment, Clahria walked in the door. Jimmy looked up and his face turned bright red. Meysah's heart started beating fast.

Clahria turned to Meysah. 'Your Greyer is safe in our stable.' She smiled, then nodded to Boreth and left the room. Meysah watched her leave with big eyes and a broad smile. He was not the only one.

Drúgan laughed. 'Come,' he said. 'We shall sit by the fireplace and talk.'

They followed Drúgan into the living area, a comfortable room filled with deep, overstuffed couches and upholstered armchairs. A bright fire was burning in the fireplace. Drúgan sat down in a rocking chair beside the fireplace and pulled a pipe from his pocket and lit it. The others found seats.

'I've lived here a very long time,' explained Drúgan. 'I established this spectral house because I knew travellers would need aid and comfort on their travels. I'm right by the Ortim River, so it's very convenient. My daughter Maria and her husband Tobias live in another house like this one, over by Zaccher Lake, quite a ways east from here.'

'You must be the greatest wizard in all of Kaulchèc History, then,' said Jimmy.

'On the contrary,' said Drúgan, glancing at Niome and the others. 'Some wizards I've trained are greater yet than me. The greatest Telorian wizardess, Elina, was trained by me. How is she, by the way? I haven't heard from her in quite some time.'

The guests bowed their heads. There was an awkward silence. 'I'm afraid she got ill,' said Niome. 'You must know she was cursed with an illness set upon her by Mirauk's powers.' She paused. Drúgan nodded and his expression grew sad. 'She passed away a few weeks ago.'

'I'm sorry to hear that,' said Drúgan. 'She was a good student of mine.'

'And a good teacher of mine,' added Niome.

'Are you the apprentice of Elina!?' Drúgan exclaimed. 'Have you set off to find the *Book of Enchantment*?'

'Sort of,' replied Niome. 'When Elina died, she told me to go to the Great Rock.'

'I am the guardian of the Great Rock. I keep magic potions there, for different travellers according to their needs. I have a special one for the bearer of the *Complement Book*.'

Niome took the *Complement Book* from her pouch and showed it to Drúgan, who smiled.

'That rock is our secret den. It is my potions lab; only I can enter it – well, I and my grandchildren. I have a dock close by and I will lend you the magic boat that will get you across the river. At that point your horses will be of no use. I will keep them safe until your return.'

'Thank you,' said Vigh, his outward calm belying the nervous lurch of his stomach as the danger of their mission sank in.

'No, it is I who must thank you, for the fate of Teloria lies in your hands,' said Drúgan, looking at the book in Niome's hands. 'Your instincts and willpower have served you well in this mission, but now you must follow through and get the *Book of Enchantment* back from Mirauk.'

'We're going to Mork!' Meysah gasped, and gulped.

'Let me advise you on the best roads to take, because once you cross that river, you will be on your own,' Drúgan warned. 'Listen carefully. You will walk along the bank until you reach a road going north. Follow that road until you reach Firlan Forest, to the north of the river. You can also reach it by going through the hills, but the river is easiest to follow. You must use your magic to enter the forest, and there you will learn the secrets for going to Mork, and secrets about Mork, from those who dwell in that forest.

'You must get to Mork and then come back to the mountains. Whatever you do, do not travel to the Islands of Mork! Strange things have happened there and in the lands farther down the coast, on the ocean. We all know that when the river splits and becomes the Malgar and Dakodol rivers, the lands become dangerous and travel, treacherous, for we approach the Morkan territories. Where the Malgar River reaches the ocean, there are myths about the evils done to others there, and of the creatures created by Mirauk that roam there.'

Drúgan crossed his arms. 'I can tell you no more. You know what you must do.'

A polc wearing a silk hat decorated with blue ribbons came in from outside with a pair of hares he'd snared.

'Ah, my grandson,' Drúgan announced. 'Tlúnëe, you've come in time to meet our guests. These are valiant knights on their way to, well, save the world.'

'I saw new horses in the barn and knew someone was here,' Tlúnëe acknowledged jovially, sweeping off his hat. He nodded at each guest as they introduced themselves. 'I'm all set to make supper, Grandfather.' With a last smile at the guests, he went into the kitchen.

'My grandson is the youngest here, though not the youngest of my grandchildren. He will go with you tomorrow to the Great Rock.'

'I thought *you* were going to guide us,' remarked Meysah.

'Oh, I'm much too old to travel such distances. It's all right, you can trust him. He's the best person to guide you.'

In the momentary silence following Drúgan's words, Clahria's voice floated into the room as she sang a soft, sweet melody accompanied by the plucking of a harp. The moment stretched on as everyone listened, utterly enchanted. Meysah and Jimmy closed their eyes in appreciation and nodded their heads in time with the melody.

'Wonderful voice,' said Drúgan. 'It gives me goosebumps every time she plays.'

Boreth stood and crossed the room to peer into a little room where Clahria sat on a tall stool, eyes closed, playing the harp. She played passionately, guided by emotion. On a table next to her was a lyre and a flute. Smiling, Boreth leaned against the door-frame and crossed his arms to watch her play. Then he realised that the way he'd left the others might seem rude, so he quietly turned around to leave.

'You can stay,' said Clahria.

Boreth turned back to face her, then actually walked into the room. 'How did you know I was there?' he asked. 'Your eyes were closed.'

'I just knew.' She smiled. 'Like there are some things you always only know. Have a seat. The next song is longer than the first.'

'Oh, don't feel obliged to play for me,' stammered Boreth, embarrassed. 'I was only listening, not wanting to disturb. If you want I can leave. I really didn't mean to intrude.'

'I know. I *want* to play for you.'

Boreth hesitated but a moment before he pulled up a chair and took a seat facing Clahria, who started again. Then she paused.

'You're not like the others, are you?' she said.

'How do you mean?'

'Oh, I'm sorry. What I mean is you look different. Are you of Dalvaran?'

'No, I'm a Telorian. I'm just a very *short* Telorian. I do have Dalvaran blood in my family, though. I've even calculated my height: exactly five feet tall and four inches, half a foot shorter than the average short Telorian, which is the average height of a tall Dalvaran. I only grew the extra half foot a few years ago, so you can imagine how short I was before that. Of course, it could be hard to judge when I'm among younger Telorians, who are about my height, or slightly taller – yes, definitely taller – and when my best friend Vigh is extraordinarily tall. But this is me. It doesn't get in the way of my fighting, mind you. I don't mean to boast, but I'm an excellent duellist.' Boreth realised he was rambling and stopped.

Clahria laughed. 'What is your name?'

'Oh, I'm sorry. I must have forgotten my manners.' *Once again,* he added to himself. 'My name is Boreth. Boreth Culmik.'

'Then I shall write a song about you, Boreth. The short Telorian who's helping the young wizardess save the world.' They both laughed, Boreth a little self-consciously. 'But you *are* different. I mean, from other travellers – you and your friends. You're special, braver . . .'

She trailed off and they shared a moment, looking into each other's eyes, and Boreth's heart skipped a beat at the intensity of Clahria's gaze.

Drúgan entered the room. 'Ah, there you are. The others have gone upstairs. I've set out new garments for the rest of the evening. You have time to wash up and change before supper. We will wash your clothes for tomorrow. Just as if you were staying at an inn,' he quipped.

Boreth rose and slowly backed out of the room. 'A pleasure,' he said to Clahria, nodding slightly, and then he turned and went to join his fellow Telorians upstairs.

The doors of two rooms upstairs were inscribed with *Comfort Room for My Guests* in bold letters, and below that, in smaller text, was written *Make yourselves at home.* The doors were open, and inside one bedroom were three beds where Niome, Meysah, and Jimmy had already put their bags down. The other room had two beds, obviously for Vigh and Boreth. Neatly folded garments rested on the beds, including a nice green dress for Niome that probably belonged to Clahria.

A third room across the hall was clearly a bathroom; a big porcelain bathtub sat in the middle of the room and a basin and a jug for water sat on a side table. A large metal kettle was on a stove on the opposite wall, heating water; several buckets sat beside the stove. Towels hung neatly on a rack. Beside it, a straw basket bore a note that read:

You may put your dirty clothes in here.
They will be ready in time for your
departure tomorrow. I hope you enjoyed
the warm bath and I hope you will be
able to sleep soundly. Enjoy your stay,
for while here, you have no worries.
Always glad to help. –Drúgan

The guests cleaned up and changed their clothes. When they went back down, the dinner table had been set and supper was being served.

'Just in time,' said Clahria as she led them to their seats.

The guests stood behind their chairs until Drúgan arrived, with Niome at one end opposite Drúgan; Meysah, Jimmy, and Clahria on the left; and Boreth, Vigh, and Tlúnëe on the right. When Drúgan had blessed their meal, he said, 'You may be seated so the feast can begin.'

Meysah and Jimmy rushed to pull out Clahria's chair for her. 'Why, thank you,' she said, smiling, though her eyes were on Boreth, who smiled in return. Jimmy and Meysah noticed their look and exchanged an embarrassed glance before returning to their seats.

Jimmy whispered into Meysah's ear as they sat down, 'Looks like we won't have to compete this time.'

'No,' whispered Meysah with a giggle. 'It seems Boreth was quicker than us to charm her.'

They ate in silence until Clahria asked, 'Are you really going to save the world?'

'We're going to do the best we can,' Vigh replied.

'Mirauk is more powerful than we can know,' said Niome, 'but once we get the *Book of Enchantment,* we can ensure freedom from evil.'

'You mean *you* can ensure freedom,' corrected Tlúnëe. 'You are Elina's only worthy apprentice, if she sent you out here. You have the magic powers, but your friends shall help you a great deal.'

'Of course,' asserted Vigh. 'We are all knights and master swordfighters – well, at least Boreth and I are.'

'Master Vigh is my teacher,' said Meysah. 'I think he is one of the finest knights in Teloria.'

'What about Boreth, Meysah?' Jimmy said with a chuckle. 'He's just as great.'

They all laughed.

'What about you, Jimmy,' asked Drúgan, 'who is your teacher?'

'I have none,' admitted Jimmy. 'Selemil doesn't believe I'd make a good knight because I'm clumsy and I learn too slowly, but that's all I want to be. I came along wanting to help and knowing I'd learn more than any sword-master could teach me.'

'You are already learning,' said Drúgan. 'You possess wisdom, for someone so young, and that is always a good sign.'

'I shall take him on as my student,' declared Boreth. 'I will be glad to, Jimmy.'

'Thank you!' Jimmy exclaimed.

'All you had to do was ask,' said Boreth, grinning.

They continued to eat in silence for a while.

'It's a shame there are so few of us on this mission,' Niome expressed. 'Selemil wouldn't let us go. He wanted us to help in the rebuilding of the wall.'

'He can think what he wants,' interjected Drúgan. 'He has yet to learn the way of magic, the deep way of magic. He is unfamiliar with its unpredictability, but that's all right. He will recognise your deed when you return, I am certain of it.' He waved his hand at her. 'My apologies. Go on.'

'I left Teloria – alone and in secret. My brother and friends came after me to help. If it weren't for them, I'd be alone.'

'Not at all,' said Drúgan. 'It was fate that brought you together; it had to happen this way.'

'Well, perhaps I could've had a bigger group, under different circumstances.'

'What different circumstances would there be, Niome?' asked Drúgan.

'You know,' began Tlúnëe when Niome didn't answer, 'prophecy says that one great user of magic will come forth to save the world from evil, and a small troop of knights will help. It was written in song by a Dragon Prophet long ago, and I believe it has come true.'

'Talking about songs,' said Vigh, 'in the song you sang us, Drúgan, you mentioned the Ghost Rider. Who is he?'

'Why, he's the rider who led you to me,' answered Drúgan.

'All this time we thought he was the enemy,' said Boreth.

'No,' replied Drúgan. 'He seems scary at first, what with his armour and hidden face, and he does not speak, but when the time is ripe, he brings those who are worthy of my hospitality to me. We reached a mutual understanding long ago, where he would keep watch for those destined to meet me and bring them to me, instead of roaming the land, haunting travellers and farmers.'

Clahria took up the story. 'He is an upstanding spirit who took an oath to help those in need. He cast a spell on himself before he died: the Lingering Spell. He's been doing it for . . . centuries, I think. He never told us his full story, or who he was when he lived, just that he was a knight with enough knowledge of magic to be able to linger on in this world to help anyone he could. He will do it until peace has been restored. That is his pledge. Then and only then can he be set free, by the one powerful enough to destroy the evil of Mirauk.'

'And strangely enough,' added Tlúnëe, 'he is a tangible ghost; we can touch him, shake his hand, and he's not even a bit transparent. But he can vanish, just like any other ghost, and do all of the other mystical actions. Weapons do not make him bleed, though they don't go right through him as they do with a normal ghost. This is probably due to the lingering spell he cast upon himself.'

Tlúnëe pursed his lips in thought. 'I've wondered if he's still partly alive. All he's ever shared of the spell is that it took years for the process of transformation to be completed, and during that time, he couldn't touch anyone or they'd transform as well. Whether he's still half alive or not, he is a polken ghost of many mysteries, and one whom we hold in great esteem for his deeds and his help throughout the years.'

'Now I understand,' said Meysah.

'How about,' began Drúgan, 'after supper, Clahria plays us another song on the harp.'

'I'd love to hear another one,' said Boreth. 'Her sweet, melodious talent should be heard at all times and by all.'

'I would love to play,' smiled Clahria, 'especially for special guests like you, about to embark on a journey to a distant land. I know just the song.'

'They have not been singing much in Teloria,' said Drúgan. 'So now, when they hear a song, it's like hearing one for the very first time.'

'Then I shall play until they go.'

The meal ended in silence and afterwards they all returned to their seats by the fireplace, except for Clahria, who went into her room to play.

'Why does she play in there?' inquired Jimmy.

'Because she feels more at ease there,' answered Drúgan. 'She is self-conscious playing in front of an audience.'

Her voice was even more beautiful than before, if that were possible, as she sang their song, written by a prophet long ago:

One day there will be
A very corrupt, evil polc,
Who will awaken in his descendants
Sorcery, you will see.

But when they try to steal
What should belong to no one,
They will be waking in others
The good, you will feel.

A great user of magic
Will set out to save the day,
With the help of a small army,
A few knights, so heroic.

So on they will go
To boundless lands,
And find more than there is to learn,
And stand up to every foe.

There she stopped, for the rest revealed the future, and the guests shouldn't know that until they figured it out for themselves. She began another song, soft and conclusive, this time playing her flute.

Drúgan yawned in satisfaction. 'Lovely, isn't it?' he said. 'Now, I'm off to bed.'

Tlúnëe joined him as he climbed the stairs to the bedrooms. Vigh followed, then Jimmy and Meysah and Niome. Boreth stopped at the foot of the stairs when he heard Clahria change instruments and start to sing the next song. This time, he felt she was singing to him alone. Boreth turned back and went into her room.

'Hu-hullo,' he said quietly. She smiled. 'Are all the other bedrooms upstairs?'

'No, mine is here, and Tlúnëe's is next door. He just went up with my grandfather to make sure everyone is at their ease.'

'Ah, yes.'

There was a pause.

'I started composing your song,' said Clahria. 'There's only one verse so far, but I'm sure it'll be done by the time you get back.'

'That's *if* I get back,' Boreth said solemnly.

'Right, if.'

'I'm afraid I can't make any promises, although I'd very much like to.' Boreth stared at her intently, wishing he could promise his return. 'I'm sorry.'

'Oh, that's okay,' Clahria said, though her eyes revealed sadness. 'At least there's a bit more hope with you than there was with the last group of travellers.'

Boreth quirked a curious brow. 'The last travellers?' he repeated, wondering if Bahvley's team had passed this way and stayed here as well.

She nodded. 'It was a while ago. The one thing I can remember clearly is that they never made it back.'

'I'm sorry,' said Boreth, suddenly worried for his and his friends' chances.

'No, I'm sorry. I know that the travellers were friends of yours. Bahvley Fairhaven was among them. He was brother to Niome and Meysah, was he not?' Boreth nodded. 'I didn't know much about him then, but now I understand more about all this.

They were the last travellers to come here, until now.'

'I'm afraid no one has dared to travel beyond the walls of Teloria until now,' said Boreth.

'When they informed us that Morkans had attacked Teloria and stolen the *Book of Enchantment,* we came to their aid. They went after the messenger who had it, but only news that Mirauk himself had killed them all came back our way. Elina was the only survivor.'

Boreth took a few steps towards Clahria. 'Bahvley was a good knight. I'd been taken captive by the Morkans and brought to one of their encampments, where I was tortured. Bahvley and his Team of Twelve freed me and others. The Morkan camp was close to Teloria, so I came back home in time to help. If it weren't for him . . . well, he was a good knight.'

'And a brave soul,' said Clahria. 'I see that same brave spirit in all the Fairhavens. Elina travelled a long way with them, only to hear and report such ill news, returning only to her own doom. She travelled back alone, and to her death; perhaps slow, but still a death.' Boreth put his hand on her shoulder and nodded in sympathetic understanding. 'She con-fronted Mirauk, you know, and laid her doom upon herself.'

'How can you say such a thing?' objected Boreth. 'You don't know what went on!'

'No, I don't, but I do know this: it has always been said that Mirauk's evil is so great that if he looks you in the eyes, you are cursed with a slow, painful, and deadly sickness. No one has looked him in the eyes and lived to tell the story. Of course, there were those few who'd barely made it back in time to tell of it, or stories of those who attempted it, but we either never hear of them again, or hear how they died – never well. Elina knew all this. She was the more fortunate one who survived the longest and resisted as long as she had the power to fight the curse. Perhaps she looked into Mirauk's eyes willingly; perhaps she knew certain things that we cannot begin to comprehend at this point in time.'

'Perhaps. I did not know all this about her,' Boreth said, his voice faint. 'Or maybe I knew but just never realised it. I trust Elina knew what she was doing, and accepted her fate.'

Clahria rose and walked to the window. 'While you were washing up, my grandfather revealed to my brother and me that she had died. He didn't want you all to see our reactions; he wanted you to enjoy your stay fully.' She turned to face him. 'Promise me that, if ever you come face to face with Mirauk, you will not look him in the eyes, that you will turn your gaze away, all of you.'

Boreth went to her and gently cupped her cheeks in his hands. 'I promise.' He leaned in and lingered an inch away from her lips for a brief moment, his heart racing as he gazed into her eyes. Clahria closed the distance, and Boreth kissed her deeply. Then he held her in his arms, leaning his cheek against hers.

They stayed like that until they heard Tlúnëe come down the stairs. Then Boreth stepped back, said good night, and went upstairs to bed.

The next morning, Niome and the others packed up before coming down to a breakfast of pancakes. But when it came time to leave, and Tlúnëe stepped out to the stable to get the horses ready, the mood shifted and they all became morose. Dread had replaced any excitement about finding the Great Rock, for now they would be going to Mork to face Mirauk.

'It will take you half a day to reach the Great Rock,' said Drúgan. 'Crossing to the other side of the river after that will not take long.'

'What potions shall we find at the Great Rock?' inquired Jimmy.

'You mean what po*tion*,' corrected Drúgan. 'It is the ultimate healing potion. You must use it only once, and only at the most critical moment. It is meant for healing if one of you is dying, or has just died. I give it to you because each of you is important to this mission. There is one dose, to be taken or administered while reciting this spell.'

He pulled a folded piece of paper from a pocket and handed it to Niome, and she began to unfold it, but he put his hand over hers to stop her.

'None of you may read it before the time of use,' Drúgan warned. 'Not even to yourselves. And remember this: it will only work if the person wishes to live and if the wound was not inflicted by Mirauk himself. Do not force the spell, or it will be in vain.'

Niome put the spell in her pouch.

'Remember,' said Clahria, 'do not look into Mirauk's eyes, for if you do, you will be cursed with the same illness that took Elina from this world.'

'We won't,' said Niome, the assertion echoed by Vigh and Meysah.

'When we return, I will expect a song,' Boreth teased, smiling.

'A song shall be written,' Clahria promised.

'And perhaps I shall write a song about you,' said Boreth.

Jimmy and Meysah shared a look and sighed. Then Meysah put his hand on Jimmy's back. 'One day,' he whispered as Boreth and Clahria embraced. 'One day.'

'Yep,' said Jimmy. 'When we're ready for love, it will come to us.'

Tlúnëe re-entered the house while they were all exchanging good wishes. 'The horses are ready,' he announced.

They went out to the yard where their three horses waited, along with three from Drúgan's stable – one for Niome and Jimmy each, and another for Tlúnëe.

'We appreciate you loaning us your horses,' said Vigh, 'especially knowing there is no stable to house them where we are going.'

'Not to worry,' said Drúgan. 'They will be cared for.'

'How are you going to bring them all back here?' asked Meysah. If Drúgan would be caring for the horses while they were gone, the only way he could do that was if the horses returned to the old polc.

Tlúnëe answered. 'I've made them familiar with the stable and I will summon them for safekeeping.'

'Well, it looks like it's the last time I ride Greyer,' said Meysah, rubbing the horse's nose. 'The last time for a long time.'

They mounted up and followed Tlúnëe, as Drúgan and Clahria stood in the doorway of the Old Grey House, waving goodbye.

They reached the Great Rock by mid-afternoon. It was exactly as it had been described: an immense boulder streaked with pink and grey, as if stroked with a brush. They all sat on their horses, silently listening to the wind, before Tlúnëe said in a low voice, 'Follow me.'

They dismounted. Tlúnëe led them to one side of the boulder where a patch of unmelted snow remained in its shade. He lifted his arms, uttering lines known only to his family.

Nelassima po srodo folessekold!
Nelassima po srodo dlogesseh!
Etel Notissimopo folerëop,
Etel Notissimopo foëlessifëi!

The outline of a door appeared in the grey surface of the rock. The narrow gaps widened as the door opened. They entered, pulling their horses in with them, and the door shut behind them.

As if they'd been expected, burning candles illuminated the interior – their kindling no doubt part of the spell Tlúnëe had uttered. Shelves lined the rough-hewn walls, and on them sat a myriad of stoppered bottles and leather bags tied with string, all containing magical potions. The room was larger than the exterior of the Great Rock had implied.

Tlúnëe walked to a shelf to the right of the door and lifted a small glass bottle containing a reddish peach-coloured liquid. 'This is the potion,' he said, handing it to Niome. 'Keep it safe at all times. Don't lose it. When you use it, drink it all at once.'

Niome studied the bottle carefully. She clasped it in the palm of her hand, then put it in her pouch.

'Wouldn't it be wise to have more than just one bottle?' asked Vigh.

'Yes,' Jimmy agreed. 'What if more than one person needs it?'

Tlúnëe put his hand on Jimmy's shoulder and looked him in the eyes. 'You will need it only once. You must learn to trust those few who can foresee events, Jimmy. It will be kept safe with Niome.'

In that moment, Tlúnëe appeared wiser and older than his years. Great knowledge mingled with the beauty of early adulthood to produce an expression so pure which Jimmy could not describe.

Niome gasped as a warm light filled the room. Now she understood: Tlúnëe was the prophet who would become *the* Prophet of Time that Henker had predicted would replace him.

'Come,' said Tlúnëe, 'the dock is not far.' He led them out of the Great Rock and the door sealed itself and vanished behind them.

They remounted their horses and rode a few furlongs before Tlúnëe reined his horse in beside a dock where a rowboat was moored. 'This boat will take you to the other side, but it will not wait for your return,' he warned.

Meysah approached it and it jostled, splashing water against the dock – Greyer clopped back quickly. 'This is a magic boat, isn't it?'

'Yes,' answered Tlúnëe. 'It will carry you where you need to go. You need no oars. Once you reach the other shore, stay on your guard.'

'We will,' said Vigh.

'Do you have weapons?' asked Tlúnëe. 'Powerful weapons?'

'We have our swords,' replied Vigh, 'and we've got knives – ours and those we took from the Morkan riders we fought.'

'And we have our magic,' Niome said, understanding that Tlúnëe was not referring to tangible weapons.

'Then you are all set,' said Tlúnëe.

The group dismounted and Boreth untied the boat from the dock and held it while Jimmy got in. Vigh thanked Tlúnëe, then clambered into the boat as well.

Meysah paused before leaving Greyer. 'Well, I suppose this is farewell,' he told the horse. 'Not for too long, I hope. I shall miss you, Greyer.' The horse snorted and stomped. Meysah rubbed the horse's nose. 'These people are our friends. They will take good care of you. Do obey them, Greyer.' He hugged his horse. 'I hope I shall see you again.'

'You will,' said Niome, who was standing behind him.

Brother and sister got onto the boat. Boreth followed.

Before the boat left the dock, Tlúnëe called out, 'Niome Fairhaven, find the *Book of Enchantment!* Meysah Fairhaven, find your courage. Vigh Nimrod, find your friend. Jimmesh Hochka, find your inner strength and valour. Boreth Culmik, find your peace of heart.'

'And you,' said Vigh, 'find your wisdom!'

Tlúnëe merely smiled. Turning his horse, Tlúnëe trotted off, and the other horses followed. He stopped at the top of a low rise and turned to look at them as the boat slowly moved out into the river. He saluted them and they saluted back. Then he rode off through the meadow, the other horses at his side.

Niome contemplated what Tlúnëe had told them. He had wished each of them the very thing they most desired, she realised: the *Book of Enchantment,* courage, a lost friend, inner strength, and peace of heart. *Perhaps these are things we shall find in time, for he can see the future.*

Perhaps Bahvley's group is still alive, Vigh thought. He suddenly knew that Tlúnëe had already found the wisdom Vigh had wished for him, for only a wise person can look into the soul of another and see their innermost desire. Vigh smiled to himself, feeling comforted.

Chapter Five:
Bob Tweedle

The light was fading in a sky turning purple as the boat floated across the Ortim River. The five travellers sat silently watching the dark forest on the far side looming larger.

'Boreth,' said Jimmy, breaking the silence. Boreth turned to him. 'Did you really mean it when you said you would take me on as your student knight?'

'I did,' replied Boreth.

Jimmy nodded, eyes downcast, thinking about the response. 'Because no one ever offered before. I guess they all thought I was a lost cause.'

'I don't think so. I can see your determination. You just need to learn patience with yourself.' Boreth smiled. 'You have shown great courage already and proven yourself as worthy as the rest of us by coming along and by fighting those riders as best you could.'

'You saw that!' Jimmy beamed. Then he sobered. 'I mean, my potential. However you put it.'

Boreth laughed. 'If you have it, someone's bound to notice it eventually.'

They fell silent again, but it was a comfortable silence. The cool breeze and the water lapping at the boat's hull soothed their anxiety and refreshed them.

However, the closer they got to the other shore, the more restless the passengers became, shifting on their seats as if trying to get comfortable and hunching their shoulders against a nonexistent cold. Niome rolled her shoulders, trying to dispel an eerie, prickling sensation on her skin. Her mouth was suddenly dry. She swallowed, to no avail.

'No!' Vigh suddenly cried, hands flying to the gunwales, his calm expression now replaced by alarm.

'No to what?' asked Boreth, swinging his head around, looking for danger. Then he felt it, and gripped the gunwales in terror.

The boat shook uncontrollably; everyone had to hang on.

'Look there!' cried Meysah, pointing to a dark figure in the water.

'The river seems to be inhabited by some sort of beast,' gasped Vigh, eyes on the dark shape.

'A beast that Mirauk set loose?' Niome quavered as the boat lurched again.

The creature slipped beneath the boat. Meysah leaned over the side and saw two glowing red eyes. Then a geyser of water spewed from the beast, creating a wave that nearly swamped the boat.

Losing his grip as the boat rocked from side to side, Meysah toppled into the water.

The boat stopped.

'Meysah!' shrieked Niome.

'Why has the boat stopped?' cried Jimmy, looking frantically at the water around them. 'We can't just float here! We have to find Meysah! What if that creature comes back?'

'The boat's waiting for Meysah to come back,' Niome said in sudden understanding. 'It won't resume until its missing passenger returns.'

They all started scanning the water, searching for Meysah. 'I can't see him anywhere,' cried Boreth.

Jimmy stood and looked around, then lowered his head in defeat and sat back down. 'Please be alive,' he mewled.

A hand suddenly shot from the water and grabbed Jimmy's arm. Jimmy screamed and threw himself away from the side to sprawl in the bottom of the boat.

'It's Meysah!' Vigh scrambled to grab the lad's hand. Jimmy and Boreth helped him haul Meysah back into the boat. As soon as Meysah landed coughing in the boat, the small vessel started off again.

Niome moved to sit beside Meysah and covered him with a blanket. 'What was it?' she asked.

'I didn't see it,' Meysah panted. 'All I know is I fell in and tried to get back in the boat.'

The boat bumped gently against the riverbank. Those in the boat exchanged nervous glances. No one moved to get out right away. None of them had ever gone this far. Even Vigh and Boreth, who had travelled to many places, had never been this far north.

'So this is it,' said Meysah. 'This is where the real journey begins.'

'I suppose so,' replied Vigh.

'We must build a fire for the night,' said Boreth. 'It'll keep us warm and it'll dry Meysah's clothes.'

'Yes,' agreed Vigh. 'We should go and gather firewood, but we must stick close together.' He looked at Meysah. 'Remain in the boat until we have unloaded our packs and gear. We don't want it leaving before we have everything.' Meysah nodded and pulled the blanket more tightly around himself.

Boreth and Vigh stepped out of the boat, Jimmy and Niome passed the packs forward to them. Then Jimmy hopped out and Niome helped Meysah get out.

As soon as they were all on shore, the boat drifted away from the bank and slowly cut across the current to the opposite shore.

Jimmy watched it anxiously. 'I don't like that it's leaving,' he admitted.

'We no longer need it,' Boreth assured him. 'Come, let's find a spot to camp for the night. I will teach you a few fighting tricks in the morning.'

The woods were eerily silent as the group walked from the river up to the treeline and set their bags down. Shivering, Meysah stepped behind a tree and changed his clothes. The dry trousers and shirt weren't all that warm, but he wrapped the blanket around himself again. Vigh draped Meysah's clothes on a branch near a small fire Boreth was starting.

As the boys set out to gather firewood, Vigh warned them again, 'Stick close together and don't wander far. This is a strange forest in a strange land.'

Although it wasn't completely dark, Niome was tired. She spread her bedroll beside the fire and lay down to sleep.

Vigh sat down beside Boreth, his eyes on Niome. 'I'm concerned with how tired she's been since we found her,' he whispered.

'Do you think it's a curse?' asked Boreth.

'No. But she lost a lot of blood when she was wounded, and that spell took a lot of energy. It could be her way of regenerating.'

'She does have a lot on her mind.'

'Yes,' said Vigh. 'She still grieves for Elina. Now I'm afraid she grieves for her older brother's death all over again. She is following in his steps and the people we meet remember him still. She will be reminded of his loss for quite some time, as will Meysah. I fear many past events will haunt her.'

'We will help her through this,' Boreth assured.

Meysah and Jimmy were making a game of gathering wood, their laughter dispelling their earlier anxiety. 'I'm excited in a way, Meysah! Are you?'

'I don't know. I'm a little afraid. Lucky for you that Boreth wants to be your master.'

'Yes,' answered Jimmy. 'I feel more confident now.'

'Hey,' said Meysah, 'the last things Tlúnëe said to us got me thinking.'

'Me too.'

'I'm a coward!'

'What!?' exclaimed Jimmy.

'I need to find courage. I always feel scared. I want to go home, that's how much I lack courage.'

'You think no one who ever set out to go to Mork ever wanted to turn back? We're all scared, Meysah. Niome most of all. And you came out here in the first place. No, the only person I know who's a coward is that boastful liar—'

'Lóim!' both Meysah and Jimmy exclaimed. They laughed.

'Hey, who do you think Vigh's friend is?' asked Jimmy.

'Beats me; you?'

'He's *your* master,' Jimmy retorted. 'I'm the last person who'd know.'

'Master Vigh has many friends, but Boreth was always closest to him. I don't know. I hope, in a way, that Tlúnëe meant someone from the Team of Twelve, that he meant . . .' Meysah paused.

'Well, who?'

'My brother.' They were silent for several moments. 'But it's probably too silly to still wish to see him again after so long a time.' Meysah's tone turned brisk. 'What am I saying? It's stupid! There were no survivors. I have to accept it.'

They continued foraging until they came to a large tree with many branches lying on the ground around the trunk. 'Stars!' cried Meysah. 'More wood!' They started gathering the branches until they both had large armloads.

'Look on the bright side, Meysah,' Jimmy began as they turned to head back to the campsite. 'One day we'll be legendary heroes, and Lóim Weedler will see who's more brave. We'll be heroes in a story of a long quest told by the fireside.'

'I can just picture it,' said Meysah. Imitating the town crier's voice, he continued. "The Quest of the Five Telorians: Will They Find the *Book of Enchantment?*"

"'Join us around the fire," it'll say in the invitations. "There you'll find out what happens next as Grandfather Fairhaven tells the story of his great-grandfather and his friends." And the entire kingdom will come to hear it.'

They both laughed, but stopped short when they heard a high voice chuckling with them. They looked wide-eyed at each other, then at the tree trunk behind them. There was now a face in the tree, a ghostly face, pale and faded, as if seen in a dream. It looked up at them as they stood motionless. 'Hello there!' it said in a friendly voice.

The two boys jumped back and dropped all the wood they had collected. 'Aaaaaahh!' they screamed, long and loud, as they ran back to the campsite.

'There's a ghost in a tree! There's a ghost in a tree!' they cried as they stopped beside the fire, gasping for air. This jolted Niome from her rest and she sat up.

'Wait, now,' said Boreth, suppressing a laugh. 'Are you trying to scare us?'

'No!' exclaimed Meysah. 'It popped out at us.'

Boreth and Vigh drew their weapons.

'Swords won't kill a ghost,' protested Jimmy. 'It's a ghost! It's already dead!'

Seeing the fear in the boys' eyes, Vigh said, 'Show us.' If there were ghosts in this forest, they couldn't hide anyway.

Meysah and Jimmy led Niome, Boreth and Vigh to the tree where they had seen the ghostly face. It was no longer there.

'It was here,' Jimmy maintained. 'See?' He pointed to the sticks they'd dropped in their fear. 'There's the wood we dropped.'

'Oh, Ghost . . . Ghost!' Boreth called, smirking. 'Show yourself.'

'There's no ghost,' Vigh chided. 'It was a figment of your imagination.'

'I don't understand,' said Meysah. 'There was a ghost right here and he spoke to us. His head popped out of this tree.'

'Wait,' said Niome. She crouched down. 'Something's written on the bark. It says: *You will need my advice before going past these trees. If you are worthy, speak these words.*' Niome read the words aloud:

Crackle Crick! Peeple Pop!
Fabble Fip! Bobble Bop!
We are travellers, and weary we are;
You know it, for we have gone far.
We need your help to go past these trees.
We wish to carry on, so summoning are we!

Crackle Crick! Peeple Pop!
Fabble Fip! Cheerful Bob!

The words summoned the ghost, who appeared fully, hands on his hips, his pale and translucent body clad in wispy trousers, shirt, and jacket. He had a round face and round ears and a short beard and moustache that nevertheless seemed to move with the wind. He chuckled and smiled. 'I am Sir Robert Tweedle. Nice to meetcha!'

He held out his hand to Meysah, who hesitated, then reached to shake it out of habit and politeness. His hand passed right through the ghost's.

The ghost laughed. 'I love doin' that! Sorry, boy, to have scared ya before. I was excited to see young visitors. A ghost can get lonely at times. I've been 'ere too many long years to remember, but I sure am glad when I meet new folks. Call me Bob, Bob Tweedle. That's mah name, and what about the rest of you?'

They exchanged glances, reluctant to speak. Then Vigh stepped forward. 'We are travellers from Teloria,' he said.

'Ah!' replied Bob, nodding. 'I see. Yes, it's to stop that nonsensical fool, that dark lord whose name I dare not mention.' He paused and seemed to shiver. 'Are ya perchance travellin' in vain?'

'What sort of a question is that?' exclaimed Niome, offended by the certainty in his tone.

'My apologies, young miss, but if I recollect correctly, last time Telorians went this way, they never returned.'

'We know,' Meysah said forlornly. The others lowered their heads – except for Niome, who caught a glint in Bob's eyes that seemed to speak of more.

When Bob Tweedle spoke again, he'd suddenly become serious. 'Except one.'

They all looked up at him. 'Who?' asked Boreth.

'Why, the wizardess. But, of course, she must've passed away.'

This last remark angered Niome. She marched right up to him. 'Why "of course"? What does that mean?'

'Perhaps we should all be sittin' at a fire while I tell the story,' Bob suggested.

The Telorians looked at each other, suspicious. Bob Tweedle seemed to know quite a bit about their affairs. *But he is a ghost, after all,* Niome told herself. *He likely has access to knowledge beyond our ken.*

Vigh settled it by saying gruffly, 'This way.' Then adding more gently to Meysah and Jimmy, 'Pick up your wood. We will need it.' He led the way back to their camp.

The ghost sat down with them and waited while they fed the fire. He did not look at them, and only gazed at the fire when he started his story.

'Long ago, I was a brave ol' knight, but I wanted to learn magic instead. So, I stopped fightin' for mah kingdom. I was a fair polc, but I deceived those who fought against Malgar. I came here to learn all the magic I could possibly learn. Soon after, mah comrade came to me and told me that Malgar was said to be destroyed, but that his grandson would probably become as great as him. We had nothin' to do but to wait and see, wait and see, and wait and see some more.'

'Yes, okay,' interrupted Jimmy, who was sitting between Meysah and Boreth. 'But how is this important?'

'Listen, young lad, we have to start with the beginnin'. Your impatience proves you are not the most worthy here.'

Niome didn't understand that remark, but like the others, who merely exchanged glances, she remained silent. The interruption seemed to have angered the ghost. Jimmy shrugged.

Tweedle went on. 'Since I'd taken no part in the victory, I set a hex on m'self. I felt awful that I'd been indulgin' selfishly in this magic that had yet to come to any good. Everyone knew that the evil of Malgar lived stronger than ever in his grandson, and all Telorians could do was build a secure wall and prepare for his might.'

'But what was the hex?' asked Meysah, forgetting the ghost's scolding of Jimmy. 'We know this story.'

'Curiosity, furiosity, bluriosity!' Bob Tweedle growled. Then he calmed himself and went on, ignoring the question. 'So they built a wall and I enchanted this place. The grandson grew quickly in power. He grew up faster than any other polc in Kaulchèc History. Instead of stayin' a child till he was twenty and an adolescent till he was ninety-five, he became an adult at thirty. His maturity and growth were both spectacular and frightening.' As Tweedle said it, his voice took on a low, spectral pitch before he resumed his narrative tone.

'When I died, I became part o' this place, if you should know, blond fellow, and curious fellow. That was mah hex. I was the guardian of this forest, keepin' evil out, makin' it a place for worthy knights to rest, where I could . . . well, help. At this point, I can't reveal yet all mah secrets, but it'll come. Don' worry.' He took a deep breath.

'When he grew up, he became Mmmmm . . . Mmmmm – I canna speak the awful name. You know. And many Telorians tried to conquer him, but he attacked Teloria, breakin' down half the wall, destroyin' so much and takin' the *Book of Enchantment*. Groups went after him, none ever returnin'. More and more of the prophecies were coming true.'

Bob Tweedle looked out fondly into the distance.

'The last group to pass this way . . . . There was a particular young fellow whom I thought might be worthy, but he didn't know what he should've known. They were all brave and courageous. This one was warm-hearted, dark-haired, dark eyed. Not enough magic, though, even though it has got to be in the bloodline, somewhere . . .' The ghost glanced at Niome. Then he went on. 'He said to me: "Whether my journey be perilous or not, someone has to set foot out of Teloria, so that others may follow."'

Meysah had tears in his eyes as he looked at the ghost. 'He told me that very same thing,' he blurted.

'And me as well,' added Vigh. 'And he was right. If it weren't for him, perhaps none of us would be out here.'

They all knew whom they were talking about.

'There was only one downfall,' continued Bob Tweedle, 'other than not knowing enough magic. He didn't have the requirement. Neither did the wizardess who, by chance, came back. If the worthy person had been with them, they might've been saved.' He paused, then shrugged. 'Or perhaps it was not meant to happen that way.

'They needed to go to the fortress not far from here. But no one can enter unless they have the magic wand. I designed it myself and made a deal with the people of Firlan that I would only let *the ones* go to them for their counsel. Of course, the wand does much more than open the fortress door, but only *one* can use it.'

Boreth leaned towards Vigh. 'Does he speak of those mentioned in the prophecies?' Vigh shrugged.

'If you are magical yourself,' began Niome, thinking aloud. 'Yes, I get it now. To be worthy, you need magic, and not just any magic – the *Complement Book*.' Niome held it out to Bob Tweedle.

'Only one must use this wand. Indeed, the one who carries the *Complement Book* and possesses great magic shall, for she holds more magic than she realises or reveals.'

He took the book and looked through the pages, as if by the book's own magic, he was able to touch it. 'This is the unique *Complement Book*. But this holds no guarantee that you are worthy.'

They all gasped.

Bob gave the book back to Niome, and with it the wand, which changed slightly upon Niome's touch. 'I put a lot of effort into fabricatin' this wand. I made it from the twigs in this forest. I call them the Tweedle Twigs from the Tweedle Woods, for I found this place myself. I made it in vain, though, for I wanted to enter and have questions answered. Questions for which I feared the answers.

'I would gladly give this wand to any traveller, but even if they were told the biggest and most important secrets, they would perish. Firlan is a sacred place; they don't speak to anyone except those with the worthy power. By now it is known to everyone that whoever looks upon Mmm . . . Mmm – you know – is cursed with a mortal illness. I was amazed that the wizardess survived, but she did not come back with the *Book of Enchantment.*' He sighed and bowed his head.

Vigh broke the silence. 'I regret to say that Elina has passed away. She was a great friend and teacher of magic to Niome here.'

'Yes, and even if I'm not worthy, I'll go anyway, because I have to,' declared Niome.

Bob Tweedle looked at her, his expression solemn yet curious. 'Before I go on,' he said, 'perhaps you should now tell me your story.'

'Well,' began Boreth, 'I don't believe we've introduced ourselves. I am Master Swordfighter Boreth Culmik, and I'm probably the one who should recount our story. My friends are all grieving, you see, more than I am, for they all knew Elina better than I did. Even so, my heart is heavy. The young polc you spoke of was the brother of two of these special travellers. This is my dearest friend, Vigh Nimrod.' He gestured towards Vigh, then introduced each of the others.

Then Boreth told their story, giving a quick account of Teloria and their travels. At last he stopped and sighed. 'That is our story, but I fear it is but a portion of a long and dangerous quest.'

'This may strike some as odd,' said Bob, 'that a ghost may grieve so much, but when you've spent so many years in the same place, waitin' and hopin' for the ones who will return with the *Book of Enchantment* . . . Only when good has come of that book will my hex be broken and I can go up to the heavens above. If evil comes to all the lands, I may be used to serve the enemy against mah will, against mah powers of resistance. I did not realise this when I set my hex.' He paused. 'I have more to tell you. And if it makes you weep, then please do so, for I can't.

'When they came to me, your brother and his eleven companions, they were full of hope and courage. Captain Bahvley and his best mates were plannin' on attacking Mork and going to the Sorcery Tower with Elina, and their minds could not be swayed from this plan.

'They told me how the Morkans came runnin' into Teloria on their great black horses, with their great black capes, and their long swords and fire torches, and set all the villages of Teloria on fire. Runnin', killin', capturin', until they came to that round hut in Teloria City.

'All they needed were the secret spells from their captives – wizards from the other towns – to know how to capture the Great Wizardess. While they worked hard to find the two books, thousands were hammerin' down the great wall day and night. So great was this attack, and for so many years did the Morkans continuously attack, I was told it was being called the Big War. And Mmmm – Mirauk!' he spat, finally speaking the hated name angrily. 'Mirauk sat on his throne with a smile of satisfaction.

'I can't imagine his fury when only *one* book came to him. His polcs had laboured a long time, but someone had hidden the *Complement Book* well.' He shook his head.

'I explained to Bahvley and to Liffwai, to Queevsil and to Tharguen, and to Elina and everyone else who was with 'em about the wand. They would not listen. I begged them to stay, but they ached with fear and grief. Perhaps it was meant to be that they went – one can only hope – for it has opened the door for followers many long years later.' Bob appraised the five Telorians.

'In any case . . . Bahvley lifted his sword high, and announced to all that he should do this alone, and it would be for the love he holds inside, not for hate. He said it was for the love he had for his parents, for his master, for his brother and sister,' Bob motioned towards Meysah and Niome, 'and for his love for Teloria. His eyes were full of hope and determination, and he shouted loud and clear, "Let us fight for the Freedom of Life!" He led his team onward that night, fired-up by his will and his belief.

'Tharguen joined him first and the others quickly followed, shouting, *"For the Freedom of Life! For our loved ones! For Teloria! For the world!"*

'I nudged Elina as she joined them. She would not stay either. If they died in battle, it would be an honourable end for them.'

Bob Tweedle smiled fondly, his eyes growing distant. 'I watched them run and yell. I was glad in a way for their high spirits. They were far from their homes, on a lonely journey to save the light from eternal shadows.'

He sobered and looked at the ground.

'Mah prayin' days were long and tedious. Alas, Elina returned marked by the curse of Mirauk's gaze. The dark land where many fell had become stronger. Mirauk had announced how he slew the leaders of the Telorian group with his bare hands. Some had disappeared and Elina had escaped. The terror grew inside her and I knew there was nothin' anyone could do.

'Few have ever returned from that evil-stricken land, and perhaps I'll never find the one who can look upon Mirauk and bear no fear, the worthy one of the wand who will set fear in *his* eyes for a change.

But at least if others wish to venture on, they take this risk, because time is short if Mirauk gets his way.

'I have lost, by my greed, the deep insight and vision that I had. I could stare into someone's eyes and see if they were the one. But I can't anymore; I will have to chance it, as you have. I will give the wand to Niome, because I see the love you have for your lost brother and for your friends. I see the love you all have for your kingdom. I see your courage, honesty, loyalty, and inner beauty, stronger within you than in anyone else. I also see the power and determination of Bahvley in you both,' he added, looking from Niome to Meysah. 'So I will take a risk. Who knows?' He shrugged, then gave Niome the wand.

'I will say to you what Bahvley wanted me to say to all Telorians who would come this way: "This is not a fight about power. It is not a fight against evil alone. It is for love that we do this. It's a fight about peace; it's a fight about magic. It's a fight to save our friends, our lands, our world. It's a fight for the Freedom of Life!"'

Niome cast her hood over her head and stared at the wand.

Boreth stared blindly into the fire, but his eyes twinkled. He had perhaps not known the previous travellers, but he had lost close friends during the Big War, and his heart had grown heavy with suppressed sorrow.

Jimmy sniffed, and Vigh's eyes glittered with tears. Meysah was the only one to weep openly. He muttered something inaudible, but Vigh caught it and answered softly in a trembling voice, 'It isn't too late.'

After some time, Bob Tweedle said, 'You may have been warned of this before, but this is the last point at which you still have a chance of returnin' home. If you wish to abandon and turn back, it's your choice. You can go back home to your warm beds, or if you are afraid because of the blockade, you can stay with the old wizard in the Old Grey House. But you must choose now.'

Boreth looked up. They all knew what terrors lay before them, what dangers lay ahead, and he dearly wanted to see Clahria and hear her sing. The yearning grew, but then he realised that if he did not go to Mork, how could he save Teloria? What good would it be to see Clahria, knowing they would die much too soon? Better to die in battle knowing she would be safe afterwards. He had to go so he could see her again, perhaps for the rest of his life.

Meysah and Jimmy exchanged looks, as if daring the other to back out first.

Niome stirred where she sat. 'I'm going,' she declared. 'My mind has always been fixed on it, and I'm not going to back out now.'

'Nor I,' Meysah said slowly. 'I long to be in my bed, in my cosy home, and see all my friends again, but I made a promise – a promise to stand by my sister and to stand by what Bahvley believed in.'

'And to not give up,' added Jimmy. 'If Meysah goes, then I'm bound to go with him, just like *I* promised.'

'They need someone with great skill,' said Vigh.

'And another to teach them,' said Boreth. 'We will all go.'

Meysah smiled and clasped Niome in a bear hug. Then he stepped back and wiped his eyes. He suddenly felt taller and stronger, and more mature. Across the fire, Vigh was studying him, and nodded with satisfaction, as if comparing Meysah to Bahvley and finding them equals. Meysah drew his sword and held it high. 'For the Freedom of Life!' he shouted, and Vigh smiled at his determination.

'Rest then,' said Bob. 'You have a big day tomorrow.'

The next morning, Boreth and Jimmy rose early and moved away from the camp for some sword practice using two sticks Boreth cut.

'You must remember to be patient with yourself, Jimmy,' said Boreth. 'You're a fast learner, but you progress slowly.'

'But I want to become as good as you!'

'See? That's what I mean. Work to your own rhythm. It takes a lifetime, you know. You improve every day. It took me a long time to get where I am now.'

'Yes, well, when I see myself beside you—'

'Don't compare yourself to me, Jimmy. Compare yourself to yourself, and how you were yesterday compared to how you are today.'

'Okay,' Jimmy said reluctantly. Then he failed to block Boreth's stick and it hit him in the thigh.

'If this were a sword,' began Boreth, 'that would have been a debilitating wound. You would have fallen to the ground, and I would have followed-through with a killing blow. Remember, it's not just skill and technique, it's survival. You must anticipate your opponent's moves. Rely on instinct and intuition rather than reflex. Let's try it again.'

They fought a while longer, then Jimmy failed to block again, oddly enough, in the same area. 'Close your eyes,' instructed Boreth, 'and see what that does.'

Rather reluctantly, Jimmy closed his eyes. They fought for a while. It helped him understand, but not to properly block the next 'killing' blow. Eyes narrowed in focus, they kept on until Jimmy blocked correctly many times, and finally thrust his stick towards Boreth's stomach.

Boreth raised his hands and let his stick drop. He smiled. 'Jimmy, I've got to hand it to you. You've won your first stick fight.' Jimmy grinned back at him.

Down at the camp, Meysah was changing back into his warm clothes. Vigh was still asleep, while Niome was studying the wand.

'I'm scared!' she admitted to Bob Tweedle.

'There is still hope,' he answered. 'One of you may be able to look upon Mirauk and suffer no ills. I believe in you, Niome. Come here.' He approached her and looked long into her eyes, then he smiled and chuckled. 'I may not see it, but there is a difference in you. I hope I'm not mistaken, but I bet you have the wand because my instinct to give it to you was correct. Yes, a ghost does have instinct.'

'How does it work?' she asked, nodding towards the wand in her hand.

'Oh, just wave it around. Here.' He gave her a small book. It looked ghostly in Bob's hands, but as soon as it touched Niome's, it turned solid, just as the wand had. On the book's cover was inscribed *Tweedle Spells*.

'Tweedle Spells!' exclaimed Niome.

'Yes, to go with the Tweedle Wand!' Bob chuckled. 'The spell for the door is called The Firlan Key. You'll see it; it's on the third page.'

Niome opened the book and flipped through the pages.

'Wave the wand and utter the spell,' instructed Bob. 'As easy as that.'

Niome turned back to the first page and read: *Dedicated to the one who will look upon Mirauk. Do not be afraid, or if you are, don't give in to fear. Look at Mirauk and make him cower.* She looked up at the ghost. 'What if I'm not the one?'

'Don't doubt,' was all he said.

Niome looked through the pages and giggled as she came upon a wake-up spell. She looked at Vigh, who was still fast asleep. 'Here is the Wake-up Spell!' She waved the wand and spoke the rhyme.

Wake mate, fake tait!

It's getting late,
For the sun is up,
The day awaits us.
So wipe that sleep away,
Save it for another day.
Wake mate. Wake!

With a jolt, Vigh leapt up and started gathering his things. He looked at Niome, Meysah and Bob, who were smiling broadly, and paused. 'Come on, get ready. We have a long day ahead of us!' They all laughed. 'What's so funny? I'm serious. Let's get our things organised.'

Again they laughed. Niome explained the joke. Vigh admitted it was funny, but he remained serious, for the sorrow that he felt was not easily dispelled. *Young souls can fly higher than older ones*, he thought. They did not realise what he knew and dreaded. He envied their bliss, but Vigh just couldn't let go just yet. The harsh reality of it was, lives were at stake.

He decided to walk over to Boreth and Jimmy. He stood behind a tree observing them for a while as they thrust and parried.

'You know, you're really ahead in a way,' said Boreth.

'How's that?' asked Jimmy.

'You took it upon yourself to learn the skills of a master swordfighter. You didn't wait for anyone's permission; you made it happen – and that's exactly what you need to do. It's *your* life; *you* decide what you want, how and when, and if you believe in yourself enough, you will make it happen.'

'And that is the most knightly thing to do,' said Vigh, walking up to them. 'It's even kingly.'

'You're finally up!' remarked Boreth.

'Yes, I was quite restless before. Now, though I may perhaps be only magically awake, I'm awake.'

Boreth frowned, not understanding the remark, but Vigh explained as they made their way back to the camp.

They found the camp packed up and the two Fairhavens waiting. 'We are all set to get going,' Niome announced.

They hefted their packs. Vigh took a deep breath and looked at the ghost who would lead them to the end of the wood. 'Let's go,' he said.

Bob Tweedle led them in single file along the Ortim River: Vigh, then Niome, Meysah, Jimmy, and Boreth in the rear.

'We encountered a creature in the water when we crossed,' said Vigh. 'Do you know anything about it?'

Bob furrowed his brows in thought. 'It might be an ancient water dragon, protecting the water. That's why few cross the river or dare to dip their feet into it on the riverbank. Morkan riders know this, so they travel along the river until they hit the shallow stream and the main road. It's the best way to creep up unnoticed.' The ghost lifted a warning finger. 'It's also possible that the creature was captured by Mirauk and altered through his dark alchemy, then released back into the river as a spy and monster.'

Vigh nodded at Bob's theory; it was most likely accurate.

Bob took them north at a rapid pace, muttering a chant to himself. Vigh thought he was just mumbling nonsense until he caught the last few verses and realised the ghost was singing about them:

From far, quite far,
They came like their mates,
Like five points of a star,
Bringing hope was their fates.

Through Tweedle's Woods they walked,
Though I can't say if they'll succeed,
Faith remains in my heart as we walk,
They need only to take the lead.

Bob halted and turned around. 'We're at the northwest edge of the forest. You're on your own now. Unfortunately mah range is limited. Walk across the hills till you reach the next forest. Don't mix it up with the smaller, more southerly one. Head north; Firlan is in that direction. There are tall trees that hide the wall of stone, so keep your eyes peeled. It'll likely take you a few days to get there. Good luck, although luck rarely has anythin' to do with these types of things. Goodbye.' He smiled and chuckled as he vanished before their eyes.

A few steps farther, they stood before a vast landscape of rolling hills that stretched to the horizon. The sunlight highlighted the bright green of new grass on some, but many of the hills were barren of vegetation and stony, and any grass was yellowed and dead. Vigh reminded himself that Winter had just ended and although there was no more snow, the land had not yet regenerated its Spring verdure.

Far off in the distance, the tall peaks of Darakön rose towards the sky. *That way,* Vigh thought. *North, to our destiny.*

CHAPTER SIX:
Many Decisions

The hills rolled on and on like great ocean waves, the scope of the landscape making them appear deceptively gentle, when in reality climbing hill after steep hill fatigued the Telorians' legs. They had to take frequent breaks to rest their tired muscles – this they did in the valleys, where they were protected from the cold north wind that swept across the crests of the hills. There in the warm lee where slope met slope, the hills loomed over them as if they were going to crash and roll over the travellers and bury them alive.

On the fourth day, they came across rubble in a broad valley that looked like thrones among ruins, and stopped there to rest.

Jimmy jumped up to sit on one of the throne-like boulders. 'Do you suppose these were built by the great kings of old?' he asked. 'The Kaulchèc kings?'

'I don't know,' Vigh replied absently, rummaging in his pack.

'The great history books claim that the last kings were sent into exile because they were greedy for power and unfit to rule benevolently,' said Boreth. 'It's possible they built these. There probably once was a castle here.'

'Ew! Morkan ancestors,' complained Jimmy, cringing in disgust, though he remained seated on the throne-like stone.

'Will there ever be a king or queen again?' Meysah wondered.

'If someone who is worthy proves themselves,' replied Vigh, 'though the *Books of Kings and Queens*, both those of old and those prophesied, have been hidden away, if not destroyed.'

'I read something about it,' voiced Niome, who had been looking through a personal spell book of hers; lowering the *Complement Book* down to rest on her knee. 'I think they even mention it in here. I could find it if there was more light.' Still bent over her spell book, she waved at the heavily overcast sky, made darker by the fact that they were sitting in the shade.

Only when Niome mentioned it did the others realise how dark it had become. 'Why is it so dark all of a sudden?' Meysah pondered, looking up. He gasped. 'Uh . . .'

The others looked up to see a massive creature with golden-red scales hovering above them. It shrieked and flicked its orange tail, and the arrow-shaped tip grazed Niome's left hand as she scrambled back, out of the way, eyes wide. It landed before them in a cloud of dust and smoke from its nostrils, blowing Jimmy off the stone throne. It regarded them with green, reptilian eyes so piercing, they seemed to see right into their souls. Everyone stood frozen in fear.

Boreth drew his sword. The creature lifted its front paw and extended a talon towards Boreth. Then with one swipe, it brushed Boreth aside, flinging him to the ground. Now everyone drew their swords and backed away to stand huddled together, watching the dragon.

The dragon advanced towards them, its feet thumping on the ground as it closed on them. The Telorians backed away.

Niome clutched the *Complement Book* tightly. The dragon looked at her, then reached out and scooped Niome up, lifting her close so it could look at the book. It inhaled and reared into the air, shrieking, but it didn't exhale flames. Instead, it released Niome, who backed quickly away, and lifted off, soaring into the sky and flapping towards the Darakön Mountains. The travellers stood transfixed, watching it.

Finally Vigh moved, then Boreth, then everyone relaxed and sighed in relief.

On the sixth day, they reached the crest of a hill and looked out over the tall canopy of the northern wood. Vigh reckoned they would reach it by the end of the day.

Indeed, by nightfall they'd reached the outskirts of the forest, its scattered trees three times as tall as regular trees, the dark trunks massive and the branches obscuring the sky with their dark green leaves, seemingly untouched by Winter. Unlike Mistoff, it was dry and cool under the trees here, with no tropical humidity, which made the lush greenness even more of a mystery.

'At last,' said Boreth, 'Firlan Forest!'

'How majestic!' exclaimed Jimmy, looking up at the towering trees.

They walked until night had completely fallen under the trees and they could no longer see their way, then they made camp within the embrace of two massive tree roots, ate, then slept.

They set out again when the sun was no more than a blush on the horizon, offering just enough of a glow to see by. The deeper they walked into the wood, the quieter it got. There was no wind, no birdsong, nothing. When one of them stepped on a twig, the resulting crack echoed eerily through the still forest. While trying to find a way through the close-growing trees, Vigh and Boreth found a path and led the others down it, only to find that it had led them to a veritable wall of trees, growing so close that they seemed to be stuck together. The Telorians went in one direction along the barrier, then back in the other direction trying to find a gap, but when they did, they found a wall of stone rising right behind the trees.

'A double wall for double protection!' deduced Vigh. 'No wonder they never get disturbed.'

'Is that a tower there?' asked Meysah, pointing up at what looked like a structure hidden behind the trees.

'Yes,' replied Boreth. 'That's probably how they see what goes on outside their castle walls. Surely they saw us coming.'

'Even if they did, they wouldn't let us in,' said Niome. 'They'll only greet us if we use the wand to enter, but I have no clue where the gate might be.'

'I hope it's not behind trees like these,' muttered Jimmy.

'In case it is, we'll have to scramble through every hole or indentation we encounter, to check,' said Vigh. 'We must walk along the wall that way.' He pointed to the right.

Their expressions uncertain, Meysah and Jimmy looked at each other and grimaced.

'There must be some simpler way,' said Meysah.

'The sooner we start, the sooner we'll find the door, but I'm afraid there isn't much else we can do,' said Boreth. 'Two of us should walk between the trees and the wall. I suggest the two of you, for now.' He nodded towards Meysah and Jimmy.

The two boys shared another look, then forced smiles and stepped forward. They plunged through the barrier of tree trunks to the narrow gap between them and the wall, and started sidling along the wall, brushing away bugs and leaves and dirt. The others walked on the other side of the trees, checking ahead for any signs of a gate.

They carried on like this for a long while, then the boys crawled out from behind the trees. Vigh and Boreth and Niome greeted them eagerly, thinking the two had found the door.

'I'm fed up with this,' complained Meysah. 'I say I run like a wild beast with my eyes closed and see where that brings me. But I am *not* going back in there. Yuck!' He crossed his arms, looking determined.

Jimmy, who stood beside him, laughed. 'I quite enjoyed the little tunnel-like space. I mean I do like insects, and if I'm honest, I felt hidden and protected from evil polcs, if any suddenly arrived. But I do like your idea, Meysah, so' – he grinned, deliberately pausing – 'why don't you run like a wild beast?' Jimmy continued, laughing, 'I'll gladly follow and check if your method is a good one.'

'Fine!' Meysah snapped. 'If that's what you all think this is – a joke! – I'll prove it.' He closed his eyes and ran about, twirling around here and there, his arms in the air.

The others followed at a distance, watching in amusement. Meysah's antics did lift their spirits; they almost forgot their dark mission. Then Meysah crashed into a tree in the tree wall and fell flat on his back. He lay there staring up at the others as they surrounded him.

'Well, maybe your method is flawed, but you sure know how to make people feel better,' said Vigh, smiling and helping him up. Meysah brushed the dirt off his clothes.

Boreth handed him his bag, which he'd dropped during his erratic trot, and playfully ruffled Meysah's hair. 'There's the hairstyle to go with a whirl-a-gig,' he said, chuckling.

They started walking again, but stopped short when a great crack shattered the silence of the forest. They whirled, their hands on their swords, thinking someone behind them had stepped on a branch. No one was there. But the cracking sound continued.

Suddenly the ground below their feet began to shake and the grass where Meysah stood lifted as a creature sprang out of the earth. It rose high above them, towering like a faceless giant root, with many smaller roots dangling from it that swayed like tentacles. Meysah dropped onto his stomach and clung to the grass that served as the creature's head. Below, the others staggered a few steps back.

Vigh drew his sword, and was immediately flung aside by one of the tentacles. Boreth was also swept aside by one of the roots before he could draw his bow.

Meysah peered down. 'Jimmy, do something!' he cried.

'Uh, sorry, but it pushed our masters aside when they went for their weapons. So far this creature has left me alone, so I'm not going to draw mine. Besides, I don't think it wants to fight.'

The creature rolled several tentacles up as though forming fists, and pounded them on the ground. Jimmy fell on his bum. Niome kept her feet, but extended her arms to keep her balance.

'You were saying?' Meysah called down.

Niome looked up at the creature. 'Are you a guardian of Firlan Forest?'

The creature's reply came as a rustling of many roots and it pounded its fists on the ground again. Niome fell to her hands and knees, suddenly feeling heavy and weak. She became short of breath and she felt her heart pounding, as she had in the presence of the Morkans. She clutched at her chest with one hand and looked towards the masters, who were also clutching their chests.

'Niome?' Meysah called out. 'Is this what the heart pounding feels like?' It seemed magic had connected them and they all felt what Niome felt.

She looked up at the creature again. A thought formed in her head, though it wasn't hers. *Are you worthy?* it asked. Niome didn't know what to answer; she didn't feel worthy, certainly not now.

'I don't know,' Niome admitted at last. 'But I'm the only one willing to do something.' She struggled to her feet, keeping her eyes on the creature. 'Elina chose me. She sent me out here. I will continue on until I find what she wanted me to find.'

The ground shook again and the creature sank back into the earth, tentacles flailing as it submerged into its underground lair. Meysah clung to the grass as tightly as when he'd been high in the air.

Jimmy approached him and extended a hand. 'I think it's safe now,' he said. Meysah reluctantly let go of the grass and slowly stood – with Jimmy's help.

Niome pointed at the wall of trees. 'The creature pointed that way as it descended back into the earth.' She walked up to the wall and reached past the trees, placing her hand on the stone wall. She could see nothing. Closing her eyes, she let her magical instincts guide her, funnelling all her magic into her hand as she focused on the wall. Her hand began to feel warm, as though the wall had become hot. Niome opened her eyes. On the wall behind the trees, a picture of a magic wand glowed yellow.

She turned to the others. 'Looks like Meysah found our gate!'

Meysah smiled in satisfaction, crossing his arms. 'I told you.'

'Don't boast,' Jimmy chided, playfully punching Meysah's arm and pointing at the grass. Meysah shifted uneasily, smiling sheepishly.

'It looks like magic lives in all Fairhavens,' Vigh said, looking at Boreth as they all joined Niome by the wall. 'And it somehow connects us all,' he added. 'That was an interesting experience, to say the least.' Boreth nodded.

Niome, focused on the illuminated wall, took out the book that Bob Tweedle had given her and turned to the third page. She waved the wand in the air and said in a loud, clear voice,

Majestic Gate of Firlan!
Open in the name of Tweedle!
The Great Ones are passing through
and need your counsel.

Open, Doors of Firlan!
Nepp orodos folnarif!

The trees cracked loudly and thrust themselves aside at her command to reveal a set of stone double doors. The travellers stepped back as the doors opened outwards, revealing many polcs, all clad in green and brown garments. They were armed with swords and bows, but lowered their weapons when they saw the five Telorians.

Niome was in the lead, holding the wand and the book. The five Telorians walked forward proudly, and stopped on the pavement around an image of a magic wand, unconsciously positioning themselves like five points of a star: Niome in the front, Meysah to her right and back a step, Jimmy to her left, also back a step, and Vigh and Boreth behind them a few steps.

The leader of the green-clad polcs walked forward – a tall, dark-haired polc with handsome features. 'Welcome,' he said as he approached to get a closer look at them. 'I see you are Telorians. That explains the guardian retreating.'

'Yes,' said Vigh, nodding. 'We've come a long way to seek your counsel, on the advice of Bob Tweedle.'

'Ah!' The polc laughed. 'Yes; what a character. My father has told me much of him. We are also Telorians . . . or were, once. We left Teloria long ago and established a colony here, building this enormous castle.' He waved a hand at the stone wall behind him. 'My father, Firnamel, is the King of Firlan. My name is

Kchalami, the Prince of this realm. Please enter. We have been waiting for folk like you. Indeed, the stars shine brightly upon us at this moment, and will until the end of your journey.'

The five travellers entered a large courtyard and the gate closed behind them. The Firlanians in the courtyard saluted them, which confused them.

After basic introductions, Kchalami announced there would be a banquet in their honour. The Telorians could only nod, still looking around in wonder. They followed the Prince up a staircase to the third floor, then down a long corridor where open doors revealed many empty chambers. Kchalami went around a corner, then stopped. Gesturing at the open doors in this corridor, which revealed bedrooms containing beds, chairs, and many luxuries, he bid them to choose any room they fancied.

'I will send someone for you when the feast is ready,' he added.

'Thank you,' said Vigh. 'It warms us to be given such hospitality.'

'A pleasure!' replied Kchalami, his gaze sliding past Vigh to Niome. 'After all, you are the worthy ones for whom we have long been waiting.' He turned and walked back down the corridor.

The Telorians washed up and returned to their rooms to each find a green tunic and trousers and a brown cape waiting for them. A yellow star with a blue wand was embroidered on the chest of each tunic.

'I'm surprised that they fit so well,' Niome remarked when they all met in the hallway.

'The Firlanians are not only skilful, they're quick,' Vigh agreed, looking down at his outfit.

'They are cool clothes, but the capes are a bit too warm,' Jimmy said, indicating the brown cape he had draped over one arm.

'Frankly, I am astonished at how honourably they are treating us,' Niome admitted, looking a little uncomfortable. 'We've done nothing to merit such treatment.'

That prompted a long, thoughtful silence.

'And there's something else,' Niome said at last. The others looked at her expectantly. She pointed to the symbol embroidered on the tunics. 'I saw Elina make a drawing of this when I was younger. She told me it was a symbol from the prophecy books.' Another silence allowed that information to sink in.

'So ultimately,' began Vigh, 'the Firlanians believe we are heroes from the prophecies? Well, everything Tweedle was saying just gained a lot more weight.'

They exchanged solemn glances. They either had to succeed and save the world, or die trying.

'Let's just wait it out and see what the Firlanians share of their prophetic knowledge,' Vigh advised.

'I kind of like the idea of being in the prophecies,' admitted Jimmy. 'I hope it's true. Then we can actually save the world and make a difference.'

The sun was going down when a dark-haired Firlanian woman went from door to door, knocking and calling softly, 'We are ready to receive you at the banquet.' She waited until they were all in the corridor, gave their garments a quick once-over, then led them to the staircase, saying, 'Your garments fit you well.'

'Yes, they're very comfortable,' said Meysah, again admiring the stars embroidered on the cuffs of the sleeves. 'These embroideries are remarkable.'

The woman smiled at him. 'We have many skilled craftspolcs and artists.'

'They're definitely very talented!' Jimmy exclaimed in awe.

She led them down the stairs and into a large hall that was brightly lit with torches on the walls and a huge chandelier overhead that must have held a hundred candles. Below that, running the length of the hall, was a long table that connected with a head table at the far end to form a T. About sixty Firlanians already sat at the long table. When they saw the Telorians arrive, they all rose to welcome them, holding tankards high or bowing at the waist.

The stout, grey-haired Firlanian seated at the centre of the head table rose and called out, 'Welcome, my dear friends! My name is Firnamel, King of Firlan. You've already met my son, Kchalami.' He indicated his son, seated to his right. On the far side of Kchalami sat another young Firlanian male, who was introduced as the Prince's war companion, Akchmassiel.

On the King's left sat a young girl soon to reach her coming-of-age, with an empty chair beside her. Firnamel introduced her as his daughter, Saffiniel, then pointed to the polc walking to her seat beside Saffiniel and introduced her as Saffiniel's chambermaid and trusted friend, Melbossli. She was the one who had come to get the Telorians.

Firnamel indicated five places set for the Telorians at the head table and waited until they were all at the front with him. Then he turned to face the crowd. 'Your attention please!' he called in a loud voice that carried to the far corners of the hall. 'I present to you our five Telorian guests. First, Niome Fairhaven!'

Niome stepped forward and bowed. Then she walked along the table until she saw a wooden *N* on a plate at the centre of five chairs. She stood behind her chair and looked out at the faces of the Firlanians, who watched her attentively. She felt heat rise to her face, and wondered what the prophecies said about her and the others.

The King presented the others and they found their seats in the same fashion. Boreth and Jimmy were to Niome's left, and Meysah and Vigh to her right. Then Firnamel gave them his blessing. 'May the heavens look upon you, and the stars shine upon you! We believe they have chosen you themselves. You are five bright and beautiful warriors like five bright and beautiful points of a star.'

'That's what Bob Tweedle meant,' Meysah whispered in Vigh's ear in sudden understanding. 'In his song: "Like five points of a star."'

'We have long awaited this moment,' Firnamel went on, 'when we Firlanians share counsel and gifts in exchange for bravery and boldness. You five have been chosen for this task. The star is your symbol. We have seated you in the way we first saw you, standing in the gateway like the five points of a star. In your honour, we will carve a star in the pavement where you stood. You will be long remembered.

'Hence, we have gifts to bestow upon you! Remarkable weapons that have been passed down from generation to generation. Relics that we shall now pass on to you.'

Firnamel paused as five Firlanians came up to stand before the head table, each bearing an object covered with a cloth.

'May these gifts connect with your souls, so that when you hold them for the first time in battle, you will instinctively know how to use them.' He turned around and took from the first of the five Firlanians a pearly white cylinder. 'To you, Niome Fairhaven, I give the Dragon's Wind, created for the one who is summoned by the dragons themselves. When you hold up this cylinder, it will blow the enemy away from you with great force. It will not kill them, but it will slow them down and blind them temporarily.'

King Firnamel passed the cylinder to Kchalami, who set it in the centre of the table in front of Niome, who studied it.

Her heart soared at the gift before her and the incredible kindness of her new allies. Yet all too soon, her heart sank again as Firnamel added, 'I'm sure it will be of good use in Mork.'

Meysah and Vigh were presented with shields.

'I carved them myself when I was young,' said the King. 'They are made of the third layer of the bark of the trees found in this forest and hewn by magic. Fire will not burn them, nor will a sword scar them. Believe me, they have been tested.'

Once again, the items were set down on the table in front of their respective owners. A picture of a great Firlanian tree had been carved into the surface of the round shields.

Jimmy and Boreth were presented with bows and many arrows.

'They were crafted by the best. You need not possess the best aim to use them, for once you've pinpointed your target, the arrow will follow that path. You may use any kind of arrow with these bows.' These also were set on the table with the other gifts.

'All of these are magical. Use them well,' King Firnamel said. 'Now I've spoken long enough. Everyone sit, and let the feast begin.'

They sat down and started to eat.

'This is grand,' Jimmy told Niome.

She didn't smile. 'I'm worried we will dishonour the Firlanians if we are not the chosen ones.'

'If so many believe it, then it must be true,' concluded Boreth. 'We mustn't let fear cast a shadow on our faith, nor our fate.'

Niome tried to smile. 'I admit I am burdened by our fate.'

'Don't worry about that now,' Vigh said gently. 'Enjoy your meal.'

They feasted and laughed for the rest of the evening. The Telorians felt welcomed, praised, and safe. Some Firlanians told them stories of their prowess and the Telorians shared past experiences as well.

After the meal, some of the Firlanians stayed to show the Telorians how to use their gifts. One lad named Elmezni, not much older than Jimmy, showed him some tricks with the bow and, assisted by his sister, Krystal, had him practice the new manoeuvres in one of their courtyards. Afterwards, he showed Jimmy where the craftspolcs worked on their art and embroideries.

'By the way,' said Elmezni, folding his arms and leaning against the wall as they watched the craftspolcs work, 'I'm developing my own signature battle move.'

'You're developing your own signature move?!' exclaimed Jimmy. 'I've never even thought of that.'

'You'll have plenty of time to come up with your own while you're away. How about this? When you return,' Elmezni suggested, 'you can show it off to me, and then we can teach each other our moves!' Jimmy nodded vigorously, already eager to exchange battle tactics with his new friend.

The Telorians took a day of rest after their eventful evening. At midday on the day after, they met with the Firlanian council in the briefing lounge. They all took turns talking, describing their journey up to this point, and revealing events from their own perspective, and the Firlanians listened attentively. The incident involving the dragon drew their greatest attention.

'A dragon!' exclaimed one of the Firlanians.

'Yes,' confirmed Vigh. 'Standing only a few steps from us.'

'That can only mean one thing,' concluded Kchalami. 'They know you travel to Mork.'

'But it didn't hurt any of you,' Elmezni noted.

'It sure scared us!' said Jimmy. 'And I'm not looking forward to going into their lair.'

'Well,' said Firnamel, 'it might be safer there than in Mork. You know, these creatures can practically read minds, so if it looked into your souls, it read your intentions. No doubt the dragons wish to stop Mirauk as much as we do.'

'But what if something goes wrong?' asked Meysah. 'The Portal is in their lair. They may not let us get near it even if we *are* chosen or worthy.'

'Maybe we're not meant to go through the Portal,' voiced Niome. 'Only the dragons know what lies behind it. There are many ways to restore peace and freedom in the land. We only know that we're meant to take the book. For the lair, we shall see when we get there.'

'I'm sure anyone in Teloria would agree with you,' said Firnamel.

'Uh-oh. Home!' Jimmy gasped. 'They don't know where we are.' He paused, looking around with wide eyes. 'And they've got Captain . . . Kàtchah to deal with.'

'It's all right,' soothed Boreth, putting his hand on Jimmy's shoulder. 'Henker knows more about the future than anyone else in Teloria. He and Gorthan must have spoken to Selemil by now, and our families. And there is the magical hideout. Don't worry. They'll be fine.'

Jimmy took a deep breath to calm himself, and nodded.

'If *we* know what your mission entails,' began Firnamel, 'then *they* know. Believe me, it's written in the stars.' He resumed his earlier discourse. 'Time presses, however. You must get to the Portal before next Colouring. Once the leaves start to change and fall, the dragons will go to sleep and block off all passageways. That will give Mirauk plenty of time to gain possession of the second book, should he make that his goal.'

Firnamel also mentioned the importance of finding the most suitable route. One of the Firlanian women seated in the circle of chairs mentioned a few routes they could take, the Ortim River among them.

A Firlanian knight fidgeted in his seat before speaking. 'Long have I studied the waters of the Great Ocean Valley in our part of this vast world, from Darakön to the ocean, from the rapids to as close to Mork as I would dare go.' He dropped his voice to almost a whisper. 'There isn't anything more unnatural than a sea monster created and sent by Mirauk.'

He identified the creature the Telorians encountered as a *goûroob*. Then, continuing in a normal voice, 'It will not eat or kill you, but it will haunt you. If you go by boat, there's no doubt it will follow you.'

The Telorians acknowledged him, and another Firlanian began to speak of the Morkan riders. Firlanian watchers had observed that the Morkans used the roads along the riverbanks, so no doubt the Telorians would be seen. And though they could make allies at the Desert of Dûnelor, their land was treacherous, despite being protected from cold, and the quicksand patches were most deadly.

'It may be a risk they'll have to take, if they're willing,' interrupted Akchmassiel. 'But it does mean walking along the ocean shores far to the west. No one knows what is in *those* waters past the borders of the Great Ocean Valley. The Islands of Mork are a staging area for Mirauk's armies. Also, if Mirauk set camps on the other side of the Malgar River, who can tell?'

'Malgar River,' Meysah mused. 'It was named after Mirauk's grandfather.' He shuddered.

Elmezni suggested travelling to the Fortress of Dalvar, where the Kaulchèc first established holdings, though it would take them close to Darakön.

Niome leaned back in her chair. 'I really don't know which way we should go.'

'We also have to consider time,' advised Boreth.

Another Firlanian predicted how much time each path should add to the Telorians' journey, allowing them to consider their options. Then, the Firlanian King offered to help them make the appropriate preparations and adjourned the meeting.

Time passed while the five Telorians thought about and discussed their options, while they prepared their things and themselves, mostly magically. Weapons were cleaned and sharpened while minds were cleared and focused. Then at last, Niome announced how she and her companions had come to a decision.

'It came to me during a meditation,' she told the council of Firlanians. 'It now seems obvious that we should go to the Fortress of Dalvar.'

The King rose. 'May strength and valour accompany you on your journey.'

A Firlanian Captain named Keeshnapalai, who had once travelled close to Dalvar, gave the Telorians a map of the area between Firlan and Dalvar.

'You will encounter a tall wooden wall that runs for many leagues, from the river to the mountains,' he told them. 'I presume it was made by the people who live at Dalvar. We call it the Fence. We will give you a knife to cut through it, imbued with a power that will cut through the wood better and more quickly than any axe. Beyond that wall, we don't know what lies on the plains, except the fortress.'

Kchalami stood. 'We will also provide you with food and medicine – and offer our prayers.'

Firnamel rose. 'We will offer you the most important of all foods, blessèd fruits that will keep the power of the Star alive.' The old King winked as he reached into his pocket. He pulled out an apple. With a small knife, he cut it horizontally and showed how its core formed a star. 'You see, now that you've arrived, everything that shows the sign of the star is sacred, for you are the Star and you've survived to come this far because of your inner strength. As long as you stay together and keep the Star whole, you will survive any danger that confronts you – you will be nearly invincible. But if you are separated, the power of the Star will falter. That is why you must persevere and reach Mork.'

His smile turned apologetic. 'I would send an army with you, but we need to protect our lands. I will do my best to prevent Morkans from coming this way to Teloria. That I can do – stop them – but the journey that lies ahead is for you five alone.'

'How can you be sure that we are truly the chosen ones?' Niome blurted.

'You doubt through your thoughts, young wizardess,' Firnamel replied. 'You should trust with your heart, trust what the stars have in store for you. You will learn, on your quest, the true nature of your destinies. But remember: reason can become the warrior's greatest bane, but will can become the unworthy polc's triumph.'

Two days later, Firnamel, Kchalami, and Elmezni bid farewell to the small band of travellers in the courtyard just inside the gate, as other Firlanians looked on.

'May the stars shine upon you,' said Kchalami. 'May the Star shine.' He looked at Niome. 'Especially its first point.' He paused, looking like there was more he wanted to say. There was a glint in his eyes as he gazed upon Niome, and his cheeks flushed before he merely smiled. 'Be careful.'

Niome nodded. 'I will.'

'I wish that you all will become memorable and admirable knights,' said Elmezni. 'Especially you, Jimmy. I will be waiting to hear the story.' They both laughed.

After exchanging a few more well-wishes, the Telorians hefted their packs and paraded through the gate in their star formation amidst the cheers and salutes of the watching Firlanians. Then the gate closed behind them, and the Five of the Star set off through the quiet wood.

Chapter Seven:
Vast Emptiness

It took the company the rest of the day to reach the endless-seeming flat expanse. No one talked; they were all deep in thought about the long and complicated journey that lay ahead of them. Before they left the forest for good, they sat down for a cold meal.

'What are these plains called?' asked Meysah.

'They are the Gord Plains,' said Vigh, consulting the map Keeshnapalai had given them. 'The old legends tell of the Gord people, who used to dwell underground. No one knows where the entrance to their tunnels is.'

'How come you didn't mention it before?' asked Jimmy.

'Because the Gord people no longer exist,' Boreth snapped, 'or at least they have not been seen in millennia. They were barbarians who did awful things.' Boreth paused. 'And inspired Morkan torture techniques,' he added under his breath. His voice softened. 'No one wants to be reminded. Let us not talk about them, and just in case, let's not let them hear us once we are on the plains.'

Meysah and Jimmy nodded.

'Niome,' said Vigh, 'you're awfully quiet. Is there something troubling you?'

'No,' she said, then admitted, 'I wonder what is yet to come.' She shrugged. 'Besides that, I have nothing to say.'

The Telorians ate the rest of their meal in silence. The sun was going down when they set out again but the moon was rising high and already shining brightly, lighting up the night.

All walked silently, but Meysah and Jimmy carried on a whispered conversation.

'I'm concerned about Niome,' admitted Meysah.

'Why?' asked Jimmy, cocking his head in puzzlement.

'Well, haven't you noticed anything strange in her behaviour?'

'No. Nothing at all. Except for her quietness.'

'That's just it,' said Meysah. 'Ever since we left Teloria, she's been quiet. And the farther away from home we get, the more withdrawn she becomes. You didn't see her at home; you don't live with her – she usually never stops talking, and she's always so happy. Now, she's . . . not herself. She's . . . grave.'

'Maybe she's relying on intuition, listening to hear what it has to tell her.'

'Maybe. I'm just concerned,' sighed Meysah. They fell silent.

The moon was full, and thanks to its light, they were able to make good time. But they all froze, listening, when the wind carried a hissing, whistling sound to their ears.

'It's as though there are sinister voices in the air,' muttered Boreth.

'It's coming from the mountains,' said Vigh, noting that the wind was blowing from the north. 'It's the shrieking of the dragons. Perhaps they are upset about something, but what?'

No one had the answer, so they walked in silence for the rest of the night, listening to the eerie sound.

They travelled for nearly a week, stopping to eat cold meals, and to sleep only long enough to stave off exhaustion. They heard the dragons' shrieking for several days before it stopped for good.

When they reached the first copse of trees, they gathered firewood, which would allow them fires for hot meals.

On the seventh day out of Firlan, they were starting to feel lost in the endless sea of green grass that seemed to stretch forever, and they still hadn't come to the Fence. Finally, at sundown of the ninth day, they saw the undulating ribbon of the Fence in the distance, but they also saw a large tent illuminated by many torches.

'Oh no!' breathed Vigh, staring at the structure from where the group crouched in the tall grass to avoid being seen. 'We have to get by before they see us. If we're lucky, the sun will go down soon and we can pass through in the dark, but if we wait here, we will get caught.'

'Ho there!' called a voice from afar.

'Quick, to the ground!' cried Boreth, flattening himself on the ground.

'There's no point, it's too late,' Vigh whispered quickly.

A polc on a dark horse came galloping up to them. He cast off his black hood and studied them carefully. 'Where are you going without your horses?' he demanded.

'Nowhere, sir,' said Vigh.

'You're not from my army, are you? Who sent you? I should inform the captain that polcs are wandering at sundown. No, wait!' he narrowed his eyes. 'Why are you dressed in such distasteful clothing?'

Meysah glanced down at his clothes; he thought he'd dressed fashionably. In fact, Telorians always dressed handsomely; even their ruggedest clothes were pretty handsome. He glared at the polc, feeling insulted.

'One would think you were Telorians!' the polc said carefully, his tone threatening. He backed his horse away and shouted, 'Telorians!'

He wheeled his horse, but Boreth quickly brought up his bow and shot the soldier down.

'They must have come from the far north,' Boreth deduced. 'Horses wouldn't be able to get past a wall like that one.' He nodded towards the towering wall-like fence. 'Quick, run for it!' he called out as, back by the tent, soldiers ran to mount their horses.

The five scurried along as fast as they could, crawling on the ground so they wouldn't be seen, but the setting sun cast its last light on them and made their swords shimmer in the purplish pink light.

Soldiers on foot were running their way, with polcs on horseback quickly passing the runners. The Fence was still too far away, and they'd still have to cut through it. There was nothing to do but fight their way to it.

Boreth and Jimmy began sending arrow after arrow into the approaching Morkans. The others waited with swords drawn. When their foes got too close for their bows to be effective, Jimmy and Boreth drew their swords as well.

Jimmy found himself facing two tall Morkans, trying to defend himself. He waited for them to come very close, then threw himself to one side and rolled away just as they were about to strike. One Morkan nearly struck the other, but the latter dodged the blow and pounced on Jimmy, sending him to the ground as his sword slipped out his hand.

'Good one!' growled the Morkan, raising his sword, 'but not good enough.'

Jimmy grabbed his sword arm to prevent him from stabbing him while groping for the knife in his boot with his other hand. As the Morkan wrenched his arm free, Jimmy brought his knife up and stabbed him in the chest, then pushed him away and scrambled to his feet, looking for his sword. As he bent to scoop it up from the ground, an arrow flew over his head, passing through the air where his torso had just been. There were archers among them! 'Archers!' Jimmy shouted, running towards where he thought the others might be, eyes searching in the twilight gloom.

Vigh heard Jimmy's warning and kept an eye on the approaching Morkans, watching for arrows as he fought off a trio of foot soldiers, the shield the Firlanians had gifted him giving him an edge over his foes. As one charged towards him, he pushed the Morkan away with the shield, and it gave so much force to the push, the Morkan flew back and landed hard on the ground, then lay still. Vigh smiled grimly. With this powerful shield, he was an even more efficient fighter.

When the enemy archers stopped, Vigh ran to help Boreth, whom one of the riders had knocked down with his horse. The horse reared, but Boreth rolled forward in a surprise move, grabbed the horse's leg above the dangerous hoof, and hung on, tripping it. The rider was able to jump free, though, and landed on his feet, his sword high for a killing blow. Vigh came just in time to put his shield between them.

Niome was fighting with a polc on foot, who slashed at her, the sword slicing her upper arm and making her cry out. She defended herself as best she could, but her arm grew numb and she could no longer hold her sword. She tried to switch hands, but blood from her wound made the hilt slippery and she dropped it. Staggering back to avoid another slash, she fell onto her back, reaching with her left hand for her sword.

The Morkan stepped on it. 'Are you trying to reach this?' he sneered. 'You won't need it anymore.'

He leaned over her, his dark stare holding her eyes as he placed the point of his sword to her throat. He smiled viciously, then whipped his head around as someone yelled.

Meysah came from nowhere, it seemed, slamming into the Morkan and dragging him to the ground with him. There was a gurgling groan, then Meysah rolled off the dead Morkan. 'And this is only one arm,' he said. 'Imagine if I had swords in both!' He jumped to his feet and helped his sister up.

Clutching her wounded arm, Niome retrieved her sword and then stayed close behind Meysah, who used his shield to protect her.

When there seemed to be a lull in the Morkan attack, Vigh shouted, 'To the Fence! Run!'

The sun had long ago set, and the overcast sky intensified the darkness. They ran as fast as they could to the Fence, but the Morkans were giving chase.

Vigh slipped the knife from the Firlanian captain out of his sleeve. 'Jimmy!' he called, 'You'll have to cut the Fence. Boreth and I will cover for you.' He handed the knife to Jimmy as they reached the landmark. 'Make the hole barely large enough for you.'

'But then you won't be able to pass through!' objected Jimmy.

'Just do it!' Vigh was the tallest and broadest of them all – if he barely fit, then the tall Morkans definitely would not be able to get through.

As Boreth and Vigh covered him, Jimmy started cutting the small passage near the ground. The magic knife went through the thick hardwood as if it were butter.

'More Morkans on the way,' Boreth warned tersely as Jimmy worked. 'And riders. They'll be here any moment—'

'It's done.'

'Quick, let Niome go through first,' Boreth urged. 'Give the knife to her. We don't want them to get their hands on it. We can't risk them following; we need some lead time.'

Jimmy gave Niome the knife just before she lay flat on the ground and pulled herself through the opening like a snake.

'You next, Jimmy,' Vigh ordered. 'Go, go, go!'

Jimmy dropped onto his stomach and slithered through.

'Now Meysah.' Vigh looked around, and a knot gripped his stomach. 'Where's Meysah?'

From the other side of the Fence, Niome heard him. 'He was with me the whole time!' she answered.

'Well, he's gone now,' said Boreth.

Before anyone could ponder on this, Boreth and Vigh were fighting again. Jimmy dropped to his belly from the other side of the hole and angled his bow parallel to the ground, nocking an arrow, taking aim and setting it loose as quickly as he could. He sent arrow after arrow towards the enemy fighters, helping the knights as best he could. They still could not see Meysah.

'Go, Boreth, go!' cried Vigh, parrying a thrust from a Morkan knight.

Boreth dove towards the hole and shimmied through.

Before Vigh could follow, a Morkan grabbed him by the neck and pushed him against the Fence. Positioning his hands around Vigh's neck, he started to strangle him. Vigh let his sword drop and tried to pull the hands away from his neck. His vision began to blur when the Morkan's gaze suddenly went blank. The knight groaned, loosening his grip, then dropped to the ground. Meysah pulled his sword out of the polc's back as he fell.

'You seem to pop out of nowhere tonight,' Vigh breathed in relief, picking up his sword.

'I guess I like the ambush thing,' replied Meysah, twirling his sword.

'Well, go. Come on.'

Meysah crawled through the opening and Vigh tried to squeeze through after him, but his shoulders got stuck. Those on the other side could hear the thunder of approaching hooves. Meysah and Boreth grabbed Vigh's shoulders and tried to pull him to their side. Jimmy had just turned to Niome for the knife to make the opening bigger when Meysah and

Boreth gave triumphant cries and Vigh wriggled the rest of the way through the hole.

'Are you hurt?' Niome asked.

'No. Maybe a little scraped,' Vigh rubbed his neck and cleared his throat, 'but I'm fine, nothing major. Let's go!'

They ran for several leagues, sometimes slowing to a trot, sometimes helping one another when one of them began to fall behind. Finally Niome staggered erratically for several steps, then fell to her hands and knees. She stayed there, trembling, her breathing harsh. As if that were a signal, the others plopped to the ground, exhausted.

Boreth laid Niome's head on his lap while Meysah tended the gash on her arm with the Firlanian herbs compounded to stop the bleeding. Her wound cleaned and dressed, Niome remained lying on Boreth's lap, eyes closed to rest them.

Vigh checked his limbs; there were only a few scrapes and friction burns, but there were tender areas on his neck and he still coughed from the choking. Boreth told him the areas were bruised, handing him a Firlanian herbal potion to rub into his neck. It did not make the marks go away, but it lessened the pain.

Jimmy held his head in his hands. 'We should've left earlier.'

'No,' said Boreth. 'We wouldn't have been able to escape the Morkans then, for they would have been on this side of the Fence.'

'It's a miracle we got away, though,' said Niome.

'It's the power of our star.' Meysah smiled.

'Do you think they'll pursue us?' inquired Jimmy.

'No,' replied Vigh. 'I think they have business at the blockade. What they were doing here, so close to Dalvar and far from the road, I cannot determine.'

'Still,' said Boreth, 'we should keep moving. They could always change their minds and go around to the north again. They've got horses; they'll catch up to us if they set their minds to it.'

'Even if they don't, I'm afraid there are a lot more shocks to come,' said Vigh.

Despite the urgency of their situation, the Telorians took some time to recover and eat before continuing on. When they resumed their journey they still felt weary and walked slowly, resting often, but after a while their energy returned and they picked up the pace.

They walked for most of the next day and met nothing unusual. For the next week or so their journey was tedious. They noticed that the days were growing longer as the nights grew shorter and warmer. Spring had fully arrived and the five travellers no longer felt discomfort or cold, but they did feel impatient and wanted something to happen.

Their wish was fulfilled on the eighteenth day of their journey, when they came to an actual road. On a post was a sign that read *'Fortress of Dalvar, straight ahead!'* with an arrow pointing up. A sign below that read *'Dakodol River, ahead and to the left!'* with an arrow curving left. No distance was mentioned, but the road and the signs fuelled their excitement, and they jogged up the road. A short distance later, the road split, with one branch going left, the other straight ahead.

'Excellent,' said Meysah. 'That must be the road to the Dakodol River—'

'Of course it is!' Jimmy interrupted. 'It goes left—'

'—and this one goes to the fortress,' Meysah finished. 'Don't make fun of me, Jimmy! I'm just deducing out loud.'

'You two shouldn't tease,' Niome said sternly. 'Come!' She started walking up the road.

'What's eating her?' muttered Jimmy. Meysah just lifted his shoulders and gave his friend a wide-eyed stare.

They walked straight up the road, which rose to a high hill upon which stood the tall stone walls with great arches and the tower of the fortress. It seemed quite beautiful from where they walked, with tall statues, perhaps of former rulers, visible above the walls. But the travellers soon discovered that it was not so.

They recognised some of the statues; in fact, the ones that looked newer had familiar faces: Bahvley; his best friend Tharguen; Liffwai; and what Meysah guessed might be Elina, though only the body stood – her head had been severed. At least they now knew that Bahvley and the Team of Twelve had been here and that they had allied themselves with the Dalvarans.

The Five reached the fortress and passed under the huge archway above the entrance. Only hinges hung, broken where the gate had been. Inside, to their dismay, they found shattered stone and burned wood scattered over the ground, and the tang of old smoke still lingered. Meysah saw the head of Elina's statue lying there too. A second tower had been completely dismantled, its tumbled stones no longer visible above the walls. Large portions of the walls within the fortress were destroyed. What had probably been a village was now ashes and soot. Bodies lay on the ground – a few Morkans, but most were Dalvarans.

The Telorians stopped in the middle of the courtyard and stared in mute shock at the remains of a great fortress crushed.

'It's the Big War all over again!' breathed Boreth, feeling dismayed. 'Catapults did this. It's the only explanation. And evil magic and Morkans.'

'How many soldiers do you think Mirauk sent here?' asked Jimmy.

'I don't know,' replied Vigh, 'but it must have been a sizeable army. I wonder if there are any people still alive here – any Dalvarans left.'

'This is terrible,' Niome almost sobbed, looking at the pieces of Elina's stone head.

'When I said I wanted more action,' began Jimmy, 'I didn't mean this.'

'I bet this is what the soldiers we encountered at the wall came here to do,' Meysah growled through clenched teeth. He was angry, but he was also trying to prevent his teeth from chattering from fear.

Vigh sighed. 'We've arrived too late to save anyone, but had we arrived earlier, we would have been as dead as them.'

'Or perhaps taken captive and sent to Mork with the returning catapults,' said Niome. 'Boreth's right, no bare hands can do this much damage, yet where are the weapons that did this?'

'This happened no more than a week ago, give or take a few days,' said Boreth, crouching to pick up a charred piece of clothing and examine it. 'The soldiers we encountered must have left the fortress last. I think it's safe to assume the main army has returned to Mork.'

'There's still hope that there are some Dalvarans alive somewhere,' said Niome. 'If none are still in their homes, then maybe they're in hiding. With such a vast stronghold, I don't think they could've *all* been killed.'

'Niome's right,' said Vigh. 'We should go looking for them and offer them our aid. We don't want them to think we're hostile.'

'True!' agreed Boreth. 'Let's search the grounds. Stick together. Hopefully we'll find them soon.'

Meysah walked quickly to one side of the court-yard but stopped dead in his tracks when an arrow hit the wall only a hair from his face. 'I think we already have.'

They slowly turned circles, eyes scanning their surroundings, but could see no one.

'Are you sure it's the Dalvarans?' Jimmy quavered.

'Perhaps not.' Vigh nodded towards a figure approaching them from across the courtyard. He was tall and clad in black, and wore a sinister sneer on his face.

'A Morkan,' Jimmy whispered.

Stopping several paces short of the group, he just stood there. They stared at him. After a heavy moment, which seemed like a few eternities to the Telorians, he drew his sword. 'Fight me, if you dare,' he taunted.

The Telorians drew their swords. The Morkan backed away towards the gateway and waited. The others didn't move.

'Come on,' he said.

Meysah took a step, but Vigh stopped him with his arm, blocking the way. 'Wait,' he warned. 'He could be tricking us. Something's not right here. What *is* he doing?'

'So be it,' declared the Morkan. He lifted his sword as if to stab himself.

Boreth quickly shot an arrow from his bow and before the Morkan could end his own life, the arrow pierced his heart. His sword clattered to the flag-stones, and he dropped to the ground with a thump.

'What was the point of that?' gasped Jimmy.

'If this is a trap,' began Boreth, 'the others are already aware of our presence. If he was powerful in magic, then he cannot become a star, for he has been slain. Better to take precautions.'

Vigh started towards the gate. The others followed. They saw Morkan archers creeping up the hill below them, moving from cover to cover.

'It's a trap!' cried Niome. On the heels of her alarm, the rumble of horse hooves reached their ears. A moment later an army came galloping towards the fortress.

'Morkans!' shouted Meysah. 'Run!'

As one, they whirled and ran back into the courtyard.

'They must have followed us,' shouted Vigh. 'I'm sure it's the same army that was camped on the other side of the wall.'

'What are we to do?' cried Jimmy, looking frantically around. 'There's no other way out.'

'Not yet,' said Niome. 'This way.' She led them along the street that exited the square on the other side and they ran along it towards the far side of the fortress, dodging arrows and ducking behind cover as they ran.

Halfway along, they paused behind an overturned cart; Niome whipped her bag off her back and plunged her hands into it, pulling out the Dragon's Wind.

The archers were closing on them.

Niome pointed the cylinder at them and a blinding light beamed from it, creating a blast of wind that nearly threw Niome off her feet with its kickback. The others' hair flailed in the wind. When it stopped, the Morkan archers were stacked on top of each other, back at the entrance.

'This should buy us some time,' said Niome with a small smile. She returned the cylinder to her bag, swinging the latter onto her back, and the Telorians ran on.

The road came to a dead end at the fortress wall. Niome lifted her arms and pronounced:

'Aiawej assahp, etalerk felesouraia!'

A section of the wall crumbled, leaving an opening large enough for them to pass through.

'You're brilliant, Niome!' exclaimed Meysah.

They ran through and didn't look back, but they heard the archers shouting and the hoofbeats of the riders behind them, as several riders came around the corner of the fortress wall. Crying out triumphantly, they urged their horses towards the Telorians.

The Five reached the edge of a wood and ran into it, dodging through the trees to elude their pursuers, sprinting as fast as they could through the underbrush and deadfall towards the sound of moving water.

The riders were getting closer. Arrows whistled through the trees all around them.

The danger that the Morkans posed had seemed like only a vague illusion in Firlan. Now the Telorians had to face the facts: they could die at any moment and had to be ready for anything.

They halted abruptly on the other side of the wood, as the land there ended in a tall cliff. Rocks and pebbles skittered down the face of the cliff from their hasty stop. With the Morkans close behind them, they ran along the edge of the cliff, seeking a way down.

Boreth slipped on a patch of loose shale and with a cry, slipped over the edge; the others stopped immediately. His fingers dug into the top of the cliff, but he was struggling with his legs to get back up, and couldn't find purchase.

Meysah and Jimmy knelt and grabbed his wrists, but as much as they tried to hold him, his hands were slipping through their grip. Meysah cried out as an arrow skittered across the shale next to his hand.

'The Morkans are nearing!' Jimmy shouted. He and Meysah tried to pull Boreth up to no avail.

'Go on without me,' Boreth urged. 'You still have a chance.'

'But you'll fall or be captured,' cried Niome.

'There's no stopping that now. Save yourselves while you still can! Save the book.' Boreth struggled some more. 'I don't intend to hang here with you around me only for us to be taken to Mork as prisoners.'

'They're close now,' Niome warned after a glance back into the woods, her voice urgent.

'I can distract them,' Boreth said. 'Run!'

'No,' hissed Vigh. He lay flat on his stomach between Meysah and Jimmy and grabbed hold of Boreth's wrists below the lads' hands. 'Now we'll see if old tricks still work. Do you remember when you flipped me over when we were still young trainees?'

'Yes,' said Boreth, 'but that was practice.'

'Well, it's time to try it for real, and it's my turn to flip you this time.' Vigh looked at the lads. 'When I say so, let go.' He positioned his hands. 'Now!'

The boys let go and Vigh rolled over onto his back, still holding onto Boreth, who flipped around to face outward. Then Vigh heaved him up, swinging him over, and Boreth followed through, swinging himself up and over like a circus acrobat. Boreth landed on the ground next to Vigh. They both lay breathing heavily for a moment, then they looked at each other and laughed in triumph.

'Now let's go,' said Vigh, and he and Boreth leapt up to follow Niome and the lads at a run along the edge of the cliff.

'Now that's a trick *we've* got to learn, my dear friend,' Meysah told Jimmy, running beside him.

'If we ever get the chance to,' Jimmy replied grimly.

Finally they came to a narrow track sloping down the face of the cliff, and stumbled down it to the river.

'Now we have to get across,' Jimmy noted, looking up and down the river

'Look!' Meysah pointed. They'd found the spot where the Morkans had left their boats.

'Excellent,' said Vigh. 'They can swim their horses across but it will take a while before they get down here – they can't bring them down that track. We'll take one of the boats and set the rest adrift.'

The five Telorians untied all of the boats, hopped into one, and started rowing across the water to the other side. By the time they hopped out of the boat and set it adrift too, they were out of range of the Morkans' arrows.

They started running again, finally stopping within a copse of trees where they were certain the Morkans couldn't see them. There, they ate a cold meal and rested for the night.

For the next day, and into the following morning, they walked a long way through a great empty vastness once more. When they heard war horns blowing in the distance, they knew trouble awaited them, though they didn't know how far away it was.

They kept on going until they saw Morkans and an unknown people – probably Dalvarans – fighting. The battle swirled around them until they were amidst the fighters in the battlefield and, unprepared to do anything else, they pushed onward.

The landscape was now half fields and half forest, with tall mounds holding caves in the distance. They darted through like stampeding beasts, dodging stray Morkans and occasionally fighting alongside the other people to get past. The Dalvarans quickly noticed their presence.

The Telorians ran and ran, finally seeking a place to hide among the trees to avoid the increasing number of Morkans. They needed to keep their arrival in Mork unknown to Mirauk for as long as possible.

CHAPTER EIGHT:
The Severed Point

The five scurried madly in different directions, trying to hide from the attackers. Boreth and Vigh climbed up a tree and hid there; Boreth strung his bow, just in case. Niome plunged beneath some shrubs. Jimmy and Meysah ran ahead, until a stray arrow hit Meysah's leg. Grunting in pain, he toppled into a mound of soft ferns and discovered a shallow trench; the ferns around it concealed him well. Meysah winced, doing his best to keep quiet, as more stray arrows flew above his hiding place. Jimmy joined him, and there they remained until the Dalvarans fled and the Morkans left the battlefield, either in pursuit of the Dalvarans or to return to their camp to rest.

When it was safe to sit up, Jimmy tended Meysah's wound, cutting off the arrowhead that protruded from the front of Meysah's leg and slowly pulling the arrow shaft back out. Meysah gritted his teeth against the pain. The arrow had hit the outside of his calf, so the wound was not severe, but it would slow him down for the next few days.

'Ow, that hurts,' Meysah hissed as Jimmy extracted the arrow.

'Quiet, you! We don't want to reveal any sign of life to the Morkans,' Jimmy chided, glancing around. He poured water from his flask to clean the wound and bandaged it quickly but well. 'Can you crawl?' he asked Meysah when he was done. 'If we crawl along the trench we'll be out of sight until we find the others.'

Meysah nodded, flexing his leg.

They crawled along the trench as far as they could to get back to where they had last seen their companions. When they thought it safe to come out, they stepped up into the field to see several bodies sprawled in the tall grass.

'Who could these strange folk be?' Meysah wondered. 'Do you think they're Dalvarans?'

'Possibly,' said Vigh, dropping from the tree he'd hidden in. Boreth dropped down behind him.

'Or just some other hostile group that happens to dislike the Morkans,' muttered Jimmy. He shrugged. 'I'm always afraid we'll have more enemies than we need.'

They stared around at the bodies in awe and dismay, then slowly walked around, searching among the dead for Niome. There was no sign of her.

'I thought she went into those bushes,' remarked Boreth, nodding towards a clump of foliage.

'I thought so too, but she's not there – she's nowhere to be found,' sighed Meysah. 'She has the . . . you know . . . most important luggage.'

'Not just that,' said Jimmy. 'Do you remember what the Firlanians said about us splitting up?'

They called out Niome's name a few times, but then realised they shouldn't have. As they moved among the bodies, Morkan riders came riding up. Boreth fired a few arrows, but there were too many of them.

'We let them know we were here!' cried Jimmy. 'What do we do now?'

'We may have no *Dragon's Wind* with us, but we do have speed. Run!' shouted Vigh. They started running, but Meysah could only hobble.

'No!' cried Meysah. 'My leg – I got shot!'

Vigh ran back to him, threw the lad's arm around his shoulder, and ran while supporting him.

'What happens when they find what Niome has in her bag?' Jimmy worried.

'You mean *if*,' corrected Boreth. 'Niome could still be hiding, somewhere safer than here.'

'This is not working!' yelled Vigh. 'They'll be on top of us before we reach that next stand of trees. There's no way we can take cover or escape them now.'

'Then there's only one thing we *can* do!' declared Boreth. He stopped and nocked an arrow in his bow. 'Jimmy, get ready. Shoot as many arrows as you can, as quickly as you can. Can you do that?'

'I can try.'

'Good.' Boreth took three more arrows from his quiver and held his bow horizontally. Jimmy did the same, praying he could make the shots. When the foot soldiers came within range, Boreth shouted, 'Now!' He drew and fired, nocked and drew and fired, nocked and drew and fired. Jimmy tried to keep up.

The runners fell. Jimmy was impressed with himself. They shot at the riders until they were out of arrows. Then they backed up and the four of them drew their swords and fought together.

His fighting limited by his wounded leg, Meysah caught a riderless horse as it trotted by, swung into the saddle, and went after other stray horses. He pulled them back to his fellow Telorians by the reins and they all mounted up.

The Morkans retreated as if surprised by the Telorians' prowess. But then they turned their horses and followed a rider that must have been their captain, because *all* of the Morkans followed him. Then they saw why the Morkans had abandoned the fight: seated on a horse in front of its Morkan rider, hands bound, Niome was being carried away. She looked back at them and reached out towards them, but then the Morkan rider brought the pommel of his sword down on her head, knocking her out, and she slumped back against his chest.

And then the riders and Niome were gone and the other four Telorians were alone. Their star had been broken at its foremost tip, the most important point of all.

Their feelings of invincibility turned to the weakness of doom. The Morkan foot soldiers were still fighting them, and unhorsed Jimmy and Meysah. Boreth's horse fell over with an arrow in its chest and nearly crushed him before he rolled into a trench, while Vigh fought against many Morkans.

Parrying with their swords, Meysah and Jimmy took arrows from the bodies on the ground and stabbed them into the Morkans who tried to attack them as they worked their way over to see if Boreth was all right. He lay in the trench, unconscious. They knelt beside him, forgetting about themselves, forgetting about Vigh. When they looked back, the master was struggling with an archer.

Another Morkan ran up, levelling his sword, and stabbed Vigh in the chest. Vigh shouted in pain, dropping his sword. The Morkan yanked his sword from Vigh's body. Vigh staggered and fell to the ground.

Meysah's eyes blurred with tears and Jimmy cried out in dismay, for their sorrow was now too great to bear. For a moment, regret and helplessness flooded their souls, but then their anger won out. The two lads stood, lifting their swords high above their heads, and shouted, 'For the Freedom of Life!'

They dashed the Morkans, slashing aggressively. The one who had stabbed Vigh knocked the two Telorians down, but they got back up and stabbed him and any others who came their way, screaming their anger until the last of the Morkans retreated, following the rider who had carried Niome away.

Meysah and Jimmy slumped their shoulders, feeling hopelessness. No one would bring Niome back or fix the harm that had been done. Jimmy had never before known such sorrow. Meysah, for his part, had experienced such chagrin once, when he lost his brother.

Boreth crawled out from the trench, wheezing but otherwise all right. The three of them approached Vigh where he lay bleeding on the ground.

'No!' Meysah wailed in despair.

'I'm still alive,' Vigh whispered with effort. 'It's only my breast, not my heart. That is too full of life for any Morkan to pierce.' He grimaced in pain. 'And on the other side,' he added, trying to smile.

Boreth got the herbs out and placed them gently on the wound, then bandaged Vigh's chest.

'They've got Niome,' said Jimmy, wiping his tears away with his sleeve.

'I thought you were dead,' mewled Meysah, 'both of you.'

'And I thought *you* were dead,' said Boreth. 'But when I heard you shout, I knew you were all right.'

'I heard it,' Vigh whispered. 'I knew there was still hope when Bahvley's words rang out.' He gasped, struggling to talk.

Meysah leaned down and gave his master a hug, careful of his wound.

'You learn well, and you defended me well, Jimmy,' said Boreth. 'I owe you one.'

Meysah sat back and put his head in his hands. 'It's over,' he mourned. 'We've lost.'

'What are you talking about!?' exclaimed Jimmy, pulling Meysah's hands away. 'Don't give up now.'

'What's the use of going to Mork when we don't even know if Niome will still be alive when we get there?'

'Your sister is cleverer than any of us,' Jimmy said firmly. 'She'll be there, and we'll find her.'

'But Jimmy, how can you be sure?' Meysah moaned.

'Because as much as I am your friend and as strongly as I love all of you, I feel it in my heart that we will see her again.'

'I feel it too, I'm just too scared,' Meysah admitted. 'I thought I was scared at the beginning, but I was supposed to gain courage. I haven't! I'm still as scared. I could've ridden after them to save Niome, but I didn't. I just didn't.'

'It's not your fault and we all know that. You did what you had to do. It's not your fault,' said Jimmy.

Meysah reached over and hugged Jimmy, who returned the embrace. Meysah sniffled back tears, and Jimmy blinked a few times, his eyes moist. Boreth bowed his head and wiped at his nose and eyes, revealing a soft side he seldom showed, not even to Vigh, his best friend.

After a few moments Boreth cleared his throat and rose. 'We must press on. The Morkans found what they've been looking for, but they'll be back for the rest of us at some point.'

Jimmy nodded, rising as well. 'We have to get out of here.'

'You should go after Niome,' said Vigh.

'And walk into a trap?' objected Boreth. 'Have you lost your mind? You're injured. We need to save ourselves.'

'Leave me,' sighed Vigh.

Boreth gave him a level stare. 'Don't do this, Vigh. You don't really want us to leave you behind. We're going to stick together. If it means slowing down or taking a different route from that of Niome's captors, then so be it. But I am not going on without you, or Jimmy, or Meysah. I know you want what's best, but that's not it.'

Vigh offered a resigned smile. 'What would I do without you?' Jimmy and Meysah helped him sit up, one on either side of him. 'Uah!' he gasped, putting a hand to his chest. 'How am I going to walk?' he wheezed.

'You need to rest,' said Boreth. 'But before that can happen, we need to get out of here.'

The lads helped Vigh to his feet and put Vigh's arms over their shoulders, then slowly followed Boreth, Meysah limping a little. They walked slowly but steadily for many leagues.

Suddenly the sound of running feet and voices came to them. As one, the group stopped. Meysah waited with a heavy heart, ready now to be slain. He feared that they were not the chosen ones; thus, he concluded that he and the others had deceived all those they loved and cared for or met along the way, all those who believed in them. He plopped down on the ground and waited. It was the end.

Jimmy plopped down beside him and Vigh had no choice but to do the same. The boys huddled together, eyes closed. As the footsteps drew closer and surrounded them, Meysah closed his eyes tighter. He jumped when a hand touched his shoulder.

'Get up!' said a voice, but Meysah couldn't bring himself to move. 'Boy, you saved my life!'

Surprised, Meysah opened his eyes and looked up at a diminutive polc standing over him.

'You took the Morkans' horses and slew them, saving us,' the polc continued. 'As is the belief of all polcs in Kaulchèc History, we owe you all our protection. *You* saved *me,* and I honour such courage.'

'Courage?' Meysah smiled.

'You are injured,' the polc said to Vigh. 'We can heal you.'

'We are Telorians, and they've taken our wizardess,' Boreth explained worriedly. 'We *can* use your help.'

'My people have met others from Teloria, though it was quite a while ago. I am Captain Holim. We are polcs from Dalvar, the greatest fortress of all. We have been at war with these fell polcs for a long time. Come, we shall bring you to our secret hideout. We will heal you as we share news. Long have I desired to meet Telorians. Come, come.'

Chapter Nine:
Surprises in the Dark

Niome plunged beneath some bushes to stay out of sight, then looked around for the others, but couldn't see them. She'd seen Jimmy and Meysah run by, but where they had disappeared to, she could not figure out. She thought she had seen Vigh and Boreth climbing up a tree.

As she watched the opposing armies fight, she concluded that the other folk were most likely Dalvarans. *There must be some way of communicating with them,* she thought. *If there's a chance we can become allies, we'd better do it quickly. But for now, I have to locate the others.* She let her mind drift, mentally recapitulating all of her friends' movements, but was abruptly brought back to the present when a Dalvaran tumbled to the ground beside her, arrows in his chest. She yelped. She had to find the others before things went too far.

A heavy hand suddenly dropped onto her shoulder, startling her. She whirled to see a Morkan looming over her – a high ranking one, going by the cut of his garments and the decorations on his chest under the black hooded cloak he wore. The Morkan's dark eyes glared into Niome's.

'We are retreating this way and I think you'd better come along,' he said, his tone threatening.

He looked at a Morkan knight beside him and they nodded to each other as the Captain deftly bound Niome's hands. He heaved Niome to her feet and the knight took her by the shoulders, half dragging, half carrying her towards his horse as she struggled against his grip. Unable to escape, Niome was unceremoniously lifted onto the horse before the knight mounted it himself. She heard him curse before bringing the pommel of his sword down on her head, and the last thing she remembered was seeing Meysah's devastated face watching from atop a Morkan's horse.

When Niome regained consciousness, the army had halted. There seemed to be a lot more of them than before, as though two groups had met and merged while she was unconscious. The Morkan with the decorations and black cape – the Captain – gave orders in an unknown tongue to those nearest to him, then walked his horse down the line and stopped beside another knight to issue an order. That Morkan uttered something to a soldier behind him and that Morkan rode down the line, pausing four more times. The army split into six groups, each going in different directions.

The first group was small, consisting of the knight carrying Niome on his horse, the Captain, another high-ranking polc, and several others. The Captain grumbled to his knight in their tongue, which sounded like an ancient form of Telorian; Niome couldn't understand the words. *So that is Morkan,* she thought. Concentrating made her head hurt. Everything seemed dreamlike.

They set off again, climbing a small hill to a cave. At this point, Niome was feeling dizzy and queasy and dozed off, dreaming of an immense, castle-like house. *Odd,* she thought. *There are no towers.*

She awoke in a dimly lit windowless chamber devoid of furniture, with only a pile of straw at one end and a door in the far right corner. She was sitting on the pile of straw. Her wrists were bound to a metal chain that was attached to the wall. Before her stood two Morkans, the same two who had found her: the Captain and the other tall Morkan. The Captain had light hair, a very strong build, and was rather ugly; the other was thin, his face shadowed by a hood, but Niome noted that his armour primarily consisted of leathers.

Overwhelmed with all that had happened, Niome reflexively stood and reached for her dagger, but it wasn't there – none of her weapons were, and her bag was missing as well. The chain she was shackled to prevented her from reaching past a certain point.

'We've taken the liberty of confiscating your weapons for safekeeping,' the Captain cooed in a voice that reminded Niome of a snake moving over dry leaves. She said nothing but backed away to stand against the wall. He pulled his lips back in a leering smile. 'Oh, we will not hurt you – *if* you tell us what we need to know. After all, we know what you guard.'

'Beshrig,' the hooded Morkan cautioned, 'I think it best not to rush into the magical matters yet. Let us start with the escaped captives.'

'Good idea, Gowtch.' Beshrig turned back to Niome. 'Perhaps you could start by telling us who your fellow travellers are. I think it's safe to assume you were all travelling to Mork.'

'Our destination is none of your concern,' snapped Niome. 'Those travellers are just . . .' – she paused – 'my fellow travellers.'

'Oh, I see,' said Beshrig. 'Trying to be difficult, are you?' He narrowed his eyes. 'We know how to play smart, too.'

'I'm in charge of safekeeping your things,' explained Gowtch. 'Since I found a magic wand, magic potion, and spell books, I'm assuming you're a wizardess. Am I right?' Niome didn't respond. 'All of this tells me you were off to steal the *Book of Enchantment*. Am I right?' He waited.

Niome pressed her lips together to keep herself from shouting what she was thinking: *Steal? Take back, you mean!* Who was he, to accuse *her* of stealing! She glared at him.

Gowtch studied her from behind his hood, his arms crossed. 'I think I'm correct. We, uh, looked through your personal things. I must say, you're very popular around Mork, Niome Fairhaven!'

Niome stared at the two Morkans, speechless with fear and rage.

'Do you know what the name Fairhaven means to us?' asked Beshrig, his tone ever threatening.

'Why would my name have any meaning?'

'Hah!' snarled Beshrig. 'Clever little Telorian, isn't she, Gowtch? Denying the young knight ever went back home to give 'em the secrets. Well, I'll tell you something, Niome Fairhaven.'

He walked up to her and stared her in her eyes. Behind him, Gowtch took a step forward, his hand dropping to the hilt of his sword, looking ready to carry out any threats.

'Whether you have those secrets or not, we can't say,' sneered Beshrig, 'but one thing's for sure: you won't succeed.'

'Beshrig!' Gowtch snapped in warning. Beshrig retreated. 'It's possible he never made it home.'

'I hope so!'

'Who are you talking about?' Niome asked slowly.

'I believe you know Captain Bahvley Fairhaven,' said Beshrig. 'In fact, I believe you are his sister. Isn't that so?'

Niome shrank beneath the Morkan's gaze and swallowed hard.

'Look, you're going to have to answer one of these questions someday,' said Gowtch, his tone conversational. 'It may as well be now.'

'Where is he? Your brother?' demanded Beshrig. Still no answer. 'Tell us, where has he gone? I know you are aware of his whereabouts; you were very close and always kept in touch, didn't you? Did he give you the secrets? Is that how you got this far?' Niome still would not answer; Beshrig scowled, aggravated. 'Where is your brother?' he bellowed, but Niome did not stir.

'I think we ought to leave the question alone,' Gowtch advised Beshrig. 'She obviously won't tell us. Of course not! She doesn't know us.' He turned his head back to Niome. 'But we sure know her, don't we! We will wait until later.'

With a last scowl at Niome, Beshrig left the room. Gowtch sat down on the ground near the door, elbows on his knees, and Niome sat in the pile of straw. The room suddenly felt a lot smaller than it had first appeared. Niome could feel Gowtch staring at her, though she could not see his face.

'You might do well to speak up soon, you know; it's for your own good,' he said. His tone almost seemed friendly. 'Don't mind Beshrig, he likes to act fiercer than he is. But he needs a Second-in-Command like me to keep an eye on you, so you'd better get used to it.' He paused. 'You can tell me the answer, you know. Whenever you're ready. Or you can sit there and say nothing. It's as you wish.'

'Why the interest in my brother?' Niome finally asked after a long silence.

'So *you're* asking the questions now?' he countered.

'No, but why my brother? What does he have to do with anything?'

'Everything. Don't you see?' There was eagerness in his voice. 'He came here, freed many prisoners, and led Telorians to battle. We need to know where he is. He's more powerful than . . . we Morkans would've liked.'

'Well, if you should know, he's dead.'

'Dead!' The shock in Gowtch's voice surprised her. 'That's impossible. He was lost at sea, so we were told,' he bumbled quickly. 'But we all knew he planned something, and we believe you have something to do with it. That's why we want to know.'

'You're lying! Your people told us he was killed by Mirauk.' Niome strove to control her anger. 'In fact, Mirauk announced it himself, to Elina.'

'No, no, we lied!' exclaimed Gowtch. 'He's out there somewhere; I'm sure of it.'

'Then there is hope after all,' Niome said softly. They fell silent again before Niome added. 'But as I have not heard from my brother in nearly fifty years, I believe Mirauk when he says that Bahvley is dead.' Niome slumped down slowly.

There was nothing else said. Gowtch bowed his head. It almost seemed an act of respect. But what respect could a Morkan possibly have for her brother?

After half the night had passed, Gowtch broke the silence.

'Captain Bahvley came to claim the *Book of Enchantment* with his fellow Telorians,' he began. 'Mirauk joined the fight to stop Bahvley from saving the wizardess, whom he had been so close to killing. Mirauk . . . he could've killed them all then and there, but a Telorian jumped in and took the blade for his captain. I was there, I watched it all unfold.'

Gowtch swallowed loudly. 'Last we saw him, Bahvley was fleeing, setting off to sea with a few mates, all of whom had managed to avert their gaze from Mirauk. When we received news from the Islands, some had been killed, but *he* had escaped. We assumed he had returned to Teloria.'

Gowtch paused. When he spoke again, his voice was casual again. 'I learnt your name when I checked in one of your books. It says *Niome Fairhaven* on the first page.' Another pause. 'Tell me about Tweedle.'

'That's none of your business!' she snapped. She shook her head, confused. 'Why are you telling me all this and where are my things?'

'Relax, it was only a question,' said Gowtch, as though trying to soothe. 'Look, I thought you should know about your brother.'

'I didn't know my older brother still lived. We all thought he'd been dead a long time.'

'A shocking surprise, is it? By the way, your things are safe with Beshrig at the moment. I want to take a closer look at them later on. Perhaps I'll learn a few spells myself.'

'Don't! You may try, but I assure you, I am quite powerful, even without my books.'

'Oh really?' Gowtch stood. 'Then why are you still in chains?' he demanded. 'Could you not make them disappear?' He walked over to her, and his voice grew menacing. 'Be assured, as powerful as you may think you are, Mirauk is even more powerful, and he will become even greater than he is once he gets hold of your books.' Something in his expression changed subtly. 'That's why I should look at them first.'

The door opened. Beshrig entered. 'I'll take over from here.' Gowtch moved to his Captain's side. 'Prepare your riders,' Beshrig instructed him. 'In the morning we will move out of the caves and ride on to Mork. We plan to take only eight to ten days. The lord's schedule is tight.'

'Understood, Beshrig. I'll go take a look at her things now and keep them with me.'

'Go right ahead, Gowtch, you're the expert in that.'

Gowtch moved to the door, eyes still on Niome.

'Oh,' Beshrig added. '*Rebkamero kitvig emeth Tene-milpakomok esson evûraia'd kekch rekh saginath; tath fisi takereth.*'

'Understood!' Gowtch acknowledged, and walked out.

Niome found no sleep for the rest of the night, though Beshrig dozed. She guessed it was near dawn when Gowtch returned. Beshrig jerked awake and looked at him when he entered. 'And so?' he asked.

'I'm afraid not,' answered Gowtch.

'What? Not there? That's impossible! Could she have hidden it with her magic?'

'It's a possibility, because it certainly isn't on her.'

'Perhaps one of those idiots back there took it.' Beshrig motioned a thumb over his shoulder. 'I'll go investigate. Meanwhile, get everything ready.'

'Understood! Oh, and she rides with me.'

'I was going to suggest that, Gowtch. You read my mind.' Beshrig left.

'What isn't on me?' asked Niome.

'The *Complement Book*,' replied Gowtch.

'Of course it isn't on me! *You* took—'

Gowtch crossed the distance between them in two strides and covered her mouth with his hand. 'Do you have to shout?' he whispered, his eyes frantic. He removed his hand from her mouth. 'Of course I took it. If there's one thing you learn in Mork, it's to trust no one but yourself. Beshrig asked me to give it to him, but I only trust myself.'

Niome stared at him. 'You lied about it being gone.'

'Of course I lied.'

There was a long pause.

'I meant you Morkans in general,' Niome said.

Gowtch shrugged, taking a step back, then he continued his thought as though she had said nothing. 'Beshrig is not as trustworthy as Mirauk thinks he is, and I know it. And you—'

'Okay, I'll stay quiet.' His strange behaviour frightened her. She didn't know what to expect from this erratic polc.

'Good!' Gowtch unshackled her wrists from the chain and bound them together behind her back. 'Today we travel. In a few days, we'll rest. By then we'll have reached the end of the caves and . . . you'll see when we get there. Come.'

He dragged her out of the room, along a tunnel, and to the mouth of the cave where the other members of the team were seated, either eating a cold meal or feeding the horses. The sun was rising, still low enough to blaze orange despite the cloudy sky. Beshrig stood waiting for them.

'None have seen it!' he complained when Gowtch and Niome arrived.

'Could it have gotten mixed up with another team's items?' suggested Gowtch.

'Perhaps,' Beshrig said, then he scowled. 'Until we meet up with the others, I want you to figure out how it could be hidden – from her!' Beshrig pointed at Niome accusatorially, then walked up to her. 'Sit down, Fairhaven.' Niome sat down on the ground and Beshrig bound her ankles together. 'Give her something to eat, Gowtch. Mirauk wants his prisoners to remain un-damaged until he decides what to do with them. Hurry up, though. I'm beginning to lose patience.'

Gowtch sat down beside Niome with a handful of fruit and a heel of bread. As Niome's hands were bound behind her, Gowtch had to feed her himself, looking as awkward as Niome felt. He tore off a chunk of bread and gradually fed it to her along with some fruit. They ate in silence. A short while later, he unstoppered his flask and put it to her lips so she could drink.

When everyone had eaten, Beshrig called out, 'Time to go! Mirauk is waiting for us. Mount up!'

Gowtch lifted Niome up and sat her on his horse, as he had before, then mounted it as well.

Beshrig took the lead, followed by Gowtch and two others. Behind them came all the other Morkan riders, including many who emerged from the caves to swell their numbers, and the Morkans from the five other groups. There must have been at least sixty Morkan riders.

They questioned Niome during the first two days, always asking about her older brother and about the 'missing' book, before giving up.

They reached the point where the hill dwindled and the network of caves ended before dusk of the fourth day. 'This is the last cave!' shouted Beshrig as he dismounted. 'We sleep here tonight.' They would no longer be camping in the caves after tonight.

Gowtch dismounted and pulled Niome off the horse, then pushed her into the cave and the next room that would be her prison. Others led the horses into an area of the cave that was clearly a stable. That's when Niome realised that the Morkans had been inhabiting the caves for a very long time.

Gowtch deposited Niome in the cell and stepped out into the hewn-stone corridor. Niome heard muffled voices arguing – Gowtch and Beshrig. Then Gowtch re-entered the cell.

'You'd better get some sleep while you still can,' he advised Niome. 'You've got a lot of exhausting days ahead of you.'

'You may try to be nice, but I'm still not telling you my secrets.'

'Did I ask for anything? No! So just keep quiet,' he growled, settling himself on the far side of the room beside the door.

Niome lay down and, after a while, pretended to sleep. Outside her cell's door, everything became quiet. She heard Gowtch rise quietly and step out of the room. He was gone a long while.

When he returned, Niome was sitting up. 'Where did you go?' she demanded.

'This is no time for questions,' Gowtch whispered urgently. He unbound her legs and helped her stand. 'You need to come with me.'

'Where? Why?'

He stopped and looked at her. 'Look, there's no time for explanations now. I just need you to trust me.'

'Trust a Morkan?' Niome backed away.

Gowtch worked his jaw. 'Look,' he snapped, 'do you want to live? Do you or do you not want to get out of here? 'Cause, we've only got one shot at this.'

Gowtch took out a knife and tested its sharpness against his thumb. Then he nicked his own leg, just enough for a bit of blood to stain the knife. He winced, giving a small grunt.

'What are you doing?' whispered Niome, confused.

'This has to look like an attack. Now, I need utter silence from you, all right?' Niome nodded. 'Good!'

Grasping her bound wrists, he led her through the labyrinth of corridors. As they neared the entrance, Gowtch let his knife clatter to the floor; the sound echoed down the corridor. They passed the stable area, just inside the entrance.

Gowtch grabbed a torch from a sconce to one side of the opening and let it fall onto a large pile of hay. It began to smoulder, and the smoke's tendrils carried back into the cave on the breeze.

He pulled Niome outside, and she looked around in surprise at the horses that had been set loose. Off to one side, just a few paces from the cave's mouth, one of them was saddled, and Niome recognised her bag on its back.

Gowtch swung into the saddle and gave Niome a hand up to sit in front of him. Then he urged the horse into a gallop and rode away from the cave.

They rode around to the far side of these hills that housed the caverns.

'Did you drop the knife there to make them believe you were captured?' Niome asked, her voice high-pitched in surprise.

Gowtch didn't answer.

'Were the loose horses and fire to slow them down?' Her tone became suspicious. 'I know what this is. You want all the magic for yourself. Stupid Morkan.'

Gowtch coughed, as Niome turned her head to glare at him. 'Stupid? I consider myself rather smart. You deduced everything but one important point. You're wrong to think I want your things for myself. On the contrary.'

Gowtch halted. He lifted Niome off the horse before dismounting it himself. He pulled their bags off the horse, dropping them on the ground, before sending the steed away where it went galloping south. Niome watched, deeply puzzled. Gowtch then reached into his jacket and pulled out the *Complement Book*. He tucked it into Niome's bag and placed it on the ground next to her.

Bending, he pulled two knives out of his boot and examined them carefully. One he put back in his boot, the other he used to cut Niome's bonds before placing it on her bag.

'I believe this one's yours.'

Gowtch reached for one of two swords that hung at his belt and unbuckled its scabbard, then handed it to Niome. 'Here's your sword.'

Niome took it hesitantly, trying to deduce this polc's intentions, but Gowtch did nothing untoward.

'Okay, I think you have all your things,' he said, taking a step back.

Niome took one quick step forward and swung her leg up, kicking Gowtch to the ground. In an instant she drew her sword, its point a mere hair's breadth from his throat as she loomed over him.

Gowtch lifted his hands in surrender. His hood had fallen back and Niome could finally clearly see his face. He was not a bad-looking Morkan, with warm blond hair that curled around his ears.

'Who are you and what do you want?' Niome demanded fiercely.

'It's a long story, so you might want to put that away,' Gowtch replied, indicating the sword with his eyes.

Niome snorted. 'How do I know if I can truly trust you?'

'Have I brought you away from the Morkans? Yes!' Gowtch retorted. His voice grew earnest. 'Listen, I'm not who I appear to be.'

'Apparently not!' Niome snapped. She didn't back off.

There was a long pause.

'Look, I'm a spy—' Gowtch began.

'I can see that,' said Niome, cutting him off.

'A *Telorian* spy!' he snapped. He continued rapidly. 'I was one of the twelve knights in your brother's team. I managed to remain undiscovered by pretending to be a Morkan, and I've been helping any Telorian who comes this way. Believe me, it hasn't been easy.'

Glaring at him with suspicion, Niome crossed her arms, adjusting so that her sword still pointed towards Gowtch. 'How do I know you're telling the truth?'

'Would I lie about something like this?' He waited for her response, then continued when none came. 'Well, *I* wouldn't, but a Morkan would; I can see your point.' Gowtch took a wooden icon from his pocket and showed it to Niome. It was shaped like a twelve-pointed leaf. 'It's the sign of the Twelve. We all had this.'

'How do I know you didn't take it from a Telorian when you killed him?'

Gowtch sighed, looking dismayed. 'First of all, if I were a real Morkan, I'd have killed you a long time ago.' His tone became one of pleading. 'Look at me carefully. Do I not look like a Telorian?'

Niome studied him carefully. 'You do have Telorian traits,' she admitted.

'You see? I never took my hood off because I didn't have that evil Morkan look in me.' He downcast his eyes. 'It is easier to look menacing when no one sees your face.' He met Niome's gaze once more. 'I couldn't reveal my identity earlier, in case someone overheard. That's why I pretended to know nothing about you or your spells, or Tweedle, for that matter. Funny fellow.'

He took a deep breath, and Niome recognised hope in his eyes. 'I was good friends with Bahvley – in fact, his *best* friend. You might remember me. Tharguen Sumperale.'

'Tharguen!' cried Niome, lowering her sword. 'That's impossible!'

'Do you remember when you were still a young adolescent – well, you were maturing – and you were scared of the Morkans? You tried to hide from them, but you got lost. I was an adolescent, too, at the time. I found you hiding in a corner, and we hid there together the entire day. We camped nearby for a couple of days.'

He smiled fondly. 'You told me I was the best protector in the world. I promised to keep you safe forever. That's why you didn't want me to leave when it came time to go after the *Book of Enchantment*. You were afraid I wouldn't be able to protect you ever again if I went. I didn't want to go; I just wanted to stay and keep you safe. I went because I promised Bahvley I'd follow him till the end. And I always keep my word. That's why I'm protecting you now.'

A slow smile formed on Niome's face. 'Tharguen?' She sheathed her sword. 'It is you! It really is!'

Tharguen stood and hugged her tightly – his embrace was as comforting as Niome remembered. Now that he could genuinely smile, he did, and Niome recognised his wide smile.

'We have to hurry,' he said, sobering. 'It won't be long before Beshrig sets out to find Gowtch and *the* captive. Fire only slows them down. Morkans are too resilient to suffocate.'

'But where are we going?' asked Niome.

'To the Dalvarans,' Tharguen replied with excitement.

'The Dalvarans!'

'Yes, they have a secret hideout on this side of the hills that the Morkans could never find. I, along with Bahvley and the others from the Team of Twelve, was allied with them when we travelled this way.'

'But do you really believe they'll recognise you in Morkan clothing? What if they shut the door on us?'

'Niome, if the present captain knew Captain Silam, he'll know me.'

'Yes! They did have statues of you at the Fortress of Dalvar.'

'Really?' Tharguen beamed. 'They actually erected statues of us?' He chuckled, shaking his head. 'Come.'

Hefting their satchels over their shoulders, Niome and Tharguen headed northeast, setting a rapid pace.

'So fill me in,' Tharguen prompted. 'Who else is part of your team?'

'Well, there's Meysah.'

'Oh, he's quite brave. Always was. Never knew it, though.'

'Yeah. He's the one who got the others to join me. You see, no one wanted me to go, so I left secretly and they came after me.'

'That's because they love you, and they believe in you.' Tharguen smiled at Niome, blushing before looking forward again and chuckling self-consciously. For a moment, they walked in silence as each of them remembered the days before Tharguen left.

Niome finally continued. 'I know. I like having my younger brother with me, even if he's sometimes annoying. He and Jimmy both – Jimmy is Meysah's best friend, who came along.'

'I never knew him.'

'He's quite the Telorian. Jolly,' she said. 'Vigh's with us.'

'Yes. I recognised him when I was riding in before we captured you.' Tharguen smiled gingerly. 'Sorry, by the way, for knocking you out.'

'It's all right,' said Niome, smiling in understanding. 'You'll make it up to me somehow.'

Tharguen chuckled, relieved. 'It's good that Vigh's with you,' he said, returning to the discussion at hand. 'You need someone with great skill.'

'We have Boreth, too.'

'I remember him. He was a prisoner at one of the Morkan camps and we set him free. He told me to always be wary and to trust my gut feeling. I took his advice, and . . . here I am.'

'Well, you may have a chance to talk to him again, if we ever find the others,' said Niome.

'Oh, we will,' Tharguen assured her.

They travelled for the rest of the night and for the next day after a brief rest, passing the time by giving an account of everything that had happened to them since they had last seen each other, since before the departure of the Team of Twelve. They stopped only to eat. They heard or saw no Morkans, nor did they hear or see the other four Telorians.

Tharguen knew that they would be arriving at the Dalvarans' secret cave soon, but Niome worried about the others, not knowing what had happened to them.

Chapter Ten:
A Perfect Birthday Gift

The Dalvarans travelled rapidly, and the Telorians, being exhausted and injured, could hardly keep up. Meysah was limping, and his pace had slowed to a trot, and then a walk. Seeing how the three Telorians were having a hard time keeping up, Captain Holim ordered that they be carried as Vigh was. After having wished for just that solution, Meysah concluded that he must have enough magic to make wishes come true, so he prayed extra hard for Niome to be protected by the stars.

With each Telorian hoisted between two Dalvarans, the party made good time, and reached their destination by nightfall.

'Our secret hideout is in the middle of these hills,' Captain Holim informed the Telorians as they were set down.

Jimmy's stomach growled loudly and he blushed, embarrassed. 'Heh-heh, I guess I'm hungrier than I thought.' He had forgotten about his hunger before, but now his stomach cramped and he felt weak.

'Don't worry about it,' said Captain Holim. 'We will all be eating soon. Just follow me.'

'Captain!' a Dalvaran called as he ran up to them.

'What is it, Weddo?' asked Holim.

'The tall Telorian's not faring so well,' Weddo said, his tone anxious.

'How so?' asked Holim; Boreth felt a lump form in his throat.

'He has a fever and he's delirious.'

The three Telorians followed Captain Holim and Weddo to where Vigh lay on the ground. A Dalvaran crouched beside him, wiping Vigh's face with a wet towel. Vigh was mumbling unintelligible words.

'Master Vigh!' Meysah knelt beside him and took his hand. 'Hang on, now. Hang on.'

'The wound must have been deeper than we thought,' Weddo said gravely.

'It was,' confirmed the Dalvaran who crouched beside Vigh. 'It stopped bleeding, but it still needs to be disinfected, for the infection goes too deep. The fever is from his body fighting a raging battle against the impurity that has infiltrated his blood. Once the wound starts healing properly, the fever will subside.'

'Thank goodness!' sighed Jimmy.

'If all goes well,' added the Dalvaran.

'No! Wait!' Vigh muttered in his delirium. 'Coullah is missing! His house burned down.'

'Who's Coullah?' Jimmy asked Meysah.

'He was his friend long ago,' replied Meysah.

'What happened to him?' asked Jimmy.

'Dead!' cried Vigh. 'I've got to go find Boreth.'

'He died,' Meysah told Jimmy, 'in the war when Mork attacked Teloria.'

'He's reliving the Big War,' breathed Boreth, worried for his friend.

'The books . . . the two books . . . need protection. Got to protect . . . Where's Boreth?'

Boreth crouched down beside him. 'Vigh,' he said gently, 'we're no longer 4717; we're 4766. And you're safe with the Dalvarans, and I'm here as well.'

'The . . . the . . . the book! The book! It's gone! They've already taken it, they've already taken Tallelah away, what more do they want! I've got to go find Boreth.'

'It's not working,' Boreth said sadly. 'He's lost in his memories, and his grief.'

'It'll take a few days,' said Captain Holim, trying to reassure.

'Captain,' said Meysah, 'we appreciate everything you're doing.'

'I'm happy to hear it,' Holim answered. 'Come into the caves. We mustn't linger out here any longer.'

They followed Captain Holim into a dark tunnel. 'Watch your step,' he cautioned. 'The tunnel curves to the right, up ahead.'

After they followed the curving tunnel, he stopped. 'You see that hole?' Holim pointed at a small gap in the wall near the ground. 'That's the entrance.'

'That tiny thing?' asked Meysah, looking unsure.

'Wait and see,' said Weddo. He crouched down and crawled through.

'I bet it's really a huge gate,' Jimmy muttered to Meysah, trying to create a cheerier mood.

They heard tapping from the other side and a few moments later, Weddo opened a large door, now obvious to their eyes, where before it had been camouflaged by magic.

'Well, it's just a pretty big door,' noted Meysah. 'Nothing compared to a huge gate.'

'Close enough,' replied Jimmy.

'This way,' said Weddo.

Everyone passed through and Weddo closed the door behind them. Captain Holim led them down a ramp and into the hideout proper: a large cavern, well lit by torches, with many doorways in its walls. Dalvaran nurses came and took Vigh into one of the rooms, where they placed him on a bed. Another came and looked at Meysah's foot to make sure it was all right. Then, the Telorians were given something to eat.

As they ate, they told their story in detail to the Dalvarans. However, they omitted the ruined fortress. Boreth had thought it best to wait until they actually knew how to word it, and Meysah and Jimmy agreed.

Captain Holim assured them that they would remain in hiding until Vigh had fully recovered. 'There is a hot spring in one of the common rooms, so you can bathe,' he told them.

'First,' began Boreth, 'we will get a whole lot of sleep.'

Before going to sleep, the three Telorians went to see their dear friend Vigh, whose wound, they were told, had started to heal a little better.

'He looks a lot better,' confirmed Boreth.

'That's good.' Meysah sighed in relief.

'Fever's still high, though,' said Jimmy, touching Vigh's forehead. Vigh was still mumbling deliriously. 'He still looks awfully bad.' He looked up at his master. 'What is he talking about?'

Boreth inhaled slowly before sighing out. 'When I was taken captive,' he explained, 'Vigh had to take on more responsibilities than he would've liked. He had too many people to worry about. It's most unfortunate that he has to relive all of that.'

'Is it possible to bring him back to the present if we speak to him?' inquired Meysah.

'I don't know,' replied Boreth. 'It didn't work before, but perhaps with time . . . I guess it can do no harm to try.'

They fell silent and watched Vigh. His eyes had dark circles around them and his face had become ashen. There was a sheen of sweat on his face. Although he was covered by many thick blankets, he shivered. When a nurse entered the room to feed him a hot herbal brew, the three Telorians lingered only a while more before leaving.

The next day, Vigh's condition was pretty much the same. Boreth sat by Vigh's side most of the day, explaining to him that the Big War was over. Vigh kept on mumbling, *'I've got to find Boreth!'* Patiently Boreth told him what had happened and how he'd gotten back, as though Vigh could hear him. Boreth hoped he could; he hoped he could ease his friend's mind.

The two boys dropped in on Vigh from time to time, but spent most of the day with the Dalvarans. They sat around and talked. Sometimes they heard Boreth singing old songs to rekindle Vigh's memory of the time before the Big War.

By evening, Vigh had stopped the mumbling, which encouraged the others, but the fever was still very high, maybe worse than before.

That night, Meysah felt sick, as if he had a rock in his stomach. He was worried about his master and about his sister. He wished Niome were there to sing a spell to heal Vigh's wound. Breathing deeply, Meysah lay in bed with his eyes wide open for a while. Then he got up and walked to Vigh's room. He sat beside him, thinking, then he remembered a song that Vigh had taught him when he was very young and he started singing it softly.

When all the world seems to be collapsing
And nothing can be reached by light,
Just remember we have each other,
And the Mighty Spirit watches over you.

When magic fails and no hope it brings
And you are lost in many fights,
Just remember we stick together,
And a hand I will give to you.

When vital, mortal wounds are bleeding,
And the dead are a dreadful sight,
Just remember you are getting better
Because I am reaching out to you.

Meysah started to sob as he sang.

When terrible everyone is feeling,
And whenever, come what might,
Just remember we have each other
And I am watching over you.

Meysah sniffled. He stared into nothingness for a while, his eyes unfocused, then rose and went to the door. He found Jimmy standing in the doorway.

'He'll come around,' Jimmy soothed.

'I know,' replied Meysah. 'But when?'

Jimmy lifted his shoulders in a shrug. The two returned to their beds and tried to get some sleep.

The next day, in need of distraction, Boreth helped the Dalvarans repair equipment in their workshop, while Jimmy and Meysah helped in the kitchen.

'I've been meaning to ask you,' said Captain Holim, as he, Weddo, and the two lads waited for the pot roast to cook, 'what was the damage at Dalvar Fortress?'

Meysah and Jimmy exchanged a glance, the question taking them by surprise.

'Don't worry about it,' reassured Holim. 'I knew long before you arrived that the Morkans had attacked. I know you want to be courteous, but now I am ready to hear the worst.'

'Well,' began Jimmy, 'since you asked . . . half of it has crumbled down.'

'Including Elina's stone head,' added Meysah.

'And there were corpses,' continued Jimmy. 'Mostly of Morkans!' he added quickly. 'The place was deserted, though.'

'They must have gone into hiding,' said Weddo. 'We have our secret ways of hiding ourselves that few polcs know of. We are too great in number for every Dalvaran to have been killed there.'

'That's encouraging,' said Jimmy.

'A quarter of us were originally sent out here, and half of those have been killed,' Holim said sombrely.

'That is a lot of Dalvarans,' said Meysah, his voice low. 'A lot of losses.'

'But a lot more losses for the Morkans,' declared Weddo.

There was a long silence while they all thought about that.

'Well,' Jimmy said at last, 'smells like the pot roast is ready. I'll go find Boreth.' He rose and left the others to serve the meal.

He found Boreth in Vigh's room. He was smiling.

'The fever is down,' Boreth announced. 'Vigh should be coming around within a few days.'

Jimmy yelped for joy and dashed off to tell Meysah. That suppertime, they all ate with great appetite, and were able to find more restful sleep afterwards.

The next day, the three Telorians sat warming themselves before a fire, for the temperature had dropped in the caves and all could see their breaths.

'Why is it so cold all of a sudden?' Jimmy complained, shivering.

'Because the sun is hidden,' replied Captain Holim, who was passing by with an armload of blankets. He stopped.

'Does that mean it's cold outside?' asked Meysah.

'Not necessarily,' answered Holim. 'It only means the sky is overcast. Here, take some more blankets.' The Telorians gratefully accepted the blankets and wrapped themselves comfortably.

'We're not used to the cold of the caves,' said Boreth.

'Nor were we at first,' said Holim.

'I'm worried that it might worsen Vigh's health,' admitted Boreth.

'I made sure myself that he was warmly covered and our nurses are checking in on him frequently. A fire burns in his room and I daresay it is warmer in there than here.'

Captain Holim looked up and saw Weddo walking past. 'Ah, time for me to go.' He left the Telorians.

'Did Captain Holim tell the others about what happened at their fortress?' asked Boreth.

'Apparently they all knew,' said Meysah. 'They just wanted to know if the fortress's structure had worsened.'

'They were all in hiding,' explained Jimmy. 'Probably the same way Selemil was able to create a magical hideout for Telorians back home.'

'Maybe,' Boreth said thoughtfully. 'That great meeting at the Governor's Hall . . . it seems like such a long time ago, yet it was less than a season ago.'

'And home,' said Meysah. 'It feels so far away, like the memory of some distant past. I wonder if we shall ever see it again.'

They fell silent.

Then, from far away came soft singing.

> *When all the world seems to be collapsing,*
> *And nothing can be reached by light,*
> *Just remember we have each other,*
> *And the Mighty Spirit watches over you.*

Meysah leapt up and ran to Vigh's room, the other two following him. It was without a doubt Vigh's voice, though croaky after his illness.

'You've finally awakened!' cried Boreth. 'Nice choice of song.'

'I don't know,' said Vigh. 'I woke up and I had it stuck in my head, so I sang it.'

Jimmy nudged Meysah's arm.

'I sang it to you,' said Meysah. 'Perhaps you heard it.'

'Perhaps, although I don't recall. I'm assuming we're at the Dalvarans' hideout?'

'You did hear us!' Boreth rejoiced, beaming, 'because I told you about this place.'

Vigh smiled wryly. 'So, I've been told a lot while I was out. Tell me, how long *have* I been out?'

'Four days,' said Jimmy. 'From the morning we travelled with the Dalvarans to arrive here until now – late afternoon, I assume.' He furrowed his brows. 'It's hard to tell when within such caves all day long. Today there's no sunshine outside – that's why it's so cold – so even if we went outside to check, we probably would have a hard time figuring out if it was afternoon or evening.'

Vigh smiled, calculating something on his fingers.

'You had such a high fever,' sighed Boreth. 'We were all so worried.'

'You were talking in your sleep,' said Meysah. 'We thought you had lost your mind!'

'You were talking about finding me,' explained Boreth, 'and of events from the Big War. We were afraid you were reliving it all.'

'Perhaps I was,' mused Vigh. 'I can't remember. What I do remember is that someone was talking to me.'

'We all were,' Meysah said happily.

'No, someone else. Someone I've never met was talking to me in my dream, as though it were real. We had discussions about many things.'

'What did you discuss?' inquired Jimmy.

'He just said, many things,' teased Meysah.

Vigh shook his head with a lopsided grin. 'Most of it is unimportant, except for one thing.' He sat up as best he could, gently pressing his hand to his chest to ease the pain while he moved. 'Could you pass me my bag?'

'Certainly.' Boreth handed Vigh his satchel.

Vigh opened it up and rummaged through it as though worried that something was missing. Then he took out the smooth stone that Gorthan had given him.

'This is the Stone of Good Fortune that Gorthan gave to me. I thought I had lost it.' Vigh held it tightly. 'It has brought me great fortune on this mission. I have been blessed with the best of loyal friends and we have lived through many dangers. We have lived! But now, after being visited in my dreams, I understand that it is not mine to keep, but mine to pass on to whomever needs it most. Someone who will, eventually, pass it down to their apprentice. Meysah.' Vigh lifted Meysah's hand and placed the stone in his palm. 'You deserve the Stone of Good Fortune.'

'Master Vigh, I couldn't possibly – this stone is maybe what kept you alive! You need good fortune just as much as the rest of us. I couldn't possibly take it now.'

'You deserve to have it now, on this journey. Besides, you're growing wiser every day. Eighty-five polken years is a long time to wait before getting the opportunity for such a gift.'

'You mean eighty-four,' corrected Meysah.

'No,' said Vigh, grinning. 'I may have been ill for a few days, but I still know what day it is today. If I'm correct, it's the one hundred and forty-ninth day of the year – the wonderful fifth day of the eighth week of Spring. Happy Birthday, Meysah! May this stone bring to you all the best fortunes of the world.'

Meysah gaped in astonishment. 'One forty-nine! I had forgotten all about it. I did not expect this. All the surprise parties of a lifetime can never match the joy of *this* surprise. Master Vigh, this is the best birthday gift ever. It's a perfect gift.' Meysah gave his master a hug.

Jimmy and Boreth smiled. 'I have to apologise, Meysah,' said Jimmy. 'The date just slipped my mind.'

'You being here with me is gift enough,' said Meysah. 'Thank you, all of you.'

Vigh smiled and coughed lightly.

'You should get more rest,' advised Boreth.

'But I feel fine!' insisted Vigh, sitting up taller. Then he grimaced. 'Then again, perhaps I'm still a little dizzy.'

Boreth chuckled. 'I'll bring you a small supper later on.'

'Thank you,' replied Vigh. 'Please be sure to bring a lot of water. I'm very thirsty.'

'That's always a good sign,' said Meysah.

They left Vigh to rest a little but later rejoined him to eat supper with him. Though Vigh ate very little, it was enough to give him some strength.

The Telorians spent a lot of time together, resting, rehydrating – at least Vigh was – joking, talking with the Dalvarans, and singing songs that they had longed to sing for a while. Vigh, although quite lively, had to stay in bed.

Two days after his fever broke, Vigh was up and about. He moved slowly, walking short distances to strengthen his muscles. Gradually, he began eating more, and was able to feel at full form. However, they decided to wait a bit longer for Vigh's inner strength to fully rebuild itself. So for the next few days, the Telorians helped the Dalvarans while planning their continued journey to Mork and to find Niome.

The Star Shines Anew

By the second day of Niome and Tharguen's journey, Niome was feeling the effects of endless walking. She stumbled and fell, placing her hand on the rocky wall next to her to try to pull herself up.

Tharguen rushed to help her up. 'What's wrong?' he asked in alarm.

'I don't know.' Niome pressed her hand to her heart. She drifted off, her vision going hazy, and when she refocused, her face was pale. 'This has happened to me before. It happens when someone extremely evil is approaching. We have to get out of here.'

As if in confirmation, they heard the thud of hooves.

'Quick, under the rocks over there,' Tharguen urged, pointing. He started running, but Niome faltered. Tharguen turned back and scooped her up, carrying her into a deep hollow in the rocks.

They waited, motionless and holding their breaths, their hearts pounding in their chests.

The thudding hooves approached and came to a halt. They heard Beshrig's voice. 'I am beginning to lose patience. I don't know if this was the work of magic too strong for me to understand, or if it was Gowtch's doing, but what I do know is that Mirauk is not going to be happy. Are you sure none of you saw or heard anything?' There was a pause. 'Capult?'

Tharguen saw the shadow of his former Morkan friend shake his head.

'I thought so,' complained Beshrig. 'Well, we have no time to waste. If they're not here, they're not here. At least with all our troops out here, they won't survive long.' Tharguen heard a heavy sigh. 'I find it hard to believe my Second-in-Command would do such a thing. Come, let us hope the *Complement Book* is not with them but somewhere with us. We'll search the luggage later. Mirauk is waiting.'

The Morkans upon their horses galloped away. The two Telorians remained in their hiding place a while longer.

'Why didn't I feel the pounding when I first met Beshrig?' Niome wondered.

'I don't know, but he sure was angry just now. Maybe that's why. Or perhaps you sensed another evil Morkan among them.' Tharguen thought of Capult but didn't say anything; that would be a story for another time. 'Are you okay?'

'I am now.'

They rose cautiously, looking around, but saw no Morkans. Tharguen sighed in relief.

'I think it's safe to say they're long gone,' concluded Niome, looking at Tharguen for confirmation.

'Yes. They've gone to Mork. They have a tight schedule and won't linger longer. I guess I must've acted more like a Morkan than I thought.'

'How so?'

'Beshrig doesn't think I'm involved – or at least he's not certain of it. A true Morkan would never betray his kind,' Tharguen smiled fondly at Niome, 'just as a true Telorian stays faithful to the ones he loves.'

'We should keep going,' said Niome, her voice a monotone.

'What is it?' Tharguen asked, catching up to her and placing his hand on Niome's shoulder. She turned. 'What's wrong?'

'I'm sorry, I . . .' She sighed and shook her head. 'I don't know what's wrong with me.'

'It's okay,' Tharguen soothed, taking her in his arms. 'I'm here.' Niome held him tightly before pulling away. Tharguen gave her a chance to rest before they set off again, walking for several more days. Continuing by horse would have drawn unwanted attention and made them more visible to patrols, but Tharguen wondered if perhaps they had sent it away too soon.

Finally they came to a cave, its opening hidden by trees. Tharguen stopped and looked around. 'I remember this place. Now let's see if my memory serves me well.'

Tharguen bent and made a torch by wrapping dry moss around a branch, then lit it. Holding the torch up in front of him, he ducked inside the cave, Niome following.

'Are you sure it's safe?' she asked.

'Oh, perfectly,' replied Tharguen, then added, 'At least it's supposed to be.'

They walked up a winding tunnel for a short while, then Tharguen stopped. The tunnel stopped abruptly, with nothing in front of them but a vast cavern.

'We're up too high to get down there,' said Tharguen, pointing towards the floor of the cavern, about thirty feet below them. 'Besides, the small opening I'm looking for isn't down there anyway. We'll have to backtrack.'

'Okay, but I hope we find this small opening of yours soon,' sighed Niome, mildly annoyed. Then her voice sharpened. 'What's that?'

'What's what?'

'Shh!' she hissed, and grabbed his arm, her eyes shifting back and forth. 'Listen.' They. Then, 'That sound!'

They heard a faint rumble somewhere above them.

'It sounds like flying dragons,' said Tharguen.

'I don't like the sound of flying dragons,' said Niome.

'Let's go back.'

There was a loud thump. Rocks fell around them and the ground shook. Tharguen grabbed Niome's hand and pulled her to him and they stood against the wall until the rocks stopped falling.

'I think the dragon landed on the hill,' stated Tharguen.

'Well, I would assume so,' said Niome, laughing at his remark.

'I mean, it can be dangerous: rocks falling, ground shaking . . . didn't it give you a fright?'

'Coming face to face with a dragon gave me a fright. This . . .' She met his gaze, her face lighting up. 'I have you to protect me.'

'Come on,' said Tharguen, trying to hide his smile. 'Hold onto my hand in case the ground shakes again.'

They started back down the tunnel. The dragon roared and the ground lurched. Niome and Tharguen stumbled into each other. When they stepped apart, Tharguen looked around. Things seemed stable again.

'I think the dragon took off.'

'Mm-hmm,' said Niome, smiling.

Tharguen gave her a sideways glance. 'What?'

'Nothing.'

'Well, don't give me that look, Niome!'

'What look?'

Tharguen looked away, suddenly self-conscious, and set off again. Niome followed. Then he saw it.

'Aha, here it is!' He crouched down and peered through the opening, then drew back and tapped the sides of the hole with his fingers. He rose and stood beside it, leaning against the wall. 'I don't know how to get in. What an embarrassment.'

'On the contrary . . .' Niome pulled a book from her bag and looked through it. 'I think there's something in Tweedle's book of spells that can help us. Ah, here: "*Knocking on a Door*." Tweedle really thought of everything!' She pulled her wand out of her bag.

'That's good. Really good,' sighed Tharguen, passing a hand through his hair.

Niome stood tall and waved her wand around while reading.

> *Hail! You there, out in the lair,*
> *Or on the stair, I call with care!*
> *Let me enter, it's for the better.*
> *I need your shelter, so please, let me enter.*

Niome's words echoed in the cave. A few moments later, with a grinding of stone on stone, the door opened.

'Weddo here to help,' the polc on the other side said. 'Please enter quickly and stand right there.' He pointed to one side. Although his tone was polite, he did have his hand on the hilt of the sword, though it remained sheathed at his waist.

Niome and Tharguen stepped through the entry and stood by the wall as instructed. Weddo shut the door.

Another polc, his chest decorated with what looked like badges, passed through an archway from a far room and stopped to take a good look at them. 'Who are you and what do you need from us?'

'We are Telorians,' said Tharguen.

'Telorians!' the other said in a sceptical voice.

'Do you know Captain Silam?' asked Tharguen.

'No,' replied the polc, 'but I've heard *of* him. My name is Captain Holim. If you knew Captain Silam, then you are definitely allies of ours.'

'My name is Tharguen and this is my friend, Niome.'

A smile slowly spread across Holim's face. 'Weddo! Get the others.'

Weddo went running, shouting, 'Quick! Hurry! Come to the door!'

A short while later, Meysah, Jimmy, Vigh, and Boreth came running into the area before the entrance. When they saw Niome, Meysah shouted, 'Niome!' and they all ran to her. Tharguen took a step to one side.

'Oh, it's so great to see you again,' cried Jimmy.

'And safe,' added Boreth.

'You have no idea how helpless we all became,' said Vigh. 'It was just like Firnamel and Kchalami had explained it: once the Star is broken, we lose our power.'

'I'm so happy to find you here,' rejoiced Niome. 'You have no idea.'

They all embraced, then Vigh noticed the polc standing in the corner, smiling at the ground.

'It can't be!' breathed Vigh.

'What?' asked Meysah.

'Am I still delirious from my fever, or am I seeing Tharguen Sumperale?'

Everyone turned to Tharguen, who looked up at them.

'It is me, Master Vigh.'

'Then I can't wait to hear the story!' Vigh said, stepping forward to embrace Tharguen. Meysah watched, wide-eyed.

'Well, you have a lot to share,' said Holim. 'Why don't you all exchange news over tea.'

'That sounds like a good idea,' said Niome. Tharguen nodded.

'You have no idea how much this means to us, you being safe and alive and here, among us once again,' Vigh told Niome when they were all seated around the table. He looked at Tharguen. 'And the same with you. It's a miracle that you're alive, after so long. That means so much to me.'

'Well, it's quite a long story,' admitted Tharguen.

'Yes,' said Jimmy, 'so much to say! So much to hear! Who wants to start?'

'Sounds like you do,' said Meysah. 'Let's tell the story together.'

They all laughed. Everyone was so happy to be reunited, they didn't care how they could all be there and well; all that mattered was that they were, regardless of the questions that were going through their minds.

'Well, as you know, Niome,' Jimmy started, 'we all hid from the Morkans. Meysah injured his ankle and we didn't know how we'd escape. When we emerged from hiding we couldn't find you. And then more Morkans came.'

'You should've seen us fight!' exclaimed Meysah. 'We were handling them pretty well.'

'And Meysah saved my life without even knowing it,' Holim praised proudly; Meysah nodded eagerly.

'But then we saw you being taken away,' said Jimmy.

'You can guess what happened after that,' said Meysah. 'We all got injured – Master Vigh was stabbed. It was bad. The Dalvarans came and helped us, but by the time we arrived at the shelter, Master Vigh had a fever.'

'He was delirious,' Jimmy added.

'He got better only the other day,' said Meysah. 'On my birthday!'

'Oh, yes!' exclaimed Niome. 'Happy eighty-fifth birthday.'

'Thank you. I had forgotten about it myself. It sure was a lucky day, my birthday!'

'The Stone of Good Fortune sure came in handy,' said Boreth.

'I am positive that Elina's spirit is watching over us,' claimed Meysah.

'But enough about us,' said Boreth. 'What about you?'

'Where to begin?' said Niome. 'I was imprisoned in the caves on the other side of the hills. The

Morkans were going to take me to Mork. The Morkan in charge of me, Gowtch, kept all my things as well as keeping an eye on me. Then one night he helped me escape and told me his story, revealing to me his true identity. Gowtch, it turned out, was a Telorian spy: Tharguen Sumperale.' Niome beamed at Tharguen. 'I sure was happy to see him again!'

Jimmy cocked an eyebrow at this information. 'A spy!'

'I made sure that Niome was safe and I hid the *Complement Book* with me so that Beshrig, my captain, wouldn't get his hands on it,' said Tharguen.

'How did you convince them?' asked Meysah. 'You look nothing like a Morkan.'

'Well,' began Tharguen, 'when the Team of Twelve and I were fighting at Tower Fortress in Mork, I was able to steal a Morkan's cloak.'

Tharguen indicated the cloak he still wore over his leather armour. He resumed his story.

'I succeeded in passing as a Morkan, and Beshrig thought I was a new soldier, so I came up with a name for myself: Gowtch. Had I known I'd be using it for the next fifty years, I would've named myself something better, something more appealing to my Telorian ears. I'm grateful for it, though; it's what has kept me alive all these years. With my hood on and a fierce tone in my voice, I look and sound like a true Morkan. I'm lucky I learn languages quickly. You see, I know the Morkan language now, but for a long time I had to be wary of how I used it, and when.'

Tharguen looked at each of his friends. 'Once I had my disguise, I was able to obtain the keys to the Sorcery Tower from Beshrig, but before I could give them to Elina, as I got back downstairs, Mirauk arrived. Elina fought Mirauk before she fled, and half our team was slain. Mirauk was furious about the few Telorians who had managed to escape.'

Tharguen looked down at his plate. 'I was alone. I felt imprisoned. No one leaves the walls of Morok without the authority of a superior.' He sighed. 'I wish Elina would've known that I still lived when she left. The only thing I could do was remain there, living as a Morkan – making sure I was menacing enough, making sure I avoided Mirauk, making sure I did *everything* I was told to do. After thirty years, Beshrig officially made me his Second-in-Command, which gave me a lot more liberty. I made a promise to myself to help any Telorian who came my way.'

Tharguen looked at Niome. 'Thanks to my position, I was able to help Niome after her capture. Had I tried to escape any time before this year, I probably would have been killed. Niome and I escaped at the only possible time – it was then or never, and I must say, it was all thanks to my Telorian instincts.'

Leaning forward in anticipation, everyone waited for Tharguen to continue – somehow the story seemed unfinished.

After a pause, Meysah asked, 'Uh, did, uh, you, um . . . '

'What is it, Meysah?' asked Tharguen.

'Did you see Bahvley slain?' Meysah blurted.

'No!' asserted Tharguen. 'I saw Queevsil and Captain Ackerley slain by Mirauk himself, along with others, but I did not see Bahvley killed, nor did anyone else.'

'What do you mean?' asked Vigh.

'Mirauk lied,' said Tharguen. 'He was so enraged about what had happened that, to elevate himself, he told Elina he had killed both captains and cursed her for life. I knew then she wouldn't last much longer. Actually, I was surprised to hear she lived so long, though I am sad she had to suffer all that time.

'As for those who escaped,' Tharguen went on, 'they took to sea. If only Bahvley had known I lived . . . I could have maybe escaped with him, but it was too risky. I decided to stay and become a Morkan. I was a good Morkan,' Tharguen mused. 'I'm not proud of it, though. I had to hide all of my Telorian mannerisms, and I regret certain actions I had to take in order to stay alive and undetected among them. I could never fully hide *all* my traits, though. I always had the heart of a true Telorian and *that*, I am proud of.'

'Wait,' began Meysah. 'I don't understand. What happened to Bahvley?'

Tharguen looked at Meysah and smiled warmly. 'He escaped.'

It took a few beats before the information sank in. Then they all rejoiced.

'Praise the heavens and stars above!' exclaimed Vigh.

'This is indeed a time of good fortune,' agreed Boreth.

'Yes,' said Jimmy, who seemed to be preoccupied. He scowled. 'Everything just seems to be falling into place.'

'Tell us, Tharguen,' said Boreth, 'would you happen to know where Bahvley is now?'

'I haven't seen him in fifty years, so I haven't the slightest idea. Of course, I'd heard news from the Morkan messengers near the Islands of Mork that a group of Telorians had escaped by boat, including Bahvley, but that was the last we all heard of him, and that was far too many years ago.'

They fell silent.

'The Islands of Mork,' Vigh said in a low voice, 'are a dangerous place to escape to.'

'But if I'm not mistaken,' Tharguen added hopefully, 'I believe he successfully reached the other side of the Islands. There is yet much to hope for.'

'There is,' said Niome.

A Dalvaran brought them hot soup and some freshly baked bread. As they ate, they continued to share their thoughts.

Afterwards the Telorians gathered around a fire with Captain Holim and Weddo. Now that they had shared their joy, the reality of their woeful fate set back in. They were not going to stay in the caves forever. They had to get themselves to Mork to fulfil their mission and then to Darakön, sooner or later.

'I hate to have to rush everyone like this,' Niome said dolefully, 'but the longest part of our journey still lies ahead of us and we must organise ourselves and focus on our goal. Tharguen has some information that may help us.'

'I want you Telorians to know,' began Holim, 'that you have the support of the Dalvaran people.'

'Thank you,' said Niome, smiling.

'If only there were secret tunnels,' said Boreth. 'There are so many Morkans out there, it seems almost impossible to get across the plains unnoticed.'

'Morkans move in groups,' explained Tharguen. 'Rarely do they travel alone. I know the pattern of their movements. Some groups guard the area, others fight the Dalvarans. They are spread out, so there must be a way to Mork without them seeing us. If I can figure out where each group is headed, I can calculate our best path.'

'But going out of the caves and exploring the area is too risky,' protested Meysah. He looked at Holim. 'You saw their attacks on us. There's no way we can go out there without getting overwhelmed.'

'We have a secret pass through our caves to the top of the hills,' said Weddo. 'From there you can see the plains all around.'

'Huh,' said Niome. 'I think that's where we were headed by accident, while looking for the entrance to this place. We got lost and ended up at a cliff above a large cavern.'

'That's the path up, all right!' Holim confirmed.

'The path around the cavern leads to the crest of the hills,' explained Weddo. 'We don't have a watch tower there, for it would be too obvious, but we can lead you up there and you can take a look around.'

'Tomorrow you shall observe the plains,' suggested Holim.

'That's fine with me,' answered Tharguen.

'Excellent. Now, we shall leave you to your meal,' said Holim. 'I must organise my troops.' Holim and Weddo rose and left.

Shortly after, Tharguen stood as well. 'You will have to excuse me,' he said. 'I am not quite used to these bright and cheerful caves. The Morkan caves are dark and gloomy and cold, and I've been in them for far too long. I need some time to myself.' He smiled at them and walked away.

'He's troubled,' said Niome, watching him depart. 'And tired. Maybe overwhelmed. He's been through so much. He confided many things to me. There must be something we can do. I'll go see what troubles him.' She stood and left the room.

'Well,' said Jimmy, 'everyone seems to be disappearing quickly.'

'I still can't believe Bahvley might still be alive,' grinned Meysah.

'It is very fortunate that we met such a great friend once again,' said Vigh.

'Indeed,' agreed Boreth.

'He's been around Morkans for a long time,' Jimmy noted.

'I know. It's amazing they never discovered his secret identity,' said Meysah, the admiration clear in his voice. 'He's a great Telorian.'

'You think?' asked Jimmy.

'I think Meysah is quite fond of our survivor friend,' Boreth remarked with a chuckle.

'Niome certainly seems more than fond of him,' Vigh observed.

'If you recall,' began Meysah, 'they always enjoyed each other's company. It's only normal that they would want to spend their time together now.'

'It seems a shame that I never knew him,' voiced Jimmy.

'How come?' asked Meysah.

'Simply because I don't know him as well as the rest of you do,' replied Jimmy.

'Don't worry about that,' said Vigh. 'In time you will know him as we do.'

'I hope so,' said Jimmy.

Niome found Tharguen standing in a dark corner, leaning against the wall, arms crossed with a hand on his chin, as he stared at the ground, pondering. 'What troubles you?' she asked.

'Nothing,' he replied briskly and turned his back to her. He leaned his arm on the wall and bowed his head, sighing.

'Tell me. Don't brush me off.'

They had been open with each other and able to communicate easily as they travelled, Niome saw no reason why that had to change.

'I'm sorry.' Tharguen turned to her again. 'I'm not used to lights everywhere. I've been in the dark for so long, and all that time I was striving to get into the light, every chance I got.' He breathed out a mirthless laugh. 'Now I'm going into the dark to hide from the light.'

'Is that why Morkans usually travel at night?' inquired Niome.

'I suppose. It works to conceal their movements and to ambush enemies, but now they are extending their movements into daylight because time is of the essence.'

'So you just left to come here because darkness is what you've grown used to,' Niome deduced.

'Because I cannot face the light, yes,' answered Tharguen, chagrin on his face. 'Not yet, anyway. I'm ashamed of the things I've done as Gowtch. They all praise me as if I were a hero, but I'm not. I don't deserve that label. If there's anyone who should be praised as a hero, it's Bahvley, if he's still alive. I have disguised myself among the Morkans for fifty years by behaving as they do.'

'You did what you had to,' Niome said softly.

'I contributed to deaths, Niome, deaths I wish I could have prevented!' Tharguen's brows furrowed in pained sadness. 'I've done nothing of merit.'

'You saved me.'

'That's true,' Tharguen admitted, and a smile quirked in the corner of his mouth. 'But I feel sadness.' He bowed his head. 'That place, its people, their beliefs and the things they do, it's enough to make you lose your mind.' His eyes met hers, glistening with unshed tears. 'Your letter, the one you gave me before I left . . . I had to destroy it so I wouldn't be found out, but your words repeated in my mind every day I was there and kept me from going mad.'

Niome smiled warmly. Tharguen stared at her with longing in his eyes. Then, his gaze grew distant and unfocused.

'I look at Meysah, who is nearly Bahvley's age when I last saw him, and I see Bahvley. I cannot see the little polc who used to fall and cry all the time; I see a polc who's grown strong and has more courage to discover than he realises, and who will be valiant and driven by passion. And although I only met him today, I look at Jimmy and I see myself.' Tharguen paused. 'I can tell he doubts me.'

'Why do you say that?'

'I see the way he looks at me. I still doubt myself now, and I doubted myself then. The difference is that then I doubted my life, and today I doubt my ability to face Mork. I have been trying to get out of Mork for many years and I don't want to return to that dreadful place. But I will, for you.'

Niome smiled. Tharguen hugged her. Then they said good night and parted.

The other four Telorians now sat by a fire in a common room. Meysah and Vigh left to turn in for the night. Jimmy sat quietly.

'What are you thinking?' asked Boreth.

'You know, after a long time away from home, people change without others expecting them to. A long time with the wrong people, and someone might be influenced. They may change to be like them. Am I thinking wisely or foolishly?'

'You don't trust him, do you?'

'I don't know him, so I don't have any reason to automatically trust him. What if he's become Morkan? How can we truly trust him?'

'I understand your concern,' said Boreth, 'but like you said, you don't know Tharguen. We trust him because we knew him then and he is now who he was then, so we trust him now. I may not know him as well as the others, but Vigh trusts him and I trust Vigh's judgement. And you should too.' Boreth smiled sympathetically at his student and left the room.

Now alone, Jimmy stared into the fire.

'Why don't you trust him?' Meysah demanded from the doorway. Jimmy turned around to see the dismay on Meysah's face. 'We can trust him.'

'Can we?' objected Jimmy. 'He's been a Morkan for fifty years. What if he's been conditioned? Can you really trust that he's still the same person?'

'Yes, I can. He is the same,' insisted Meysah, taking a step further into the room. 'You don't know him. I do!'

'You knew him fifty years ago. What if he's a spy for the Morkans, pretending to be a Telorian spy. What if he's corrupted.'

'Have you lost your mind, Jimmy!?'

'No, but have you?' Jimmy stood, suddenly feeling affronted.

'This is Tharguen we're talking about. Bahvley's best friend.'

'Which is precisely why we should be wary, why it would be easy for him to—'

'Does anyone else share your views?' Meysah interrupted.

'No. I don't know,' Jimmy shrugged. 'I don't think—'

'Then there you go!' declared Meysah.

Jimmy sighed, deflating. 'I can't talk to Vigh, he's too overwhelmed by his joy at seeing his friend – like Tlúnëe predicted. Boreth, as you heard, does not share my doubt. Niome, she's in bliss as well. I suspect that she may be in love, by the way she looks at him. I thought I could talk to *you*. Though I wasn't expecting you to have heard what I said to Boreth, I still thought I could share with you my fears and doubts on the matter in more detail. I'm only concerned for everyone's well-being.'

'Well, being away from home sure has changed *you,*' sneered Meysah.

'What do you mean by that?' demanded Jimmy.

'Jimmy, I don't know why I trust Tharguen, but I do, we all do. He's a brave Telorian, always was and still is.' Meysah crossed his arms.

'I'm not . . .' Jimmy threw his hands up in exasperation. 'I don't know how to make you understand, Meysah. I'm not saying he's a fraud, a fake. All I'm saying is, he might have been influenced or tempted or—'

'Just don't talk to me, okay?' Meysah stalked out of the room.

Jimmy plopped down in his seat by the fire, leaning forward and burying his head in his hands before eventually falling asleep.

On his way to breakfast the next morning, Jimmy intercepted Meysah and asked him how he was doing, hoping to sort out any misunderstandings, but Meysah only glared at him and said nothing. Jimmy realised that he had hurt his friend more than he'd thought. He had killed Meysah's joy. Tharguen meant a lot to the others, but Jimmy's fears had gotten in the way of his own appreciation of the lost and found friend. *There must be something wrong with me,* he thought. *I wonder if Boreth's tendency to doubt strangers is contagious.*

At the table, the two boys stayed quiet. Although Jimmy tried to concentrate on the conversation the others were having, his mind replayed the previous night's argument, and he and Meysah glowered at each other. Afterwards, Jimmy retreated to be alone for most of the day, wishing he were in Firlan. At least there, he had Elmezni to keep him company.

No one seemed to notice Jimmy's absence, except for Boreth, who came looking for him. He found him on the steps that led to the second level of the Dalvaran system of caves.

'I presume you had a chat with Meysah,' said Boreth.

'He heard what I told you. I tried to explain, but I'm bad at explaining what's in my head and he won't talk to me anymore. He hates me now.'

'He doesn't hate you,' Boreth said gently, sitting next to Jimmy on the step. 'He simply doesn't understand how anyone could doubt such an admirable Telorian. You need to understand why he feels that way.'

'I *know* why,' protested Jimmy. 'I'm not saying Tharguen is completely evil, just that we should keep an eye open *in case* he's not the same person anymore! Anyone would see why; why don't you?'

'To tell you the truth, I really can't argue against your reasons,' admitted Boreth. 'Perhaps we are all clinging to the past, expecting a miracle. To Meysah, the possibility that Tharguen has been affected by the Morkans, even in the slightest, has shattered his dreams and hopes about Bahvley – hopes he now has thanks to Tharguen. There is nothing we can do but wait. Give Meysah time. He will come around.'

'I hope so,' muttered Jimmy. 'Is there anything you can do?'

'I'll see what I can do, and if he mentions it to me, I'll advise him well.'

Jimmy sulked. Boreth stood and left. In truth, Jimmy was afraid of Tharguen because he was afraid of Morkans, and Tharguen had been one. He probably could trust the Telorian, he admitted; he just chose not to.

Hearing footsteps coming slowly up the stairs, Jimmy stood and waited. It was Tharguen. Jimmy's heart skipped a beat. He wouldn't be caught dead being alone with Tharguen, he thought. *On second thought, I'll be caught dead after having been alone with him.*

'Ah, Jimmy,' said Tharguen. 'We were wondering where you were. Has Weddo come by this way? I've been looking for him.'

'No,' Jimmy replied. He moved his hand to the hilt of his sword, just in case, but nothing was there. He had left his sword in his room.

'Is there something wrong?' asked Tharguen, puzzled.

'No!' Jimmy replied nervously.

'Well then, I'll see you later.' Tharguen went back down the stairs. A short while later, Jimmy went down to be among the others.

'It is right this way,' Jimmy heard Weddo telling Tharguen. 'You must be careful.'

Niome and Meysah were with Tharguen. They did not see him, but Vigh noticed Jimmy, and his confused expression. When the others had gone, Vigh approached Jimmy.

'Tell me,' he said, 'what is the cause of your silence these days?'

'Oh, nothing, really.'

Vigh looked unconvinced. 'I should think that if it was nothing, it wouldn't trouble you so much.'

'It's complicated,' Jimmy sighed. 'It's something and I might tell you, though I don't know if you will understand.'

'I have faced many complications in my lifetime. I may or may not understand. Either way, it's up to you.' The master smiled in sympathy. 'If you don't wish to tell me, that's fine. I simply thought I could help you out.' Vigh turned and began away.

'It's about Tharguen,' Jimmy blurted. Vigh turned to look at him. 'Meysah is upset at me because I'm afraid we may be clinging to an illusion; that maybe Tharguen is not what he appears to be. What if he has changed and become a Morkan? I know it sounds stupid, but I just don't want us to be walking into a trap – literally into Mork, and into a trap.'

'I never thought of that,' admitted Vigh. 'I know Tharguen extremely well, for I trained him, and I can guarantee that he is the same Telorian he was before, but you are right to be cautious. Perhaps we should all be cautious from now on. On our guard, just in case.'

Vigh stood in silence for a long time. 'It is true that we have been greatly blessed, but we have also been greatly cursed. I should not wish for Tharguen to betray us and we should not betray him. But we should be mindful of what is yet to come on our path.'

'I'm relieved you understand. Perhaps I've gone about it the wrong way. I have a great fear of Morkans – more of a phobia, really – and the fact that Tharguen was a Morkan, even if in disguise, makes me shudder.'

'I understand your feelings, Jimmy. I will talk to the others. In the meantime, don't worry about it. Your mind should not dwell on such fears.'

'I think I might go spend some time with the Dalvarans to clear my head,' said Jimmy.

Offering Vigh a relieved smile, he left. Though he walked around for a while, he couldn't find any Dalvaran who wasn't busy, so he went to train with Boreth.

Meanwhile, Tharguen, Niome, Meysah, and Weddo climbed up to the hilltop by way of the passage Tharguen and Niome had taken the previous day, although Weddo showed them a ramp just below the cliff that wound up to the summit.

A dragon passed overhead but only snorted at them.

Tharguen walked to the crest and peered over. 'Can they see us up here?' he asked Weddo.

'No, we are too high up. But they may notice if we move around too much.'

Tharguen nodded. He looked off into the distance.

Niome and Meysah were observing the terrain below them. 'There seems to be an army over there,' observed Meysah, pointing southeast.

'There are many armies over there, but they are going to Mork,' said Tharguen. He looked around. 'The army that is farthest east must be going to the Telorian border, for it is not moving in the same direction, nor at the same pace as the others. There should be no more Morkans at the caves, although some might be lingering in hiding.' Tharguen peered north towards Darakön, and shivered. 'As for those who are not going to Mork, they will not get in our way if our timing is precise.'

'What do you mean?' asked Weddo.

'We must make for Mork, right? Those armies east of here will arrive in Mork in less than five days, if they don't slow their horses. We must not intercept them. The armies to the south are guarding the area and they move in triangles. They will go east next, then move around where we are, and then back south,' Tharguen explained, gesturing with his hand. 'We must leave before they reach this general area, but we must look like we are Morkans, arriving with an army of Morkans. They may get here in four days. There are more armies guarding the way to Mork. I shall provide the password to get us through. We should arrive very soon after the armies east of here arrive.'

Tharguen turned his attention to Niome and Meysah. 'The best way is to walk in independently. They will think we were guarding the way. All we need are black capes and a diversion. I will speak to the Morkans when we reach Mork, but only if I am spoken to.' Tharguen paused. 'Planning this is not so easy. I should speak to Captain Holim and everyone else. But one thing remains certain: we should leave in three days.'

'Then we should start preparing immediately,' said Weddo. 'There is much to do before then.'

They started back down, Weddo passing first through the hatch, then Meysah. Tharguen lingered, staring into the distance.

'Can you see over there,' he asked Niome, 'where the clouds seem to gather?'

'Yes,' she replied.

'That is Mork. I can almost see Mirauk's Sorcery Tower from here. That tower is the most dreadful place there is in Mork; that and his Sacred Grounds, where no one is allowed to walk. That tower is worse than the Prison Tower, worse than the Command Tower or the watch towers or any other. Worse even than the Torture Tower. It frightens me still.' He looked down, and continued in a half-whisper. 'I know I may not be entering it, but you will, and that frightens me more than anything.'

Niome took his hand and held it in hers.

'Niome!' Meysah called out, his voice drifting up from the hatch. 'Tharguen! Are you coming?'

'Yes, we are,' Niome called back. 'We were only double-checking.'

'Of course,' replied Meysah, popping his head out to look around.

They all descended, then gathered to make plans. Tharguen explained the Morkan movements to Captain Holim. Then he said that having black cloaks like those worn by the Morkans would help conceal their true identity.

'You're in luck,' said Holim. 'We took some hooded capes from the Morkans we'd killed to use as a disguise if necessary. I believe we have just enough for you and my tallest soldiers, whom I'll send with you.'

'Excellent,' said Vigh. 'Now we need to plan a distraction.'

'I'll lead an attack on the armies that patrol the area, to draw their attention away from you,' said Holim, 'a day or half a day after you've left. We will probably intercept any army that would otherwise be on your tail. That will be one less worry left behind you.'

'This means a lot to us,' said Vigh. 'We hate to have to part with you. I feel I owe you for healing me. I am ever thankful for that.'

'You owe us nothing,' Holim assured. 'It is we who owe you. You will be walking into Mork. That is a very brave deed.'

'If I may suggest something,' voiced Jimmy. 'I know we must avoid talking to Morkans, but if one should speak to us in their tongue, what are we to do? Perhaps you could teach us some basic phrases.'

'Good idea,' agreed Tharguen. 'I don't know how effective that will be, but it will be better than knowing nothing. We should start right away.'

'That should take care of everything, then,' said Boreth.

'Well, not exactly,' said Niome. 'I have a certain concern that must not be ignored. What are we to do if we run into Beshrig?' In the silence that followed, she looked at Tharguen.

'Who's Beshrig?' Meysah asked quietly.

'Tharguen's Captain,' replied Niome.

'Oh, right. Yes, I suppose that would cause a bit of a problem,' conceded Meysah.

'Should we ignore him and pretend to be random Morkans, or what?' asked Niome.

'I am still Gowtch to everyone in Mork,' stated Tharguen. 'Everyone knows a Morkan alone cannot fight an army of Dalvarans. I shall improvise.'

'Very well,' Weddo said with optimism. 'I'm sure you will be successful and the task will be much simpler than it seems. You are strong Telorians! Magic is on your side.'

Boreth smiled at the Dalvaran, but the others could not see the optimism in the situation. The meeting broke up, with the Telorians going with Tharguen to learn some of the Morkan tongue and Holim going to organise his troops for their surprise attack; timing was of the essence.

The next day, the Telorians continued to learn from Tharguen, then Vigh suggested they all go to the largest hall to practise their melee skills. Vigh and Boreth partnered up, and Niome sparred with Tharguen, leaving Meysah and Jimmy with no choice but to partner up if they wanted to practise. Vigh and Boreth thought it might rekindle their friendship.

After he had spoken to Boreth, Niome and Meysah about being cautious about Tharguen, Vigh thought he saw a touch of sympathy in Meysah's expression, and hoped that would translate to a desire for reconciliation.

All seemed to be going well until Meysah delivered a bruising blow to Jimmy's hand.

Jimmy paused and glared at Meysah. 'You did that on purpose, didn't you?'

'Really, no!' protested Meysah.

They reluctantly resumed their sparring, exchanging harsh glances. Their thrusts and swings gradually grew stronger until suddenly their mock duel seemed to turn into a real one.

Jimmy disarmed Meysah, which Meysah did not appreciate, so he stalked over and snatched Jimmy's weapon out of his hand as he was putting it away, and sent it clattering to the floor.

'What was that for?' demanded Jimmy.

'Well, you disarmed me, so I disarmed you,' answered Meysah.

'Really? Or is it because you're upset at me?'

'Are you accusing me?' taunted Meysah.

'What?'

'You are!'

The others had now stopped what they were doing and moved closer to see what was going on.

'You just don't want to trust Tharguen!' declared Meysah.

'I am only concerned,' protested Jimmy. 'What's wrong with you? You can't even accept the possibility – you don't *want* to even consider the possibility. You're believing an illusion.'

'That's not true!' Meysah retorted, and he pushed Jimmy to the ground. Jimmy knocked Meysah's legs out from under him and the two lads grappled and punched each other.

'You're just jealous!' shouted Meysah.

'As far as we know, he could be playing you all. A con!'

Jimmy rolled and landed bestriding Meysah's chest. Meysah struck Jimmy's mouth; Jimmy did the same to Meysah.

Boreth grabbed hold of Jimmy and hauled him away from Meysah. When Meysah leapt to his feet, Vigh grabbed him, interlacing Meysah's arms behind him to hold him back. As the two lads kicked and struggled, eager to continue their fight, Niome and Tharguen each stepped in front of one to block their view of the other.

'Don't exhaust yourselves,' Niome scolded Jimmy. 'It's not worth it.'

'Please,' Vigh reprimanded. 'This is ridiculous! You can't even get over a disagreement. You are no longer children. Please be civil towards each other. Come on; we are going to Mork, and the two of you are acting just like Morkans.' Meysah opened his mouth to say something, but Vigh cut him off. 'I don't want to hear who started what or who said or did what. I think we all know the reason, but it's between the two of you. Solve it.' He and Boreth released the two lads.

They all went their separate ways, though they made sure Jimmy and Meysah were not in the same room until it was time to learn more Ancient Morkan. For the rest of the day there was no mention of this, nor did the two young Telorians speak to each other.

The next day, Tharguen gave lessons only in the morning, but Jimmy skipped the lesson and spent time with Weddo instead. He had already met the tall Dalvarans who were going to join them, for they also were learning the Morkan tongue, but Weddo introduced him to the Dalvarans who were going to attack the Morkans with him and Captain Holim. Jimmy thought them very brave.

Jimmy realised what he'd thought was boredom was really melancholy. He did not look forward to going to Mork at all. *How did I get myself into this situation?* he thought as he wandered about. He counted the days he had been away from home so far. *Sixty-six long days and sixty-six long nights.* He went to his room, wanting to be alone.

He hadn't been there long when there was a knock on his door and in came Tharguen. 'You missed today's lesson,' the polc said gently.

Jimmy had nothing to say. Here was the polc he'd accused of being a Morkan, who knew what Jimmy thought and feared about him, yet he seemed to be passing none of his own judgement on Jimmy.

'That's all right, I suppose,' Tharguen continued after a short pause, 'since you've picked up most of the language more easily than the others. You must be good with languages.'

Tharguen sat down next to him. Jimmy didn't move; he just glared at the ground.

'You know,' began Tharguen, 'I understand why you don't trust me.' That brought Jimmy's head up.

'I wouldn't trust me if I were in your shoes. I could tell, even before your fight with Meysah, how much you doubted me. And I've deduced that it's the reason why you and Meysah aren't talking to each other, why you haven't been talking to each other since my arrival.' He breathed out a small chuckle. 'I have to admit, he's quite stubborn sometimes, just like his brother was.' He shook his head. 'Don't let this ruin your friendship. What if this was the last time you were to see Meysah?'

'How dare you suggest such a thing!' seethed Jimmy.

'I know what I look like to you: a Morkan, or traitor, or stranger if you like; you feel that I'm an impostor imposing on you and leading you into a trap. But I am a friend. I don't know how to prove it to you, but you *can* trust me. I understand it is difficult for you and I don't expect you to trust me anytime soon.'

Jimmy gave no reply. He merely continued to glower.

Tharguen went on. 'You're much like me in a way, distrustful of strangers, wary of others' opinions, but brave and warm. I'm sorry you feel like this, I'm sorry if I've contributed to it, but . . . ' Tharguen paused.

'I don't see your point,' snapped Jimmy. 'You don't know what it feels like for your best friend, your truly best friend in the world, to be angry at you for . . . misjudging, if you like . . . someone. You don't know what it feels like to be so far away from home and your best friend won't even talk to you anymore.'

'I do,' said Tharguen, his voice tinged with sadness. 'Before walking into Mork, I had a fight with Bahvley. It's quite stupid when I think of it now. We each wanted to handle the attack in a different way. I didn't trust his judgement and he got upset and accused me of doubting the whole trip.'

Tharguen brought his hands together and stared at the floor. 'We said some hurtful things to each other. Bahvley stopped talking to me, except to give me an order here and there. We didn't talk for days, stubborn lads as we were. I told myself he'd get over it, that I didn't need to talk to him.

'And then it was too late, we were in Mork, not speaking to each other, angry at each other, fighting at Tower Fortress, watching our friends die for the polc whose future role had been prophesied, the very polc I loved as a brother. The next thing I knew, he was gone and lost.' Tharguen closed his eyes for a moment, when he opened them again, they were glistening with tears. 'If he is indeed dead, I will never be able to forgive myself.'

Tharguen heaved a sigh and stood. He glanced at Jimmy, who was staring at the ground. 'Don't let it happen to you, Jimmy. Don't go into Mork without having reconciled with Meysah.' He left.

After thinking about it for a long time, Jimmy decided to go talk to Meysah, except when Jimmy approached him, Meysah didn't want to hear him out. He told him to leave him be and not to speak to him.

'I'm sorry, Meysah,' pleaded Jimmy.

'Just go.'

A long silence hung between them. They stared at each other, hearts heavy. Then Jimmy left. It was no use.

Shortly after dawn, the Telorians rose, made their final preparations, and ate a large breakfast. They had only to put on their black cloaks.

'What about our Telorian cloaks?' asked Meysah.

Vigh laughed. 'Don't worry about that! We'll get new ones when we get back home. For now, we have no other choice but to leave these behind.'

They passed through the archway to the room just inside the entrance to the caves. A tall Dalvaran approached and said, 'Hello, I am Rimid.'

The Telorians acknowledged him with a bow from the waist.

'I would like to say that on behalf of my seven friends and myself, we are honoured to be walking into Mork with you,' Rimid went on. 'If we die in battle, we know that it will be after defeating many Morkans, and we know that you will recover the *Book of Enchantment.* I wish you six brave polcs good luck in advance. As for us, we do not expect to return.'

'It is such a sacrifice for you to stay behind so that we might go back home,' Niome said solemnly. 'But I do hope you make it back to Dalvar alive.'

'We chose to come with you. We do this for you and for Teloria, *and* for Dalvar.'

The other seven Dalvarans stepped forward. They were wearing the black cloaks, their hoods thrown back. All eight knelt down on one knee. 'We will do whatever is necessary,' said Rimid. 'We are your servants.' Then they all rose.

Holim and Weddo arrived. 'It has been an honour knowing you,' said Holim. 'I will miss you.'

'We will miss you, too,' said Vigh.

'You must now set off,' continued Holim. 'Time is passing and you must hasten. Our duty awaits. I shall lead my troops tonight, right after dusk. When you return, I shall make sure that the path to Darakön is cleared of Morkans.'

Captain Holim turned to Niome and bowed deeply, taking her hand. 'You will retrieve the book,' he asserted. He straightened.

Weddo gave the Telorians their black cloaks. 'I shall escort you out.'

Donning the cloaks and pulling up the hoods, the Telorians took one last look around and said their goodbyes. Weddo led them out and bid them good luck and farewell, then he ran back inside. The group of fourteen polcs were now on their own.

CHAPTER TWELVE:
The Path Darkens

The team travelled for many days, always carefully looking ahead to make sure there were no Morkans in their path as they got ever closer to Mork. Only once did they come close to encountering a Morkan army, but they sped up and detoured several miles out of the line of march to stay out of sight. They had left the hills behind and were now travelling across open prairie, with few places offering concealment.

The sun shone brightly on the eighth day, but the dark skies of Mork could be seen from afar. In a week or two they would reach Mork.

Not long after midday, they saw a cloud of dust on the horizon behind them that indicated a band of Morkans on the move.

'We must pick up the pace,' Vigh urged.

They quickened their pace but they had already been walking fast and they were getting tired.

'I can't continue like this,' muttered Jimmy. 'I fear all my energy will be spent and I will not be able to defend myself.'

'You're right,' said Vigh. 'The Morkans are moving far too quickly for us. They will intercept us before too long. Perhaps we should wait for them and attack.'

'Is that a good idea?' asked Meysah, uncertainty in his voice.

'Do we have any other choice?' asked Niome.

'They may attack us,' said Tharguen, 'and by now, they know we are here.'

They all looked towards the approaching Morkans, now in plain view. Drawing their swords, they waited.

'Hang on,' objected Jimmy. 'Morkans attacking Morkans? Remember, we're supposed to be on *their* side.' He lifted a section of his dark cloak.

'That's true,' Vigh realised. 'Put your swords away! We will stand and wait for them. There may be no need for fighting. As Tharguen mentioned earlier, Morkans regroup all the time, so that's what we might have to do. But first, let's wait.'

The Morkans caught up to them and stopped several feet away from the Telorians. The tallest of them stepped forward. His hood cast a shadow over his face.

'Are you on your way to Mork?' he asked.

Tharguen tensed. 'Yes,' he replied as Gowtch, his voice pitched lower. He could not see the Morkan's face but he recognised his voice, and it irked him that he could not place him.

'Why do you stand around, then?' a second Morkan demanded.

'We thought you wanted to speak with us, since you were hurrying to join us,' explained Tharguen. 'But if that is not the case, we shall see you later.' He turned and started walking away. The others followed suit.

'Where are your horses!' asked the first Morkan, his tone suspicious.

'They sound like they suspect us,' Jimmy whispered to Boreth.

Tharguen turned back to face the tall hooded polc and realised the Morkans themselves had no horses. A sudden dread came over him. Had these Morkans been following them for days, perhaps spying on them the whole time? Tharguen had to think up a convincing lie.

'Well, probably for the same reason as you,' he replied carefully. 'Mirauk did not think it necessary.'

'What is your business here?' the Morkan asked.

'That is confidential,' Tharguen said flatly.

The Morkan stared at him for a long time, as if trying to bore into his soul. 'Correct me if I'm wrong, but it would appear that you are hiding something.'

'*Si tûkhyusk conkif dekenital!*' Tharguen said firmly.

'Very well,' the Morkan said after a long pause. He backed away and signalled his companions.

Tharguen turned around, and the Telorians and Dalvarans started walking again at a casual pace.

'I think he convinced them we're Morkans,' Meysah whispered to Vigh. 'Good thing he knows the language.'

After they'd walked a short distance, Vigh stole a glance back. The Morkans still stood staring at them, as though waiting.

'I don't think we convinced them,' Vigh told Tharguen. 'They may be preparing to attack. Be ready,' he told the others.

They continued, on their guard.

Vigh looked back again. As one, the Morkans turned and started towards their group again, gaining on them quickly.

'Draw your swords!' shouted Vigh. 'They were not fooled by our disguise!'

The Telorians and Dalvarans turned to face the oncoming Morkans, swords drawn and ready, as the Morkans sped towards them.

'Looks like they were planning an ambush,' Niome hissed.

'Some ambush,' muttered Boreth.

'Yes, well, they're going to fail,' declared Tharguen.

The Morkans attacked without hesitation. The tall Morkan swung at Tharguen. Before he could be caught off guard, Tharguen countered the attack with one of the techniques he'd mastered during the decades he'd spent in Mork.

These Morkans were especially skilled and it was difficult to get inside their guard, but the Telorians were also able to fend off the Morkan blades, at least at first.

Niome's sword clashed with the tall Morkan's, the one who had spoken to Tharguen; he seemed to be the captain. He parried, and pushed her back.

'You have no idea who you're dealing with,' Niome confidently declared.

A smirk crept to his lips as he lifted his head just enough for Niome to see his mouth. 'No,' he answered, 'I'm afraid it is *you* who does not know with whom you are dealing.' With a flick of his sword, he disarmed her.

'Back off!' yelled Jimmy, coming to Niome's aid.

The Morkans surrounded the pair, and one of them grabbed hold of Jimmy from behind, holding a knife to his throat.

The others were quickly overpowered by the Morkans.

'Capture the rest of them,' the Morkan leader shouted. 'They can give us some answers about—'

'If there's one thing I hate most,' seethed a voice from behind him, 'it's when someone threatens the lives of my friends.'

The Morkan whirled to find Meysah standing behind him, hood thrown back, his sword now inches away from the polc's chest.

'So tell your filthy knight to let go of my friend Jimmy, here, or I might just have to kill you.'

The polc took a step back in surprise. 'Stop!' he shouted in a loud voice. 'Let them go!'

'Is this a trap?' shrieked Niome.

'No,' declared the Morkan Captain, almost smiling. 'I believe this is a misunderstanding.'

'You'll tell us anything to save your skin!' Meysah taunted, taking a step forward, his sword still pointing at the Morkan's chest.

The polc stared at him a long time, as though speechless. Finally, bewildered, he breathed, 'Meysah!'

Meysah backed away, stunned. 'How do you know my name?'

The polc cast off his hood.

'Heavens!' exclaimed Tharguen, just as bewildered – he had crept up behind them and come to stare at the polc. 'I can hardly believe my eyes. Chance and fate have let you live.'

'Tharguen!' the polc breathed out, his eyes glistening. 'I thought you had been killed.'

'What's going on?' shouted Vigh as he and Boreth hurriedly approached them. Everyone gaped at the polc in astonishment.

Meysah knew that this almost mirror image of him was his brother.

'Is it really you, Bahvley?' Niome asked slowly.

Bahvley turned to her. 'Niome!' He smiled and laughed. 'You were right, I had no idea with whom I was dealing.'

Fighting back tears, though unsuccessfully, they all hugged. Bahvley held his brother and sister in a tight embrace.

'How beautiful you've grown, Niome. I always said you would. And how handsome and strong you've grown, Meysah. You look . . . like me when I was your age.' Bahvley laughed, though it was a bit of a sob too. He could barely contain his excitement at being reunited with his sister, brother, and best friend, let alone his master too.

'Fifty years and you haven't changed, my friend,' said Tharguen. 'Still pulling the same tricks.'

'And what about you? I didn't think you had escaped.' Bahvley stared in awe at his friend. 'I thought I knew your voice – no, I knew it right away, yet I could not believe it could be you. When you spoke the Morkan tongue, I was convinced you were a Morkan, for even if I'd recognised your voice completely, I thought you were dead.' He hesitated. 'I really did not think you had escaped.'

'I didn't,' replied Tharguen, grinning. 'Looks like we both thought of the same thing: disguise.'

'Are you telling me you've been pretending to be a Morkan since . . .' He let out a breath.

'Yep, and in Mork too, until recently. I tell you it has not been easy, nor entertaining, for that matter. Morkans are rather . . . dull and boring and un-sociable.' They laughed, relief washing over them.

'And Tharguen saved me when I was captured,' added Niome. 'That's how he's here now.'

'Well, well, well,' said Bahvley. 'How pleased am I to hear it.'

'Oh,' Tharguen hesitated, 'you aren't angry at me anymore, are you?'

'Of course not! I overreacted. Had another day gone by – or week, after days already – I would've already forgotten about it. You didn't think I was still—'

'No, I know you far too well.'

They smiled, embracing each other tightly, as a tear ran down each of their cheeks. They would probably need to address some of the details of their past quarrel at a later time, but both Bahvley and Tharguen knew and felt they were reconciled.

Jimmy and Meysah looked sheepishly at each other. 'Did you really mean it when you said *friend*?' asked Jimmy.

'Yes,' said Meysah. 'I don't want to be angry with you anymore. I'm tired of not talking to you. I'm sorry.'

'Me too. I misjudged Tharguen,' admitted Jimmy.

'And I misjudged your doubts – or concerns, I should say. Besides, the last thing I want is to march into Mork with a chip on my shoulder.'

'Yeah, tell me about it.'

They smiled.

'I want you to meet my friends,' expressed Bahvley. 'They come from a land beyond the Islands of Mork. We've been travelling a long time, and we prepared for a longer time before we left their continent. They are called Kikies. Meet their captain, Phynd.'

A Kiki stepped forward – the second 'Morkan' from before the fight. He seemed cheery and his eyes squinted when he smiled. 'Our apologies for the misunderstanding that caused this fight,' said Phynd. The Telorians were about to answer when he added, 'I understand. It is a pleasure for us as well to meet you. Bahvley was the first polc we met.'

'We didn't say anything,' said Vigh, eyeing the Kiki with curiosity. 'How did you know—'

'We are telepathic,' replied Phynd. 'That is how we learnt your language so quickly, by reading Bahvley's mind. Amongst ourselves, we communicate telepathically or through our spoken language, which you would consider only squeaks and funny sounds – tongue and teeth sounds, your friend here calls them.'

'Yes,' chuckled Bahvley. 'They create the most astonishing and adorable sounds, either through their teeth or with their tongue placed against their teeth. They also use facial expressions. It's difficult to explain; you have to experience the Kikiness for yourself. I'm sure if they were to be written down into words though, there would be more words in Kiki-language than in the Common Tongue.'

'Well,' began Vigh, 'as eager as we all are to hear the story, we still must hurry to Mork, so you may share as we travel.'

'Very well,' said Bahvley.

After introductions were made all around – with the Telorians introducing the Dalvarans and Bahvley introducing the rest of the Kikies – they started off. The Telorians explained the reason for their haste and, when they all stopped for supper, they summarised their journey so far. In turn, Bahvley told them of his.

After Mirauk had tried to kill him, Bahvley revealed, the surviving Telorians had taken to the sea. In truth, Mirauk had killed Bahvley's decoy; Elina had revealed that Bahvley's future role had been prophesied, and the Morkans knew his description but not his face. Thus, Bahvley's friend Queevsil who matched that description had volunteered to stand in as his decoy, for they all knew Bahvley mustn't look at Mirauk. Since Tharguen had donned a disguise unbeknownst to Bahvley, he thought Tharguen had been killed as well. He had looked for Tharguen as long as he could but never found him.

Bahvley and Tharguen shared a few sad glances as Bahvley recounted his tale, for both had witnessed the deaths of their friends. Each knew the hearts those deaths had broken and the hopes they had shattered.

Disguising themselves as Morkans, Bahvley reported, the remaining Telorians had stolen a boat and gotten past the fifth island by sailing west. However, by then the Morkans knew that Bahvley had escaped and took a small ship to follow in pursuit. The Telorians were intercepted, and their ruse was discovered. They managed to defeat their pursuers and travel past the Islands, but afterwards more Morkans boarded the ship and attacked them once more.

Bahvley had very little recollection of what had happened to them next. He'd been knocked unconscious when fighting Morkans and lost part of his memory, he admitted. He knew that he and Liffwai had been the only two left when their boat finally reached the Kikies' shores. Bahvley recollected that Liffwai had died from an injury to the stomach; he was already dead when Bahvley finally awoke, having passed that very morning despite the efforts of the Kikies to heal him.

While Bahvley's blow to the head explained the missing pieces in his memory, something about it all troubled him, and it irked him not to be able to remember.

When the boat miraculously reached the shores of an unknown continent, Bahvley was found and healed by the Kikies. These new beings learnt to communicate with Bahvley and they became friends, Celor being his first and closest friend there. Bahvley grieved for a long time – for Liffwai, for Queevsil, for Tharguen, for the other Telorians – but the Kikies took care of him for so many years that he became one of them.

They explored the seas and found ways to counter Mirauk's magical reach. With this, they devised plans for their great journey while Bahvley settled for a time, preparing to return home.

'On top of being mind readers,' Bahvley told his friends, 'they are versed in peculiar magical ways. They have a special ability to vanish into thin air when they please.'

'Vanish!' Jimmy exclaimed, eyeing one of the Kikies accompanying them. 'How do they do that?'

'In reality, they shrink to fairy size,' explained Bahvley. 'Some of them can fly as well, but only when they're in that smaller size; otherwise they jump or simply walk. But they can all shrink to about an inch.'

'Amazing . . .' said Niome, studying the Kikies with interest.

It had taken many years for Bahvley to heal, to grow accustomed to the Kikies, and for them to form a strong bond. The Kikies closest to Bahvley gradually learnt the Common Tongue from him. Then they showed Bahvley their kingdom.

'I drew a map of it,' he said. 'I also drew a map of Teloria and of Mork for them, so I could explain the importance of my going back.' Although he enjoyed their beautiful, warm country and its hearty inhabitants, he dreadfully missed his home, Teloria, and needed to go to Mork to finish what he had begun and be who he was destined to be.

The Kikies assured they would help Bahvley finish the mission. They set sail, following the shoreline, then travelled north and west, making a large, circular detour so they wouldn't be seen by any Morkans. They landed at the Colama Valley, just north of Darakön. Although magnificent, it was deserted, its kingdoms completely abandoned. Bahvley and the Kikies learnt from a hermit polc living on a remote hilltop nearby that the polcs who had lived there had moved far away to escape the threat of the Morkans.

Bahvley and the Kikies scaled Darakön, travelling through a high mountain pass, then they travelled around the hills, having descended closer to the Dakodol River than anticipated.

They managed to avoid Morkan armies, on the most part. They were acknowledged by one at one time, passing as Morkans as they were. If they did need to hide, Bahvley found concealment and the Kikies shrank. Eventually, they reached the other side of the hills and up ahead, not far from where Bahvley remembered the Dalvaran caves to be, 'we saw you.'

'No wonder it took fifty years,' said Vigh.

'They will undoubtedly recognise Bahvley in Mork,' Meysah pointed out.

'Disguised as he is, no,' replied Tharguen. 'I didn't even recognise him.' He smiled at Bahvley. 'I thought I recognised his voice, though, but I didn't realise it was him. No,' Tharguen became serious again, 'they will recognise no one.'

For many days the infiltrators travelled. The skies grew darker and cloudier the closer they came to Mork, often coupled with rain and chilly temperatures. Yet, as the team approached their destination, heat lingered in the air.

On one of those days, a strong, warm wind blew.

'What is this hot wind?' asked Niome.

'Some say that it is Mirauk's raging, fuming breath,' said Vigh. 'Of course, in the prophecy books a lot is exaggerated, but the wind does blow strong from the west.'

'Why do the days seem shorter?' asked Jimmy.

'Because they are getting darker,' replied Tharguen. 'As we approach Mork, we approach the darkness of its evil. The thick clouds of Mirauk's malice cover the skies and stop the light from coming through. Some say Mirauk has summoned an ancient magic that causes this, others believe Mirauk's power is simply that formidable. Regardless, remember that in Mork, it is almost always night.'

The wind blew stronger and stronger before subsiding, while the rain continued until the clouds were too dense to rain anything but darkness. During the day the skies were grey, but at night everything seemed pitch black – no moon, no stars, only darkness. Vigh had to use the light-cube; it seemed to lift the darkness off the ground and light the way for everyone.

Bahvley and Tharguen organised pairs of Kikies to scout ahead of the larger group to make sure they didn't blunder into a Morkan patrol. On the fourteenth day since the Telorians left the Dalvarans' secret cavern, one of the Kiki scouts returned to report that one of the six Morkan patrols moving in their area – four on horseback and two on foot – was up ahead. Worried that the band's number was great enough to draw unwanted attention, the Kikies shrank to their fairy size gand would return to their polken size only if they needed to fight.

'Things sure have changed since I last was here,' Bahvley told Tharguen. 'There weren't nearly as many patrols here last time, were there?'

'Let me take care of this,' said Tharguen. He turned to Niome, Boreth, and Vigh. 'I need you two to hold Niome as though she were a prisoner. That should convince them to let us through.'

Niome took her cloak off and Tharguen put it in his bag, then he lightly bound Niome's hands in front of her. Vigh and Boreth stepped up on either side of her and gripped her upper arms, and started forward with Bahvley behind them, then Jimmy and Meysah and a few Dalvarans to either side of Tharguen. The Kikies floated along unnoticed.

Meysah swallowed and muttered to Jimmy, 'I hope this works.'

The patrol came in sight and swerved towards them when the riders saw their group. They stopped a few metres in front of Niome and the masters, blocking the way. The Telorian party stopped.

'Ho,' said a Morkan, urging his horse forward. '*Wekherek reka kuyokh gokinag?*' he asked them.

'*Ihakhev semokhin thigo kitvig ekhokit Mirauk hemilefkech,*' replied Tharguen, stepping forward and quelling his fear.

'Who is your superior and what is your sector?' demanded the Morkan.

'My superior is Beshrig, from Sector 3-5-9-8,' stated Tharguen. 'I am following orders for Mirauk's personal affairs with the Telorians, as instructed by those above me.'

'And what is your name?'

'Gowtch. I am in charge of these Morkans sent to assist me.' He waved towards the others without looking at them.

'Gowtch! You were reported missing.'

'I was captured by a secret army of Dalvarans, but they were soon intercepted and we succeeded in recapturing the prisoner. I went after her as soon as she made her escape. The error was mine in thinking I could take her alone. Nevertheless, here she is, and subdued.' Tharguen continued, his voice silvery. 'I'm sure Beshrig will be very pleased, as will Mirauk.'

'Perhaps he should meet you here,' the Morkan suggested. 'Beshrig will want to . . . give her the necessary consequences for her actions.'

Niome closed her eyes and muttered something to herself. No one heard.

'It would be best not to,' asserted Tharguen, careful not to let his worry seep into his voice. 'Mirauk is waiting, and my orders come directly from the Inner Circle.'

The Morkan nodded. 'Proceed.'

The Morkan shouted a command at the other Morkans and the Telorians walked through the patrolling army, hearts pounding. When they were far enough away, Meysah and Jimmy breathed sighs of relief.

'We shall reach the gates in a few days,' Tharguen informed everyone, as he gave Niome her cloak. 'We will have to follow the same procedure. Once in Tower Fortress where the Command, Prison and Sorcery towers are, we won't have to anymore.'

'Good thing he's been in Mork all this time, so he knows the secrets,' Jimmy muttered to Meysah.

Meysah nodded. 'Good thing he speaks their language.'

* * *

The days continued to darken and by the time they had reached the gates, they could no longer tell the difference between day and night. The gloom made nighttime lighter than normal and daytime darker than normal, although some nights were pitch black.

On the eighteenth day since they parted ways with Captain Holim, the group of Telorians, Dalvarans and Kikies reached the main Gates of Mork.

There was a tall, black metal gate lit by torches, and many Morkans on horses stood guard in front of and behind it. There was a series of other gates past the first one, which Tharguen had explained worked as one mechanism.

The Telorians and the Dalvarans assumed the same formation as before.

Tharguen stepped forward. 'I have something to bring to Mirauk,' he told one of the guards.

The Morkan turned his horse and examined Niome with cold, calculating eyes. She felt the pain in her chest and pressed her bound hands against it. Vigh made it look like he and Boreth were steadying her, but in fact they were holding her up, supporting her trembling body. Behind them, Jimmy and Meysah were shaking, doing their best not to look at the Morkan without arousing suspicion.

Tharguen went on. 'I am Gowtch from Sector 3-5-9-8. I am Beshrig's Second-in-Command.'

'Is this a prisoner?' the Morkan asked, pointing his sword in Niome's direction.

'This is *the* prisoner,' declared Tharguen. 'I am to bring her to Mirauk myself.'

'What is the password?' the Morkan asked nonchalantly, as if speaking from habit.

'*Passakwokhdero kit Morok: thme gakhit yiliw ezzir! Sekotor passakwokhder: ûsse thwe kakho kit goworo!*' said Tharguen.

'*Penoth gatesse!*' the Morkan roared. '*Akhnad khetel thme passak!*'

The gates swung open with a harsh metal squeal. First the largest and foremost gate, then the others, moving in unison.

'*Kelarth ewaia!*' the Morkan told the others behind him. '*Tikhis pirosern sifo gater mipotar-kacheno kit Mirauk.*' Then he turned to the cloaked and hooded Telorians. 'The path has been cleared for you.'

'Thank you,' said Tharguen.

Keeping a level head and his gaze stern, Tharguen led the group as they passed through. The gates closed behind them.

They walked through the city of Central Mork for another day and a half; they had entered Mork but had yet to reach Tower Fortress, which held the three main towers. They ate as they walked, though none of them felt very hungry. They were hot and scared and surrounded by Morkans staring at them – at least that was what it felt like – and all they wanted was to get their task over with.

When Tower Fortress came into sight, Tharguen led the Telorians into an alleyway where they could check their weapons and allow Niome to collect herself. Then, they marched to the entrance of the looming fortress.

CHAPTER THIRTEEN:
Rushing In and Out

They stepped into an immense square hall from which many corridors led off into darkness. Torches everywhere drove back the gloom in the square. The Telorians looked around. Very few Morkans were passing through and those who did pass seemed to be in a hurry.

'_This_ is where you spent the last fifty years?' Meysah whispered to Tharguen.

Tharguen gave a short nod, then waited as several Morkans passed them.

'There is a secret corridor from the Prison Tower to the Sorcery Tower, but everyone goes to the Command Tower only, except those of exceptionally high rank,' Tharguen said in a low voice when the square was empty of Morkans again. 'We cannot be seen entering the Sorcery Tower – no one is allowed up there except the highest lords and those of Mirauk's Inner Circle. We may have to split up.'

'Is it possible for us to enter the Prison Tower without being noticed?' asked Vigh.

'No, we are too great in number,' replied Tharguen.

'We'll stay behind,' said Rimid, 'but will come to your aid if needed. We will also prepare horses for your escape.'

'Thank you,' said Niome. 'I don't know how long it will take us. Who knows how long we'll have to wait before Mirauk leaves his quarters? We must be ready for anything.'

'The stables are down that east corridor.' Tharguen nodded towards the corridor in question.

The Kikies, still hovering close by and unseen in their fairy form, understood what was required of them.

A couple of Morkans came into the hall and nodded to the group. Then, the infiltrators split up, the Dalvarans setting off in one direction, while the Telorians followed Tharguen into another corridor, which curved around before ending at a set of large winding stairs.

'Where are you going?' a young Morkan who was coming down the stairs asked condescendingly. He held his chin up as he eyed the group.

'To relieve the guards,' replied Tharguen.

'All of you?' The Morkan narrowed his eyes in suspicion.

'Well, no,' Vigh said sharply. 'Mirauk wishes to speak to some of us.'

'Oh, he wants to meet you at the prison cell,' the Morkan deduced. 'Then this must be important.' He tilted his head upwards, as though he were an important polc, and continued in a boastful manner. 'I hear the Telorian carrying the *Complement Book* has been captured.'

'Indeed,' said Boreth. 'Mirauk has specific orders for us concerning that book.'

'Well,' said the Morkan, 'I hear he is at supper now, but it *is* good to arrive before him. The Lord has been impatient of late. Of course, it is not my place to say.'

'We shall disregard your comment,' said Tharguen, a threat and warning in his voice. 'But you should know not to criticise the Lord's behaviour. He surely has reason to be impatient if he is.'

'Yes, of course.' The Morkan continued down the stairs and past them.

'A very young Morkan who is still ignorant and innocent,' sighed Tharguen.

'If innocence can exist in a Morkan,' Jimmy muttered to Meysah.

'Yeah, word spreads fast too, eh.'

'He has revealed to us that Mirauk is not in his private study,' said Tharguen. 'That means we don't need to wait around; we can avoid a confrontation. Come, we must hurry.'

As they climbed the wide staircase, they passed many doors. Some of them were guarded, others not. The guarded ones contained prisoners, Tharguen informed them in a whisper.

'They have that many prisoners?' gasped Jimmy.

Tharguen nodded. 'Many polcs from different places. Some from long ago, others from yesterday.'

'I shudder at the thought that this is where I might have wound up had the Team of Twelve not freed me from captivity,' Boreth whispered to Vigh.

They climbed for a long time. Then they reached a point where the walls formed alcoves. There were two cells on either side of the stairs between the alcoves.

'These aren't real cells. They serve as a decoy,' said Tharguen. 'This is the secret passageway.'

'Boreth and I will remain here to keep watch,' said Vigh. 'If we hear anything, we'll run to the other side.'

'It would be best if you didn't,' said Bahvley, 'leave your posts, I mean. We will need you once we get back.'

'You mean you're going up with me?' asked Niome.

Bahvley turned to her. 'I'm not leaving you to go up those stairs alone. No matter who goes, I'm going with you.' He placed his hands on her shoulders. 'A Fairhaven is prophesied to retrieve the *Book of Enchantment*. That Fairhaven is you. I will ensure that you do indeed retrieve it.' Niome smiled at her brother.

'All right, then,' said Boreth. 'We'll guard the way for you.'

'What about us?' asked Meysah.

'You are a Fairhaven, are you not?' smiled Bahvley. 'We're in this together.'

'You're coming with us,' confirmed Tharguen. 'We're going to need the two of you.'

Meysah and Jimmy looked at each other nervously.

'Don't be scared,' Niome said soothingly. 'You're going to stay with us the whole time.'

Vigh and Boreth took up positions in the alcoves and the others slipped through a trap door in the landing and closed it without being seen. They ran across the secret corridor to the other tower.

When they reached the secret door at the other end, Bahvley hesitated. He stared down the stairwell. 'I'll stay here.' He looked back at the others. 'I'll be well hidden. If I hear Mirauk coming up these stairs, I'll be able to run ahead and warn you.'

He took Niome's and Meysah's hands in each of his and gently squeezed. The three siblings nodded to each other. Tharguen, Niome, Jimmy, and Meysah then continued up the stairs towards the top of the Sorcery Tower as the Kikies returned to the Prison Tower.

Niome felt very hot, for the heat of evil was unbearable. They all cast off their hoods to breathe better.

They heard footsteps coming their way from farther up. Jimmy and Meysah quickly pulled their hoods back over their heads, but Niome's cloak snagged on a hook in the wall and fell from her shoulders. Tharguen quickly picked it up but didn't have time to pass it back before the Morkan was in plain view.

'Is this Niome Fairhaven?' the Morkan asked in astonishment. His voice sounded familiar to Niome.

'It is,' asserted Tharguen, as Jimmy and Meysah took hold of Niome as though they were guards.

Niome felt the pain again and the two lads propped her up as best they could.

The Morkan came closer to take a better look under the torchlight. 'Gowtch?'

'Beshrig!' Tharguen acknowledged, swallowing nervously.

'I knew you'd get yourself out of any entanglements the Dalvarans threw at you.' Beshrig beamed at him. 'Well now, there isn't much time for explaining – you'll do that later. You can give me the prisoner. I'll take her from here.'

'I'm afraid I can't do that,' said Tharguen. 'I have to bring her to Mirauk. I went to great lengths to find her again.'

'Remember that I am in charge of her, not you, Gowtch,' Beshrig warned. 'I've given you many liberties, but this is one I am not prepared to allow; the last time you were alone with her, she escaped and had you captured. Gowtch,' Beshrig's tone became one of reassurance, 'it is not you I don't trust but her. You have done well, as you always have. I know Mirauk will reward us both for this, and I will vouch for you, as I always have.'

'I know, Beshrig,' replied Tharguen, bowing his head. 'And I appreciate all you've taught me over the years.'

'That's my Gowtch.' Beshrig clapped Tharguen on the arm. 'Mirauk is at supper now. I shall bring our prisoner to the Prison Tower.' Beshrig grabbed Niome by the arm.

'No! You can't,' Tharguen objected a little too quickly, pulling on Niome's sleeve. 'I must bring her—'

'It's an order, Gowtch. I know you would prefer to take care of this yourself, but you must still follow my orders.' Beshrig tugged and Tharguen let go of Niome. 'Besides, you don't want to jeopardise any chances of becoming Captain, do you?'

Beshrig took two more steps down the stairs, pushing and shoving Niome ahead of him.

Meysah tried to go after her, but Jimmy stopped him with a hand on his arm. 'Don't do anything foolish,' he whispered.

'I'm sure you would be honoured to get a promotion, Gowtch,' continued Beshrig, turning to look at Tharguen, 'and be in full command.'

'Yes, I would,' said Tharguen, resolved, 'but not in Mork.'

'What do you mean?' asked Beshrig, scowling in confusion.

'It has been a great privilege serving you, Beshrig,' said Tharguen, 'but all must come to an end sooner or later.'

Tharguen unsheathed his sword and stabbed Beshrig so qiuckly, the Morkan had no time to react. Beshrig fell to the floor with a grunt of pain, eyes wide in surprise.

'You have given me the key to help in protecting my friends and my kingdom,' said Tharguen, crouching by Beshrig. 'I could not have done this without you.'

Tharguen pulled his sword from Beshrig's body and sheathed it, letting out a shaking breath. Beshrig toppled onto his side, dead or close to it.

'The keys!' said Meysah, dropping to his knees beside Beshrig to search the body. He pulled a set of keys from Beshrig's pocket. 'Keys to Mirauk's chambers, maybe?'

Tharguen didn't answer. Stunned by his actions, he accepted the keys Meysah gave him. 'I had no choice,' Tharguen mumbled. He looked up. 'I just killed the person who looked after me all these years and taught me all I needed to know to help you. But I had to do it.'

'You saved my life,' said Niome, 'once again.'

'I, uh, can't believe I just did that,' breathed Tharguen, still shocked. Then, he rose and he shook himself. 'We need to get rid of the body before anyone finds out.'

'We can take care of that,' assured Meysah. 'We'll find a room to hide the body in.'

'Here, take the keys.' Tharguen threw the keys to Jimmy who caught them immediately. 'You'll probably need them more than us. Besides, neither my set of keys nor a captain's can unlock the door where we're going, only magic can.'

'By the way,' said Jimmy, 'that was brave.'

'Thanks. Now, hurry. Don't stay gone too long, and catch up quickly.' Tharguen took Niome's hand and continued up the stairs.

Jimmy lifted the dead Morkan by the arms, and Meysah took the legs. They half carried, half dragged the body down the stairs to an isolated door they had previously passed.

Setting the body down in a position to minimise blood pooling on the floor, Meysah tried to turn the doorknob. It was locked.

'One of these keys must open this door,' said Jimmy, as he began trying each key.

'Hurry,' urged Meysah.

'There are too many keys to try out,' complained Jimmy. Finally, they heard a click. 'Ah-ha!' Jimmy pushed the door open.

The two lads looked inside the room. It was small but packed with huge chests. There were also three wardrobes, and shelves holding weapons, the likes of which they had never seen before.

'Is this where Mirauk stores all his weapons?' Meysah wondered. He shivered.

'Or torture tools,' Jimmy added.

They picked the body up again. 'Should we hide it in one of the chests?' asked Meysah.

'In a wardrobe, maybe?' suggested Jimmy.

'Let's see.'

Once again, they had to use the keys to open the chests and the wardrobes. One of the wardrobes contained armour; another held axes and spears. The third would not open. There was no room to fit the body in any of them. They found a chest with nothing but cloth in it, so they emptied its contents and put Beshrig's body inside, then put the cloth back on top. They locked the chest.

'That should be good,' said Jimmy.

'Okay,' Meysah said nervously, 'let's get out of here.'

They turned around in time to see the door close.

'Uh, what was that?' asked Meysah.

'Oh, probably just . . . wind?' Jimmy reached out to turn the doorknob, but the door would not open. 'Wait—'

'There is absolutely no wind at all,' quavered Meysah.

Trembling, Jimmy looked at Meysah, feeling dread. 'We're locked in.'

'That's impossible!' Meysah tried to open the door. He jiggled the knob angrily, then stepped back. 'Use a key.'

'Where? There's no keyhole!'

'What are we to do!' Meysah wailed. 'We have to get out of here.'

'Don't panic, Meysah! We'll figure something out.' But Jimmy was also panicking.

Meysah brought his hands to his head, grabbing his hair. 'This is not good.'

Niome and Tharguen climbed to the top of the tower; Niome wondered what was taking the lads so long.

They came to a large black door with an arched top. 'It's locked,' said Tharguen.

Niome rested the palms of her hands gently on the door and spoke a few lines of a spell, her voice low and soft.

> *Ej usis lacalef,*
> *dece tep torë,*
> *ejtu norë lacalef,*
> *eptu siëj neret.*

The door swung open.

The room was empty of Morkans, but it was full of books – on shelves and in piles scattered around the room. Niome scanned the room with her eyes. It looked like a mix between a study and a library.

'How am I to find the book when there are so many, all scattered and disorganised?' she sighed, feeling despair. 'The shelves are three times my height, at least, and the piles on the floor go up to my waist!'

'Do you really think Mirauk would leave the *Book of Enchantment* piled with less important ones, where it could easily get lost?' asked Tharguen. 'He would surely place it in a special place, a secret place. I don't know where it is but I do know that after a while, he stopped carrying it on his person because it was too much of a hassle to guard it. It was better kept in his private study – in other words, here.'

'He has many secret and private places, from what I hear,' replied Niome. 'He knows I will come for it. You said yourself he'd seen the identity of the one who guards the *Complement Book* in Elina's eyes.' Niome nodded at the stacks of books before her. 'This is where he put it, to lure me here. He doesn't think we can escape, but something tells me he doesn't think I'll find it before he gets back.' She looked at Tharguen. 'I'll do my best to hurry.'

'I'll stand guard.'

Niome immediately started looking through the desk drawers. Tharguen went to the door and stood by it to keep watch.

Vigh and Boreth kept silent watch. Boreth suddenly turned to Vigh. 'Did you hear that?'

'Hear what?'

'Thumping. It was like the dream I had in Mistoff. It started off faint. It'll become louder and louder.'

'You do have better ears than most polcs,' noted Vigh. 'We should remain vigilant.'

One of the Kikies appeared as if out of thin air. Luckily, no Morkans were around to see the phenomenon, nor the startled reactions of the two polcs.

'Mirauk has just entered the Sorcery Tower,' she informed them.

'Right this very instant?' Boreth asked urgently.

'Yes,' she answered. 'We can fly at tremendous speeds.'

'Thank you . . . ?' began Vigh.

'Mië. I don't believe I gave you my name when we first met.' She smiled delicately and inclined her head politely. 'I shall go and inform Bahvley now.' Mië vanished and the door of the secret passage moved a fraction.

'Mirauk's the thumping,' Boreth realised. 'I might have known before, but—'

The thump came again, still very faint, but louder than before. Then the two masters saw the door move again and Mië appeared before them.

'I'm afraid Bahvley is not there,' she said.

'Not there!' exclaimed Vigh.

'It is possible he heard the thumping and went right away to inform the others. I must head back down to report.' Once again, Mië vanished, and Vigh and Boreth exchanged worried glances.

Bahvley ran quietly up the stairs of the Sorcery Tower until he was close enough to see the open doors of the large room at its top. He paused to survey the situation. He saw Tharguen standing guard at the entrance, but Tharguen did not see the two concealed figures moving along the wall towards the door.

Sprinting the rest of the way, Bahvley ran up to Tharguen and pulled him against the other wall. He only had time to hold a finger to his lips and point towards the other wall before he grabbed the first Morkan to come within reach and clapped a hand over his mouth. Seeing the other Morkan, Tharguen moved to trip him and sent him collapsing onto the floor. Tharguen dropped down on top of him and drove a knee into his back, covering the Morkan's mouth with his hand.

Inside the room, Niome turned around, alarmed.

'Keep looking!' Tharguen called to her. 'We'll get rid of these filthy Morkans.'

The Morkan Tharguen was restraining bit the Telorian's hand; Tharguen yanked his hand away, and the Morkan yelled, 'Thieves!'

The other Morkan pushed Bahvley off him and shoved him through a door that was hidden in the shadows. Tharguen followed them in, dragging his Morkan with him. Bahvley grappled with the Morkan, who drew his knife. Punching the Morkan's wrist, Bahvley knocked the knife out of his hand, and the blade skittered across the floor with a metallic hiss . . . followed by a chilling silence, and then a sudden splash.

'What in the Kurssus—' breathed Tharguen.

'There's a drop-off here,' Bahvley remarked, still grappling with the Morkan. As if to punctuate that revelation, a strange, beastly moan rose from the water below them.

'I don't like the sound of that at all,' quavered Tharguen.

They continued wrestling with the Morkans. The one fighting Tharguen slammed him against the wall and tried to stab him with a dagger, but Tharguen kept swaying and bobbing from side to side.

The other Morkan grabbed Bahvley, attempting to push him over the ledge; Bahvley ducked, pulling on the Morkan to add to his momentum. The Morkan fell over him, grabbing Bahvley's sleeve as he toppled past, taking Bahvley with him.

Grabbing the edge of the drop-off with one hand, Bahvley stopped his fall. Down below, there was a splash and a rumble, followed by a hideous snort. The Morkan cried out in sudden fear, and his grip was yanked free of Bahvley's sleeve. Bahvley heard the snap of the beast's jaw and the Morkan's screams stopped abruptly.

Meanwhile, Tharguen was holding off the Morkan with the dagger. As the Morkan slowly started stepping back to avoid Tharguen's blade, he stepped on Bahvley's fingers. Bahvley gave a loud cry, but never let go, instead gripping the edge more tightly. Tharguen kicked the Morkan hard in the chest and he too fell into the water. Another snap-crunch followed, and the sound of teeth munching flesh and bone.

Tharguen grabbed hold of Bahvley and pulled him up. Bahvley crawled away from the ledge before standing.

'How are your fingers?' asked Tharguen.

'Only bruised,' replied Bahvley. 'I've been through worse.'

'Thanks, by the way.'

'I saw them coming up, so I followed. They got stealthy when they spotted you.'

Tharguen gave him a lopsided grin. 'Good thing you were there then.'

They moved to exit the room, but discovered they were locked in. They exchanged an alarmed glance.

'Now what?' asked Bahvley.

The thumping was growing stronger, until it seemed to be right next to Vigh and Boreth. The same thing for Meysah and Jimmy. They had been trying to break down the door with whatever makeshift tool the room presented, but the door proved unbreakable and unopenable.

Soon they could tell the thumping came from the tread of heavy boots, accompanied by a clank whenever their owner took a step. Jimmy and Meysah realised at the same time that the sound was coming from right outside the door they were trying to open – one key was now being inserted into the keyhole with a metallic scrape.

The two lads quickly set aside the objects they'd been using on the door and dashed to hide in the wardrobe, pulling the garments that hung inside around themselves.

The door creaked as it swung open.

Meysah's heart skipped a beat.

All became quiet. The only sound was heavy breathing. Then the clang of a weapon.

If Mirauk found them and looked them in the eyes, Meysah and Jimmy were dead polcs.

The door closed again and the thumps slowly got fainter as they continued up the stairs. Reluctant to breathe out sighs of relief, Meysah and Jimmy emerged from the wardrobe. They were still locked in the room, but thankfully they and the body had not been discovered.

'Now what?' asked Meysah.

Tharguen and Bahvley pushed on the door, straining against it with all their strength. It wouldn't budge. They hacked at it with their swords but could not cut the wood.

'This is not an unbreakable door,' complained Tharguen. 'Or at least it's not supposed to be. This is evil magic.'

'Niome!' yelled Bahvley. His voice echoed in the room. 'Well, that's not working.' He sighed. 'I have just been reunited with my family. I will not let Mirauk take my sister and brother away from me.'

'Nor I,' declared Tharguen.

They heard thumping as it grew louder and louder. Memories from long ago, when they'd heard those same thumps, conjured images of their dying friends in Tharguen's mind. Despair flooded his heart.

Bahvley bowed his head, leaning his forehead on the door.

'I just hope she's well hidden,' whispered Tharguen, his breath shaking.

Niome was ready to give up. She closed her eyes and took a deep breath. When she opened them, she was staring right at the *Book of Enchantment*. It was concealed behind the bookshelf she'd been looking at, lying on a shelf that looked like part of the brick wall but was clearly a special slot for the book. Niome pulled it out and put it in her pouch.

The thumps got louder.

Niome's heart started pounding hard, almost in time with the thumps. She felt weak, light-headed and dizzy. *I'm going to die,* she feared. Her entire body started shaking, and she swallowed against nausea. Her face felt hot. *Am I going to pass out?*

The physical ailments kept worsening. It was an attack like she'd never had before – and perhaps never would again if she didn't survive it. Piercing pain stabbed through her chest like a needle.

Then, suddenly and instantly, it subsided, as though it had all been an illusion. Niome was no longer trembling, her heart was beating normally, and she felt abnormally calm. Except there was one new feeling: she sensed a presence. In the utter silence, Niome felt the vibrations of her nemesis. She knew Mirauk was standing right behind her, yet somehow it did not disturb her.

'At last you meet me,' she said, her voice surprisingly calm. There was no answer. 'Do I surprise you?'

'No,' said a deep yet normal-sounding voice. 'I knew you would be able to feel my presence. I have been expecting you. You must face the facts: you cannot defeat me. No one can. You are weak.'

'I think you are mistaken,' declared Niome, turning around to face him, though she kept her eyes downcast. 'You underestimate my chances of survival.'

'It is you who overestimates them,' Mirauk sneered. 'Look into my eyes if you truly believe you are as strong as I am.'

Niome looked up. A very tall polc clad in black and gold armour stood before her, normal-looking at first glance, even resembling a Telorian, but with eyes that glinted with evil, anger, and all-knowing power. Fear and despair chilled her heart, like a poison dart piercing her soul. Mirauk grinned, confident. He looked no older than Vigh, though Niome knew he was many centuries old. His magic kept him young, it seemed.

As frightened as she was, Niome did not back down. Mirauk scowled at her, as if trying to make her cower. Still Niome kept her eyes fixed on his. A part of her did not understand why she was risking death, yet she kept on staring.

'I don't believe I am as powerful or as strong as you, Mirauk,' Niome said firmly.

He chortled, his satisfaction harsh and ugly. 'Oh no, you aren't. Now give me back my *Book of Enchantment*, and the *Complement Book* as well.'

Niome said nothing, though she wondered if she should dare tell him they were never his to begin with.

'Give me the two books!' he bellowed, impatient.

'No!' screamed Niome, defiant.

Mirauk unsheathed his sword. Niome took a step back.

'Very well, if this is how you want it to be.' Mirauk peered deeply into Niome's eyes, then pointed his sword at her. 'So you have come with four others.' Niome's eyes widened. 'Yes, Niome Fairhaven, I can read your mind. Something that comes with great *power.*'

'No, stop it!' Niome cried, pressing her hand against her head. 'I can feel you probing my mind! Stop!'

'A pain like you've never felt before,' Mirauk sneered with satisfaction. He laughed sinisterly. 'An uncomfortable tickle. A discomfort all should have the privilege of experiencing when in my presence.' He paused. 'You believe in the prophecies, Niome? I don't! You don't actually believe that the Five of the Star are going to restore the Freedom of Life, do you?'

He let out a breath. 'Oh, I see, Bahvley Fairhaven has returned. Well, well, this is most interesting. The prophesied King of Teloria, come to finish what he started. What else can you tell me? Oh wait, you're not telling me; I'm hearing your thoughts, seeing in your mind's eye.' He laughed loudly.

'Stop it! Ah!' Niome had tears trickling down her cheeks.

Mirauk let go of her mind and stepped forward, his sword levelled. Niome staggered back, her balance failing. The wizard swiped his sword through the air in challenge but Niome cringed away, weak and on the edge of consciousness. She struggled to hang on, trying to fight the sudden fatigue, trying to gather her strength.

Still, she somehow kept her gaze on Mirauk, trying to understand what he was sensing from her, what he was thinking, what he was planning, but his face was emotionless and expressionless. He seemed to be waiting for something.

A crooked smile crept up the side of his mouth. 'Watching someone suffer and making them suffer passively is so much more satisfying than using any weapon.'

He walked towards her. She did not move, did not have the energy or willpower to move.

'Magic is such a great thing to have, Niome.' He teased her with the tip of his sword, sliding it down her face. 'You don't know how to use it. You are not powerful at all. You'll never wield such power. How can anyone put the fate of this world in your hands! They've sent you to your death. I will take your mind and use it for my own.' He lifted one hand, open and slightly cupped. 'I will take your power from you, suck it out, and then you will do my bidding. You will obey my every order, willingly, because you will know who is the true master.'

He put his hand on her head and continued his probing.

'Ahhhh, no!' Niome cried in pain and fear.

As Niome screamed in agony, Mirauk's face became sterner. He clenched his teeth and scowled in concentration. Then he suddenly let go and stepped back.

'What's this? Treason! A Morkan really a Telorian?' Mirauk seethed, letting out a guttural breath. 'Oh, and

I was this close to elevating him to a most honoured rank.'

Niome gathered herself and drew her sword.

'Oh, no – you aren't going to have the time to fight me with that!' declared Mirauk. He threw a spell from his open palm at Niome without speaking any words. A flick of blinding light flew towards Niome's chest.

Niome lifted her hand reflexively and cried out words she did not even know she could pronounce. The bolt of light vanished into oblivion with a pop. Niome could not explain how she had done that. She was trembling violently. She kept her hand out in a blocking position, her sword in her other hand.

Gradually Niome became aware that the trembling feeling came from within her. It was a different kind of trembling, not physical but metaphysical, and she felt it grow. It was her own magic within her fighting back.

Niome looked deeply into Mirauk's eyes. The worst was over. She had suffered something inexplicable, and she was no longer afraid of looking into his soul to see the evil that threatened the entire world. Her jaw hardened as she concentrated. They glared at each other for a long moment. Mirauk tried to probe her mind once more, yet Niome instinctively blocked him.

Niome lifted her sword and took a deep breath, squaring her shoulders.

Suddenly Mirauk's gaze lost its harshness; she saw worry in his eyes. He staggered back. 'You don't believe you are *stronger* than I am?' he asked, now understanding what Niome meant.

She smirked, resolute. 'I believe it.'

* * *

The door that Tharguen and Bahvley had been struggling to breach suddenly opened on its own. They didn't stop to wonder why, they simply ran out. Niome rushed out of the larger room.

'Run as fast as you can, while you still can,' Mirauk bellowed, 'because I can assure you, you won't get very far! Not you, Niome Fairhaven, nor you, Bahvley Fairhaven!'

Niome joined the other two, who did not look back to chance a glance at Mirauk, though Bahvley's face paled when he heard the evil lord mention his name. He knew what it meant, and so did Tharguen – especially Tharguen. He knew what Mirauk had done to Niome to find out that Bahvley was here. The look on Niome's face revealed that she had just spent all her energy and that she had seen the evil and rage in Mirauk's glare.

Meysah and Jimmy heard the thumping of running footsteps just before the door opened. They cautiously stepped out and saw the other three.

'Run!' cried Bahvley. 'And don't look back!'

They all raced to the secret passageway. When they met up with Vigh and Boreth, Tharguen yelled, 'Niome's got the book! But I believe Mirauk looked her in the eyes, and now he's pursuing us!'

They dashed down the stairs, almost tripping and stumbling. Niome yelped when she fell and rolled down a couple of steps.

'I feel it again! The pounding!' she screamed.

'Why did you have to look at him?' Tharguen mewled, desperation in his voice. He tenderly picked her up and carried her in his arms, holding her tightly. She wrapped her arms around his neck.

'I felt it before too,' she murmured, 'but I felt relaxed when I was looking at him.'

Tharguen blinked back tears. He knew that Niome would soon die. He couldn't quell the feeling that he had failed her in some way, even though he had been unable to influence what occurred in Mirauk's private study.

When they ran out of the tower, the Dalvarans were waiting for them with horses.

'Go! Quickly – ride! We shall hold them off,' assured Rimid. 'We shall hold Mirauk off. Farewell!'

The Telorians mounted the Morkan horses, Tharguen with Niome in front of him as he took the reins.

'After them! They are Telorian trespassers!' Mirauk's voice boomed out behind them, and they heard the hiss of many swords leaving their scabbards.

With a last wave at Rimid, and an internal prayer for him and his fellow Dalvarans, the Telorians kicked the horses into a gallop and rode off.

It took them half the night to reach the gates, where once again Tharguen spoke to the Guard Captain, claiming they were on a mission to intercept and fight Dalvarans. After much silent worrying, they were let through.

By this time, Niome had recovered enough to ride her own horse, and the group looked like Morkans on an urgent mission.

The Guard Captain waved them all through.

The Telorians rode on for two more days before encountering a Morkan patrol. Word of their deception had now spread faster than they could ride, and the Morkans were waiting for them.

Chapter Fourteen:
Slipping Away

*A*ll of the Morkan soldiers were facing their way as the Telorians rode towards them. Tharguen took the lead. The Morkan Captain rode out to meet him.

'I have orders not to let anyone pass,' the Captain said.

'And I have orders to fight the Dalvarans,' Tharguen countered.

'Very well, but first I shall inspect your squad,' said the Morkan.

Some of the Telorians stirred, but Tharguen quickly gave them a warning glance. The Morkan studied each of them carefully. He walked his horse by Boreth and nodded, looked at Meysah a while longer than was comfortable, then nodded, and stopped in front of Niome, then nodded. He paused a long time before Bahvley, narrowing his eyes as if he recognised something about him. *That might explain why he spent so long studying Meysah,* Bahvley thought. *My brother quite resembles me from back when I first entered Mork.* The Morkan slowly rode by Jimmy and Vigh, nodding slowly. Then he turned and walked his horse past Niome again.

He rode up to Tharguen. 'All right, you may go.'

The Telorians began forward, but the Morkan Captain stopped them again, his expression doubtful. He walked his horse up to Niome again.

'You're quite a young lad,' he said. 'Who sent you with this squad?'

'Beshrig,' Niome answered in a low monotone.

'Uh-huh. May I?' the Morkan asked as he took hold of Niome's bag. She nodded. He opened it, peering inside, but didn't touch anything. He closed the bag. 'You're quite equipped!' he remarked, tapping her chest with his hand.

Tharguen stirred uneasily, suspecting the Morkan knew something, and wanting to remove that Morkan's hands from Niome.

The Morkan Captain moved his hand and felt the outline of a book in Niome's pocket. 'What's this?' As he took the book out, he casually added, 'Did you know that Beshrig was killed by Telorians?' He looked at the book and his voice changed. 'I think you should hand me the other book as well, if you care for your life.'

'Never!' Niome defied, grabbing the *Book of Enchantment* and pushing it into her bag.

The Morkan drew his sword, yelling, 'Attack!'

Before he could do anything else, Tharguen was behind him, pulling him away from Niome. Once she was safe, he stabbed the Morkan in the chest.

The rest of the Telorians took their weapons out. Boreth fired arrow after arrow into the Morkan ranks, but they were outnumbered. The Morkan archers shot the Telorians' horses from under them and the Morkan soldiers advanced towards them.

To the Morkans' surprise, twenty-six Kikies appeared before them, popping in and out of sight, which confused the Morkans even more.

Phynd sliced a Morkan down, relieved as he witnessed his and his comrades' skills. After decades of training, the Kikies were finally engaged in a real fight, and the rush of adrenaline quelled any fear that had arisen since stepping foot into Mork.

Niome took out her Dragon's Wind and aimed it at the Morkans, blowing them back a fair distance, which allowed Boreth and Jimmy, and many of the Kikies, to shoot arrows at the approaching Morkans. Other Kikies moved among the Morkans, gathering arrows and disappearing with them to bring them quickly to their friends. Soon the Telorians and Kikies had retreated as far as a copse of trees where they could take cover.

'We're going to have to run north and travel along the mountains,' Tharguen told Bahvley. 'If there's one thing fifty years in Mork have taught me, it's that Morkans are petrified of dragons. They won't go anywhere near them. They may eventually follow us, but it'll slow them down and stall them for a while.'

'I take it we have better chances of reaching the Portal in one piece by taking that route, then' Bahvley surmised. 'Personally, I'd rather be attacked by a dragon than by Morkans. I'll tell Phynd.'

Jimmy, Boreth and a few Kikies continued shooting arrows, while other Kikies were fighting the Morkans or protecting the Telorians.

One Kiki approached Niome. 'I'm Celor. I have been assigned to be your escort. We shall be the first to leave.'

'What do you mean?' objected Niome. 'I don't want to leave the others behind. We mustn't be separated!'

'Don't worry,' Celor reassured. 'Each of you has an escort. You're just the first to be escorted because you're the most important and, with all the commotion, the Morkans are more likely not to notice your absence if we leave first.'

'Oh.'

Celor took Niome's hand, and the pair ran so fast, it almost seemed they were flying – or maybe they were. Perhaps Celor had shrunken her, too, Niome mused. They had obviously travelled a great distance quickly, for when Niome looked back, she could only see specks moving chaotically in the distance.

When Morkan archers began shooting at their location, Meysah grew concerned for Jimmy. 'Please take shelter!' he cried, pressing his back against a tree and peeking out from behind it.

'I have to keep shooting,' insisted Jimmy.

'No, you don't! There are many Kiki archers; they'll take care of that. Come, Bahvley says that you are to be escorted next anyway.'

'Escorted where?'

'Far away. It's like flying with the Kikies, except it's their secret and they won't tell me all the details of how it's possible to get so far so fast without being seen. Come.'

'Okay.' Jimmy retreated.

'Look out!' cried Meysah as an arrow flew towards Jimmy. Meysah pounced on his friend, bringing him to the ground and taking the arrow meant for Jimmy in his ankle. 'Argh! Not again,' shouted Meysah as Jimmy got to his feet.

'What is it?' Jimmy asked anxiously, then he saw the arrow. 'Oh no.'

'The same leg as last time!' complained Meysah.

Jimmy knelt. 'This is going to hurt.' Meysah gritted his teeth and nodded. Jimmy broke the arrow shaft off so it wouldn't snag and cause Meysah more pain. Even so, Meysah cried out as the shaft snapped off.

'You two are next,' a Kiki announced. Another Kiki stood next to him. They took the lads' hands and dashed away to join Niome and Celor.

Boreth kept shooting arrows. The Kiki next to him looked back at the others behind the trees. 'It will soon be our turn to go,' the Kiki informed him.

'Our turn to go?' inquired Boreth.

'Yes, I will escort you. Don't worry, it's quite safe. Fast travel is the safest.'

'Oh, I'm not worried,' said Boreth. 'And I am very grateful that you are helping. It's only a shame that I haven't had the chance to become better acquainted with your people. It seems we've spent more than enough time together to get to know each other, yet I know so little.'

'I know what you mean, but when we are in our shrunken size, it is difficult to chit-chat with others, let alone in mid-battle,' noted the Kiki.

'I understand,' said Boreth.

'My name is General Tithil, one of three leaders of this group of Kiki explorers. Celor and Phynd are my superiors.'

'Very nice to meet you, Tithil. My name is Boreth, master duellist and Knight of Teloria.'

'Come, it's time to go.' Tithil took hold of Boreth and off they went.

'You may be interested to know that we Kikies have a special ability that allows us to regenerate,' Tithil said as they ran. 'When we are wounded, we heal within moments. However, if we are badly wounded, we lose our ability to shrink. That is why so many of us are archers – ranged combat means there is less risk of that happening. And believe me, to have something that great taken away is like having a vital piece of my being stripped away. I have fought in close combat before, but because we have not encountered many hostile people in our history, we are not accustomed to such battles; only those with the quickest reflexes survive such battles. That is why we trained for many years before we were ready to embark on Bahvley's journey.'

'I completely understand. It would be comparable to me losing my ability to use my sword. I could teach you how to duel when we get back to Teloria. In fact, I would be delighted to teach you.'

'That would be greatly appreciated,' smiled Tithil.

They joined the others. 'Hello, brother,' said Tithil to one of the Kikies who was tending Meysah's wound. He looked very much like Tithil.

'Not too much trouble in departing from the battle, I hope?' Tithil's lookalike inquired.

'We've had a very successful escape; no one noticed,' replied Tithil. 'This is my twin brother, Forthil,' he told the Telorians.

Vigh and Mië arrived, followed by Tharguen and another Kiki. Then, many other Kikies arrived.

'What are we to do now?' asked Meysah.

'We are to wait for our captains to arrive,' said Celor. 'Then we shall be on our way.'

'What about the other Kikies?' asked Jimmy.

'They will meet us later,' replied Celor. 'Don't worry, Bahvley trained us well.' He chuckled in Kiki fashion.

'Why not now?' asked Meysah.

'If everyone came now,' explained Mië, 'the Morkans would discover our little secret. They will be fine; they'll join us when they feel the time is right.'

'Your mind is full of questions,' said Tithil. 'Ah, I understand. Like Celor said, don't worry about it.'

Meysah fidgeted. 'I don't like it when people read my mind,' he muttered to Jimmy.

'This is the first time that—'

'Well, anyhow, it makes me feel uncomfortable.'

'They don't constantly—' continued Jimmy.

'Still, I don't like it.'

'You know, it's their way,' said Jimmy, speaking very fast so he wouldn't be cut off. 'They said they'd train to do it less, but it's their second nature. And I don't like it when people—'

'Well, I'm not the only one who cuts you off like that. You cut me off too.'

'Can you read my mind?'

'Huh?'

'By the way that you . . . it's as though . . .'

'No, my dear friend,' sighed Meysah, smiling mildly. 'I just know you far too well.'

'I guess that's what taking a trip together does,' said Vigh, who had been eavesdropping on their exchange. He laughed. 'I know all about it, for I have been on many trips with Boreth. We always know what the other is thinking. Most of the time.'

Bahvley and Phynd joined them. 'It is time to go,' said Phynd, as Bahvley took a moment to get his bearings following the fast-fly. Dawn had passed, though the group hardly noticed, for the sky was so dark.

They travelled for two days, stopping only for brief rests and food. The remaining Kikies had joined them by this time.

'It's Half Year's Day today,' noted Vigh.

'How do you know this?' asked Niome, who seemed abnormally out of breath. 'We have not seen the sun or moon in days.'

'I have been keeping count in my notebook, and today is the first day of Summer,' replied Vigh.

'Some Summer's day!' muttered Jimmy, looking at the overcast sky.

'That means we only have one season left,' noted Boreth. 'Ninety-two days before the dragons start back into their homes, perhaps less.'

'Let's hope we won't meet too many obstacles there,' said Phynd. 'During our travels, we saw that the dragons fly as much in the Colama Valley as in this one.'

'We will meet several,' said Niome. 'I sense that this will not be an easy road.'

'More Morkan patrols!' exclaimed Bahvley, feigning enthusiasm.

'I don't think so,' said Tharguen. 'Morkans don't patrol that area.'

'Not Morkans,' said Niome, 'but magic.'

'Regardless, we must press on,' said Bahvley, 'and prepare ourselves for anything.'

They travelled for perhaps a week with little incident. Just when they thought the sky would clear, dark clouds rolled across it. They weren't many days away from Darakön, but they would still have to travel past the Dakodol River and onwards to the entrance of the cave that gave access to the Portal.

Furthermore, they had to ensure Morkans could not follow their trail as they walked along the edge of Darakön as it zigzagged north and south and up and down. To walk in a straight line would shorten the trip, but it would make it much more dangerous.

What had begun as a small excursion to the Great Rock to find out what lay hidden there had become so much more. They needed to reach the dragons, and they knew Niome was the only one strong enough to go through the Portal. But what now weighed on everyone's mind was that before she'd had the chance to walk into the other realm, she had been forced to confront Mirauk and look into his eyes.

A heavy rain started to fall. Soon the water was ankle deep. It poured a long time and yet the clouds never seemed to be empty of rain. The wind picked up and blew violently. Niome developed a fever. She was already weak, perhaps weaker than she showed, and she was falling every so often during the storm. Her mind had weakened to the point that she could not think clearly. She seemed to be getting sicker and sicker. The Telorians wondered if she would ever make it home, let alone to the Portal.

After two days of hurricane-like weather, they implored Niome to cast a counterspell while she still could. Niome's previous attempts had resulted in no change, so she had opted to conserve her energy. The rain was so dense they could hardly see each other. They were drenched and tired. It was so dark that even the light-cube could not lift the gloom, and the water had risen farther. If it rose too high, they feared they might drown or be swept away by some new current.

'Mirauk is trying to show he is stronger than you,' Tharguen told Niome. 'That is why you must prove him wrong.'

'I suppose I *could* try another spell,' Niome conceded. She stood and spoke loudly.

Laila ëaia satiri pasfolod, pehlëimi! Evales ëimi!
  Evileg suila ethelt thaginest oteg üirath siëth!

Nothing happened.

'Why won't it work?' cried Niome. She grimaced in pain and staggered, holding one hand on her head, the other pressed over her heart. She began to moan. 'I can't take this anymore!'

Tharguen stepped up and steadied her. 'You must hold on,' he pleaded. 'Take more herbs. We're almost at the foot of the mountain.'

'How do you know?' asked Vigh. 'We cannot see a thing!'

'There are trees here,' Tharguen pointed out. 'There is a small forest around the base of the mountain. We are but a few days away.'

'Surely it will take us longer,' said Tithil, panting. 'We are walking against the wind.'

'Just remember this is not real wind,' said Tharguen, turning to the group. 'Perhaps if we put our minds to it, it will cease.'

As if in protest, a great gust of wind buffeted them so hard that the Telorians fell to the ground and some of the Kikies had to hold onto the trees to avoid being blown away with the wind. The wind swirled up like a tornado and then came back down, and died away. Everyone climbed to their feet and made sure everyone else was okay.

'At least that dispersed the water at our feet,' said Jimmy, looking at the ground. 'I think it kind of helped.'

'Where's Niome?' cried Meysah. Everyone looked at each other, dread in their eyes. They searched everywhere in the immediate vicinity. 'Maybe she was carried back to Mork.'

'Nonsense,' objected Bahvley. 'Niome is strong. I'm sure she's here somewhere.' He swallowed hard.

Another search did not find her.

Bahvley let out a shaking breath. 'What has Mirauk done to my sister?'

Tharguen took out a knife and stuck it in a tree. 'We split up and search in several directions. This tree is our starting point. We meet back here. We're not going to find her by standing around.'

Jimmy and Meysah and their Kiki guardians went north; Boreth and Vigh with Tithil, Celor, and several other Kikies went south. Bahvley and Phynd and more Kikies went west, and Tharguen and the others searched east. The remaining Kikies stayed at the tree.

They searched carefully for the better part of the day. Tharguen felt something in the tall grass with his foot. He crouched down and found Niome. His stomach lurched. She was unconscious, lying on her stomach.

'Niome!' he cried.

He rolled her over and lifted her head to wipe the dirt off her face. Her brow was damp and hot with fever.

'Oh, why did you have to look?' he sighed in grief. 'Why did you have to look into Mirauk's eyes!' He took her in his arms and whispered in her ear, 'Stay with me. Please don't die. We need you.' He heaved. '*I* need you.' He kissed her brow, willing the Mighty Spirit to keep Niome alive. He turned to the Kikies. 'I need blankets.'

The Kikies produced blankets from their satchels and Tharguen wrapped Niome in them. The blankets, though they were damp, had mostly been protected from the rain by the leather satchels. They would help.

Niome coughed. 'Niome, hold on,' Tharguen whispered to her. He looked at her a long time. 'I love you.' He closed his eyes and a tear ran down his face. He caressed her cheek, brushing her hair away from her face. With an arm beneath her knees, Tharguen stood and carried Niome to the designated tree.

Vigh and Boreth had already returned when Tharguen arrived. 'Oh, my!' gasped Vigh. He took out some herbs and fed them to Niome, who was still in Tharguen's arms.

'She won't last much longer if that rain doesn't stop,' quavered Tharguen.

'She has exceptional strength,' said Boreth. 'Usually.'

'Do you think this is a test?' Vigh asked gravely.

'A test! Mirauk is testing Niome?' Tharguen gently placed Niome on the ground.

'If it is,' began Tithil, 'then I'm afraid each of you Five of the Star may get one.'

'Why do you say that?' asked Boreth.

'Tithil is one of our wisest loremasters,' said Celor. 'He foresees many unexplainable things. I bid you to consider the possibility.'

'My brother is seldom wrong,' added Forthil. 'And if this is a test, then there is hope yet.'

'But it can't be,' insisted Vigh. 'Mirauk knows nothing of us. He doesn't know about the star that the Firlanians created in our honour. He doesn't know who the Five are.'

'Doesn't he?' asked Tithil.

'I agree with Tithil,' said Tharguen. 'If Niome looked at Mirauk, he saw her soul. He has abilities none of you can even begin to imagine. We don't know what he put her through. She would not discuss it, but I am ready to bet my life on it – he read her mind. And believe me, he knows more than we will ever think he does.'

'If this is correct—' began Boreth.

'Oh, I promise you, it is,' declared Tharguen.

'Well, in any case, we may face perils more dangerous than this.'

'And then again,' said Celor, 'if this is a test, as Forthil said, Niome will recover shortly.'

'In the meantime,' said another Kiki, 'we should take very good care of her. We should carry her and keep her warm. As a healer, I know we cannot do much, but this will help.'

'Thank you . . . ' began Vigh.

'Dessimë.'

'Dessimë,' Vigh nodded, feeling great concern, 'are you certain there is nothing else we can do to help her condition?'

Dessimë shook her head. 'Just continue on,' she replied. 'We must keep going no matter what. Especially if you are all to face a test.'

'How will they know if it's their turn to be tested?' asked Tharguen.

'This is not something anyone knows,' replied Tithil. 'A test will arise at any time – before, during, or even after a mission has been completed. A polc or Kiki may get one and think if they took the other way they would not have been tested, but no matter which path you choose, the test will be there. It is inevitable.'

'Well, we can't really go anywhere right now,' said Boreth, 'if the others are not here. I hope they haven't gotten lost.'

'Well, I know *I'm* safe,' said Bahvley, coming up to the tree. When he saw Niome, he put his hand on her forehead. 'Hold on, little sister. You always wanted to prove to Mirauk that he wasn't the most powerful. Well, now's your chance. Prove to him that you are stronger yet. I know you are. I always have. Don't slip away.'

There was sadness in Bahvley's voice, but he straightened and said, 'We're all in this together now. We're going to help Niome save the world. We're doing this for Teloria, for our loved ones, and—'

'For the Freedom of Life!'

Everyone turned around and saw Meysah, Jimmy and others standing a few feet from them. 'Let us fight for the Freedom of Life,' Meysah repeated softly yet confidently, echoing what Bahvley had declared fifty years ago.

The two brothers looked upon each other now with a different understanding and affinity. They stared into each other's eyes as the rain soaked their hair and trickled down their cheeks, and it seemed the two mirrored one another in both appearance and intent. Their heartfelt intentions were expressed in that one phrase, and Bahvley knew his younger brother had heard his story and that he had followed Niome because Bahvley had gone that way a long time ago. Bahvley was proud of his brother. And Meysah knew that Bahvley knew, and *he* felt proud. It was almost as though they could read each other's minds. They had been apart for fifty years, but in this moment, they saw that their relationship remained unchanged.

'Come then, brother,' said Bahvley, tears mixing with the rain on his face. 'Let's fight side by side, as partners, for the Freedom of Life.'

Meysah smiled. 'As partners,' he repeated softly, and the two brothers embraced.

The rain continued to fall. The Kikies lifted Niome and lay her on their shoulders as if they were a bed. Tharguen walked beside Niome.

The company walked for five days in the rain and wind, even though they were far from Mork now, with only the magic of the Kikies to sustain them and prevent them from falling ill. Jimmy yearned to see the blue Summer sky dotted with puffy white clouds.

On the fourth day, they reached Darakön, and were now walking along the base of the mountain.

No amount of hoping or praying helped Niome, for every day she seemed to slip a little farther into the spirit land. Tharguen prayed to his father's spirit, for his father had been one of the wizards of Tassar. Vigh kept giving Niome herbs, but he couldn't tell if they made any difference at all. Meysah constantly held the smooth stone that Gorthan had given Vigh, who had passed it on to him.

Bahvley consoled his brother. He only wished he could have spent more valuable time with his sister. Had he not been gone all this time, he thought, things could have been different. He felt he had failed in Mork, despite Elina's insistence back then that all that would occur was written in the stars and dictated by the dragons. Still, Bahvley could not shake the feeling that had he been there to care for his younger siblings, perhaps Niome would have a stronger hold on this world, and more of a reason to fight off any curse. But she was not as powerful as Elina had been when Elina had looked upon Mirauk's evil visage and fought off the illness for fifty years. Bahvley tried not to let his worry show – doing so would not help anyone.

Boreth, on the other hand, had hope yet, and insisted they press on. However, on the sixth day, they could no longer keep pace as they had been. They needed rest and food.

The Kikies gently placed Niome on the ground and Tharguen crouched down beside her. 'She's slipping away,' he sorrowed, his voice shaking. There was still so much he wanted to say, so much that had not been said when he had the chance. 'What can we possibly do?'

'She stopped coughing,' Boreth noticed.

Tharguen looked at Niome and saw that her mouth was shut and her chest no longer rising and falling. He placed his hand under her nose.

'No!' he gasped. 'She has stopped breathing!' Tears began to pour from Tharguen's eyes. 'She's dying,' he sobbed.

Everyone gathered around. Meysah looked at Dessimë as if to get answers.

'There's nothing left to do,' she said.

The Telorians knelt beside Niome and bowed their heads, the rain mingling with their tears.

Chapter Fifteen:
The Prophecy Comes True

*I*t felt like an eternity had gone by before Jimmy noticed that the rain had stopped. He cast off his wet hood and looked up into the sky. The clouds, now lighter in colour, parted and let the sunshine through. A sunbeam lit up Niome's face for a few moments and then the clouds were gone and the sun shone so brightly that everyone had to squint.

A cough drew everyone's attention back to Niome, who slowly opened her eyes and sat up.

'You're awake!' exclaimed Tharguen.

'You're alive!' exclaimed Meysah.

'Of course I am,' said Niome, as though they were merely stating the obvious. 'I guess I passed out when I hit my head.'

'You hit your head?' gasped Vigh. 'Where?'

'It doesn't hurt,' replied Niome. She brushed some dirt off her sleeves as she spoke. 'It gave me a strange dream, though. And at the end of my dream,

I saw Elina. She spoke to me and gave me a lot of information that will help us a great deal.' She paused, noticing that everyone had tears in their eyes. 'Why is everyone crying?'

'Heh, you scared us so much,' wept Tharguen.

Niome inclined her head to the side. 'I don't understand.'

'You were unconscious for many days, Niome, and every day you got worse and worse,' explained Bahvley. 'We thought you were going to die.'

'That's a scary thought,' Niome said, feeling un-easy. 'I'm happy I didn't. I'm not ready to die.'

'I sure hope not,' Boreth said with a tearful chuckle.

'Tithil believes this was a test set upon you by Mirauk,' said Vigh. 'And I must say, you sure proved your power. We all thought you were dying because of Mirauk's curse. But it looks like there was no curse.'

'Elina told me that I *was* cursed, but in my dream, I broke the curse. I don't know how I did that, but Elina told me that I should be able to use my magic without losing energy now. I don't know what that means. Normally that comes with training, but . . . She also said that somehow, I cured my anxiety and I won't feel the pounding anymore. She mentioned that when Mirauk connected his mind to mine—'

'So he did torture you,' Tharguen disdained, reflexively placing his hand on Niome's. 'He read your mind.'

'Yes. It was strangely painful. He threw spells at me, but Elina told me that by doing that, he opened a connection between us that may eventually allow me to acquire certain powers that he has. She told me a lot of other things. Before she left, she told me something very odd. She said, "The strong have become the weak." But I don't feel weak.'

A wide smile slowly spread across Vigh's face. 'I don't think she meant that you became weak, Niome. If anything, you've grown much stronger. I can see it in your face; it is different.'

'I think she meant Mirauk has grown weak,' Boreth agreed.

'I'm with Vigh and Boreth,' said Meysah. 'The proof is that Mirauk did not seek you out, you faced *him.*'

Niome looked around at the mountains. 'Wow, I *was* out a long time.'

'The prophecy books said that the One would look into Mirauk's eyes and make him quiver,' said Bahvley. 'And that the One would grow very strong. All my life I have hoped for this One to come soon. Now my wish has come true. Niome, you are the One.'

'Am I? I guess what the Firlanians told me is true, then. I believe that we are the Five.' Niome rose. 'I do feel different.' She looked around at the others, at herself. 'I am!' She smiled. 'I am the One; we are the Five! That's how I survived, that's what Elina meant. I don't feel afraid anymore. I feel . . .' She breathed in deeply, feeling a new sense of purpose, and smiled.

That night, for the first time in a long time, the company made camp and sat down to rest. They made a large fire and ate what little food they had with such relish that it felt like a feast. Afterwards everyone went to sleep under the stars, caressed by a warm breeze.

Niome woke up in the middle of the night and took a stroll a little way up the mountain, settling on its steep incline to look at the sky. She felt refreshed.

A short while later, Tharguen arrived. 'You couldn't sleep?' she asked as he sat down very close to her.

'I wasn't sleeping,' he admitted. 'I was watching . . . I was keeping watch.' He looked up at the sky.

'It's a nice night,' voiced Niome.

'Yes, and it's thanks to you,' replied Tharguen, dropping his gaze to her face. 'You brought the weather back to normal. You brought the sunshine back.'

'I never realised how magical I was,' Niome admitted. 'At least not to that extent. It's quite the interesting feeling. One day I'm just a young student arguing with Gorthan about a journey of a few weeks, and the next thing I know, I'm walking out of Mork one hundred and six days later, the most powerful wizardess of all.' She breathed a short laugh. 'That's something.'

'You have a very special gift,' said Tharguen.

'I'm still a little unsure of myself. I don't quite know how to go about life now.'

Tharguen laughed. 'The same way you always have. In time you will learn to control and effectively use your power. I'm not the expert on that matter,' he sobered, his gaze growing intense, 'but you always knew how to enchant someone.'

'Well, I'm very grateful for my natural abilities and for everything that's happened to me. I'm very grateful you're here ... to protect me.' They both smiled.

'You know, I was really frightened before,' began Tharguen. He looked at the ground. 'I never doubted your strength, but when you'd almost completely slipped away, I got so scared. I don't know what I'd have done, had you not survived. It was like I was losing a piece of myself.' Tharguen looked at Niome. 'My life stopped then and there, and panic and melancholy invaded my heart, for I thought I was losing you. And that must be the worst thing in the world, to lose the one person you love most.'

Niome's expression changed as she looked into Tharguen's eyes and saw that familiar longing she so often noticed when he looked at her. As Tharguen leaned in a little, Niome's breath hitched and her stomach fluttered. She tilted her head towards him and their lips met in a warm kiss, both fiercely leaning into the other as the tug in their hearts turned to relief.

Tharguen put his hands on her cheeks and then held her tightly in his arms. The two spent the rest of the night kissing greedily as though making up for lost time and lying in each other's arms, looking up at the stars.

Meysah was the first to waken, feeling bright and refreshed. He stretched mightily and yawned in satisfaction, as though he were sleeping in his own cosy bed instead of a blanket on the grass. He felt so relieved and safe now, even though he was far away from home. Noticing that Niome and Tharguen were absent, he looked around and then up, and saw them lying together on the mountain bend.

'Finally!' he sighed.

The others gradually awoke and got up. By then, Niome and Tharguen had returned. Meysah just couldn't keep himself from teasing them a little.

'Well, you sure look rested,' he cheekily teased Niome. 'Did you sleep well?'

'Yes, I did,' she replied.

'Uh-huh, I'm sure you did.' Meysah laughed. Then he lifted an eyebrow at Tharguen and wandered away.

'Is he feeling all right?' Tharguen asked Niome, watching Meysah as the polc sauntered over to Bahvley.

'It's Meysah,' laughed Niome, nodding. 'He's always like that.' Smiling, she went to join her brothers.

Bahvley beamed at Tharguen, and Tharguen felt his cheeks flush. The polc walked over to him with a knowing expression.

'It was about time,' said Bahvley. Tharguen chuckled shyly. 'I mean it, Tharguen. I'm happy you and my sister have finally declared your love for each other.'

'You and me both,' admitted Tharguen.

'I bet.' They both laughed.

'Bahvley,' Tharguen sobered, 'it means a lot to me that you're happy about me and Niome.'

'Of course! You're like a brother to me, Tharguen. Your happiness is important to me. For all the times I've teased you in the past, it's nice to see the two of you together. Really.'

Tharguen smiled. 'Thank you.' Bahvley clapped him on the back.

The Kikies set up breakfast. Though it was customary for the Kikies to be helpful, the Telorians felt like they were being unduly pampered.

'Well, you are such special Telorians, we feel you deserve to be treated like royalty,' said Phynd. He winked at Bahvley, who chuckled. 'I have spent many days with the Kiki King in his abode, and his hospitality was always comforting and pleasant.' He glanced at Celor and smiled knowingly, as though sharing a telepathic joke of some sort. Still smiling, Phynd turned back to Niome.

'Perhaps we will become royalty,' stated Niome. 'If all prophecies come true,' she added, glancing at her older brother. He shrugged.

'And how would *you* know?' Jimmy demanded in a teasing tone. 'It's one thing to dream and hope the prophecies come true; it's another to *see* into the future. But if you ask me, it has a very nice ring to it: Jimmesh Hochka, Royal Knight.' They all laughed.

They finished breakfast while fantasising about their royal futures, reiterating to the Kikies that there had not been a ruler in Teloria in millennia. The Kikies then explained how in their society, they had a leader who willingly made difficult decisions and sacrifices for the good of the people with the counsel of many wise Kikies by their side.

'Though we are a free people and our rulers don't exactly rule per se,' said Phynd. 'We all work together as equals in our community, even though our King is very well served. He can even live his life as a commoner, only making decisions on behalf of his people every now and then. What determines who becomes a leader, the Kiki who guides our people, is their power in magic and telepathy.'

After breakfast, as they were packing up, Boreth approached Vigh. 'Niome's strength has returned quickly and she seems stronger than ever.'

'Yes, of course,' agreed Vigh.

'You truly believe she's the One?' asked Boreth.

'Yes, don't you?'

'Oh, yes! At least I hope she is. It's just, I worry that we might be jumping to conclusions. And we don't know if she's completely cured from the curse. The prophecy books also speak of—'

'Yes, I know,' said Vigh.

'Until all has come true, we cannot say for sure.'

'I know,' replied Vigh. 'And we mustn't expect too much of her at this time. Let's not worry about that, though, eh – her role, our role. Time is all we need now. Let's wait and see if what is prophesied will come to be.'

They joined the others. 'I hope everyone is well rested,' said Vigh. 'We have many long days ahead of us.'

They set off. At midday they had to pack away their cloaks, for it was that hot. That night was also very warm. They only rested a short while, for they didn't want to risk the Morkans catching up to them.

The next day was another hot day – the Telorians loved the weather. However, the Kikies, who came from a country with seasons varying from hot and humid to cool and breezy, were not used to such dry heat.

'We can no longer continue like this,' sighed Mië.

Tithil agreed. 'I feel like I'm going to melt.'

'Or burn to a crisp,' added Forthil.

Phynd explained. 'Our magic has difficulty in such weather.'

'But there isn't anything we can do about it,' Niome argued, worry in her tone.

'Of course not,' said Phynd. 'But we can shrink. We will all need to be put in our magical jar together and kept in the shade.'

'I have extra room in my bag,' suggested Jimmy, 'but you're still going to cook.'

'Oh, no.' Phynd laughed. 'We brought a *special* magical glass jar from home. Our jars are per-manently cool, unless put in the sun for too long. In a dark bag, even a hot bag, we shall stay cool. We created such jars especially for this trip, knowing we would be travelling outdoors for long days such as this one. Bahvley knows about it.' Bahvley nodded. 'However, if you need our help, just let us know.'

'No problem!' said Niome.

'Excellent.'

'Will you not get hungry, or thirsty?' asked Jimmy, sounding a little unsure.

The Kiki chuckled. 'Oh, how there is so much to teach polcs about Kikies. Thnn-thnn!'

Phynd took a large, sparkling glass jar from his pack and opened it. He handed it to Jimmy, who held it as all of the Kikies shrank and flew into it – it was remarkably light in weight. Jimmy stoppered the jar and placed it in his bag.

'Well, I hope they'll be comfortable,' he said.

Two weeks passed without incident. The mountain track had become rougher and the Telorians had to watch out for falling rocks.

'I hope no Morkans have followed our trail,' said Meysah, looking back at the path behind them.

'If they have, what are we to do?' asked Jimmy.

'Why the sudden worry?' Boreth queried.

'I don't know,' replied Jimmy.

'It's because they *have* been following us,' said Niome. 'They're very far behind, but they're there. Even so, I sense that there are dragons nearby, and the dragons will take care of things. I'm sure of it.'

'How would you know?' asked Meysah.

'Well, I *don't* know,' Niome admitted. 'It's just logical reasoning. Dragons don't like Morkans and they seem to have been helping us so far.'

'Don't question her abilities,' whispered Vigh. 'Same as you don't question your instincts or inspiration. Never ask why.' Meysah nodded.

Niome looked up into the sky as a roar reverberated from the mountains around them. A dragon flew overhead, wings beating rapidly. It landed farther down the mountain from them and walked ponderously along the trail.

Meysah gaped at it and then at Niome, then looked back at the dragon. 'I-I-I don't understand.'

'It's simple,' said Jimmy. 'As Niome said, the dragon is blocking the path against the Morkans.'

'There must be more to it than that,' remarked Meysah.

'It's basic reasoning,' said Jimmy.

Meysah still stood staring. The others had continued up the path and Meysah and Jimmy were the last in line.

'Come on!' Jimmy grabbed Meysah's arm and dragged him along as they trotted to catch up to the others.

Then Jimmy suddenly stopped, eyes wide, as he realised something. He quickly opened his bag and took out the Kiki jar and opened it. One of them flew out and grew into his normal size – it was Phynd.

'What is it?' the Kiki asked.

'I might have forgotten to give you an update last week,' blurted Jimmy. 'Sorry.'

'Oh, that's all right,' chuckled Phynd. 'Time passes differently for us when in the jar. We thought only a few days had gone by. Do not worry about it.'

'Jimmy!' Meysah called out. 'Are you coming?'

'Yes!' Jimmy sighed with a chuckle. He and Phynd started walking. 'Well, two weeks have passed,' he told the Kiki, 'and not much has happened. A dragon just passed overhead and landed down on the trail behind us.'

'Is that all?' inquired Phynd.

'I believe so,' replied Jimmy.

'All right. I shall see you in a while.' Phynd shrank and flew back into the jar.

These are complicated beings, Jimmy thought as he replaced the lid and put the jar back in his bag.

The team navigated the rocky path, sometimes having to wait as rolling pebbles became a tumbling cascade of rocks. Other times, they deviated from the path to avoid boulders. Ten more days passed this way until they came to a fork in the trail.

'We have to decide which way is best for our safety,' said Vigh. 'To our right we have the plain. It may take us too close to the Morkan caves or the Morkans themselves. On the other hand, it brings us closer to the Dalvarans. Straight ahead, the path climbs steeply. We would stay close to the mountain, safe and away from Morkans, but in danger from falling rocks with nowhere to shelter from them. Then again, that route keeps us watched over by the dragons. What do the rest of you prefer?'

'I certainly prefer the field,' said Meysah. 'I'd rather fight my way through than be crushed at the start.'

'Me too,' agreed Boreth.

'I prefer the path,' said Tharguen. 'No more Morkans for me, not for now at least.'

'I say tumbling rocks are far less dangerous than armies of Morkans,' expressed Jimmy.

'I just have a bad feeling about the mountain,' voiced Vigh. 'Something tells me awful things will come of it.'

'Far worse things may come from the Morkans,' noted Bahvley. 'Falling rocks are a little more predictable.'

There was a long pause.

'Niome,' said Vigh, 'so far it's tied. Your opinion will decide the road we take.'

'I choose not according to my personal opinion, but by what is best for us all,' Niome began. 'What must happen will happen, and we may have the power to change the outcome, but we cannot change the outcome of that which none of us know. It is not safe anywhere, but' – she looked at Vigh – 'some of us are due to learn some magical lessons, and avoiding them will not help any of us. Another opportunity for such a thing may arise again, but it might not be overcome so easily, and it might be even more dangerous than the initial trial. Thus, we will deal with whatever lies ahead of us on the mountain.'

Vigh walked to Niome as the others stared at the steep slope. 'I don't understand—'

'You will later.'

Niome started up the path. Vigh and the others followed, some more reluctantly than others.

So far they had been very lucky, but that night an earthquake struck. It began gently, like the rumble of thunder, and then the ground began to vibrate.

'You want to bet this is Mirauk's doing?' Meysah complained to Jimmy.

'No,' Jimmy replied bluntly. 'I know it is.'

Vigh stopped and turned to Niome. 'I knew something like this would happen!' he growled.

'So did I,' Niome replied just as heatedly, as she stood facing him. 'Look,' she calmed, 'somehow I know all that will happen tonight. But you must trust fate.'

'Trust fate, yes, but if you knew of this, then you could've changed it!'

'Changed it by jumping into far worse dangers? Or changed it by dealing with it and not letting it happen?'

Vigh hesitated for a beat, then blurted in sudden understanding, 'You can see into the future!'

'Now that I've told you that something will happen, *you* can change it – and only you.'

'How?' insisted Vigh. 'What will happen?'

'Look out!' shouted Tharguen.

A great boulder came crashing down as Tharguen and Bahvley leapt to grab Niome and Vigh. Many boulders followed with a roar and a rattle of pebble dust. Niome and Tharguen fell to the side, coughing. When the dust had settled, everyone was safe and unhurt, except for Vigh and Bahvley – they were nowhere in sight.

'Quick!' cried Meysah. 'We have to do something!' He ran to the pile of rocks and started kicking and pulling at them, trying to move them.

'There's nothing we can do, Meysah,' implored Niome. 'It's not up to us to—'

'But our brother is in there, or under there, and so is my master!' Panic rang in Meysah's voice as he vehemently struggled with the boulders. 'I'm not losing him again, Niome. I'm not losing Bahvley!'

'Meysah!' insisted Niome. 'This is something that they must go through. This is a test.'

'A test!?' cried Boreth.

'How unlucky this is!' mewled Tharguen.

'Luck has nothing to do with this,' said Niome. 'It almost never does.'

'I don't understand,' said Jimmy.

'Luck rarely interferes with the way things happen in life. It is a word we use too often and take too lightly, not knowing the true meaning of it,' explained Niome.

'And what is the true meaning of it?' Meysah seethed through his teeth. He stopped trying to get through the rocks. He sighed, defeated, leaning his head on the boulder.

'It is not explained but understood,' Niome replied calmly. 'In time you will understand, but you will never be able to explain it.'

'What shall we do, then?' asked Boreth.

'Nothing,' replied Niome. 'There's no point in worrying, so let's sit and wait and . . .' Niome sighed. Tharguen gently placed his hand on her shoulder.

'All right then,' said Boreth. 'You know best, so we shall wait.'

They waited most of the night. Some of them slept; others could not find rest.

'Maybe Vigh was right,' Niome worried. Only she and Boreth were awake. 'Maybe I could have changed the course of this event. Who knows how long they'll be in there.'

'You have a gift, Niome,' said Boreth. 'Do not doubt it. Often the initial impulse or feeling is the right one. You have received a new blessing. It is new to you. It is new to us all. In time you will learn to use it well.'

'You're right,' said Niome.

'I have also noticed that you are growing very wise.'

'I am not yet used to that, either,' Niome admitted.

'In due time,' assured Boreth. 'I now counsel you to rest. A wizardess needs her sleep. I shall keep the watch. Sleep, like all the others. You should clear your mind. Maybe meditate as you fall asleep.'

Niome nodded. Allowing herself to relax, she lay down next to Tharguen, who instinctively wrapped an arm around her, and fell asleep.

CHAPTER SIXTEEN:
Regrettable News

Vigh lifted himself off the ground in the pitch darkness. At first he thought it was night, but he noted there were no stars in the sky. He walked forward, hands out, and felt a wall. He walked along it, his hands tracing the rocks all around a small space.

He didn't know how long he had been unconscious. He also thought he was alone. He found his bag and pulled the light-cube out of it. It lit up the tiny area, confirming that it was surrounded on all sides by rocks.

Vigh saw Bahvley in a corner. The polc was lying on his back, one leg stuck under the rocks.

Vigh hurried to his side and tapped his face. 'Bahvley!'

Bahvley moaned, wincing. 'My leg is stuck,' he said faintly. He slowly opened his eyes.

'Let me help you sit up.' Taking hold of Bahvley's hand, Vigh placed his other hand under Bahvley's back. 'Come on.' He propped him up. Bahvley turned at the waist and leaned his back against the rock behind him. 'How are you feeling?'

'My head hurts like it's never hurt before,' replied Bahvley.

'What about your leg?' asked Vigh.

'It feels numb, but I don't think it's been crushed or broken . . . it doesn't hurt quite that much. It might be trapped in the space between two rocks and not directly under one. It's stuck at the ankle – that's where I feel a squeeze.'

'Well, at least you can feel it.'

Vigh wiped his forehead with his hand, thinking it was dripping with sweat, but he felt a gash above his brow and his hand came away covered in blood. Retrieving the Firlanian herbs, he took some for himself and gave some to Bahvley. Then he rose and started pushing and pulling on the rocks to try to move them. Nothing helped.

'Hey!' he yelled. 'Can anyone hear me?'

'I can,' Bahvley said matter-of-factly.

'Well, at least you're not dying.' Vigh exhaled a chuckle. 'You have the same sense of humour as Meysah.'

'That's normal. It runs in the family.'

'Niome is more serious.'

'Oh, that's just because she's preoccupied,' said Bahvley. 'Wait till we get home; you'll see the three of us joking around. We must have been quite a bunch as children. I don't know how our parents put up with us.'

'Home is so far from here, yet it feels like we've been out here for far less time than we actually have,' said Vigh.

'Normally it's the opposite,' remarked Bahvley. 'But I can't judge, I've been away from home longer. Teloria.' He sighed. 'We should get out of here before we suffocate.'

'Yes,' agreed Vigh. 'I don't think they can hear me on the other side. Before we get out, let me free your leg.'

'How?' asked Bahvley.

'I'll try to lift the rock for a brief moment so you can pull out. On three – one . . . two . . . three!' Vigh heaved and pushed, but the rocks did not budge. He only hurt his hands.

'It's not working,' sighed Bahvley.

'I have an idea,' said Vigh.

He took out his sword and his shield. He squeezed his sword in between the two rocks to create a small space, then he slipped the edge of his shield, face-down, into the gap.

'You're going to break your shield!' protested Bahvley.

'Oh, no, not this shield. This is a special Firlanian shield, made from the third layer of the bark of their trees, if I recall correctly. It doesn't break, nor does it get scratched or burned.'

Vigh pulled his sword out from under the rocks. 'I'm going to jump on my shield now,' he explained. 'If all goes well, it should lift the rock enough for you to get your foot out. You've got to be fast, though.' Bahvley smiled wanly and nodded. 'One. Two. Three.'

Vigh jumped on the opposite edge of his shield, the other side popped up, and Bahvley cried out in pain as he pulled out his leg.

He breathed deeply to ease the pain. 'Well,' he said, wincing, 'I'm still alive.'

Vigh chuckled. Rolling up the pant leg, he put herbs on the lacerations on Bahvley's ankle. Then he pulled his shield out from under the rocks.

'So it worked,' said Bahvley. 'Do you think you could get us out that way?'

'No,' replied Vigh. 'We would need a much bigger shield and more than just the two of us to lift and move a few of these rocks.'

Vigh sat down to think. He looked through his bag to see if there was anything he could possibly use and found the knife that the Firlanians had given him, the one they'd used on the Fence. He hefted it in his hand, then held it firmly. *If it cut through the Fence, could it cut through these rocks?* There was only one way to find out.

Gripping the knife tightly, he rose and stabbed it into one of the rocks. It went right in. He had to wriggle it out, but he was able to stab the rock again and again in different spots.

'What . . . *are* you doing, Vigh?' asked Bahvley.

'An experiment.'

Vigh kept repeating the sequence until a piece of the rock fell down at his feet. 'Now we're getting somewhere.' He grinned.

He studied the rocks for a good while. Then he felt the rocks in the top half of their rocky cave to find the thinnest point between a couple of them. He stabbed at those for a while. The two rocks moved closer together, falling upon each other ever so slightly. He figured if he did this long enough, their shifting would create an opening.

Vigh kept at it for a long time.

Finally a large rock from the top fell with a loud thud, leaving a large enough opening for Vigh and Bahvley to crawl through.

'You should go first, Your Prophesied Highness,' Vigh said, smiling, as he put all his things away.

'Stars! Am I glad you were befriended by the Firlanians,' smiled Bahvley. 'They gave you a lot of special and useful weapons!'

Vigh helped him stand. They looked up at the sky. The vibrant oranges and pinks of dawn glowed through the hole.

'It looks like we're just in time for breakfast,' Bahvley quipped.

'Good; I was working up an appetite.' Grinning, Vigh lifted Bahvley up.

Bahvley squirmed through the opening and pulled himself out. He looked down at the astonished faces of his companions; however, Niome was smiling.

'Hi,' he said. 'Could I get some help here? My leg is still numb.'

Meysah and Jimmy scrambled up to help him, then went back to help Vigh.

'We're all right,' Vigh reassured them as he clambered to the bottom of the mound of rocks. 'Bahvley's leg is injured and we're quite hungry.'

'Master Vigh Nimrod,' said Tithil, 'you have been tested on your strength—'

'And intelligence,' Forthil finished.

'And his patience,' Bahvley added, laughing.

'Another test from Mirauk, I suppose,' said Vigh, sobering.

'Yes,' replied Niome. 'And had we gone the other way, I don't know what would have happened. These tests will only make the five of us stronger. We should thank our enemy; he is doing us a favour.'

'I also saved my friend,' added Vigh, nodding towards Bahvley.

'If it hadn't been for you, my old master,' said Bahvley, 'I *would* have lost my leg.'

'We will carry you,' said Mië. 'Your leg will heal quickly, but for now, you shouldn't put weight on it.'

'Excellent, I can catch up on my sleep,' Bahvley quipped. Mië made a Kiki sound which Bahvley echoed.

They all sat down to have breakfast.

'So tell me,' began Tharguen, 'how *were* you able to get out?'

'With the knife from Firlan,' said Vigh. He explained the whole procedure.

'Clever,' said Boreth.

Although Vigh seemed fine, he admitted that the experience left him a little shaken. He had begun to feel claustrophobic, and what had frightened him the most was the possibility of not getting out in time, of not being able to help Bahvley in time.

To Bahvley, the night had gone by quickly, but to Vigh it seemed to have lasted for an eternity. He was accustomed to suppressing all his worries so he could function efficiently; now, however, sharing them with the others made him feel much better. This experience had taught him that there was a solution to everything, no matter how impossible it seemed – it only *appeared* impossible, and one only had to find *the* solution.

After breakfast they set off again. The Kikies decided to endure the warm air, for they needed fresh air again now. A drizzle of rain kept the air cool for a few days before the sun shone again. The path levelled out now and meandered through green grass and flowers.

On the morning of the fifth day since the incident, Meysah snuck up behind Jimmy and shouted, 'Happy birthday!' He gave his friend a candle – unlit, but a candle still. 'I was saving it specially for you.'

Jimmy laughed. 'This is wonderful!' He hugged the candle. 'I'll treasure this candle till the day I die. It will remind me of our journey and my first birthday away from home.' He and Meysah chuckled boyishly.

It was a plain white candle, but Jimmy took out his knife and carved in it: *7th day - 7th week - Summer - 4766 - my 1st B-day away from home - Darakön.*

The day was a very pleasant one for everyone, and by the next day, they could all see the Dakodol River from afar. They knew that once they passed it, they would soon arrive at the cave's entrance.

The following evening, they met a party of Dalvarans. They were extremely happy to see them. They introduced them to the Kikies and told them about their successful travels since they'd last seen Captain Holim.

'It is very fortunate that we've met,' said Boreth. 'I long to hear news of Captain Holim and Weddo.'

'I am afraid things have been more grave on our end,' replied the Dalvaran.

'How so?' asked Jimmy.

'Well, we have cleared your path of Morkans, and you'll be pleased to know that our friends who were hiding at the fortress have begun rebuilding it. Some are still in hiding, but many of them have joined us here on this side of the river.'

'Perhaps we can stop by the fortress on our way home,' Meysah suggested to Bahvley. 'There are big statues of you and Tharguen and others among the ruins.'

'It may be out of our way, but we can always make a detour,' said Bahvley. 'I would like to see these famous statues myself.'

'That's about the only good news we have,' the Dalvaran said gravely. 'Captain Holim is now farther south, but we can clear you a path if you wish to see him again.'

'You've already done a lot for us,' said Vigh. 'And we are pressed for time, I'm afraid. But thank you. And tell Captain Holim that we thank him and that we are safe.'

'I will.' He took a deep breath and continued grimly, 'Many Dalvarans died fighting the Morkans. We killed many more of them, yes, but they are good at creating havoc, and our deaths and casualties are severe. Captain Holim's unit alone was reduced to half.'

'This news saddens me,' expressed Boreth. 'It's bad enough that the eight who came with us to Mork sacrificed their lives so that we could get away! Captain Holim and Weddo have our deepest sympathies.'

The Dalvaran messenger and his comrades exchanged sad glances. 'I'm afraid Weddo has little need for sympathy.'

'Why?' asked Meysah.

'Weddo was killed in battle.'

There was a long pause as the Telorians bowed their heads. Weddo had been a brave soul.

'But that's not all,' the messenger continued. 'We sent an envoy of thirty to Teloria shortly after you left for Mork to inform them of the happenings. They sent word out to additional parties to escort you home if they encountered you. It is pure chance that we've met you first and heard your news.'

'It is our pleasure,' Niome said diplomatically.

'So what is the news from Teloria?' asked Vigh. 'What do the brave Dalvarans who went there have to report?'

'Only seven of them returned, and three were gravely injured.' He paused. 'News from your home is doleful. The Telorians went into hiding when the Morkans began their assault – Morkans who had created a blockade on the main path into Teloria.'

'Kàtchah!' said Vigh in a low and severe tone.

'Him,' Tharguen disdained. 'I knew he was heading to Teloria, though I did not know the details of his mission, at least not all of them.' He shook his head. 'He's never good news.'

'I'd like to meet him face to face and give him a piece of my mind,' declared Vigh.

'No, you don't,' replied Tharguen, remembering all the times he had to deal with the Morkan. 'Believe me, you don't.'

'What did Kàtchah do?' asked Niome, concerned.

'Not all Morkans from this blockade got into the kingdom. The wall was untouched, but those from your home who were captured were instantly killed or tortured. Some who died were from the south.'

'The south!' cried Boreth. 'Do you know anything about the polcs from Oleréla?'

'I'm sorry, are you Boreth Culmik?'

'Yes!'

'We received a list of those who died, one of them was named Pilanna Culmik.'

Boreth gaped at the Dalvaran, then bowed his head. 'At least she's reunited with my father now. He died during the Big War fifty years ago.'

'Many from Oleréla were killed, many with your name. I'm sorry many from your family have died.'

'Most of my family died during the Big War. The few of us who still lived . . . Well, I'm the only one left now.'

'One Telorian was not instantly killed; he was kept alive a long time for interrogation, for he was of great value to the Morkans: Gorthan.' The Telorians looked up in shock.

Tharguen drew in a sharp breath. 'I was hoping Gorthan would survive an encounter with Kàtchah. There was nothing I could do to warn Teloria, to warn Gorthan.'

'The Morkans tried to get secrets out of him,' the messenger went on, 'secrets about the five of you. I am told they executed him just before our troops arrived. His death remains unconfirmed but he has been declared fallen. I'm sorry. That is it.'

'That is it?' spat Boreth. 'Nothing more! I suppose wishing for better news is hopeless. This is most disturbing and most upsetting!' He balled his hands into fists. 'Oh, how I hate Mirauk and all Morkans.'

Boreth turned to the messenger. 'Thank you for these reports. I am greatly grieved by the loss of my family and by Gorthan's death, but you went through great pains to get this information to us.' He bowed his head. 'I don't know how I should react to this. This is most unforgivable.' He clenched his teeth. 'Kàtchah did this.'

'Boreth,' Vigh said gently. 'I am so sorry.' He put his hand on his friend's shoulder. 'Boreth, you're going to get through this. We're the Star; we'll help you through these emotions. This is as much a shock to all of us as it is to you. I grieve for your family. You mustn't let yourself be overwhelmed by the anger we all feel.'

'But I am very upset!' seethed Boreth.

Though his voice was shaking, it was still quite level. His angry calm worried Vigh, who feared Boreth would snap in an explosion of suppressed emotions.

'I am not angry, Vigh,' Boreth grated through clenched teeth. 'This . . . that I feel . . . is rage.'

Boreth drew a breath and let out a soft shout of desperation. 'My entire family is gone, Vigh. To hear such news about them devastates me! And my mother – she . . . she had centuries ahead of her still – gone before her time. If I'd stayed, if I'd been there for them—'

'You might have been killed as well! There is no reason to blame yourself, Boreth.'

'You clearly don't understand,' Boreth snapped at his best friend. 'None of you seem that upset and I don't understand it.'

'We *are* upset,' confirmed Tharguen, 'I assure you.'

'We are all sad,' said Niome, 'and we are grieving with you. I understand—'

'You *don't* understand!' Boreth's brows furrowed in grief. 'How *can* you? You all have your families. Whereas mine . . .' A sob escaped him. 'My entire family was from the south, and now they are all dead. You can't possibly understand! None of you can,' he growled. Whirling, he stalked off.

'Boreth!' Vigh yelled after him.

Boreth spun around. 'Just let me be!' he shouted. 'For pity's sake, give me some peace and quiet!'

They fell silent, letting Boreth go.

'I apologise for this news,' the Dalvaran messenger said after several moments. 'I wish I had better news to report.'

'It's not your fault,' assured Vigh. 'Boreth has reason to be more upset than any of us. We must give him time alone.' He turned to the others. 'We'll wait for Boreth here.'

Boreth walked briskly up the mountain path and finally stopped. He leaned against a tree, gazing out over the Dakodol River without really seeing it as he wept. He seemed frozen in the past, his memories conjuring images from the Big War in his mind. Not only had he lost his father in the Big War, but many friends and cousins as well; his closest cousin had been tortured and killed before his very eyes while he was a helpless captive. Now he had lost more family, more friends, and his master.

'Your wisdom has been blinded by your woe,' said a soft voice.

'Hullo Niome,' said Boreth without turning around. 'You startled me.' His voice was a monotone as he tried to hide his emotions from her.

'I wish there were something I could do, some way I could use my magic to make everything better.'

'Thank you.' Boreth's voice softened as he spoke. 'It's all right. It just scares me. If only I had been there, I could have done something.'

'Like what?' asked Niome. 'Could you really have done anything more than what you're doing out here?'

'I feel so foolish now to have shouted at you all – I know you feel my pain with me. I . . . I regret it all. Not being out here – I regret not having the opportunity to help at home. Hearing such news . . . I feel like there is a huge weight on my heart.' Boreth placed a hand on his chest. 'I keep wondering if this is one of those abhorrent tests from Mirauk, and wondering what I have to do to make it go away. I would have expected something more . . . physical, like hand-to-hand combat, or one-on-one battle with a Morkan.'

'But that would not be a test; it would be too easy. Your strength is not in doubt, not even by you. These trials challenge what we ourselves doubt about ourselves, the enemy feeds on our fears. You lost most of your family in the Big War and . . . '

Niome shook her head. 'Mirauk has hurt you in a very cruel way. We mustn't let him win. We must remain strong, even though it may seem difficult at times.'

Boreth bowed his head and looked over his shoulder at Niome. 'I'm sorry I was so angry at everyone. Tell them I'm sorry.'

'There is no need for you to apologise for your anger, Boreth, but I will tell them if it solaces you that I do.'

'Thank you. I'm still very upset . . . . I just need more time alone before we continue.'

'I understand.' Niome turned and walked back down the trail.

The sun was beginning to set. Boreth sat down on a rock. He heard, as if from far off, a melody echoing in the wind. It was soft and soothing. He closed his eyes and took a deep, slow breath. In his mind he saw Clahria, for the music came from a harp. Then it dawned on him: the melody in the air was the song that Clahria had composed for him. He heard her voice singing the song, singing to him. It gave him hope.

Boreth started to hum, but the humming that came out was a different song, a new tune, the song that he was composing in his head for Clahria. He had not come up with words yet, but that did not matter. His tune was soothing and it complemented the other one. He knew that when the time was right, the words would come to him. Despite his grief, his heart was now at peace, even if just a little.

When he was ready, Boreth walked down the path and joined the others. The Dalvarans had already left to give the news of the Telorians to the rest of their people. Boreth was still filled with sadness, but he was calm and would accept his grief soon enough.

'I am ready to go on,' he said. He looked at Tharguen, who seemed most regretful. 'Tharguen, before you ask, I don't blame you.' Tharguen shifted uneasily. 'I know you did all you could for Teloria from your position in Mork.' Boreth turned to the others. 'I know Gorthan's death hits everyone here hard. And I know you all grieve with me for my family.' He paused. 'You . . . are my family now.'

Vigh clapped a hand on Boreth's shoulder and the two friends embraced.

The group set out the next morning. At times they heard the soft squeaks and murmurs of the Kikies, but otherwise, all was quiet. The Telorians did not speak amongst each other, for they remained deep in thought. By evening, they reached the shores of the Dakodol River and camped on its bank.

After spending the night and the next day crafting a raft, the Kikies shrank and the group started their journey across the river. By evening, they had reached the Dalvar side.

CHAPTER SEVENTEEN:
Mission Accomplished

'We have reached the border of Dalvar,' said Vigh. 'Straight ahead lie the caves of Dara-kön. Who knows how long it will take us to get there.'

'Hopefully not that long,' said Meysah. 'We need to get this over with.'

'Where are the Kikies?' asked Niome, noticing that they weren't floating in the air.

'They went back in the jar,' said Jimmy. 'They say we'll be less visible that way, but we are to inform them when we need them, of course.'

'They sure are a quiet folk,' said Tharguen.

'That's because they can be quiet when necessary,' replied Bahvley. 'You don't know them as well as I do. They can be quite noisy, you know. Since they're telepathic, they can go a long time without beeping or squeaking, but once they start, there's no stopping it.' He chuckled. 'When on a mission, they concentrate and keep to themselves and they become very serious compared to their usual state. They mind their own business, that's all. Once we are safe at home, they will liven up and share more with others and you will see how fun and . . . well, *Kiki* they are.' Bahvley laughed.

'I wonder what the origin of that name is,' Meysah mused. 'Kiki.'

'It means cute and funny in their language,' explained Bahvley. 'In case you haven't noticed, they are all cute in their own way. Of course, some of them, like any polc, are beautiful, but . . .' He paused, searching for the words to express what he was trying to convey. 'Their faces look like . . . how can I put it?'

'Kikies!' teased Meysah, in a highly exaggerated tone.

'Yes!' Bahvley exclaimed, holding out his hands, fingers outstretched. Meysah chuckled. 'They can be very serious and polc-looking too,' Bahvley went on, 'but with pointed ears, of course. Some Telorians are almost like Kikies.'

'Like who?' inquired Jimmy.

'Like Meysah, or Niome,' said Bahvley. 'Meysah certainly acts like one sometimes. Tharguen, on the other hand, looks very much like one.'

'Of course, I'm more *handsome* than cute,' bragged Tharguen, looking at Niome.

'He acts like one, too,' added Niome, 'if I under-stand their behaviour correctly.' She smiled at Tharguen and kissed his cheek, brushing a curly strand of hair from his face.

'They may be quiet now, but you'll see later,' repeated Bahvley. 'I don't mind their silence, but I admit it's more pleasant when they're *not* serious.' He laughed. 'I'm Kiki. They told me so. They said, "You look and act like a Kiki. Telorians must be related to us in some way. Perhaps from very ancient times. You are Kiki. Hnthnnn!"' Everyone laughed at his funny impersonation.

'And what about me?' asked Jimmy, looking almost worried. 'Am I Kiki?'

'You certainly act it,' said Niome. 'Silly and funny.'

'Well, let's see,' began Meysah, striking an old wizard's pose: knees slightly bent, back hunched over, one hand on his lower back and the other rubbing his chin. He walked around Jimmy, then paced to and fro, observing Jimmy as he spoke. 'Hmmm, I think he looks like a Kiki.' Long pause. 'Yeah, he looks like a Kiki.' Shorter pause, a step and a little giggle. 'He – he *is* a Kiki.' Turning to face the others, he pointed his thumb back at Jimmy. 'He's a Kiki.' Short pause. 'Do you think he looks like a Kiki?'

Everyone had wide grins, even Boreth. The two lads looked at each other, attempting to maintain a serious and puzzled composure, then slowly smiled and burst into laughter.

Bahvley joined in. 'My stomach hurts, you make me laugh so hard!'

'These two certainly are phenomenal,' expressed Boreth, smiling fondly. 'I feel so much better just watching them.'

'We shall have to write a song about them,' expressed Bahvley.

'And you will be in it as well,' said Meysah, 'because you are just as strange!'

'Of course,' agreed Tharguen. 'He's family.'

'I do admit it,' said Bahvley.

The rest of the day was extremely pleasant. They ate from the fruit trees at lunchtime. They had come across a few before, but now these trees were plentiful and the Telorians gathered many of their fruits for the road.

Meysah thought it would be a good idea to dry the fruit for later. Bahvley sliced the fruit up and Meysah placed the slices on his shield to dry in the sun as they walked, with Bahvley and Meysah taking turns carrying the makeshift tray. By the end of the day they had dried fruit to keep for later. They repeated the procedure during the next days before rain moved in.

On a clear night as they settled for some sleep, the team heard the shrieking of the dragons carried on the breeze. It was faint but enough to distract them from any other sounds around them.

As the others slept that night, Boreth was awakened by a strange sound. He could not tell what it was, nor where it came from, so he remained vigilant. In the morning he told only Vigh about it; he didn't want to alarm the others, nor did he want to alert whatever or whomever it was that he had heard it. He and Vigh remained on their guard. The sound stopped near the end of the day, but then Boreth heard it again in the evening.

That night, Boreth realised what the sound was: footsteps. Belonging to what or whom, he did not know, but he had his suspicions and he woke everyone up and told them they had to move. They complied, rising and immediately packing up their things, but they were confused, for Boreth refused to tell them what the hurry was about. They travelled the rest of the night.

In the morning, while Tharguen walked beside Niome, he glimpsed a flash of something in the bushes alongside their path. He increased his pace until he could sidle up next to Boreth.

'I fear it is a Morkan,' he whispered surreptitiously, 'but I only see the light from the sun reflecting off his sword and cannot judge the distance. If we make any sudden moves, it will let him know that we are aware of his presence.'

'I believe he is alone,' Boreth replied in the same manner, barely moving his lips. 'I have a good sense of hearing and I've only heard one set of footsteps.'

They both looked around at their companions. Vigh and Jimmy were walking in front of them, Meysah behind, then Bahvley, while Niome was last. They turned forward again.

'He could be after the books,' deduced Boreth.

'That's why I don't want to leave Niome's side. If anything should happen to her, I don't know what I'd do.'

'I'll keep an eye up front,' said Boreth.

Tharguen turned to return to Niome and saw a Morkan sneaking up behind her. With a growl, Tharguen rushed to Niome and past her, sword raised. He swung it so hard he nearly sliced the

Morkan in two. As the enemy crumpled to the ground, Tharguen turned to Niome and placed his hand on her arm.

'Are you okay?' he gasped.

She stared back at him with wide eyes. The Morkan had been so quiet that no one had heard him. Niome had not seen his shadow, for all their shadows were behind them still.

'Yes,' she finally managed.

'That was close,' breathed Meysah, nudging the corpse with his foot.

'No, this is close,' a voice behind him sneered.

Meysah whirled towards the flashing sword of another Morkan as it descended towards his head.

With a war cry, Jimmy leapt forward and swung his sword, blocking the Morkan's with a loud clang as the weapons met. The Morkan staggered back, and Jimmy swung again, dropping the Morkan dead to the ground.

'It's my turn to save you,' Jimmy said with relief, turning to Meysah.

'Where did they come from?' gasped Vigh.

'Look out!' shouted Bahvley.

Sensing the Morkan behind him, Vigh grabbed him and flipped him forward, then stabbed him at full tilt in the chest with his knife.

'How many are there?' Vigh shouted as the Morkan dropped.

Weapons drawn, the Telorians stood back to back, poised and alert. Another Morkan leapt out of the underbrush, knife raised. He pushed Niome to the ground with his boot.

Niome screamed as the Morkan slashed at Tharguen, who blocked the knife with his sword only to have it fly from his grasp. Grabbing the Morkan's arm, Tharguen grappled with him. As the others ran to help, the Morkan disengaged and backed away, producing knives from concealed pockets on his person and throwing them at the Telorians with quick precision, forcing them to take cover.

Tharguen charged him from the side, tackling him, but the Morkan twisted around, pinning Tharguen beneath him, intent on bringing the knife down into Tharguen's neck.

Niome lifted her hand and pointed at the Morkan, shouting out,

'Liveië reiûeh op, hish inim eid!'

The Morkan was thrown back like a ragdoll, landing hard a good distance away from Tharguen who rolled onto his stomach.

Bahvley pressed his boot down on the Morkan's chest to hold him in place. 'How many of you are there?' he demanded. The Morkan only laughed. Bahvley bent and pressed the point of his sword against the Morkan's throat. 'I said, how many of you are there!?'

'You really think killing us is going to change anything?' the Morkan sneered. 'We are going to kill all of you, one by one, until *she* is alone. She will have no one to protect her or the books she carries. If it isn't today, it will be another day. You are all going to die!' He burst into harsh laughter.

Bahvley jabbed his sword into his throat and the Morkan's laughter turned into a gurgling grunt before he died.

Niome ran to Tharguen, who rolled onto his back. 'I'm okay,' he said.

Niome urgently pressed her lips to his, still feeling so afraid. 'I just got so scared,' she whispered when they pulled apart.

'That's how I felt when you were unconscious those many days,' expressed Tharguen as Niome helped him up. He gently brushed her hair from her face and wrapped his arms around her.

'We have to get out of this place,' said Vigh, looking at Bahvley who was still hunched over the Morkan's body. 'Let's hope there are no more Morkans following us. These ones were exceptional trackers for us not to have discovered their presence earlier. They were also skilled duellists, for them to fight all of us so well.'

'Their goal must have been to slow us down and, failing that, to kill some of us,' concluded Bahvley. Tharguen confirmed his friend's assessment. 'There may be more spies like these,' Bahvley went on, 'gathering information to send back to Mirauk, and others bent on killing us. We must be vigilant. I'm afraid we may have to skip a few nights of sleep.'

Continuing on, everyone remained on their guard. At night, they slept only briefly and took turns keeping watch; during the day, they were as anxious as they had been in Mork. Everything suddenly seemed so quiet.

Jimmy noticed a hole in the mountainside that looked like a cave entrance from far, but Boreth thought it was an observation post. Jimmy thought he had seen a dragon's tail quickly flick by. They later saw another observation post. They quickened their pace and slept very little for the next four days.

On the fifth day, Meysah froze and began shaking when he saw two big eyes looking through another hole in the mountain. He knew the dragons were watching them. His legs felt weak and his teeth began to chatter. Everyone was frightened by those big gleaming eyes, but Meysah was the most affected. It took Bahvley's stories about the Kikies to get him to walk.

Two days later, they finally reached the entrance of the caves. There was a wide opening, big enough for a dragon to pass through. From outside, they could hear the dragons' heavy breathing coming from far within the cave.

'They know we're here,' said Niome.

'Will they try to stop us?' asked Meysah, remembering the gleaming eyes.

'I don't know,' answered Niome. 'They haven't before. If their intention was to stop us, they would have already done so. The caves are quiet. They are waiting.'

She turned to face everyone, which included the Kikies, who were about again and ready to follow the

Telorians' lead. 'From here on, I am in charge of this expedition. Vigh, I appreciate the leadership you've provided us so far, but now matters require a wizardess's mind.' Vigh nodded.

'We have to be extremely quiet, as quiet as a dragon,' Niome went on. 'They won't bother us unless we disturb them. I don't know how long this will take, but there will be times when we will have to wait or walk extremely slowly. No more rushing. Haste is not to our benefit.' Everyone nodded, listening attentively.

'We are here now; we are no longer in a hurry to get here. For safety purposes, we will keep the same order: I will go first, Boreth and Vigh behind me, then Jimmy, then Meysah, then Bahvley and Tharguen. Last up, I need a few Kikies, but most of you will have to stay outside to guard the entrance.'

'I will send Tithil, Mië, Celor, and Dessimë with you,' said Phynd. 'I will stay out here with the other Kikies.'

'Excellent,' acknowledged Niome.

'See you in a while, brother,' Tithil and Forthil said in unison. All the other Kikies shrank.

Niome took a deep breath. 'Let us proceed.'

They entered in single file. The interior was not as dark as they thought it would be, for they could see quite clearly. A powdery glow resembling light fog hovered above them near the ceiling throughout the cave. It looked like smoke, but when they touched it, it felt like powder. It was indigo-purple, at times coruscating to blue, and it seemed to be produced by the dragons.

The cave narrowed to a wide tunnel. After they'd walked for a while, the tunnel curved left, then straightened, then curved right. It ended at a *T* junction with tunnels running left and right.

'Which way should we go?' asked Meysah.

'When in doubt, always stick to the right,' said Niome. 'It's a little trick I learnt from Vigh at Firlan.' Vigh smiled.

Niome led the way down the right tunnel, which continued its gradual curve towards the right before sharply turning left and upwards. They climbed for a long time.

'I wonder if it isn't night yet,' Jimmy told Meysah.

Meysah gave no reply, being lost in his thoughts. He was terrified of this place. He felt the cold of the dragons and felt as if their gleaming eyes would pop open at any moment and stare right at him.

'No, it isn't,' replied Tharguen, overhearing Jimmy. 'When the air cools, then it will be night, for the temperature drops when the light stops feeding its warmth.'

They continued to climb, but their pace was slower now. They had to stop and rest from time to time, but they eventually emerged onto a wide cliff high above a wide open space. A higher cliff rose straight ahead of them, giving access to a set of stairs. The stairs were technically behind them, but they could only reach them if they followed a narrow path along the perimeter of the cavern. Niome led them along that path.

When they reached the other cliff they could see the steep tunnel they had taken to get up there. Vigh bade them wait, as he sat down and recorded their route in his notebook so they wouldn't get lost on their way back. Then they kept going.

'I think it's night now,' Jimmy said, shivering.

'It is,' confirmed Tharguen.

Their new path took another turn and widened, then descended gradually for a long time. The featureless tunnel made for a boring trek, yet no one broke the silence, afraid to draw attention to the group. Niome sensed that attention was already upon them but said nothing, instead concentrating on her goal.

Finally they reached a wide area at the bottom of the slope. Here the openings from which the dragons had watched them were visible. There were no dragons present as far as they could tell. In the middle of the cavern floor was a big dip with sloping sides, and the only way to the other side was by walking past this dip. Large entrances to tunnels were visible around the perimeter of the dip, as though they were entrances to a basement area. The party walked across quietly. Meysah was all the while dreading those peering eyes.

'I hope the dragons can't see us,' Jimmy whispered to Meysah.

'Quiet!' Meysah whispered harshly. 'You'll disturb them.'

'With one sentence?' protested Jimmy. 'That can't disrupt the peace.'

'It will eventually, if you keep at it!'

'Your whispers are louder than mine!'

'Jimmy!'

'Sorry. You shouldn't be so worried,' Jimmy reassured. 'As if a dragon will pop out of nowhere—'

'Jimmy!' Meysah hissed, staring at one of the tunnels.

'Because we had one little conversation—'

'Jimmy,' repeated Meysah, 'I think . . .'

'And that just really—'

There was a loud thump and a snort. Meysah gulped. Everyone stopped abruptly and looked at the two lads, though their whispers had not been loud at all.

Jimmy looked around him. Another thump resounded. And another.

Out of the shadows of a tunnel stepped a huge dragon. Its green reptilian eyes glared at them all and then focused on Meysah. It snorted again, smoke steaming out of its nostrils. Slowly but steadily they all started up the slope on the other side of the dip. The dragon leapt at them and grabbed Meysah in its claws, lifting him off the ground.

'Go!' cried Meysah. 'Save yourselves.' He looked at the dragon. 'That's right, you understand me perfectly. You deal with me first!' He tried to give the dragon a scowl, but his fear still came through.

The dragon let Meysah drop into the dip, almost as though challenging him. Meysah quickly rose and drew his sword, holding it with both hands. The dragon backed up and spat fire at him. Although the fire did not reach Meysah, he nevertheless lifted his arm to hide his face, so intense was the heat of the flames.

Meysah whipped his shield off his back. The dragon spat fire again and Meysah ducked, covering himself with his shield. The dragon walked towards him; Meysah whacked its claw and it retreated. It took another deep breath. Meysah ran under the dragon to avoid the fiery breath, then he ran back out to face the dragon. It shrieked in anger.

'Meysah!' cried Vigh. 'Quickly, run this way.'

Meysah started running, but when he got near the slope, the dragon set its foot down and blocked the way. Meysah had been running so fast that he bumped into the dragon's leg. He slowly backed up down the slope. The dragon flicked its tail and Meysah was thrown to the other end of the dip, landing on his back and sliding across the ground.

The others tried to help, but each time they got near the dip or even moved, the dragon flew past them and spat fire or clawed at them.

Meysah stood again. There was no point in running away; it wouldn't work. He had to face his fears.

'So this is how you want it, eh,' he told the dragon. 'You want to fight? I'll fight!'

He ran to the dragon and slid under it, slashing its underbelly. The dragon shrieked and launched itself into the air, then shot back down and landed on Meysah, pushing him to the wall. Meysah got back to his feet with effort, panting.

'We have to do something to help,' cried Jimmy, stringing his bow. The others stood ready to jump down and help Meysah. 'I'll take this dragon down myself if I have to.'

The dragon flew up again and spat fire at the high ceiling of the cave. It seemed to open up a water flow of some sort because water started cascading down like a wide waterfall. It flowed down in front of the Telorians and Kikies, all along the edge of the dip. Before they could go anywhere, to their great amazement, the dragon spat ice at the waterfall, freezing it into a wall that separated them from Meysah and the dragon. Water kept falling from the opening in the ceiling, freezing as soon as it touched the wall of ice.

'What are we going to do?' gasped Jimmy.

Meysah was on his own now.

The dragon walked towards him again. Meysah threw one of his knives. It landed on the scales of the dragon's back and bounced right off. Meysah ran under it again, picked up his knife, and ran to the other side of it.

Before it had time to whip its tail at him, he stabbed the dragon's tail. The dragon turned towards him. It lifted its foot and scratched Meysah's arm with its talon. Meysah slashed its palm as it withdrew. It spat fire again and Meysah protected himself with his shield, stabbing repeatedly at the dragon. He screamed in pain as the dragon slashed his back and right leg.

Meysah ran under the beast and slashed at its hide again. He tried to dart to the other side, but the dragon slammed its foot down and its talons landed on either side of him, pinning him down. His sword arm free, he tried to stab the dragon but it ripped his sword away, scratching his face in the process. Meysah took a deep breath, then kicked one of the dragon's talons with so much force that it broke. He slipped through the gap that remained and grabbed his sword, then hobbled across the dip. He was weakening.

The dragon turned its head and breathed so powerfully that the gust knocked Meysah off his feet and he rolled across the ground.

'Meysah!' cried Vigh from the other side of the ice wall. 'Can you hear me?'

'Yes,' Meysah answered weakly.

'You don't have to fight it,' said Vigh.

'What are you talking about?' argued Meysah. 'I have to finish it off if I want to survive.'

'There are other ways of gaining victory,' replied Vigh.

'What am I supposed to do?' demanded Meysah. 'Talk to it?'

'That's right,' insisted Vigh.

'What, should I tell it about our mission?'

'It could work!' Vigh hollered.

'I'll try negotiating then,' Meysah reluctantly relented, trying to smile fearlessly.

Meysah had no time to ponder, no time for diplomatic niceties. He walked right up to the dragon and looked it in the eyes. Whether he had found the solution or not, he didn't care anymore; he merely wanted to buy himself some time, to maybe distract the dragon so he could slay it if possible.

'Listen,' he told the dragon, 'I don't want to kill you, not unless you want to kill me.'

The dragon snorted and smoke streamed out of its nostrils. Meysah turned his head slightly to the side. The dragon came closer and looked straight at him.

'We are not evil polcs,' he continued hesitantly, stammering slightly. 'We are simply on a mission. We only want to save our home, Teloria, and the rest of the world from the evil of the Morkans.' Meysah glanced down and back at the dragon. 'Mirauk wanted to have power over all the lands and we Telorians . . . we are stopping him, uh, by . . . Well, we are carrying the *Book of Enchantment* and the *Complement Book.*'

He looked up at the others. Vigh motioned for him to continue. 'We want to prevent Mirauk from gaining ultimate power and—'

The dragon flew up into the air and spat fire at the wall of ice, then spat ice at the hole in the ceiling from which the water had been falling. The ice melted and the cascade stopped. The dragon flew back down, as Meysah collapsed to the ground.

'Meysah!' cried Bahvley.

Then, up the slope Meysah came, crawling on all fours. The others helped him up.

Niome looked around while Dessimë tended to Meysah's wounds and burns. The young wizardess was curious about this dragon's rare magic, but the dragon had disappeared back into the shadows.

The group continued on.

'Why does the road have to be so long and dangerous?' Meysah complained. 'Look at me! I look like a Telorian come back from the dead, with all these cuts and bruises.'

Bahvley chuckled. 'You look like a young Telorian who faced his biggest fear to gain greater courage,' he remarked, wrapping an arm around his brother's shoulders and smiling with pride. 'And that says a lot for a polc like you.'

Meysah smiled under his grimace of pain, thinking of Tlúnëe's departing words. 'I still think the path in this cave is too complicated,' he muttered.

'That is why only the wisest could come,' said Niome. 'Yet I believe the direct and original passage has been destroyed or barred. To find the right way to go, you don't necessarily need a map, you just have to let your heart guide you. Your emotions are as essential as your senses, for magic guides everyone everywhere, always.'

'Well, that's a good thing,' said Jimmy. 'Although I do agree with Meysah. I can't wait to get out of this place, and be at home and granted the title of Knight!'

'That is your dream, isn't it?' asked Boreth. Jimmy nodded. 'Keep visualising, for it will come true if you do. Although I do agree about this cave. I cannot wait to get out. I have been composing a song for Clahria in my head and I want to hear what it sounds like out loud. Though we should remain silent for now.'

They continued silently up a curving hill that soon turned into a narrow path; this time it did not hug the wall but crossed the middle of the big open space like a bridge. It was a lot higher than the other had been, and a lot longer too.

'I don't like the looks of this,' voiced Bahvley.

'Is it just me,' began Jimmy, 'or did it suddenly get warmer in here?'

'It has been daytime for a while,' noted Tharguen, trying to sound reassuring for Jimmy, who was sweating with anxiety.

'All right,' said Niome, 'we have to go in single file, very slowly. Don't look down.' She stepped out onto the stone bridge and, slowly and very carefully, started across. One by one the others followed.

Meysah's leg was feeling better thanks to the Firlanian herbs, but even so he had to pretend he was walking on solid ground and look straight ahead. Pebbles and stones, dislodged by their feet, skittered off the edges of the bridge, even more when Jimmy slipped and recovered with a gasp and muttered curse.

At one point, the path narrowed so much that they had to carefully lower themselves to their hands and knees and crawl. Tharguen's hands slipped and he would have fallen if Bahvley hadn't grabbed him and steadied him.

Thankfully, the four Kikies following them hovered nearby in their fairy size, ready to help if need be, but even they were uncertain how effectively their magic could help with the dense and magical dust that floated in the air.

Meysah was relieved when the bridge widened to a comfortable width for walking, and he felt like he could breathe more easily.

'Finally,' Tharguen breathed behind him, voicing Meysah's and everyone else's relief.

However, when they got to the end of it, they still couldn't reach the set of stairs. First Niome and then the others stood staring at a gap before them – about a metre between the stone bridge and the landing for the staircase. Jagged stone on both sides of the gap suggested the bridge had been broken.

'How convenient,' Meysah said sarcastically, trying to hide a new surge of anxiety.

'I don't think this gap was here fifty years ago, before the *Book of Enchantment* was stolen,' Boreth observed.

'Neither do I,' agreed Vigh. 'This looks recent. Perhaps Morkans have attempted to investigate and the dragons prevented them from getting through to the other side by breaking the bridge at this point.' He looked around and sighed. 'Well, there isn't anything we can use to span the gap, so I suppose we're just going to have to jump.'

'Looks like we don't have any other choice,' said Niome. Meysah grimaced.

'Actually, there is one other option,' said Tithil. Everyone turned to look at the Kiki. 'Flying!' He grinned and uttered a squeaky chuckle. 'As you jump, we Kikies will jump with you. It will feel as though we are flying, except we cannot really fly when we are this size, only run fast, so you'll need to give yourselves a big push when we leave the edge of the bridge.'

'If you can't fly when in this size,' began Jimmy, 'what's the difference between jumping with you or jumping alone?'

'A big difference,' assured Celor. 'Our speed will add to your liftoff to carry you over the gap with less effort.'

'What about the weight?' asked Meysah. 'Won't you just be adding weight and therefore . . .' He made a crashing sound.

'If you jump alone,' began Celor, 'unless your liftoff is powerful, you will not cover the full distance. You will fall to your death . . . if you are lucky.'

'That bad, eh?' asked Jimmy.

'I am afraid so. But if you jump with one of us,' continued Celor, 'our magic will allow us to reach a speed that will propel you to the other side. Let me demonstrate. Who wishes to be first?'

'I shall go,' declared Bahvley. 'I have done this before when we were crossing over the mountain from the Colama Valley, and I must say, it's quite a thrill.' He glanced at Celor. 'Ready when you are, my friend.'

'All right!'

Celor stood behind Bahvley and put his hands on his shoulders. They backed up a few steps, then ran rapidly towards the gap and leapt. They got to the other side so quickly that if Meysah hadn't been intent on the gap the whole time, he would have missed it.

Bahvley turned towards the others. 'You're scared the first time, but then it becomes sport.'

'Some sport,' muttered Meysah.

'Come, Meysah,' said Mië. 'You will be next.'

Meysah took a deep breath. Mië followed the same procedure as Celor. They backed up and then they ran, faster than Meysah had ever moved before. They were on the other side before Meysah had time to be afraid, though he *was* a little shaken.

Mië shrank and appeared again beside Niome. She and Niome got to the other side as well. Dessimë got Jimmy through, although Jimmy slipped while landing, and Celor grabbed him by the arm and hurled him to safety next to Bahvley. Dessimë went back for Vigh. Tithil brought Boreth and Tharguen over in turn.

'You see,' said Celor when they were done, 'that wasn't so bad.'

The Telorians looked down from the top of the staircase; from this angle the height was intimidating. They started down the steps within the new tunnel.

The stairs twirled and circled as they went down; by the time the Telorians and Kikies reached the bottom, they were all rather dizzy. Once their heads had stopped spinning, they walked through a long, winding tunnel. The air grew chill as night fell outside.

Rumbles overhead reverberated in the tunnel, knocking a few pebbles loose above their heads. At one point there was an enormous *BANG* and Jimmy jumped, almost hitting his head on the low ceiling. He leaned against the wall of the tunnel for a moment, calming his hammering heart.

'My bones nearly popped out of my skin!' he told Meysah as he pushed away from the wall. They started walking again.

'Wait!' said Bahvley, and the others turned to him. 'There's something inscribed on the wall. I think when Jimmy leaned here, he rubbed the dirt off and uncovered something.'

They all hovered around as Niome stepped up and rubbed the spot with her sleeve. There was indeed something inscribed there and it was written in the Ancient Telorian tongue.

'Whoever wrote this wrote it such a long time ago that most of it has faded away,' she said, leaning forward and peering closely at the inscription.

'Do you believe it's a warning?' asked Vigh. 'Perhaps people died venturing farther than this. Perhaps the prophecies were true when they said that the dragons would do anything to prevent anyone who wasn't worthy from getting near the Portal, in the event a dark and evil lord came to exist. I believe it has come true. Due to Mirauk, they are doing everything in their power to prevent any polc from entering.'

'Well, this might shed some light on things. What does it say?' asked Tharguen.

'I don't know,' replied Niome. 'But I'll try to decode some of it.' She observed the characters for a long time. 'I think it says "lonely" here,' she said, pointing. 'Or is it the word for "alone"?' She looked at another word. 'Oh, this is definitely "pass". This . . . I really don't know; it's too faded. And that one I forget. Um, this one here is . . .' She paused. 'This doesn't make any sense.'

'What is it?' asked Meysah.

'It says "five",' answered Niome. She began to rub the wall beside, above, and below the inscription.

'Alone, pass, five,' echoed Vigh. 'Could it mean us?'

Niome stepped back. On the area she'd rubbed clear of dirt, below the inscription, someone had drawn a five-pointed star. 'Without a doubt,' she said. 'We are the Five of the Star. Only we may continue from this point on.'

'Well, here we go again,' said Boreth. 'Just the five of us, like at the beginning.'

'It looks like you are all in the prophecy books,' said Bahvley.

'In our culture,' began Tithil, 'it is *the* greatest honour to be in a prophecy. None of us have ever spoken of this before, but Bahvley was in *our* prophecies too.'

'I was?' exclaimed Bahvley, cocking his brow in curiosity. 'This is the first I'm hearing of it.'

'It was said that a stranger would come to us, out of nowhere,' said Mië. 'He would be in need of our care, and he would bring us and his people together.'

'I didn't even know you had a prophecy book,' remarked Bahvley.

'You'll find that Kikies are very much like Telorians in some ways,' said Celor, 'and in others we are very different.'

'Tell me about it,' chuckled Bahvley.

'And I suppose some of us are more strange than different,' said Meysah, grinning. 'Like Bahvley.'

'It looks like I'm the only one who hasn't been prophesied about,' said Tharguen.

'You don't know that,' Bahvley pointed out. 'Perhaps you're in the old books at home.'

'I'll have to look through the *Prophecy Book* when we get home,' said Niome. 'Whether you *are* in the book or not, we are all here for a reason. I mean, you didn't survive all those years in Mork as a spy for nothing, and you certainly will be in the *Great History Book.*'

'Not if we keep procrastinating,' said Vigh, his tone serious. 'I don't know what awaits us, but we'd better get this task over with before it's too late.'

The five who had set out from Teloria looked at one another. They were on their own now; Bahvley, Tharguen, and the Kikies would have to wait for them here, and no one knew how long it would take them to return.

'Don't be scared,' Bahvley reassured Meysah. 'Everything will be fine. The worst is over. You've fought your dragon.'

'I know,' replied Meysah. 'I'm dreadfully frightened, just not like before.'

The Five started forward.

'Niome!' Tharguen called. She paused to look at him. 'Be careful.'

'I will,' replied Niome. Smiling tenderly, Tharguen brought his hand to his lips and extended it towards her. Niome mimicked the motion, sending him a kiss of her own.

'You know you can just walk over there and kiss him, right?' Meysah teased Niome as the Five resumed their journey. Niome blushed, smiling.

They walked steadily down the tunnel, turning sharp corners that gave them the impression they were backtracking – five corners, to be exact.

'Do you realise we've been walking in the formation of a star?' remarked Vigh as they got to the end of the tunnel.

However, their one tunnel did not end at a destination but at the junction of many more tunnels – five, to be exact, with a bright light in the distance at the end of each. They looked at each one carefully.

'There are five tunnels and five of us,' Boreth noted. 'We should split up and each take one tunnel, walk to the end and observe what's there, then come back and report to the rest of us.'

'What if some are longer than others?' asked Jimmy.

'Then we will count a hundred long strides forward,' replied Niome. 'If the tunnel goes farther, we will just have to turn back.'

Vigh took note of this in his book. Then, the Five began down their respective tunnels; Niome took the centre one, Jimmy took the tunnel to the left of hers, with Meysah to the immediate right, Vigh took the rightmost tunnel, while Boreth walked down the far left one.

At first, they counted aloud as they walked, all in unison as they could hear the others counting as well. Then they could only hear themselves. Maybe twenty steps or more before they would have reached one hundred steps forward, they heard the others again, and moments later, the Five were reunited when their tunnels merged into a circular room with a domed ceiling.

There was light all around them, though it did not come from the fire pit in the centre – no, this was a magical glow. Rumbles rose from below the floor.

Jimmy decided to be the first to enter. He'd taken only a few steps when the floor shook and crumbled before him, throwing him off-balance. Seeing Jimmy on the verge of falling into the resulting crater, Meysah lunged and grabbed his arm. The two lads teetered on the edge, looking down at the dragons and fire below them. More and more of the floor crumbled away as Boreth and Vigh quickly yanked them back to the wall.

'They want us to go down there,' said Niome.

'Who?' cried Jimmy.

'The dragons!' she replied.

'They want us to die!' shouted Meysah.

'If we don't go down on our own,' Niome explained, 'they will make this entire place crumble.'

'But how are we to get down there from here?' protested Meysah. 'We can't fly!'

Niome's face lit up. 'Perhaps we can.'

She quickly looked through the *Book of Enchantment* as the others stared at her, but she found nothing that could help them in this situation. Jumping down would be dangerous, but they couldn't just stand there on the ledge and wait. Something inside Niome told her there was a solution, the *perfect* solution. She looked through Tweedle's book of spells and paused at an odd spell near the end of the book that read '*This one needs five!*'

They didn't have time to lose. 'Listen,' she said, 'I think I found what we need: "This one needs five!"'

'How curious is that!' expressed Jimmy. 'He thought of everything, that Bob Tweedle, didn't he?'

Niome nodded before continuing to read. '"One for a wand and five for a voice. A moment once long awaited now elicits surprise and anger, for endless time has buried it in oblivion and evil has destroyed the Way. Dragon eyes may not recognise, but five voices spoken as one summon them."'

They all huddled around Niome as best they could, as she held the book up so they could all see the words. Then they read the spell aloud, in unison.

Their voices melded to one resonance, strong and beautiful, ringing out through the domed room and the crater below it.

Dragons of Darakön!
Masters of Magic!
Fair creatures of the world
And rulers of the Portal,
We come to give back what has always belonged to
you.

We wish not for power;
We are here to stop evil.
We present to you the books
That contain the Portal Key Spell.

Guide us to the Portal!
Edilûga sui ot ehelt Lanitorep!

The dragons gradually stopped roaring and batting their wings, settling down and growing quiet.

The floor stopped crumbling.

Niome read the final sentence: *The dragons now recognise you and will cooperate. Speak to them as you would to each other.*

She looked down, hesitating. 'Uh, could we have some help? We need to get down.'

A dragon flew up and presented its back to them, hovering in the air, wings flapping lazily. The Five climbed on and it brought them down safely – so smoothly and quickly, even Meysah enjoyed the descent. They jumped off and looked around.

A large fire burned in the centre of the immense space. Eight dragons stood quietly, staring at the Telorians, observing them with one eye, then with the other. They stomped the ground lightly with their front paws. Behind the dragons there seemed to be another tunnel, shorter, its opening a large arch. Niome knew that was where the Portal lay.

'Why are they looking at us so strangely?' Meysah asked, feeling uncomfortable.

'They are recognising us,' said Niome, 'looking into our souls and making sure we are truly the Five benevolent Telorians.'

'If you want my opinion,' began Boreth, 'someone at some time in Kaulchèc History must have had some way of communicating with the dragons. We all seem to be part of the prophecy; even Bob Tweedle knew about us, though he couldn't reveal anything. I have read parts of the *Prophecy Book* and nowhere does it mention us, or Bahvley; only briefly does it mention Niome. So perhaps we are in the one and only book that only the wisest are allowed to read: *The Dragon Prophecies*.'

Vigh marvelled at the dome around them. 'Do you think that all along, we really were written about, but almost no one knew because no one was supposed to know?'

'There's only one way of finding out,' said Jimmy. 'We check in the book when we get home! I mean, technically we are allowed to now, right?'

'Niome may be the only one wise enough to read it,' replied Vigh, 'but she *will* read it and be selective in knowing when to stop reading.'

'Yes, I will,' Niome confirmed. 'But where has it got to; is it still around? We don't know how much damage was done to Teloria. I don't even know where the book was before.'

'As long as it's somewhere,' said Jimmy. 'I'm dying to know about my long life as a master-knight!'

The dragons snorted.

'I think they know who we are now,' deduced Meysah. 'Thank goodness. I didn't appreciate being thrown around.'

Niome turned to the dragons. 'Could you please show us the way to the Portal?' she asked politely.

The dragons all turned their necks so their snouts were pointed at the arched tunnel opening. The Telorians walked over to it, but when they reached the entrance, the dragons blocked the way. It gave the impression the dragons had changed their minds and were objecting to their passing. The Telorians didn't understand.

'Maybe they want you to say thanks?' suggested Meysah, not liking the looks of this at all. Niome thanked the dragons, but still they would not move.

The Telorians slowly walked closer to the tunnel, the circular portal at the far end now visible as it coruscated purple light.

'Could you please clear the way?' Niome requested. 'Could you let me pass to the Portal?'

Instead, more dragons stepped in between them and the tunnel.

'Now I really don't understand,' expressed Vigh.

'Maybe they want proof,' Jimmy offered. 'Show them the two books.'

Niome took out the *Book of Enchantment* and the *Complement Book*, presenting each one to the dragons. The largest dragon approached her and observed the tomes, then snatched them out of her hands. Turning its head, it uttered a stream of groans and grunts to which the other dragons responded.

'What's it doing?' Meysah asked carefully.

Even as she shook her head, revelation came to Niome in the form of memories – words of advice from various times and previous thoughts she had voiced.

Maybe we're not meant to go through the Portal.

Could you please show us the way to the Portal? And they had.

Only the dragons know what lies behind it . . .

There are many ways to bestow freedom upon the lands.

All we know is, we're meant to take the books . . . as for the lair, we shall see when we get there.

We come to bring back what has always belonged to you.

Now Niome understood what everything meant, and in her mind, she magically let go.

She spoke these thoughts out loud to the others. They were still taking it all in when Niome exchanged a look with the largest of the dragons. She nodded, and the dragon nodded back. Then, it cast the two books into the fire.

'Oh no!' cried Jimmy.

The other four watched in shock as the books burned. Now there were no more books, no more Key Spell. They were destroyed.

'We've lost our chance!' exclaimed Boreth.

'No,' said Niome, 'we have not. Mirauk has. Now, there is no risk of him passing through.' Everyone turned to her in puzzlement. 'I was not meant to pass through the Portal – no one ever was. It is for the dragons, and the dragons alone. We don't need to go through it anymore. I know enough magic from those books. In this way, ultimate power can never be gained. Mirauk has lost, so at least in part, we have already won.'

The dragons shifted, agitated, drawing the Telorians' eyes to them; they were gazing at the fire. The Telorians looked at the huge fire, looked into it beyond the flames, and saw Elina's spirit standing tall, floating in the flames. She looked down at them, smiling proudly. That's when the other four of the Star understood why the books had to be destroyed.

Elina bowed to them before she vanished.

'Our task is done,' said Niome, smiling. 'Let's go home.'

A dragon flew the Five back up to the platform where they then took the five tunnels back. The others were shocked to see them returning so soon.

The five Telorians weren't certain how to explain what they had experienced. Thus, the Kikies read their minds and then described what had happened as best they could to Bahvley and Tharguen. The overwhelming feeling all shared was relief, for they knew they wouldn't have to go back to Mork for quite some time. Teloria would be safer now.

The seven Telorians and four Kikies walked through the tunnel, back to the stairway. They walked confidently and proudly, especially Niome, Jimmy, Meysah, Boreth, and Vigh.

When they reached the stairs, a dragon flew down from a higher tier and indicated that they should climb onto its back. When they were all on, it flew to a tunnel near the dip where Meysah had been attacked. The dragon pointed towards the tunnel, so they got off its back and walked through the tunnel.

A short while later, they arrived at the mouth of the cave, where Phynd and the other Kikies were waiting for them. They did not need to explain what had gone on inside Darakön; the Kikies read their minds and knew it for themselves.

It was a hot, sunny day, which pleased Jimmy most. They set off for Firlan.

Bahvley and Tharguen decided that the Morkan armies at Teloria were now their top priority, and that there would be plenty of time to visit Dalvar once things had been settled back home – their beautiful home where they most longed to be.

They all stopped, wary, when they heard a noise in the underbrush near the path.

Bahvley called out, 'Who's there?' There was no answer. He turned to the Kikies who had been guarding the area. 'Did you see or sense anyone before?'

'No,' replied Phynd. 'I wonder now which skilful demon snuck up on us.'

A Morkan charged from behind some shrubs, catching the Telorians by surprise. They quickly drew their swords, but he was too quick for them and dodged their attacks. The Morkan leapt past Vigh, who charged towards him, and grabbed Jimmy, driving his sword through his chest.

Jimmy shouted gruffly in pain as the sword tip emerged through his back and then the Morkan pulled his sword out, almost casually. Jimmy groaned again and stood there for a moment, breathing irregularly, before he dropped his sword and fell to his knees.

Roaring his fury, Meysah threw himself at the Morkan and killed him with one blow to the heart. Behind Meysah, Jimmy toppled onto his back, blood spreading rapidly across his clothes. Meysah turned to his friend, and a deep, overpowering sorrow descended upon him.

Everyone ran to Jimmy, crouching by his side. He was still conscious and had tears in his eyes. Meysah cradled his friend's head in his lap.

'I don't want to die,' Jimmy wheezed, trembling. 'I'm supposed to . . . be a . . . knight. A master. Please! The . . . po . . . tion . . .'

He exhaled his final breath. He was dead.

Meysah covered his mouth with his hand and mewled into it, as tears blurred his vision. Bahvley wrapped his arms around his brother who wept in his arms, still holding Jimmy.

Boreth knelt down next to Jimmy and passed his hand over Jimmy's still open eyes.

'He would have made a brave knight,' Vigh said softly, crouching beside him.

'No,' Boreth corrected, 'he *was* a brave knight. I shall miss him greatly.'

The others bowed their heads.

Niome suddenly gasped, smiling through her tears. 'Yes, the potion! Jimmy remembered. We can save him! It didn't occur to me until now, but yes. Yes!'

She opened her bag and took out the peachy potion and the folded paper their friends at the Old Grey House had given them. Meysah watched his sister with renewed hope.

'Let's hope this works,' she said in a low voice.

She slowly poured the potion into Jimmy's mouth. Then she read clearly – and carefully, for her voice was quivering:

Lelamey stissipre voleba,
essolith taheiw tarelimag lerëop,
I limassa cuyo!

Evilam egkalab lelametel tehenelissam irest.
Evilam egkalab etel êlessifëi
fosiliath galen uyo lomos,
I gelimë buyo!
Siliath humos sehilûis otevilëi,
Daneleiew sehiliûti otvelië salalelw.
Niralami ter otus, galen uyo lomos!

Everyone waited, looking at Jimmy. Then, they witnessed the miracle: all the blood that was streaming out of Jimmy stopped, and the blood on his shirt dried. The wound closed up, and when Dessimë approached and checked Jimmy's chest, only a faint pink spot marked where the wound had been.

Jimmy suddenly drew in a loud, deep breath and exhaled, then again, a few times. He opened his eyes, then sat up and looked down at his chest. The faint scar remained.

He looked up, gaping. 'Am I a ghost?'

Laughing and crying for joy, Meysah rejoiced. 'It worked! The potion worked!' He gripped his friend by the shoulders. 'It's a good thing you thought of it, Jimmy. We had all forgotten! It's truly amazing – you're alive. You're perfectly fine!'

'Well, if you continue shaking me, I might not be!' muttered Jimmy.

Meysah hugged his friend as if he had been lost for years. Then Jimmy began to laugh and to cry too, realising how important he was to the others, to the Star, and how loyal they were to him.

'I could not have wished for better friends, or a better adventure than this,' he expressed. 'Thanks to you, I'm going to become what I've always dreamt of becoming. And that makes me the happiest Telorian alive.'

'You are indeed a knight,' Boreth told him. 'You've been given a second chance to prove your abilities.'

'Now you can live and see for yourself how everyone will honour you,' Meysah added.

'I thought it was the end,' admitted Jimmy. 'I didn't want it to be. But I now understand certain things about life I didn't before. I can't explain it, but somehow I know it. I am truly grateful to have you, all of you.'

'And we are truly grateful to have you,' said Boreth, patting Jimmy on the back.

'This magic is beyond our understanding,' said Phynd, 'but we are truly grateful it exists. You may not realise it, but you Telorians inspire us all – especially you, Jimmy. You are very Kiki-like – even more so now, for Kikies don't die easily.'

'I *am* brave, and I feel wiser. You were right, Boreth, this trip has made me more – you know, just *more*.' Jimmy laughed. He unbuttoned his shirt and took a look at the pink mark more properly. 'I don't understand it either. It doesn't even hurt,' he added, touching his chest. He pressed here and there, first gently and then a little harder. 'Okay, perhaps it does just a tiny bit.'

He returned his attention to the others. 'But in that moment, when all was becoming blurry and dark, I remembered that Tlúnëe and Drúgan gave us a spell and a potion, and Tlúnëe was particularly kind to me about the matter that one of us may die, and that's when it became clear to me: he knew. Tlúnëe knew. He predicted it.'

'Hey!' Meysah nudged Jimmy with his elbow. 'Now you have something to boast about to Lóim Weedler! And you have the shirt to prove it.'

'And you as my number-one witness,' grinned Jimmy.

'I wouldn't be so quick about showing off,' Vigh cautioned. 'You won't need to, really. You'll just come home after having been to Mork *and* Darakön, and that will be enough. But I understand you want to prove yourself knightly. You don't need to boast for that, you just need to be who you are. A true knight never boasts, he just is.'

'Okay,' said Jimmy, 'I understand.'

'But hey, you told Lóim you'd cut off his tongue,' objected Meysah.

'Except on certain rare occasions,' Vigh confessed.

Offering him a hand, Meysah helped Jimmy to his feet. Then, laughing and teasing each other, the group of Telorians and Kikies marched on south to Firlan.

Chapter Eighteen:
A Few Short Rests

It took the team almost eleven full days to reach Firlan. They arrived at the forest in the early afternoon. As the days had passed, the air cooled and the leaves started yellowing, for Colouring was on its way.

They encountered two bands of Morkans who were heading back to Mork. One group ignored the Telorians and Kikies, although they must have known very well who they were; they rode quickly past, intent on their original mission, whatever that might have been. The second band stopped to fight them, but then retreated and rode off.

During this short encounter, the Telorians and Kikies learnt that Mirauk had ordered all Morkans to return to Mork. The Telorians knew that Mirauk was planning something and that his armies would grow stronger, but it was going to take time, time enough for Teloria to grow stronger as well.

Untouched by the weather, the leaves of the trees of Firlan glowed at night, reflecting the moonlight. The company camped for the night just inside the forest and arrived at the gate a little after dawn.

This time Niome didn't need to utter the spell, for before she could take out the wand, the trees parted and the doors opened for her. Before them stood Firnamel and Kchalami to welcome them. Behind them, many other Firlanians waited in the courtyard, smiling.

'Welcome back,' said Firnamel, ushering them in. The doors closed behind them as everyone stopped just inside the entrance. 'It is great to see you once again. We knew you would succeed.'

'We did have a few worries,' admitted Kchalami. 'But when our watchers sighted Telorians far off, we knew it was you.' He smiled fondly.

'It is good to see you,' said Niome. 'We were worried as well, but I believe we did well.'

'Quite, in fact,' boasted Meysah. 'And we sure showed those Morkans.'

'I daresay,' laughed Firnamel. 'I gather you've had quite a few encounters with them. So have we. They tried to attack us and we stopped many armies from going to Teloria, but those are details we will talk about later.'

'I see you are more than just the five of you now,' noted Kchalami. 'Who might your companions be?'

Tharguen and Bahvley stepped forward. Tharguen shook hands with the King and his son. 'I am Tharguen Sumperale. I was once part of a team of

Telorians, a great many years ago, who made their way into Mork. I became a spy in Mork and it was fate that let me live. I thought I was the only survivor until we encountered my friend.' He nodded towards Bahvley.

'Bahvley Fairhaven.' He shook hands with Kchalami and Firnamel, both of whom beamed at him. 'I am the older brother of Niome and Meysah. I, too, was part of the Team of Twelve, as we called ourselves. I, too, thought I alone had survived. It is sad that only two of us lived, but I will eternally be grateful that it was my best friend who survived with me.' He turned and gestured towards the Kikies. 'I was adopted by these people. They are the Kikies from far away, and they have joined us in our battle against Mork.'

'So it was true,' smiled Kchalami. He looked at Tharguen. 'The first and only Telorian to survive in Mork for those many years.' He looked at Bahvley. 'And the first Telorian to ally with a new people from a distant land. One of the prophecy books spoke of you, but no one believed it could actually happen.' Bahvley and Tharguen smiled at each other.

Firnamel turned to the Kikies. 'Welcome to Firlan. I am King Firnamel and this is my son, Prince Kchalami. We are honoured to meet you. I hope you will feel comfortable during your stay here.'

'We are pleased to meet you also,' replied Phynd, respectfully inclining his head. 'Our people have a lot in common with polcs. We will have a lot to share.'

The two Firlanians led the group further into the courtyard. Firnamel turned to his people and declared loudly, 'The Telorians have successfully returned!' His announcement was met with raucous cheers.

Then Firnamel pointed to the ground, and the Telorians and Kikies looked down. The wand that had been carved in the pavement was now in the centre of a star, and at each point was the first initial of each member of the Star.

Niome walked to her spot in the front and stood on her letter. Then she raised her head to look up at the Firlanians and saw on all their faces great admiration. She turned around to face the others. Meysah walked to his letter, then Jimmy, Vigh, and Boreth went to stand in their respectful places. And at that moment, all the Firlanians, including Firnamel and Kchalami, bowed to them. Smiling proudly, Bahvley and Tharguen bowed as well, as did the Kikies.

When she saw that even those who had helped them succeed were bowing to them, Niome's heart swelled.

'Come,' said Firnamel. 'You must all need rest. We shall help you settle in. I hope you're up for a big meal.'

'Oh, certainly,' Jimmy enthused.

'You can stay here as long as you like,' Firnamel continued as they crossed the square.

'Thank you,' replied Vigh. 'We will certainly stay a while, although we must carry on home.'

'Of course,' said Kchalami. 'You must be quite eager to go home.'

'Oh yes!' exclaimed Tharguen. He and Bahvley looked at each other. 'I can hardly wait until my memories of that dark place are replaced by fresh new memories. I long to see Teloria's orange morning skies, and the bright colours and people of our home.'

'Yes,' Bahvley mused fondly, daydreaming of his home. 'I have but a vague memory left. I have been waiting so long for this day when I would be on my way back home. It fills my heart with joy.'

Tharguen agreed. 'Although hazy, I remember all the wonderful things from home. We were not much older than Meysah, Jimmy, or Niome when we left.'

Tharguen reached for Niome's hand as he continued to walk side by side with Bahvley led by Kchalami, who clocked the gesture of affection. The Prince's smile never faltered, but he averted his eyes.

'I remember those afternoons after lunch on our days off from training,' Bahvley said wistfully. 'We would hide in the trees and spy on everyone.'

'*That*'s why you weren't surprised when I organised a surprise party for you!' realised Vigh. 'That explains it. A lot of questions answered.' He laughed.

'Soon you will arrive, and Teloria will welcome you warmly.' Firnamel smiled.

'Yes, though we shall enjoy our stay here greatly,' expressed Boreth.

'And there's lots to do, too,' added Meysah.

'Like showing off your signature battle moves!' said Elmezni as he joined them. He seemed to have popped out of nowhere.

'Elmezni!' exclaimed both Jimmy and Meysah.

'It's good to see you!' said Jimmy.

'I'm very happy to see the two of you,' said Elmezni. 'And in one piece!' They laughed.

Elmezni led the heroes to their rooms. He helped them settle in and chatted with them while Firnamel and Kchalami went off to oversee preparations for the feast. Since the original band of five Telorians had grown to a band of seven Telorians and almost thirty Kikies, the Firlanians added an extra large table to that evening's banquet.

The next day the Firlanians gathered in the garden to hear their guests recount their tales. It was just as interesting for the travellers as it was for the Firlanians to hear their different perspectives of the mission.

The Firlanians, in turn, told their story. They had prevented a few squads of Morkans from continuing on to Teloria, but then the Morkans started travelling across country instead of by road, and they attacked Firlan, killing quite a few Firlanians. For such a tiny kingdom, that was a high price to pay. Firnamel and others had stayed in the castle to cast protective spells while the others, like Kchalami and Elmezni, fought fiercely. Many Firlanians, Elmezni among them, had been gravely wounded – and the Morkans had continued on anyway. When they noticed that the Morkans were retreating to Mork in a hurry, the

Firlanians let them go uncontested, and remained inside the walls of Firlan.

Afterwards, Elmezni brought Jimmy and Meysah to the sparring ring. The lads each showed off the moves and stances they had mastered over the seasons, as promised, enjoying being more playful without the worries or complications of war.

On the fourth day, the Telorians decided it was time to go home. They left in the afternoon of the fifth day, and had reached the Hills by nightfall. They felt so rested from the four days they'd spent in Firlan that they kept on going, travelling by the bright light of the stars shining in a clear sky.

Niome looked up and knew that the brightest star was Elina, and that she and a star near her were watching over and protecting the travellers. *Who is the second star?* she wondered. *Could it be Gorthan?* If so, then he had died before the Morkans could kill him. Gorthan had always been very clever in how he used his knowledge of magic.

They finally did stop to sleep at some point in the night, finally tired from climbing up and down those hills.

On the third day they stopped at dusk and rested at the top of one of the hills. Tharguen looked up into a deep purple sky marbled with yellow and blue and smelled the air.

'It is Cool Quarter Day,' said Boreth. 'Tonight will last as long as today, and from here on, the days will shorten, the air will cool, and the colours will become vibrant.'

'I can hardly remember the last time I saw a beautiful Colouring,' Tharguen voiced.

'I'm sure you've seen nature's beauties while travelling,' said Niome.

'In the past fifty years, the first beautiful sight I encountered was in those caves: a peaceful sleeping beauty.'

'Woo . . .' quipped Meysah and Bahvley simultaneously.

'Even though I was all tied up, and my clothes were torn and dirty?' Niome teased playfully.

'Even though all that,' replied Tharguen. 'You brought hope back to me.' He smiled and took her in his arms.

'You brought hope back to *me*,' she said, closing her eyes and resting her head against his chest.

Looking into the distance, Tharguen thought he saw some dragons entering their lair. He certainly saw dragons flying to Darakön, their movements peaceful and untroubled now, and he felt comforted.

Shortly before dusk on the sixth day since leaving Firlan, the group of travellers reached the Tweedle Woods. Jimmy and Meysah now knew not to be afraid if Bob Tweedle popped out of a tree at them. Except this time, he was waiting for them beside his tree, and greeted them excitedly.

'I knew it!' exclaimed Bob, after acknowledging every Telorian individually. 'No one else'll need mah help again. Everythin' will be fine. I must admit, I grew fond of this forest, but now I need not be here anymore. I wish you all a merry journey back home and safe journeys to follow.'

'We wish you a happy journey to the stars,' expressed Meysah. 'Although there isn't much journeying, I guess. I've never been a ghost, so I can't say.'

Bob chuckled. 'Thanks, Meysah.' He held out his ghostly hand. Once again Meysah tried to shake it and his hand passed right through Bob's. Bob laughed and so did everyone else, especially Meysah. 'I just had to do that one last time before goin' up. Do tell the Firlanians thank you from me, next time you see 'em. Even if it was their ancestors who made the deal with me, they let you in.'

He smiled, and then in a flash he was gone, like a shooting star flying up into the sky.

The travellers camped overnight in Tweedle's Woods and set out the next morning for the shores of the Ortim River. As they approached, they heard people walking along the riverbank, talking. Vigh motioned for everyone to conceal themselves. The Kikies vanished from view.

'I say we kill them on sight, then we have nothing left to worry about!' said the first voice.

'But sir, don't you think you're overreacting a little?' argued another voice.

'Don't talk out of line, you.' Pause. 'Lakht!'

'That sounds like a Morkan name,' Jimmy whispered.

'It is,' Tharguen disdained.

'I'm afraid he's right,' another voice, possibly Lakht's, said. 'I'm afraid Mirauk made his orders clear. He knows what he's doing.'

'Looking like a scared old wizard? Lakht, I could be as great as him if I wanted to.'

'You haven't heard the stories,' said another voice.

'What stories?' asked Lakht.

'These are not your ordinary travellers. It isn't for nothing that Mirauk sent so many messengers to warn us to return. Nor is it for nothing that there were so many of us sent out here to try to catch them before they got to Mork in the first place. It isn't for nothing that we are slowly, one squad at a time, creeping back to Mork. These Telorians have powers. They are practically invincible when they are together. And one, I hear, a wizardess, is the strongest – she is more powerful than Mirauk himself.'

'Did you hear that, Lakht?' the first voice laughed. 'More powerful than Mirauk. And I suppose they passed through the Portal, too! Mirauk has had visions and knows they did not. They are not stronger than him. Don't listen to rumours.'

'But it's true!' objected the other. 'How do you think they got the *Book of Enchantment* from Mirauk in the first place?' There was a pause. 'I tell you, it's true.'

'Yes, well, not for long,' said Lakht. '*Mirauk si ost kerlevar, ost pokhewlurf akhnad gornazdekh, ekh iliw goworo ost chronotgosk nwotath ekh sakh metekecht rikavlekh. Ekh sash lokedoc nikit kekh sulo achnad konowes alafokekh wassekesen. Ekh iliw goworo trilebek, osiliw alafosu. Akhnad rebkamereth tagkitach, fiethest Telorians reka chronotgost otegarthdekh, alaew nekedo kitodsi pilkhsit ethme yarpat akhnad khikli ethme nidikhviadlayu. Ethye wokhnit ebkabelo kit suvirkire lanoë. Ethye iliw pershikh, kuyokh hakhev yim worod akhnad Mirauk konowesit.'*

'What is it?' the first voice asked cautiously. 'Do you hear something?' He lowered his voice, but the Telorians could still hear him. 'It's them, isn't it?'

A long silence followed. So intent were the Telorians to hear what was said next that the Morkan attack took them by surprise as many Morkans pounced at the Telorians.

Creeping up from behind, a Morkan grabbed Meysah. He jerked free and shoved his attacker off him, running with the others for the water, but Morkans there tried to push them in and drown them. One held Vigh's head underwater, but Vigh managed to push the Morkan off him.

'You!' Lakht glared at Tharguen.

'Me.'

Tharguen blocked the incoming strike, steel clashing against steel, and pushed the Morkan back. Tharguen feigned defeat for a moment, taking a weak step back, then slashed high. Lakht wavered for a moment before he fell dead.

The Kikies then reappeared, surprising the Morkans and making quick work of what was left of them. A few managed to escape, but the Kikies and

Telorians decided to let them go; for now, they were more concerned with simply being safe.

'Why did that Morkan look so surprised to see you?' Bahvley asked Tharguen as they stood recovering from the battle beside the river. 'Did you know him?'

'Lakht?' replied Tharguen. He nodded. 'He was above me in rank before I became Beshrig's Second-in-Command. We never got along. He was always jealous of everyone else and somehow he knew I didn't belong. He transferred to another battalion when I got promoted.'

'Well, you got even with him once and for all,' said Meysah.

'No,' replied Tharguen. 'I got him because I hate it when people threaten my friends, especially when *Morkans* threaten them!'

'What did he say?' asked Boreth

'Terrible things that are so frightening and disturbing that I remember it word for word,' answered Tharguen. 'But I take it as a warning.'

The others gave Tharguen curious looks, so he translated 'Here's what he said in the Morkan tongue: "Mirauk is clever, powerful, and organised. He will grow in strength now that he has met his rival. He has looked into her soul and knows all of her weaknesses. He will grow terrible, and we will too. And remember, if these Telorians are strong together, all we need to do is split them up and kill them individually. They won't be able to survive alone. They will perish, you have my word. And

Mirauk knows it.'" He scowled as he delivered this information.

'This war is not over,' said Vigh. 'We must prepare constantly. It has been a good beginning for us – we have to make sure it comes to a good end. We know we are stronger than Mirauk and so does he, but he will do everything in his power to contradict the facts, especially if he can see things and knows we have not passed through the Portal, as that Morkan claimed.'

Vigh paused, looking apologetically at Niome. 'I also believe that Mirauk did see a lot of information valuable to him when he looked into Niome's eyes. We have to continue to train and gather allies. I know you said we have already started to win, Niome, but we have not won yet. As troubling as this news is, better we know now than too late.'

Tharguen sat down on the bank and put his head in his hands. 'Why do I feel the darkness of Mork will haunt me forever?'

'What do you mean?' asked Bahvley, coming to stand beside him.

'I don't want to hear or understand that tongue anymore,' complained Tharguen. 'I don't want to know secret passwords or overhear plans of execution and how to destroy those I love. I don't want to be a part of that anymore; I want to have nothing to do with it. I had to put up with it for so long; my heart is so weighed down. It's hard to stay yourself in there, without losing hope, without losing your mind or succumbing to evil.'

He stood, and turned to face everyone. 'I don't want anything to happen to any of you. Mirauk will try, but he won't succeed – I won't let him. I need you to promise me that you won't let him either, that you won't give up and that you will always stick together.' His voice quavered and he leaned against a tree, head in his hand, his eyes glistening.

Niome walked over and put her hand on his shoulder.

'I'm sorry,' lamented Tharguen, 'but the fear you felt in Mork is nothing next to the constant fear I felt and still feel, after the terrors I have seen.'

No one could respond to that; no one could fully understand how Tharguen felt.

He straightened and took a deep breath. 'I want to go home.'

'Looks like we'll have to build a raft, then,' said Bahvley.

Niome looked across to the other side of the river. She raised her hand and muttered inaudible words. Then she stepped back. The magical boat appeared, coming from the other side of the river. Everyone looked at Niome in surprise, then back at the boat, understanding her power.

As the boat carried them to the other side, Meysah fidgeted in his seat. 'I hope the beast is gone,' he muttered. It was.

They reached the far shore safely and walked towards the Old Grey House.

That night, Boreth could not shut his eyes. While the others slept and the Kikies kept watch, he took a short stroll a few paces away from the camp until he paused and propped one foot on a large rock, looking far into the distance. He began to softly sing his song for Clahria. A few phrases later he paused, hearing someone approaching behind him.

'You can keep singing,' a familiar voice said. 'Don't let me disturb you.'

Boreth turned around to see Clahria leading their horses from atop her own silver-white horse.

'I was singing . . . your song,' he said.

'It's lovely,' replied Clahria. She pulled the reins and stopped the horses.

'I'm surprised to see you,' admitted Boreth.

'I thought you might arrive faster by horse,' Clahria said as she dismounted.

'How did you know?'

'Tlúnëe knew. And somehow, so did I.'

Boreth walked over and embraced her. The horses neighed.

'I'm glad you've returned,' said Clahria, as they continued to hold each other. 'I missed you.'

'I missed you too,' said Boreth, tightening his arms around her.

'I hope you'll stay longer this time.'

'I hope so too!' replied Boreth. He hesitated, looking deeply into her eyes, and leaned his forehead on hers. Then he kissed her tenderly. As their kiss deepened, so did his joy. They pulled away smiling.

'Is everyone all right?' inquired Clahria. 'How is Jimmy?'

'Alive and well,' replied Boreth. 'You knew what was going to happen to him, didn't you?'

'I knew, Tlúnëe knew, my father knew. Henker knew. That's why he sent you to us.'

'I'm glad he did.' Boreth smiled.

'Me too. But what happened to Jimmy was one of those inevitable surprises. It could've happened to any one of you, but that's not what was in store for you.'

'Those dreadful tests from Mirauk – you knew about those too?'

'We knew a lot but could not speak of it – at least not most of it. We knew that if Niome was powerful enough to look into Mirauk's eyes and live, his powers would permit him to see into Niome's mind, and he would know way too much about you and Teloria. He would have to test you through his evil magic to study your strengths and see if what he had seen in Niome's eyes about you was true.'

'I have to say, Jimmy sure did give us a scare. It happened so fast. We were walking along, and then we were attacked and he was gone. And then he was back.' Boreth smiled. 'I've grown extremely fond of him. I'm glad to be his teacher now. I don't know what I'd do if I lost any of my four friends. We've grown so close through this journey. I guess we truly are the Five of the Star. I can't lose them.'

'You won't.' Clahria took Boreth's hand and they walked back to the camp.

They found the others standing with weapons in hand, their eyes wide, except for Meysah.

The lad grinned. 'I knew I heard Greyer. I knew I wasn't going mad.' He motioned towards the others. '*They* thought you were Morkans.'

Clahria smiled, her golden hair shimmering in the moonlight.

'Oh, I think Clahria's beauty far surpasses the beauty of any Morkan's,' Boreth said, admiring Clahria and passing a hand through her hair.

Jimmy fell back down on his blanket in a dramatic display of relief. He put his hand on his heart and said, 'I'm still alive! I'm still safe! Thank the stars!'

Chuckling, Meysah helped him up. Then he bounded to his horse. 'Hi, Clahria,' he said as he passed her.

Greyer neighed happily and lifted his front hooves into the air. 'I told you I'd come back!' Meysah exclaimed. 'I'll race whoever's willing!'

'I'll race you,' declared Bahvley. 'But I don't have my horse.'

'I brought enough horses for everyone,' said Clahria.

Soon they saw that not only had she brought Greyer, Boreth's and Vigh's horses, and horses for Jimmy and Niome along with her own, but she had also brought steeds for Bahvley and Tharguen. The Kikies, of course, would fast-fly.

Meysah and Bahvley were the first ones up the next morning, and the first ones to leave.

'Come on, Greyer,' said Meysah. 'Let's show Bahvley that we're faster than him!' Chuckling, the brothers left at a gallop.

They arrived at the Old Grey House around midday, and a short time later, the others joined them. Drúgan and Tlúnëe had been expecting them, and gave them a very warm welcome. The house seemed magically bigger, with enough room for all the guests, including the Kikies. Jimmy and Meysah asked how this could be, but Drúgan would not tell them his magical secret. Not even the Kikies could read his mind to find out. Drúgan was one mysterious wizard and would remain so for a long time.

The travellers spent a short but merry time at the Old Grey House. They stayed long enough to let a few more Morkan battalions ride by without encountering them. Boreth and Clahria spent most of the week together, and he knew he would be making many more trips in the future to see her.

Outside, more green leaves turned yellow, yellow ones turned orange, and some of these turned red.

On the morning of the eighth day, they left for home. Accompanied by the floating Kikies, the Telorians rode peacefully for many days until they came upon a Morkan battalion – but not just any battalion.

'Kurssus,' Tharguen breathed in a tight voice as Bahvley urged his horse up beside Tharguen's, 'that's Captain Kàtchah – the last Morkan I want to see right now.'

Captain Kàtchah shouted an order and his soldiers wheeled their horses around to intercept the Telorians. 'I order you to stop!' he yelled at them.

The Telorians kicked their horses to a gallop and rode past.

'I said stop!' bellowed Captain Kàtchah as the Morkans urged their horses forward. 'If you want to avoid an attack, stop!'

'As if you are open to negotiation,' Niome snapped. 'It is *you* who should avoid an attack. You know who we are and you know you cannot defeat us.'

The Telorians kept on riding.

'Oh, I wasn't talking to you, Fairhaven!' sneered Kàtchah. 'You'll try to hide, but I know of your betrayal now and Mirauk knows too.' He snorted angrily. 'You're the first one we'll kill!' he shouted.

'Who are you talking to?' Bahvley demanded as Kàtchah's horse caught up with them.

'I'm talking to Gowtch. Do you hear me, Gowtch? You taught me to be this perceptive!'

Tharguen turned his head to face Kàtchah, who was riding alongside him. 'I see hiding from you is of no use, Kàtchah. If you remember correctly, you tried to kill me on many occasions and you always failed. Who betrayed whom? I may not know magic lore as you do, but I know combat. Oh, and if you should know, I never betrayed anyone, for I was always a Telorian, a true Telorian.'

'You!' snarled Kàtchah, raising his sword. Tharguen blocked it with his own, the blades connecting with a ringing clang.

Kàtchah suddenly fell off his horse, as though a gust of wind had pushed him off. Everyone stopped their horses. The Telorians looked at Niome, thinking she'd used her Dragon's Wind, but she held no cylinder. Instead Niome's eyes were focused on Kàtchah. It took him several attempts to stand, as if he were weakening. He finally staggered to his feet and held onto the stirrup of his horse's saddle to stay upright.

'I don't know what kind of magic you're using,' he seethed gruffly, 'but if *I* can't finish you off, Mirauk will.'

After three attempts, Kàtchah got back on his horse, turning his attention to Thargen.

'I always knew you were different from the others, Gowtch, and I wasn't the only one to think so. I couldn't say anything then, for you trained me for a time, and it never looks good to question one's master.'

'I was the subordinate who helped you get your title, Kàtchah,' retorted Tharguen. 'It would have reflected poorly on you to question me after that.'

'At least I now know the truth – and have a good reason to kill you!' Kàtchah shot back. 'Now I know why you were so good at Telorian techniques, why you were the best to train me.' His lips curled into a sinister smile. 'How does it feel knowing your training went into killing your mentor?'

'I didn't know you'd be tasked to torture and kill Gorthan,' Tharguen said with disdain. 'Things would have been very different had I known.'

'At least now I'll get to fight you – the real you, the Telorian whose name is Tharguen Sumperale. And if I don't today, I won't stop until I do!' Kàtchah glared at Tharguen. 'You will be hunted down until the day you die.' In one fluid motion, he turned his horse and rode back to his battalion of Morkans.

'You trained him?!' exclaimed Niome, her voice tinged with disgust.

'I had to train him in certain melee techniques, that's all. I was exceptionally good, and doing so allowed me to gain prestige among the Morkans and earn a reputation for my team. It helped me gain knowledge – knowledge that allowed me to help you, Niome. Had I known then he would be tasked to capture and torture Gorthan . . .'

Niome's expression softened. 'I understand.'

Tharguen bowed his head. 'I kept my true allegiance hidden for so long, and many secrets were kept from me that I vied to learn . . . but there are no longer any secrets where I'm concerned. I was never truly his master, and it was only for a very short period of time. He knows a certain form of magic and is held in high esteem by Mirauk; he is part of Mirauk's Inner Circle.' Tharguen looked up at everyone. 'He's right. Everyone will be after me.'

'Well, everyone's after all of us,' said Bahvley. He clapped a hand on Tharguen's back, smiling in sympathy.

They reached Mistoff six days after leaving the Old Grey House. King Woob met with them to give them news. The Pleessies' shield was growing stronger, he told them, and soon it would protect the whole forest once more. The travellers then continued on and rode out of Mistoff, and two days later, they reached Teloria.

'Almost home,' announced Meysah. He and Jimmy shared a smile.

'Home,' said Jimmy, grinning.

'Home,' echoed both Bahvley and Tharguen, sharing a smile of their own.

Chapter Nineteen:
The Arrival

The gate of Teloria was shut fast and the guard towers seemed deserted. Silence hung heavy in the air, as if no other living being existed. The Kikies had vanished for practical purposes.

'I hope Teloria isn't completely abandoned,' muttered Bahvley, feeling a pang of worry as he recalled the abandoned kingdoms from the Colama Valley.

The Telorians slowly approached the portcullis.

'Stand back!' called a voice.

The travellers stopped and backed away from the gate. The doors of the guard towers opened and spewed Telorian soldiers, weapons in hand.

'Get down from your horses,' the same voice as before commanded. Its owner strode out onto the battlement and they recognised the insignia of a captain on his chest. They did as he requested. 'Now stand still. If you make any sudden moves, we will respond accordingly!' The soldiers surrounded them.

Several of them stepped forward and led the horses off to the side. 'Please identify yourselves. Who are you and what do you want?'

'We are Telorians,' said Vigh, taken aback. 'We've come back home.'

'Impossible. No Telorians have left the kingdom in years,' the Captain countered.

'We have,' asserted Niome. 'There were guards who knew of our departure.'

'Yes, well, most of those guards have been killed by Morkans. I am in charge now and no one spoke to me about any departure.'

'That's because it was a secret,' explained Niome. 'We left to go to Mork and retrieve the *Book of Enchantment*. I was Elina's apprentice.'

'Mm-hmm . . .' The Captain eyed them looking unconvinced. 'Those Telorians died. Don't try to fool me – it won't work.' He smiled knowingly. 'Show me this *Book of Enchantment*, if you really have it.'

The Telorians exchanged uncomfortable glances.

'How convenient,' Meysah muttered sarcastically.

'That's what I thought,' the Captain sneered.

'Uhm,' hesitated Jimmy, 'we sort of destroyed the books in Darakön.'

'Uh-huh, sure. Actually, there were five who left. There are seven of you.'

Meysah laughed inside. *More like thirty-three*, he thought, *counting the Kikies*.

'We retrieved two of our friends who had been gone for much longer,' explained Vigh.

'Just identify yourselves,' the Captain snapped. 'I don't want to waste my time with any more Morkan spies.'

'Have spies infiltrated Teloria?' Tharguen wondered under his breath. It was possible, given Kàtchah's reputation, and although their hoods were cast off, the Telorians wore black capes and could very well be taken for Morkans. Tharguen knew, though, that Morkans would have attacked the guards a long time ago, yet the Captain disregarded this. Therefore, the Telorians did as the Captain requested and each said their names in turn.

The Captain merely sniffed in disdain. 'Whoever you are, you are well informed, but not well enough! Bahvley Fairhaven and Tharguen Sumperale left Teloria some fifty years ago in our polken reckoning and died in Mork.'

'No, we did not!' Tharguen growled in annoyance.

'We *have* been gone that long, risking our lives for Teloria,' Bahvley argued, appalled, 'and this is the welcome we get?'

'What a nightmare!' sighed Tharguen.

'You don't know what we've been through,' Jimmy said calmly.

'We fought for Teloria,' added Meysah.

'You could at least say thank you,' suggested Jimmy. 'And especially to Bahvley and Tharguen.'

'Listen,' began Boreth, 'we left not knowing what was in store for us and we have witnessed terrible things. We long to be back home.'

'We went to Mork,' stated Vigh. 'We went there to save everyone and everything. And now we can't even get the recognition we deserve? Could we at least speak with Selemil?'

'Selemil doesn't negotiate with spies,' the Captain snapped, crossing his arms and looking away.

'*What?*' cried Meysah. 'You still think we're spies!?'

'Wait!' insisted Niome. 'Arguing won't help us.' She turned to the Captain. 'I don't know how to convince you that we truly *are* Telorians, but ask yourself this: why have Mirauk's armies all retreated? What threatens them?' She paused. 'It is us. We are stronger than them. I don't mean to boast, but I know now that I am more powerful than any other wizard in Kaulchèc History. I can see the doubt and fear and confusion in your eyes. You have no need to be afraid, for we have successfully returned. Bring us Selemil so he can prove it. I know you are being very cautious. I don't want to have to use my magic against a fellow Telorian just because of a misunderstanding.'

The Captain hesitated, looking confused. He turned to a soldier behind him. 'Go get Selemil. Tell him it's an emergency. Try to be back before tomorrow.'

'Understood!'

The Captain turned to the other soldiers. 'Put them in one of the guard towers. They don't *appear* hostile, so you may keep them unbound for now. Just make sure they don't make any sudden moves.' He looked back at Niome and the others. 'It's a precaution. We'll keep your horses nearby.' Then he added, 'But if you do anything . . .' And he let the warning hang.

The soldiers stripped them of their weapons and bags and escorted them into a large room in the tower and set guards over them. They waited as patiently as they could, all things considered. Evening came and Selemil still hadn't arrived. The Telorians were tired of waiting, tired of not sleeping, and tired of being treated like the enemy.

Finally, sometime during the night, when they were half asleep, their heads bobbing low, the door to the room opened and Selemil's voice drifted in. It came as a comfort to them, even if the voice was scolding.

'What do you mean, an emergency concerning Morkans passing as Telorians? I want more details.'

'They're Morkan spies, sir, claiming to be—'

Selemil walked in and saw the seven travellers and stopped, mouth agape. They all rose to their feet.

'Oh my,' breathed Selemil. He turned to the Captain. 'These are not Morkan spies! I appreciate that you were only being cautious, but I highly recommend you apologise,' he turned back to face the Telorians, beaming at them, 'for these are Teloria's greatest heroes!'

The Captain opened his mouth to speak, still looking at Selemil.

'Not to me! To them! We owe them our praise.' He walked farther into the room. 'How is this possible?'

He shook his head and answered himself. 'I don't know, but you are alive and well. We'd heard news from Dalvaran scouts and assumed – but anything could have happened to you between then and now.' He looked at Bahvley and Tharguen. 'This is a story I have to hear!' He smiled. 'Welcome home!'

Embarrassed for misjudging them, the Captain had food and drink brought to them. Selemil pulled up a chair, eager to know everything about their journey. The Telorians called for the Kikies to return to their normal size and introduced them to him and the shocked Captain, who had not realised there were even more of them than the seven travellers standing before the gate.

'I'll admit it,' said Selemil 'when I heard that you'd gone, my first reaction was anger, but it soon turned to worry.' And he told them what had happened while they were gone.

'The repairs on the wall around Teloria were proceeding well, but then we started to suspect that the Morkans were cooking up something. So we started to gather all of the Telorians, which was a good thing – many were in hiding already when the Morkans attacked. First they attacked in the north, but they left because too many Telorians, the important ones, could not be found.

'The Morkans were gone a long while, which gave us time to get everyone from further south up to the magical hideout – the ones who hadn't already left their homes. But the Morkans hadn't really been gone; we discovered they'd been making their way south undetected. Our knights fought them off when the Morkans entered Teloria there, but many still died.

'Gorthan was one of those fighting them. They captured him and tortured him for information, but he wouldn't answer their questions, and weeks later, we learnt that he was dead.'

'Kàtchah,' Tharguen disdained, feeling guilty.

Selemil resumed. 'The problem was, *no one* could answer their questions, for they were questions about *you*.'

Niome, Meysah, Jimmy, Boreth, and Vigh exchanged unhappy glances.

'The Morkans knew we were on a mission to retrieve the *Book of Enchantment*,' said Niome. 'They were after the *Complement Book*.'

'Yes,' replied Selemil. 'And no one here knew of your whereabouts. Many Morkans had been informed of Mirauk's visions and of what he'd seen through Elina's eyes. They knew if they could bring you to Mirauk, they would be richly rewarded. That was why they captured Gorthan.'

'I'm sorry,' said Niome.

'As am I,' said Tharguen, his tone solemn.

'Gorthan knew the risks,' Selemil reassured. 'And he knew yours was a mission of utmost importance.'

'Who now fills his role?' inquired Vigh.

'Nsarmön, the next High Master of Knights, assumed Gorthan's position,' replied Selemil.

He continued with his tale of Teloria. 'Many soldiers kept fighting the Morkans. A Dalvaran envoy came and we exchanged news with them. They were able to update us on you.

'Then one day, the Morkans stopped fighting and slowly started retreating. Even so, many Telorians remained in hiding, not knowing if the end of the world was approaching or not. Henker, however, said that something good was on its way, that something good was to come of this.

'We continued our work on the wall and since then Teloria has been heavily guarded – you got a dose of their caution when you arrived at the gate.' Selemil smiled. 'But today is a fine day, for the five travellers have returned, bringing hope and good news.'

Tharguen told Selemil what he'd heard the Morkans saying back at the riverbank. Selemil knew what everyone would have to do, but first there was more to take care of.

'We Kikies wish to help,' declared Phynd. 'I can leave half my crew here and bring more Kikies from our homeland – many will come if they are needed.'

That made Selemil very happy. 'We will discuss this later,' he told Phynd. 'First, you and your people are welcome to stay and rest as long as you need to.'

By this time morning had arrived, and the sun was up and shining brightly. 'Come,' Selemil beckoned, 'we must go see Henker. He is at home.'

They arrived at Henker's house a little past midday. He had been awaiting them and had already prepared many comfortable houses for the Kikies to stay in, not far from his home. The seven chatted with him a while and they supped together.

The sun was setting when the seven travellers at last walked towards home. Meysah looked up into the sky and took a deep breath. They were home at last.

Coincidentally, as they had before they left, they met Lóim Weedler clopping down the road on his horse. He reined the animal in and stared at them.

'Meysah! Jimmy! You're back!'

'Yes we are,' asserted Meysah, smiling at the lad who had bullied him when they were younger.

'That's impossible! They said you were dead!'

'Well, I did die,' said Jimmy, 'and thanks to the potion and spells that Niome had, I came back to life.'

'That's not true,' objected Lóim, narrowing his eyes in suspicion. 'It can't be!'

'It is,' confirmed Bahvley. 'I saw it with my own eyes.'

'Who's this?' Lóim asked Meysah, jerking his thumb at Bahvley.

'This is my brother,' replied Meysah. 'Bahvley. You remember him, yes?'

Lóim stared at him. 'Either I'm not feeling well, or . . .' He shook his head. 'It's just so hard to believe . . .' After another moment of gaping, he smiled, bewildered. 'Well, welcome back. I hope you rest well. I'll probably see you around.' He pressed his knees to his horse's flanks and the beast clopped away.

Meysah and Jimmy looked at each other and shrugged.

'No boasts?' remarked Jimmy.

'Friendlier?' guessed Meysah.

'He's changed,' concluded Jimmy.

'No, he knows you have,' said Vigh. 'I believe I saw respect in his eyes.' He rubbed his chin. 'Or was it admiration?'

Chuckling, and bewildered as well, the group continued on their way.

They came to Boreth's house. He said good night and went in through his back door. His pipe was still on the table, waiting to be smoked. He sat down, leaned back, and lit his pipe.

The others kept on trotting. They came to Tharguen's hut. He embraced Niome before going in, taking his time to kiss her tenderly. Soon after, Jimmy went into his house. Then Vigh was home.

The three siblings continued towards their home.

From down the street Niome could see their father sitting on the porch, looking up at the stars. Then he looked across the way and saw them clopping up the street. Ceymi rubbed his eyes, then stood and blinked a few times.

Niome picked up her pace. Meysah and Bahvley did too.

'Hi Dad,' said Niome as they came up the garden path. They dismounted their horses. 'We're back.

Sorry if we worried you by simply disappearing like we did.'

He could only grin at them, speechless.

'Niome saved the world!' declared Meysah. 'She's the most powerful wizardess of all.'

'And Meysah fought so many Morkans that they were frightened by his courage,' added Bahvley.

'And Bahvley united Telorians with a people called the Kikies,' said Niome.

With tears of joy in his eyes, Ceymi stepped forward and hugged his children, holding them in his embrace for a long time.

'Your mother is sleeping,' he said after a while. 'Let's wake her up to a nice surprise.'

The next day, the travellers met up and walked to the Governor's Hall where hid the entrance to the magical hideout. Before they entered, Selemil took Niome to a small room whose walls were lined with many old books.

'These books have not been looked through in a long time,' said Selemil. 'I was recently looking through some of them and I came across this one here.' He picked up an old leather bound book and handed it to Niome. 'I thought it had been destroyed.'

The title on the cover was in the script of the ancient Telorian and Kaulchèc tongues. Niome translated it: *The Dragon Prophecies*. She stared at it for a long time.

'Well, open it!' Selemil encouraged. 'Inside it has been translated into the Common Tongue.'

Niome opened the book in the middle, where a bookmark had been placed, and read aloud.

'"There shall be five who will travel to Mork together. Five who will save the world. Five brave

Telorians; five points of a star. These five will be guided by magic. Together they will be as powerful as the stars. Only if they separate will they be weakened. If they spend too much time far away from each other, their strength will diminish."'

Niome skipped ahead a few pages, for the book described how she left Teloria and how their title, Five of the Star, was created in Firlan, and she already knew this, as did everyone else by now. She continued to read.

"'This Telorian will know every one of Mork's secrets. He will open the key to Mork.'" She looked up. 'They're talking about Tharguen!' There were many pages about him.

"'But he will not have been the only survivor. There will have been one other who will have travelled to a distant land by chance and been taken care of by the people of that place. He will unite his people and this new people together.'" Niome skipped ahead. "'He will be destined to—'"

'Perhaps you should stop reading there,' said Selemil, closing the book in Niome's hands.

'Why? Even Bahvley knows what comes next.'

'Perhaps, but what is left to be read has not happened *yet*. Don't worry, it will soon enough, for all that is in here *will* happen. Anyway, next week there will be a celebration for you all.'

Niome handed the book back to Selemil, who returned it to its place. When they exited the room, Niome told the others what she had read.

'It seems we are special enough to be in the *Dragon Prophecies*,' smiled Vigh. 'I never realised our importance was foretold to this extent. We will be celebrated, and now there are Telorians waiting to hear our story and their destinies.'

'So come,' said Selemil. With a snap of his fingers, he opened the entrance of the secret hideout. He led the seven Telorians down the stairs to a grand dormitory, larger even than the Governor's Hall, where Telorians waited on chairs and on beds.

'How will all the Telorians hear us?' asked Niome.

'Ah,' said Selemil. 'There are many crystal spheres – all the wizards have them. The crystals show all and allow everyone to hear all from afar. One day you will create your own crystal, Niome, and you will see.'

Selemil took out his crystal sphere and activated it by passing his hand over it. He got everyone's attention and within moments, they all settled down to listen.

'I have great news!' he announced. 'We have begun to win the war. And this is all thanks to some very special Telorians. I will let them tell you their story.'

As Selemil spoke, his voice echoed through the room and wherever there was a crystal sphere, it projected his voice, loud and clear, to all the Telorians in its vicinity.

When the seven travellers spoke, everyone listened intently, as though it were storytime. They took turns telling their story, and they spoke for a long time. Snacks were brought to them throughout the day, and they were still speaking as night fell. When they finished, Telorians were no longer afraid to come out of hiding, and many went home.

The people of Teloria called the return of the seven a miracle, and indeed a miracle did happen in Teloria that week, for Telorians began to sing. Telorians, young and old, sang and laughed. They sang songs that hadn't been sung in over fifty years. The soldiers building the wall began to sing as they laboured. All who had feared being heard by Mirauk all these many years were now singing loud and clear, challenging him to hear their hope and joy. Merry tunes rang out all throughout Teloria, just like before the Big War.

The sun shines bright again,
There is beauty all around,
The stars have given us another day
To laugh and play, hoorah, hurray!

And as Selemil had planned, exactly ten days later, on the first day of the fifth week of Colouring, on their Colouring Feast Day, a party was thrown in honour of the seven Telorians.

It started early in the gardens of the Governor's Hall, which was the only place big enough to hold everyone. It was also the only place that had remained untouched by the Morkans.

Clahria surprised Boreth by riding to Teloria for the occasion, as Tlûnëe had foreseen the event, and many of the knights who had trained and fought with Bahvley and Tharguen long ago were also in attendance. Together, they held a small ceremony for all those who had died in Mork – the other ten from the Team of Twelve, Captain Ackerley and the army of three hundred Telorians who had followed them.

When the merriment resumed, music played loud and people danced long.

As evening approached, Selemil took the stage and addressed the crowd. 'I have an announcement to make,' he began. 'And I think now is a good time to make it.'

He opened his arms, motioning to the gardens around him. 'First, I must tell you the history of this hall and these gardens. This is the Governor's Hall today, but long ago it was the Royal Halls, and these were the Royal Gardens. And in fact, from now on, that's what they shall be again. The thrones in the Governor's Hall were made for the ruler and their consort, and yet all this time governors like me have been sitting in them. But now, on the throne should sit a king. Someone with leadership abilities – someone who fought for freedom for Teloria! Someone who has truly proven himself worthy.

'Our new King has done all that. He has also united our people with another people. He has always been powerful, in everything he's done and everywhere he's gone. Even the Morkans knew he would be dangerous to them, were he to survive, for his royal title was prophesied long before he was born. And he not only survived, but accomplished much as well.'

Selemil looked at Bahvley. 'Bahvley Fairhaven, do you accept the honour and responsibility of this position?'

Bahvley was speechless. To hear a vague prophecy was one thing, but to actually arrive at this day where he would be named King was an honour he could not put into words.

'Say yes,' Niome whispered, smiling.

'You are exactly what everyone hopes and imagines a king should be,' whispered Meysah, grinning.

'If anyone deserves to be King,' whispered Tharguen, 'it's you.'

Tharguen and Bahvley beamed at each other, remembering things said to each other long ago, and Bahvley's heart swelled.

He took a deep breath. 'Yes!'

'Then please step up,' invited Selemil.

Bahvley came and knelt before him on one knee. Selemil drew his sword and placed it on Bahvley's shoulder, then on the other shoulder. 'Bahvley Fairhaven, I pronounce you King Bahvley Fairhaven, ruler of Teloria.' He sheathed his sword. 'You may rise, my King.'

Blinking back tears, Bahvley rose to cheers and applause. Henker stepped up and Selemil turned and opened the box Henker held. He lifted out a golden, gem-encrusted crown and placed it solemnly on Bahvley's head. Bahvley smiled. Selemil stepped down.

'Now that I am King,' began Bahvley, 'I have a few requests to make – or are they more like nominations of others to office?' He laughed. 'To start, I would like Selemil to be my seneschal. In the past, every ruler had a seneschal and advisors, and since you have been a good governor for Teloria, I feel it only fair that you and Henker become royal members of my court. I only wish Gorthan were here with us, but I know he is watching us, as Elina is.'

'It will be an honour,' declared Selemil.

The crowd cheered.

'It is an honour to be made King,' Bahvley beamed. 'I will do my best to rule Teloria fairly and to meet all the needs of my people. We will win this war, and the Great Ocean Valley will be safe again. We will all, once again, have our Freedom of Life!'

More cheers erupted, a roar that rose to the heavens.

'Next,' continued Bahvley, 'I call upon my dearest friend, Tharguen Sumperale. You have always been there for me and my family. You were the first to volunteer to follow me to Mork. You were there when we thought all hope had been lost. You spent fifty difficult years as a Telorian spy in Mork. How you weren't discovered, I do not know, but you learnt all the Morkans' secrets there were to know. And you saved and protected my dear sister, the most important person in Teloria, for she guarded the *Complement Book*. Now you shall be *Captain* Sumperale of the Royal Court.'

Tharguen stepped up and embraced his friend. 'Captain is what I have always wanted to be, and here – in Teloria.' He beamed at Bahvley, arms still on his arms. 'You honour me by granting me that title.' They hugged again before Tharguen stepped aside.

'Next,' Bahvley went on, 'there are the most important five Telorians we need to thank. They form a star and are as powerful as a star; they are the reason why we are all here and alive today. They are the reason why I and Tharguen have returned home after our . . . personal exploits, if you wish.' He smiled fondly before he grew serious again. 'It is all thanks to my sister, Niome, my brother, Meysah, his friend, Jimmy, and their masters, Vigh and Boreth.'

Bahvley presented the two masters. 'I'll start with Boreth and Vigh. You two are exceptional knights and masters. I don't think anyone has as much skill as you. Even Gorthan, when I was young, told me that you had exceeded the abilities of your masters – and he was one of your masters. Your training and wisdom inspired me, which helped me make many tough decisions in Mork, and helped me when coordinating with the Kikies for our return to Teloria. Thank you both.'

Vigh and Boreth bowed in acknowledgement, smiling at Bahvley.

'Thus I promote you to a new level of mastery. You will no longer be referred to as Sir Boreth or Master Vigh, but as Lord Boreth Culmik and Lord Vigh Nimrod.'

'We thank you for this,' said Vigh. 'To be a Lord in Teloria is one of the greatest honours of all.'

Bahvley smiled and turned to Jimmy. 'Someone else deserves recognition. Someone who is very skilled and learns well, and whom I *admire*.' Bahvley paused for a beat to emphasise 'admire'. 'I think it only fair to recognise you as an apprentice-knight.' Jimmy laughed. 'You truly are remarkable, Jimmesh Hochka, Apprentice Knight of Lord Boreth Culmik.'

There were more cheers.

'Now, I know you already have a master, Meysah, but you deserve recognition as well.' Bahvley chuckled. 'You are very brave; you faced many dangers and overcame them all. I have not seen such courage in a long time. Meysah Fairhaven, I make you partner-knight with your dear friend Jimmy.'

Both lads whooped, jumping into the air and embracing each other, eliciting laughs from the cheering crowd.

'Last but not least, the most important person of all, Niome Fairhaven.' Bahvley walked to his sister, smiling at her. 'You are now the new and only Great Wizardess of Teloria, and I officially bestow that title: Great Wizardess Niome Fairhaven.' Bahvley took Niome's hands in his, speaking more softly now. 'This party today is for you, Niome. Thank you.'

Niome enthusiastically wrapped her arms around her brother and kissed his cheek. The two laughed, hugging tightly.

The crowd roared and cheered, and music and singing resumed.

Bahvley stepped down from the stage and joined his dear friends. The greatest gift of all for all of them was being together, and being home.

THE END

<u>THANK YOU SO MUCH FOR READING!</u>

If you enjoyed this book,
please consider taking a few moments
to write a review on Amazon or Goodreads.
It would mean so much.

Thank you.
May the stars shine upon you!

<u>The Journey Continues</u>

When Tharguen and his team travel to Dûnelor in an attempt to secure an alliance with the desert dwellers, they discover a sinister plot, and some of the most dangerous Morkans are behind it.

Tharguen is forced to face the darkness of his past, Niome must unlock more of her newfound powers in order to protect her kingdom, and Bahvley is shaken by truths uncovered when Teloria is faced with a deadly and undefeatable new foe.

Map of the Great Ocean Valley

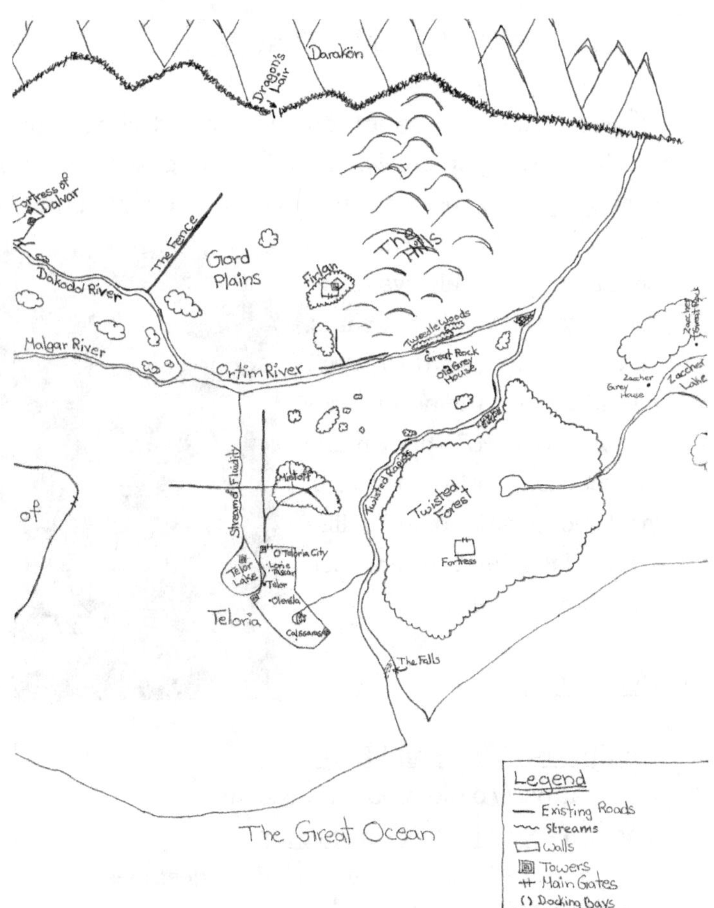

Darakön
Dragon's Lair
Fortress of Dalvar
The Fence
Gord Plains
Firlan
The Hills
Tweedle Woods
Zacchet Forest Rock
Dakodol River
Great Rock of Grey House
Malgar River
Zacchet Grey House
Zacchet Lake
Ortim River
Stream of Fluidity
Mistoff
Twisted Roads
Twisted Forest
Telor Lake
Teloria City
Lone Rascal
Telor
Olenda
Fortress
Teloria
Colosseum
The Falls
The Great Ocean
Legend
Existing Roads
Streams
Walls
Towers
Main Gates
( ) Docking Bays
Bridges

Celinka Serre is an indie writer and video producer working in freelance and sharing short stories of various genres, as well as anecdotes, on Medium. She believes in the freedom of creativity and always continues to pursue her dreams. Having begun *Stardust Destinies* at age 19, the novel series is but one of her many projects, being also a writer of fan-fiction, various indie film screenplays, and a few collaborations as well.

Connect with Binky:

Wordpress Website and Blog:

https://binkyproductions.com

Medium - Stardust Destinies Extras:

https://medium.com/stardust-destinies

Medium - Main Profile:

https://medium.com/@binkyinkwriting

Twitter: https://twitter.com/binkyinkwriting